Derek Hansen is the author of several bestselling novels and collections of short stories. He divides his time between his home on Sydney's northern beaches and his winter hideaway in Doonan, southeast Queensland. He's one of those authors who has to know how a story ends before starting it. This is hard going and involves endless hours of lonely contemplation, exiled on his boat with a couple of lines over the side and a cold beer in hand. It's tough, but someone has to do it.

SOMETHING FISHY

DEREK HANSEN

HarperCollins*Publishers*

HarperCollins*Publishers*

First published in Australia in 2005
by HarperCollins*Publishers* Pty Limited
ABN 36 009 913 517
A member of the HarperCollins*Publishers* (Australia) Pty Limited Group
www.harpercollins.com.au

HarperCollins*Publishers*
25 Ryde Road, Pymble, Sydney NSW 2073, Australia
31 View Road, Glenfield, Auckland 10, New Zealand
77–85 Fulham Palace Road, London W6 8JB, United Kingdom
2 Bloor Street East, 20th floor, Toronto, Ontario M4W 1A8, Canada
10 East 53rd Street, New York NY 10022, USA

National Library of Australia Cataloguing-in-Publication data:

Hansen, Derek
  Something fishy.
  ISBN 0 7322 8195 4.
  1. Fishing - Fiction. I. Title.
A823.3

Cover design by Michael Killalea
Typeset in Garamond 11.5/16 by Helen Beard, ECJ Australia Pty Limited
Printed and bound in Australia by Griffin Press on 70gsm Bulky Book Ivory

6 5 4 3 2 1   05 06 07 08

It is really a pleasure to be able to dedicate this book to a good mate, Peter Trethewey. Year after year, Captain Pete has taken me aboard his Salthouse sportsfisher and shown me the wonders of the Sea of Cortez. I've seen sights that John Steinbeck wrote about in *The Log from the Sea of Cortez* back in 1938, sights I thought no longer occurred — striped marlin in their hundreds free jumping off the island of Cerralvo; porpoises in their thousands jammed in an area the size of a football field chasing bait fish, with yellowfin tuna up to one hundred and fifty kilograms leading the charge; and manta rays leaping from the water like giant tossed pancakes. Utterly amazing. Sometimes just being there is enough and catching fish irrelevant. Peter, this is a heartfelt thank you.

Contents

Something Fishy

'All mankind descended from fish,' said Everton Sweet.

His wife sighed and slipped away to look for another group talking about more sensible things, like spring fashions. She noticed her friend, Al, who'd heard Everton's party piece before, also slip away. She waited for him to catch up.

'That's not nice,' she said facetiously. 'Walking away while my husband is speaking.'

'Good God, Francine, what are you going to do about him?'

'What can I do, Al? I married a genius and live with a fool.'

Francine had married Everton some twenty years earlier, recognising that his special abilities could keep her a valued Chanel and Gucci customer for life. He hadn't disappointed her. She'd spent his money enthusiastically and not always wisely, but the cost of her extravagances was no impediment to their steady accumulation of wealth. What Francine couldn't understand was how her husband, who was a luminary in genetics and related fields and whose patents raked in millions of dollars a year, could be so socially inept.

Al, on the other hand, was handsome, socially adroit and reasonably successful in a salaried sort of way. Unfortunately for Francine, Al's success couldn't even begin to compare with Everton's. She spent the equivalent of Al's gross annual salary in a single month. What she wanted was for Everton to become more like Al, or Al to become as successful as Everton, whereupon other arrangements could be made.

'Man descended from apes, surely,' Francine heard an unwitting guest say. She took Al's arm and walked away. She knew exactly how Everton would respond and also knew that he would keep the hapless guest and those around her baled up for another thirty minutes unless they had the sense to sneak away. Everton's problem was that he knew too much about one thing and not enough about anything else.

'Ah, but what did the apes descend from?' said Everton. 'What is the ancestor of all primates? If you follow that thought back far enough, for three hundred million years, you'll reach the instant when the first creature left the sea to live on dry land. Now, think about that creature and where it came from, and try to imagine what its ancestor would have been.'

'A fish,' said a young lady who clearly hadn't heard Everton's party piece before.

'Exactly,' said Everton. 'When the *coelacanths* — the fish with legs — broke away from the main order of fish you could argue that they took the first steps on the evolutionary ladder that led to mankind. All land vertebrates are simply highly modified fish.'

'Why not a reptile?' said her young man.

'The first creatures to stray onto dry land may well have been primitive forms of reptiles,' said Everton tolerantly. 'But still it would have been the result of a genetic mutation of an extremely primitive form of fish.'

'So you're saying we're all fish?' said the young lady.

'Not at all,' said Everton. 'God knows, when I look at you, young lady, I don't see anything remotely fish-like. I see a beautiful example of the most intelligent life form on earth — a woman.' He waited for the predictable chuckles to die down. 'However, if I put you under a microscope, a very, very powerful microscope, guess what I'd find?'

'Something fishy?'

'Exactly. You might think the genetic make-up of human beings would be vastly more complex than that of a fish but in fact it isn't. Human DNA is made up of around three billion pairs of four nucleotides arranged like rungs on a ladder. Fish have close to the same number. So, for that matter, have fruit flies. We're really not as special as we like to think we are.

'All the various species on earth evolved by genetic mutation. Where the mutation was benevolent, a new, successful species emerged. Where it was unsuccessful, the mutation resulted in extinction. When you consider that this process of mutation has been going on for hundreds of millions of years, it is no surprise that we have so many divergent species, both of animals and plants. Yet, despite these millions of years of mutations, I can look at your genetic code and still see clear evidence of our common ancestor. I can look at the DNA of a lionfish or a queen fish, a snapper or a John Dory, and know that, but for a series of genetic accidents, there go I.'

'Is that what you do?' asked the young lady.

'It is indeed,' said Everton. 'I believe that fish carry in their genes the answer to almost all of mankind's problems.'

This was the prompt for Everton to launch into a long monologue of how certain fish genes had the potential to treat various human diseases and extend human life. In his enthusiasm he'd fail to notice people's eyes go glassy, their jaws drop and their minds not so much wander off as implode. By the time he'd got into the use of fish genes in the production of new wonder drugs, half of his audience had usually found an excuse to be elsewhere. By the time he'd got to the use of fish genes in modifying food, he was lucky if he didn't find himself talking to the wall.

'But if you transplant sand shark genes into potatoes to stop them going soft and mouldy, won't they taste fishy?'

Everton blinked hard and looked around. He wasn't accustomed to people staying to the end of his scintillating mini-lectures. It was the young lady and she was gazing at him with genuine interest. Her young man had gone elsewhere. Everton's eyes flicked quickly around the room and found him engaged in deep and meaningful conversation with a scantily clad beauty, from a position where he was free to gaze down her cleavage.

'Well?'

Everton's attention snapped back to the young lady in front of him. He owed her an answer, having more than likely cost her a boyfriend.

'It can happen,' he said reluctantly. 'The sand shark gene didn't affect the natural taste of the potato, but things like that can happen.'

'If potatoes tasted fishy, we wouldn't need fish with our chips,' said the young lady brightly.

She had, Everton had to concede, hit a very annoying nail right on the head.

* * *

Psychiatrists claim that the line between genius and madness is the finest ever drawn. Everton managed to keep to the right side of the line although there were times when he appeared to straddle it. His obsession with fish genes was a good example. There had been a time when he'd taken a much more catholic approach to solving problems and fish were no more favoured than, say, fowl, foxes or fungus in providing DNA.

Everton was a specialist in xenotransplantation, which meant he mixed and matched DNA from different species. Just as orchardists might splice a branch of a mandarin tree to an orange tree, or one type of apple tree to another, Everton spliced animal DNA to plant DNA and vice versa. One of his triumphs was to splice a strand of DNA from rapeseed into the DNA of a pig and, as a consequence, reduce the amount of saturated fat in pork products to the point where even crackling got a Healthy Heart tick. He patented the relevant genes and sold the concept to pork producers around the world. He did the same with hens, except that he spliced in a strand of DNA from a Spanish olive so they produced mono-unsaturated eggs which, he liked to joke, fried themselves.

These were the more sensational examples of the sort of thing Everton did. On a more mundane level, he used a flounder gene to quadruple the shelf life of tomatoes, and a gene from pyrethrum to make cotton and grain crops like wheat, barley and maize naturally resistant to insect pests. The royalties just kept coming in.

Nobody could pinpoint when he became obsessed by fish genes, but it may have been during his research for a Swiss drug company specialising in dental pharmaceuticals, when he developed a local anaesthetic from the Patagonian toothfish. The anaesthetic was five times more effective than novocaine and had no known side effects. In studying the DNA of the toothfish in such minute detail, Everton may have recognised the patterns that hinted at his own — and all of mankind's — origins. There again, it could have happened when he found an enzyme in the common pipi which stopped Polyfilla drying out before you've finished patching the hole you're working on. It could have been any of a hundred projects. Whatever it was, it convinced Everton that fish genes held the answer to just about every problem.

He became increasingly fascinated by the medical possibilities of fish genes. He became convinced that they had the potential to cure, treat or arrest every known human ailment, but he was continually frustrated by the need to test his new drugs in clinical trials, all of which took years. Invariably, his drugs would produce a side effect and the process of engineering out the fault put the testing program back to square one.

However, enough of what Everton did worked, and worked without side effects. He became richer and, as he became richer, he also became more obsessed with fish genes. Everton took his obsession home with him, took it into the lounge, the library, the dining room, the games room and, yes, into the bedroom. His beautiful wife became more convinced she lived with a fool.

Francine thought about leaving him but also thought of the wealth Everton had yet to amass, and decided an affair with Al offered her the best of both worlds. Al was happy to oblige. Nobody bothered to ask Everton what he thought of the arrangement. When Francine and Al were together they never mentioned fish and never ordered it to eat, either. The strength of their relationship lay in the fact that it was entirely fish-free.

Everything went swimmingly for Francine and her fish-obsessed husband until the day Everton's hand wobbled of its own accord. Most people would have dismissed the occurrence as an aberration or the result of an excess of wine or spirits, but Everton sat up and took note as every good scientist should. When the tremor recurred two weeks later, and for a more sustained period, he realised the aberration was not a transient thing but the product of physiological malfunction.

A number of diseases that he'd tried to cure or arrest with his fish-gene-based therapies scrolled through his mind, and he was distressed to realise his tremor might have something to do with Parkinson's disease. He hadn't had much success in finding a drug to arrest, relieve or cure Parkinson's. His relief at discovering that he wasn't suffering from Parkinson's disease was short-lived. His doctor informed him, with much regret, that he had a tumour the size of a gull's egg buried deep in his brain. The shaking was caused by the tumour impacting on his cerebral cortex. Unhappily, Everton hadn't had much success in finding a treatment for brain tumours, either.

Everton looked at the scans and MRIs of his brain and agreed with the surgeon that excision was not an option: operating would not remove enough of the tumour yet remove too much of his healthy brain. He agreed with the oncologist that chemotherapy and radiation therapy offered limited benefits and that intervention would only buy him a few more months to live. He used his contacts and rang eminent researchers in the US, scientists working on 'magic bullets' and laser treatments, and agreed with them that they could not yet offer him anything remotely approaching a cure. Having exhausted all his options, he went home and told his darling wife.

'What about me?' she said in horror. 'What's going to happen to me?'

Everton pointed out that the trusts and royalties would provide her with more money on an annual basis than she could ever hope to spend, unless she was inconceivably reckless or stupid or both.

'How much more?' she wanted to know.

'Angel heart, if there were two of you, there'd still be more than enough.'

That was the answer Francine was looking for. With Everton out of the way she could formalise her relationship with Al. Everton's royalties would take care of his extravagances as well.

'What about you?' she asked, now that her concerns were alleviated.

'I'm going to die in seven months,' he said.

'Can't they do something?' Francine wanted to make certain he was really checking out.

'They? Yes. They can keep me alive for another two or three months with chemo and radiation therapy.'

'Three months?' said Francine. In her head she was adding three months to seven, working out what season it would be when he died and what season it would be when she subsequently married Al. She had her wedding dress to think of.

'But chemo and radiation therapy are out of the question.'

'Really?'

'The fact is, I have only one chance left.'

'One chance? You've still got a chance?'

'An outside chance.'

'How far outside?'

'In the time I have left, I have to find a way to get rid of my tumour myself. It isn't going to be easy, but it would be impossible if I let my system be blasted with radiation and poisoned by chemotherapy. I'd be too sick to work. Although I've got seven months to live, I don't have seven months to work. I'm not exactly sure what will happen as the tumour grows or when it will happen, but I know whatever happens won't be pleasant.'

'So seven months, right?'

By Francine's calculation, seven months would take them to the beginning of winter which, following an appropriate period of short black dresses, would clear the way for a spring wedding.

'That's right. Seven months,' said Everton. 'Unless . . .'

'Unless you find a cure,' said Francine bluntly. The prospect of that happening didn't worry her in the least. She wasn't stupid. She knew some of the best brains on the planet had been working on cancer cures for decades. What could Everton do in seven months? No, Francine saw no impediment to her wedding plans.

Everton worked day and night, but not exclusively, on trying to find the genes that would save his life. He wanted to make sure his dear wife was properly taken care of in the probability that he wouldn't find the gene he was looking for in time. He wanted her financial security to be absolute:

fireproof, bombproof, recession-proof, conman-proof and well-meant-advice-proof. He saw his poor bereaved wife living alone in their many mansions and condos for the rest of her life, mourning his demise. He couldn't bear the thought of her worrying about money as well. It never occurred to him that his death was exactly what Francine needed to make her life perfect. So while he trawled through the DNA of amberjack, bass, catfish, dhufish, eels, flathead, etcetera, etcetera he also took time out to work on commissions.

New Zealand lamb producers asked him to change the taste of lamb to make it taste more like pork so that they'd have a better chance of cracking the US market. Meanwhile, pork producers asked him to alter the taste of pork so that it tasted more like beef, which was far and away more popular than pork. The pork producers also slyly hoped to exploit a marketing opportunity created by outbreaks of mad cow disease, which had put a lot of people off their steak. At the same time, beef producers asked him to rid beef of flavour altogether so that it didn't interfere with the taste of fried animal fat and salt, which was actually what people most liked about their product.

Unfortunately for the lamb, pork and beef producers, all of these innovations were scrapped during testing on the grounds of the confusion they caused. The changes drove people mad and, in turn, they drove the marketing experts back into their boxes.

Still, Everton collected his fees because he did what he was asked to do. It wasn't his fault that what he'd been asked to do was stupid. And every day, he grew ever closer to drawing his final breath.

Sometimes his shaking hands made work all but impossible and, as the months passed, he also had to contend with fits that struck without warning. Everton worked his way through three of his remaining seven months, through the alphabet of fish to the sharks, and through the species of sharks to the great white before he made his breakthrough. The answer was so obvious that he was stunned he hadn't thought of it earlier and angry with himself that he'd wasted three valuable months.

Nature had made the great white shark wonderfully efficient, so efficient in fact that its DNA had remained substantially unchanged from the moment the first great white had taken its first tentative bite out of its neighbour. It had never had reason to change or adapt because it had sat pretty well at the top of the food chain ever since. Everton should have realised that. He should also have reasoned that a killing machine as efficient as the great white shark had no need for a big sophisticated brain and could get by with a brain the size of a pea.

On the other hand, Everton had a big sophisticated brain and it should have been obvious to him that a big shark with a minuscule brain could not afford to suffer brain tumours. Not even a small tumour, not even one the size, say, of a grain of rice. It was only logical that, in order to have survived for one hundred million years, the great white shark would have a defence against brain tumours. It was this defence, spread over a number of genes, that Everton found.

'Eureka!' he cried. Despite the fact that Everton had made innumerable discoveries he'd never shouted 'Eureka' before. He wondered if corny exclamations were another symptom of his tumour.

Having isolated the shark genes that produced the proteins that attacked brain cancer cells, he knew he could go the next step and create a form of therapy that would save his life. Naturally he wanted to share his wonderful discovery with someone and the one person he most wanted to tell was his darling wife. He could imagine the look of sheer joy and relief on her face when he told her the good news. He picked up the phone and immediately dropped it back on its cradle. Why imagine the look on her face when he could witness it? He checked his watch. It was only two thirty in the afternoon. What the heck? Even a brilliant scientist deserved an early mark occasionally. He raced out of his lab and into his car.

Often when people have exciting news to tell, they drive like maniacs. Everton did the opposite. Having just saved his life, he didn't want to lose it in a head-on with a Mack truck. It was just after three when he pulled into the driveway of his home. He tried to park in his garage but there was a strange car occupying his place. He figured it belonged to his wife's hairdresser, beautician, personal trainer, personal astrologer, *tai chi* instructor or interior decorator. He let himself in quietly so that he could surprise her, tiptoed into the lounge, the library, the home theatre, the solarium and the games room before tiptoeing upstairs. He figured if she wasn't downstairs, she'd be in their bedroom having her nails done. He tiptoed up to the door and gently pushed it open. He was about to shout out 'Surprise!' but the word jammed in his throat.

He was wrong. His precious wife wasn't having her nails done.

Or her hair.

Or her make-up.

Oh, no.

Everton quietly pulled the door closed in a state of stunned disbelief. His wonderful, precious, devoted wife was in bed with Al. Al — in her bed, *his* bed, *their* bed. On this momentous day, when he and Francine should be celebrating the prospect of his reprieve, tears flooded his eyes. He snuck out the front door, managing to avoid being spotted by the maid, the cook or the gardener, and quietly drove back to his lab.

Everton was hurt. No, not hurt so much as devastated. But overwhelming everything was a numbing sense of disbelief. After all, he thought he'd been the perfect husband by providing his wife with everything she could ever want. He'd thought they were the perfect couple, a complementary match of her beauty with his brains. He couldn't even begin to imagine why Francine could possibly be unhappy with him or why she'd allow Al into her bed. Unless . . .

Unless she was distraught at the prospect of losing him and had turned to Al for comfort. Maybe she was more terrified by the prospect of living alone than she'd let on. Maybe she'd begun planning for life after his demise. Yes, he thought, that was the probable explanation. After all, they'd been so close. Francine couldn't bear the thought of living the rest of her life in an empty house, or indeed several empty houses. But couldn't she have waited? In four months he would either have found a cure or be dead. Four months didn't seem long to wait before planning the next phase of her life. It saddened and angered Everton to think that his illness had driven his wife to take such drastic action. He decided there and then that he couldn't leave her, that he'd never leave her. He reached the lab determined to rescue his wife from Al's clutches. He was determined to turn his discovery into a cure.

Later that night when Everton returned home and told his wife about his discovery, she burst into tears. Everton's big mistake was in thinking they were tears of joy, that they were grounded in feelings of relief that she wouldn't have to face the rest of her life without him.

'I'll turn my discovery into a cure,' he said soothingly. 'Trust me. I promise I'll never leave you.'

Francine cried even harder.

The following day, when Everton told his oncologist what he intended to do, the doctor was outraged.

'You can't do that!' he shrieked. 'Not without proper trials. Not without testing for side effects. Not without formal approval.'

'I haven't got time for any of that,' said Everton.

'But what if you're successful?' said the oncologist. 'You'll make us all look like fools.'

It took the promise of a lot of money and endless assurances that no one would know of his involvement before the oncologist agreed to help by harvesting Everton's brain cells and injecting them back into the tumour once they'd been modified with shark genes. But first Everton had to work out exactly which parts of which white-shark genes were implicated in his cure, and how to use them to modify his own DNA. The task looked formidable. He thought about the problems ahead of him while the oncologist drilled a tiny hole in his skull to draw off some brain cells. That night

Everton fitted so badly his darling wife made him sleep in the guestroom.

Everton's biggest fear was that he'd left his run too late, that the trembling and the fitting would become so bad that he'd no longer be able to work. In desperation, he involved his senior lab staff in the project without telling them exactly what he was trying to do. (After all, it was unethical, illegal and could get them thrown out of the profession.) He also took short cuts he'd never normally countenance. He took whole sections of great-white DNA because he didn't have time to isolate precisely which part of the genes he needed. He did a lot of this to a lot of genes. He took risks no scientist in their right mind would ever entertain. But Everton was hardly in his right mind and the short cuts offered his only chance of salvation.

Each night when he finally dragged himself home from the lab, he found Francine waiting anxiously for him.

'How'd you go today?' she'd ask.

'Better than expected,' he'd say. His reply was always the same because he didn't want to upset her. 'Don't worry, Angel heart, I'll keep my promise. I'll never leave you.'

It always touched him deeply that Francine would then cry herself to sleep.

After four weeks, the oncologist injected Everton's modified brain cells directly into the tumour and into the surrounding brain tissue. At that time, Everton had less than three months to live. He went to bed hoping that he'd wake up to evidence that his gene therapy was working, but woke instead to a blinding headache, fever and nausea. Even Francine was moved by his distress. She wanted to send him to hospital, though privately she thought a hospice would be more appropriate. She was convinced Everton's sickness was the beginning of the end for him.

To Francine's dismay, the headaches, fever and nausea went away after five days. Their cessation marked the end of what she'd hoped was her new beginning. Everton rose from his bed to shower feeling weak but optimistic.

'I'm hungry,' he said.

'I'll order you some breakfast,' said Francine through gritted teeth. 'What would you like?'

'Sashimi,' said Everton.

Two days later Everton felt well enough to take a limo to the oncologist's private rooms for a second shot of modified brain cells.

'Are you sure you want me to do this?' said the oncologist.

'As sure as anyone can be when there's no other option,' said Everton.

'Do you think it's working?'

'I don't know.'

'How is the trembling?'

Trembling? Everton looked at his hands. Through the headaches and fever he'd forgotten about his hands trembling. He held them out in front of him. Both were as steady as a rock.

'Coincidence,' said the oncologist. 'What about the fits?'

Fits? Everton tried to remember when he'd last fitted. He couldn't be sure whether or not he'd fitted while the fever raged but he knew for a fact that he'd suffered no fits since the fever broke.

'Temporary relief,' said the oncologist dismissively.

He pressed the plunger on the syringe and fired another few million modified brain cells into Everton's tumour.

For the next three days Everton lay in bed racked by headaches and fever. On the fourth day he woke up hungry and ordered steak tartare. Poor Francine didn't know what was going on. She'd had her hopes raised once more only to see them dashed. Her spring wedding was beginning to look decidedly shaky.

Three days later Everton had the last of his injections and suffered only twenty-four hours of headaches and fever. He ordered seared tuna for breakfast and, after circling the plate a few times, attacked it.

Everton grew stronger with each passing day on a diet of sashimi, barely seared tuna and salmon, and steak tartare. It reached a point where Francine contrived to dine out as much as possible because she couldn't stand watching him eat. It wasn't just the fact that most of the food he ate was raw, it was the way he ate it. Where once he had been uninterested in food and hardly picked at it, he now wolfed it down. Great quantities of it. She put the change down to his tumour but that explanation lacked conviction. Cancer patients were supposed to lose their appetite, not discover it. Other things began to annoy her, too. One night she shook him awake.

'What's up?' he said sleepily.

'You're flapping!' she said. 'How can I sleep with you flapping all night long?'

'Flapping?' said Everton.

'Well, whatever it is you're doing.'

'I'm not aware of doing anything.'

'You're flapping,' said Francine. 'That's the only word I can think of that fits.'

'Okay,' said Everton, 'I'll try not to flap.' He rolled over onto his back.

The following morning Francine found him searching through his drawers for a swimming costume.

'But you never go swimming,' she said. They kept their pool heated all year round but Francine was the only one who ever swam in it.

'I need the exercise,' said Everton.

'Why?' said Francine. She couldn't figure out why anyone who was scheduled to die in eight weeks would bother doing exercise. What good was a beautiful body when you were about to be cremated? Besides, cancer patients were supposed to grow weaker not stronger. It was so typical of Everton that he did everything the wrong way around.

'What harm can it do?' said Everton.

Francine wanted to examine that thought further in case Everton was hinting at suicide, but she was running late for her yoga class.

Everton found a swimming costume, slipped a bathrobe on over the top, grabbed a towel and headed down to the pool. He'd sat around it many times but had never been tempted in, not even when it was insufferably hot. Swimming simply wasn't his thing. But on this autumn morning the water looked utterly irresistible.

He dived in. Until then he didn't even know he could dive. He surfaced and began to butterfly-stroke his way to the opposite end. This amazed Everton. Until that moment, he hadn't even been aware that he knew how to do the butterfly. But what astonished him most was the power of his kick. He kicked like a dolphin, his whole body rippling like a sine wave. And he had another surprise in store. As he ducked to make his turn he discovered he could swim faster underwater than he could on the surface. He felt himself able to glide like the space shuttle and cover the length of the pool without apparent effort. This thrilled him as much as any scientific discovery he'd ever made. He decided to see how many lengths of the twenty-five-metre pool he could do on a single breath. He did seven. Seven! One hundred and seventy-five metres on a single breath.

As soon as he was dry, Everton rang the oncologist. He wanted to share the discovery of his astonishing talent. He was euphoric.

'You'd better come in,' said the oncologist.

He put Everton through a series of CT and MRI scans, looked at the results and shook his head in disbelief.

'Your tumour has disappeared,' he said. 'Gone, vanished. I can't find a trace of it.'

'Has it metastasised?' asked Everton. 'Did it spread to any other parts of my body before it disappeared?'

'There is no evidence of metastasis.'

'That's fabulous news!' said Everton. 'That means my therapy has worked. It means I'm cured. It means I'm not going to die! Francine will be overjoyed. I can't wait to tell her.'

'Maybe you should wait,' cautioned the oncologist. 'I want to do more tests. I want to check your chemistry and make a closer examination of your brain before either of us start talking about a cure.'

'Whatever you say,' said Everton. What were another few days if the delay brought unequivocal confirmation of his cure?

'Can I get you anything to drink?' asked the oncologist.

'Got any saltwater?' said Everton.

New commissions rolled in but Everton ignored them. He couldn't get his head around them. He'd faced death and rediscovered life, and along the way realised what a joy it could be. He stayed home and swam, even managing ten lengths of the pool on a single breath. Five weeks from his scheduled death he looked fitter and stronger than he had at any other time in his life.

'What's going on?' demanded Al when Francine met him for lunch.

'I don't know,' said Francine. 'Maybe, just maybe . . .'

'Maybe what?' said Al.

'It doesn't bear thinking about,' said Francine.

'What?' said Al.

'Just maybe he's found a cure. Maybe he's not going to die after all.'

'The selfish bastard!' said Al.

'Everton, you'd better come in.'

'Why?' said Everton.

'I've got your test results back,' said the oncologist.

'On my way,' said Everton. It worried him that the oncologist didn't sound at all excited. There again, Everton consoled himself, the oncologist hadn't sounded excited when he'd discovered that the tumour had disappeared. He put it down to professional jealousy and took a limo to the clinic.

'You'd better sit down,' said the oncologist.

Everton sat.

'What's up?' he asked.

'The good news is your tumour has not only shrunk but gone altogether.'

'That's great news,' said Everton.

'Wait,' said the oncologist. 'The bad news is your brain has started to shrink as well.'

'What?' said Everton.

'Your brain, it's shrinking.'

'Shrinking?'

'Quite rapidly,' said the oncologist. He overlapped the scan of Everton's brain when the tumour had first been diagnosed with the scan he'd done when the tumour had first disappeared. The brain shrinkage was obvious. When he overlapped the follow-up scan the shrinkage was even more obvious.

'Tell me,' said the oncologist. 'Exactly how big is the brain of a great white shark?'

Everton lay perfectly still on the bottom of the pool. If he lay perfectly still he could remain there for up to ten minutes without having to surface for breath. But time was irrelevant to him as he could no longer measure it or even grasp the concept. Language, imagination and thought also eluded him. He still made discoveries but they weren't the kind people got excited about or which generated royalties. For Everton, every journey around the pool was a voyage of discovery. His memory had abandoned him too.

As Everton's brain had shrunk, his cerebrum — the centre of intellectual thought and conscious activity — had closed down. The remaining part of his brain was fully occupied with autonomic functions like heartbeat and respiration, sensory perception like seeing and feeling, and registering things like hunger and pain, hot and cold. Everton didn't know who he was or what he was. He was only dimly aware that he was.

'What are we going to do with him?' asked Al, as he gazed down into the pool. 'Can't we send him away somewhere?'

'He's still my husband,' said Francine. 'And, for all his faults, he was as loyal as any man could be. He promised he'd never leave me. Helping him keep his promise is the least I can do.'

She tossed a handful of raw tuna and salmon pieces into the pool and watched as her husband rose slowly to investigate them.

The Ripple Strip

Aubrey listened with a mixture of awe, envy and dismay as the young woman presented her paper on *The Final Frontier: the structural and physiological adaptations of fish at extreme depths.* The auditorium was packed. Every seat was occupied and the overflow perched cheek to cheek on the aisle stairs. Aubrey hadn't seen anything like it since he'd presented his paper on *Variations in Jaw Bones: a key determinant in the classification of fish*, some twelve years earlier. He sighed. Twelve years. Had it really been that long? That was when he'd been a luminary, a world authority, much praised and sought after for his work in settling long-standing disputes among ichthyologists about which fish belonged to which class, sub-class, order, superorder and so on. Since then his system of classification had been largely superseded as the science of ichthyology had moved on, propelled forward at an ever-increasing rate by a new generation of bright young brains, of which the young woman speaking was but one example.

Aubrey suddenly felt old. When he'd chosen his career he'd been so certain that it afforded security for life. He'd been the first of a new breed, a brilliant young man intruding into a world of grey-beards and lifetime tenure. But everything had changed and, unwittingly, he had been one of the agents of change. The young woman was a consequence of this change.

Her audience sat enthralled as she concisely, logically and confidently presented her discoveries, providing the first comprehensive look at, and understanding of, life ten thousand metres below the surface of the ocean. Her work was brilliant, she was brilliant, and Aubrey was no less enthralled even though each slide and each well-researched observation drove another nail into the coffin of his career. At the relatively young age of forty-two, he found himself treading water and in danger of sinking. His position as senior lecturer in zoology, specialising in ichthyology and herpetology, was under review.

Aubrey didn't know what he would do if his tenure was not renewed, as seemed most likely. He'd made too many mistakes. When his brighter students and burgeoning talents from other institutions had come up with ideas on classification that challenged his, he should have embraced their insights and, in embracing them, contrived a degree of ownership. He'd seen other faculty members do exactly that and had been contemptuous of them. Now he understood their wisdom. Instead of emulating them and ensuring his retention, he'd resisted every idea that threatened a dimming of his light, with the inevitable consequence that he came to be thought of as out of step and behind the times, a fuddy-duddy, an obstacle in the way of progress. He'd tried to shore up his flagging career by extending his expertise to all vertebrates, thinking the extra strings to his bow would increase his value to a university perennially strapped for funds. In hindsight, it was another mistake. The university wanted a mistress, not a wife. It wanted excitement, glamour and the 'sexiness' of new discoveries. Discoveries generated publicity and publicity generated grants. Aubrey's diversification only took him a step closer to the door.

Aubrey had every reason to be concerned about his future. Outside of academia his knowledge held questionable commercial value. His most recent paper had been a highly derivative study of the Patagonian toothfish, a compilation and analysis of other people's work. As an attempt to gain a degree of ownership it had failed dismally, but it had acquainted him with the peculiarities of the species. His work had been based on a desire to preserve the toothfish in its subantarctic environment for all time. Now it offered him a shred of a lifeline. Maybe he could sell his specialised knowledge of the fish's feeding habits, growth rate, breeding cycle and whereabouts to the companies that fished for it. With luck, he might even score a consultancy. The downside was that the personal cost would be considerable. Everybody he'd ever worked with or taught would shun him for ever after. And they were the only friends he had.

He started at the sound of applause. Somehow, his mind had drifted away from the dissertation to his own predicament. He was aware of people standing to applaud and shot to his feet, desperately hoping his indiscretion had not been noticed. Fortunately for him, the auditorium lights were slow in coming back up to full power. He looked down to the stage where the young woman acknowledged the accolades and felt the arrow of envy pierce his heart. A new luminary had been born and now shone where once he'd stood.

*   *   *

Aubrey had some serious thinking to do and did what he always did when the need arose. He checked the tide and moon charts and his own diary of what fish should be where and when, and prepared to go fishing. Fishing for Aubrey involved a six-point-three-metre Bertram half-cabin, which was capable of the fifty-kilometre run out to the edge of the continental shelf in the right conditions, but was also ideal for fishing in Broken Bay and the lower reaches of the Hawkesbury River. He noted that high tide was due at 11.03 pm on a moderate flood and that the new moon would be only briefly visible in the western sky between 8.15 pm and 10.00 pm. His lunar charts indicated that the best time for fishing would occur around midnight, although the fish were not expected to be voracious. That was fine by Aubrey. He was more interested in thinking than fishing and only wanted a couple for the pan to justify the expedition and confirm his expertise.

He motored to his special flathead spot near the conjunction of the Hawkesbury River and Broken Bay. He'd found the spot by accident and had kept it secret ever since. He never fished there in daylight, even when he knew big flathead were in residence and eager to wrap their jaws around anything that moved. The Royal Australian Navy had been responsible for his discovery. They'd begun a program to map the sea bottom in Pittwater, Broken Bay, Sydney Harbour and for three kilometres out to sea as an anti-terrorist measure. The idea was that if they knew what the bottom looked like, they'd be able to spot anything that might subsequently be planted there — smart mines or nuclear bombs, for example. Aubrey thought the navy's concerns were a bit over the top, but he welcomed the opportunity to take part in the program as an observer. He also wanted to know what the bottom looked like to get a clearer idea of fish habitats, likely species and population densities. It was his good fortune that he was aboard the naval launch the night they mapped the ripple strip.

The ripple strip was a series of bumps on the sandy bottom of a kind you'd expect where an outgoing river met an incoming tide. Certainly the naval officers saw nothing worth remarking upon. But Aubrey did. Typically the ripples the sonar identified should have been in shallow water and no more than ten centimetres apart, rising no more than three or four centimetres. But the ripples were actually in a deep trough, up to three metres apart and rising as much as fifty centimetres. Aubrey had never seen a profile like it and had no idea what had caused it. What he did recognise, however, was its potential for harbouring flathead and jewfish, and he took a quick reading from the GPS. With the coordinates noted, he could find the spot again on the darkest of nights, which was precisely his intention.

Aubrey anchored a buoy upstream of the trough and drifted backwards from it, slowly paying out line until he was positioned directly over the ripple strip. He rigged up two rods with enough lead to hold bottom thirty-five metres below, with four-metre traces set one metre above the sinker so his bait would move about in the current. He put a live yellowtail on one line and a gang-rigged pilchard on the other, and sat back to wait for a bite.

The night was even more perfect for thinking than it was for fishing. Once the new moon slid behind the dark mass of Ku-ring-gai Chase the darkness became almost absolute. He left his anchor light on as the law required but with his canopy up he was shielded entirely from its glow. He held his hand in front of his face and grinned when he couldn't even see its outline. With the still water and lack of wind or distraction, the night really was ideal for letting his thoughts run.

Perhaps encouraged by the conditions, his thoughts began optimistically as he considered consulting with the navy, the fisheries department, fishing companies, companies that farmed fish such as tuna, snapper, barramundi, trout, Atlantic salmon and Nile carp, and others that farmed prawns, yabbies, marron and trochus. The possibilities seemed endless until he remembered that the Atlantic salmon farms in Tasmania were in dire financial straits, tuna farmers were under attack from conservationists, snapper farmers were struggling for viability, and yabbies and marron were proving a lot trickier to farm than anyone had imagined. But the really depressing thought was that all these options took him away from where he most wanted to be — lecturing in a university where his knowledge was valued, or as principal research scientist of the fish or reptile section of a reputable museum.

The last possibility was the most attractive but also the most remote because he lacked contacts and, even more to the point, newsworthiness. He had to accept that he'd done nothing in the past twelve years that was outstanding or deserving of such a role. He simply wasn't 'sexy' any more.

The ratchet on his starboard reel announced that a flathead had taken the bait and he rose to wind it in. At one-point-five kilos it was hardly a monster but perfect for the pan. Its arrival did nothing to lighten Aubrey's mood. He simply dropped the flathead into a slurry of ice and saltwater after spiking its brain to kill it, rebaited with another live yellowtail and sent his line back down to the bottom. He returned to his seat, opened a beer and tried to regain his thoughts. But instead of thinking constructively, he allowed himself to wallow in all the 'if onlys' and 'might have beens'. There were lots of them, far too many, and he couldn't help wishing he'd been smarter, or that he could have his time over again. He surrendered to his reveries, and why not? His past was immensely more promising than his future.

He was deep in his memories, almost on the verge of sleep, when he was jolted out of his chair. The Bertram dipped momentarily towards the stern before settling. Aubrey grabbed a torch and raced aft. His first thought was that a log had collided with his boat, but logs drifted downstream not upstream and would have hit the bow not the stern. His second thought was that a large shark had homed in on the weak electrical current generated by the incompatible metals in his stern drive and taken the leg and propeller in its mouth. He'd heard of this happening, had seen photographs, and knew enough about how sharks located their prey to realise this was a very real possibility. He was also aware that he was fishing in the corridor for sharks tracking south down the coast and up into the Hawkesbury River. It was only five short steps from seat to stern but, by the fourth, Aubrey was convinced that when he shone his torch into the water he'd find himself eyeballing a large tiger shark or bronze whaler. Instead he caught a glimpse of a bald head, a beaked mouth, two beady eyes and a carapace over three metres long. A carapace over three metres long! His brain refused to process what he was seeing.

The night was black and the water even blacker but there was no mistake. The top of the carapace was out of the water and the beam of his torch revealed details so unexpected, so improbable, that Aubrey stopped breathing. He noticed his line wrapped around one of the creature's flippers, heard the ratchet on the port reel suddenly scream, saw the carapace dip, heard his line ping as it snapped, and saw the object of his attention disappear so abruptly and completely that he only had the broken line to confirm that it had ever been there in the first place.

'No!' he shouted. He needed more time, time to confirm the impossible, to confirm his instinctive identification, to confirm to his complete satisfaction the miracle that had occurred.

'No!' he cried again.

He'd seen salvation, looked it in the eye, only to have it abandon him as quickly as it had come — but maybe not! He covered the five short steps back to his seat in four large strides and stared at the screen of his fish finder. There the creature was, in mid-water, still diving, a red splotch on his screen at fifteen, sixteen, seventeen metres. Suddenly another red splotch came onto the screen from the side at ten metres, followed by another at twelve metres. There were three of them! Aubrey looked on, incredulous, certain that what he was witnessing was momentous. The upper two splotches were rising. Rising! Coming up to breathe! They exited to the left of his screen at six metres. Aubrey rushed to the side of his boat, tried to judge their trajectory and waited, torch poised, peering into the blackness.

Bluh!

He heard the creature exhale and directed the torch beam further to the left.

Bluh!

This time the sound was further right and out a bit. The torch beam caught disturbance on the water and he briefly glimpsed a dark round shape. Then, frustratingly, it was gone.

Bluh!

Bluh!

Aubrey spun around. This time the sound — no, two sounds — came from the starboard side and closer to his boat. His heart slapped into his ribs like a loose piston and his hands shook so badly he had to rest the torch against the canopy struts to steady it. And there they were, two beady eyes staring back at him as though fascinated by the beam. Even five metres away, with the night and the water swallowing up the light, Aubrey could make out the distinctive ridge and mounds on the anterior carapace. He studied it, suppressing his disbelief, concentrating with all of his might, willing the creature to remain where it was while he logged every single detail into his memory. He couldn't risk another mistake, couldn't afford to base all his hopes on an error of judgement, couldn't stand the ridicule if he was proved wrong. The creature hung there, looking up at him for what seemed an eternity but was probably no more than five seconds. Then slowly, ever so slowly, it submerged.

The dawn light made Aubrey look up. He hadn't worked so hard since he was a brilliant young ichthyologist out to make a name for himself. His desk and the floor around it were covered by reference books, and his printer was stacked high with material downloaded from the net. The first book he turned to had provided the confirmation he sought and everything subsequently had confirmed the confirmation and filled in the gaps in his knowledge.

Unlike fish, turtles had never really been a passion for him. Green turtles up to seventy centimetres in length frequently popped up to say g'day when he fished on the edge of the sandbank just south of Portuguese Beach. He welcomed their company but wasn't drawn to figure out what they were eating or what had attracted them to his boat. While an authority on both fish and reptiles, Aubrey was widely regarded as being a fish man. But that was then and this is now. Turtles were suddenly the most fascinating and exciting creatures on earth and Aubrey couldn't learn enough about them.

The ancestors of turtles first appeared in Africa three hundred million years ago and quietly went about the business of evolving and adapting while dinosaurs came and went. The first primitive ancestors of tuataras, lizards, snakes, amphibians and crocodiles emerged around a hundred million years later. Throughout their steady plod through evolutionary time, turtles had changed very little in basic structure.

Aubrey knew all this, had even taught it, but forced himself to check back over his data in case he'd missed something, or in case some other bright wunderkind had come up with a new theory that changed everything. But he hadn't missed anything, and bright young things had added nothing significant to the sum total of knowledge about turtles.

Aubrey rose from his desk and made himself a pot of strong coffee. He was dizzy, not from lack of sleep but from excitement. The young woman had blown everybody away with her paper the day before, but he was in possession of facts that made her discoveries look more mundane than fish and chips wrapped in yesterday's news. Yesterday's news — a criticism often levelled at him, but never again! The university wanted sexy and, boy, could he give them sexy! But even as he enjoyed this thought and tried to imagine the look his discovery would bring to the faces of the vice-chancellor and the governing board, he realised the inherent problem confronting him: nobody would believe him.

Nobody would believe him!

Aubrey's excitement collapsed in panic and horror. Why should anyone believe him? He could picture himself standing before his department head, telling her that he'd discovered not one but at least five and possibly an entire community of Archelon marine turtles, alive and thriving less than seven kilometres from his back door. He could see her smug, supercilious face and knew exactly what she'd say. He could already hear her patronising voice and its all-too-familiar ring of impatience.

'Really, Aubrey,' she'd say. 'A living Archelon! Sorry, a *community* of living Archelon. You are aware, of course, that the Archelon has been extinct for the last thirty-eight million years. Doubtless you are also aware that no turtle fossils of any of the major groups have ever been found in Australia, none from the Cretaceous or Tertiary periods, and certainly no Archelon or any other species from the family *Protostegidae.*'

She'd dismiss his request for funding and resources out of hand. She wouldn't go so far as to accuse him of fabrication but he knew she'd dismiss his discovery as a pathetic attempt to save his job. Any hopes of resurrecting his career would be washed away in a flood of contempt. Suddenly the glorious morning of his triumph became the dawn of just another sad day.

Aubrey stared into his empty coffee mug. When had he drunk the contents? He poured himself another and slumped down at his desk. What had he been thinking? Did he really believe he could rush into the university, announce he'd just discovered a species of giant turtle from the Cretaceous that had been extinct since the Oligocene and be showered with accolades and plaudits? No, he needed proof, conclusive proof, before he even opened his mouth. He knew some herpetologists who'd even require a live specimen, plus full documentation of its habitat, diet, breeding cycle and favourite TV show before they'd be convinced. He groaned aloud. Without funds or resources how could he ever provide adequate proof?

He was on the verge of surrender when he realised that was exactly what he'd been doing for the past twelve years. Success came at a price and that price was application, diligence, persistence and industry. Damn it! There was a time when he'd had those qualities in abundance and he could see no reason why he couldn't demonstrate them again. He, the forgotten man of ichthyology and herpetology, had the opportunity to deliver the greatest discovery in the history of biological science, to shine once more and bask in international fame and glory, to regain the professional security he craved. All he needed was proof, enough proof — but how much proof was enough? And what kind of proof could he provide?

The answer was so obvious he felt ashamed of himself for even contemplating giving his discovery away. How had he confirmed the identity of the Archelon? By checking his recollection against photographs of fossils. Photographs. He was an accomplished underwater photographer, a skill he'd developed and polished on innumerable field trips with students. Selling reproduction rights of his photos even made a worthwhile, though hardly substantial contribution to his income. All he had to do was take a photograph.

Provided his Archelon returned to the ripple strip.

He groaned again and with good reason. He'd been brought up in Pittwater, still lived in the Clareville home he'd been raised in. He'd fished there for most of his forty-two years and knew people who'd fished there longer. He'd fished the ripple strip at least a dozen times, always at night and always just before the flood and two hours into the ebb. So how come he hadn't discovered his Archelon before? Clearly, to have survived undetected for so long, the turtles had learned to avoid contact with mankind. Was his discovery an accident, a freak event not to be repeated for another thirty-eight million years? There was only one way to find out.

Aubrey's lecture that day did nothing to enhance his reputation. He came home the moment his duty was done and slept for six hours, after which he laid out his wetsuit, face mask, fins, tanks and regulator, camera and underwater light. He checked his equipment thoroughly and found no fault. Aware of the risks in diving alone, particularly at night in a known shark corridor, he considered inviting one of his old students along. The guy was a good diver and often teamed with him on recreational dives. But Aubrey hesitated. Even one diver might scare the giant turtles off; two almost certainly would. He weighed the risk of diving without a buddy against the possibility of results and opted to dive alone. Results took priority over safety.

The moon sat higher in the sky and lasted a little longer, but it was soon as dark and still as it had been the night before. Aubrey sat in his diving gear, his camera and light close at hand, ready to drop over the stern the instant the turtles showed on his fish finder or he heard the telltale bluh of their breathing. A school of tailor passed beneath, followed by a school of what Aubrey was sure were jewfish. Normally this would have had him on the edge of his seat in anticipation of a hook-up. Instead he felt only disappointment. Midnight came and brought with it the peak of the tide. The water around his Bertram settled as the force of incoming tide and outflowing river held momentarily in balance.

That was the instant the first red splotch appeared on the screen. Aubrey grabbed his camera and light but hesitated, eyes glued to the screen. The single red splotch could signal the return of the turtles but also the presence of a large shark. He waited for another splotch, hoping to see a repeat of the pattern of turtles rising to breathe.

Bluh!

The moment he heard that wonderful, priceless sound he climbed over the transom onto the swim platform and gently lowered himself into the water. He let his weight belt take him down to five metres before releasing air into his buoyancy vest to arrest his descent. He adjusted pressure until he'd achieved neutral buoyancy and turned on his light.

Nothing.

Suspended sediment washed down by the river limited the range of his light to around five or six metres. Would it be enough? He began to revolve, moving his torch slowly up and down, desperate for any sign of movement.

Still nothing.

He completed three-sixty degrees and contemplated his next move. If he descended visibility would probably decrease. If he ascended visibility would improve but he'd probably also lessen his chances of spotting one of the turtles. Yes, they rose to breathe but, according to his fish finder, they tended to congregate in mid-water and lower. He decided to stay where he was and complete another revolution. As he began his turn he felt something grab the fin on his right foot. He almost screamed in fright. It had to be a shark! He jerked his leg away and shone the torch down where it had been . . . just in time to see a giant turtle glide gracefully away into the depths, out of range of his light and of his camera. The instant rush of fear and the sudden excitement at seeing his quarry combined to make his heart race at a rate it hadn't achieved for years. He felt the onset of dizziness and light-headedness and forced himself to calm down. After several deep breaths, he continued his turn. He hung there, peering into the beam of light, searching for movement. Would they return or had his sudden movement when he'd withdrawn his foot scared them away?

Something closed around his left fin, surprisingly gently for a turtle noted for its powerful beak and the large crushing surfaces of its jaws. Aubrey slowly directed the beam of light towards his feet, camera poised for what may be his only chance of a photo. The turtle let go moments before the full beam reached it. Aubrey spotted it gliding calmly back down to the depths, pointed his camera and released the shutter. The range was extreme for the conditions but he felt sure he would have captured something. But would it be enough?

He resumed his rotation. Obviously something in the way he moved or the play of the light interested the turtles enough for them to nip his fins. The scientist in him wondered if the nipping was part of a mating or bonding ritual. He was thinking about this curious behaviour when another turtle descended in front of him, not close but in the range of his light. But was it in range of his camera? He had time to fire off two shots before the turtle was lost in the depths. Aubrey hung there for another twenty minutes but made no more sightings and felt no more tugs on his fins. He surfaced, elated, tired, anxious, drained.

Did he have proof?

He placed the camera inside his dive bag and undressed. The evening was warm enough but immersion had lowered his body temperature. He shivered as he towelled down and changed into his tracksuit. He slumped into his seat knowing he'd done something no man had ever done before: he'd swum with Archelon turtles, creatures that had inhabited the oceans along with marine ichthyosaurs and plesiosaurs at a time when the most ferocious carnivore the world had ever known, *Tyrannosaurus Rex*, had held dominion over the land. He wanted to sit quietly in the stillness of the night and absorb that wonderful fact. But there was purpose behind his presence and that purpose could not be denied.

Had the turtles come close enough?

Were the shots good enough?

Did he have proof?

'Well?' said Aubrey.

'Interesting,' said Nigel noncommittally. Nigel was a senior research scientist in the department of herpetology at the Australian Museum. He examined Aubrey's photos through a powerful magnifying glass and checked them against the negative.

'Interesting?' said Aubrey. 'Is that all you can say? For the love of God —'

'What do you expect me to say?' said Nigel. 'If everything you've told me is true I'd give my right arm to be the person who confirmed your identification.'

'Everything I've told you is true.'

'I accept that,' said Nigel, 'on a personal level. But on a professional level I require proof, in fact I demand it.'

'There! There's your proof!'

'If only that were true,' said Nigel. 'I see three indistinct photographs of turtles which possibly have interesting, even intriguing features. But I can't be sure of that. I could be looking at a new species of modern sea turtle or a variation on a known species. That is the most likely explanation. If pressed I'd have to say family *Cheloniidae*.'

'What about the scale? Those turtles were between three and four metres long and that's allowing for underwater magnification. There are no modern turtles remotely that size.'

'Prove it,' said Nigel. 'There is nothing in the photographs to indicate scale. You say three metres long but they could be thirty centimetres. If you'd left your foot in the shot you might have been able to make a case.'

Aubrey groaned. Another 'might have been' to add to his collection.

'Can't you be more positive?' he asked. 'You know me and you know I wouldn't invent something like this. All I want is for you to commit to the point where I'd be justified in requesting resources to conclusively prove their existence.'

'On a lesser matter, perhaps I could be persuaded.' Nigel shook his head apologetically. 'But what you're proposing is that I commit to the existence of a species that has been extinct for thirty-eight million years on evidence which, at best, is ambiguous and could not possibly stand up to rigorous investigation. I'm sorry, Aubrey, and I wish it were otherwise. You're asking me to take a road fraught with peril and I will not do it.'

'My whole life, my career and everything I care about comes down to these three photographs,' said Aubrey.

'Take some more,' said Nigel brightly. 'This time leave your foot in the photo. And tempt the creatures closer. You give me more definite evidence and I'll give you more definite backing. It's as simple as that.'

But Aubrey knew it wasn't.

Aubrey refilled his tanks and checked his equipment in preparation for another attempt to photograph the Archelon. He did it knowing he was destined to be no more successful than the night before, but he could think of no other course of action. There was no point in waiting for clearer, cleaner water because the water over the ripple strip would always be full of river- or tide-borne sediment. The sandy undulations, he now saw, were the result of sediment being deposited over thousands and probably millions of years. He guessed that the trough had probably once been a deep trench that had gradually filled in.

The suspended sediment created another problem. It reflected light back at the lens of his camera. Even if he managed to get reasonably close to one of the giant turtles, the result would still be a grainy, indistinct print, which would inevitably be viewed with scepticism. Throw in the outrageous nature of his discovery and his colleagues and peers would automatically — and rightly — suspect a hoax and his grainy prints would only serve to confirm their suspicions. He thought of the supposed photos of the Loch Ness monster and of flying saucers — all grainy and indistinct like his. Contriving to get a diving fin in the shot would not help his cause either. It could be dismissed as a model, a balsawood or plasticine miniature designed to inflate the dimensions of a common sea turtle.

Aubrey's spirits sank to a new low. Clearly, he would need to be freakishly lucky even to get Nigel's qualified endorsement. He'd not only need to get within two metres of one of the giants but have a yellowtail or a tailor or some other common species of fish in shot at the same time to provide evidence of scale. The chances of that happening were laughable.

Nevertheless, he reloaded his camera, donned his gear and set out once more for the ripple strip. The worst possible breeze had picked up, a sou-westerly, strong enough to put a steep chop on the water and lift spray into his face. He motored along steadily at the most comfortable pace for the conditions. When he reached the coordinates he realised he couldn't anchor upstream as usual because the breeze would blow the boat away from the ripple strip. So he lined up into the breeze, hoping the windage of the boat would outweigh the force of any current. The result was not entirely satisfactory and the Bertram swung capriciously from the anchor buoy. He played out enough line so that he swung in an arc over the ripple strip. The only positive thing about the conditions was that his fish finder would cover more territory and, theoretically at least, improve his prospects of getting a read off the turtles.

If they were there.

He left his navigation lights, stern light and anchor light on to make his boat easy to find after surfacing from his dive. The moon was up somewhere in the western sky but its whereabouts were completely lost behind a leaden overcast. Aubrey opened his flask of coffee, poured himself a drink and sat staring at the screen of the fish finder. An hour passed and the tide reached full flood. Nothing. He watched and waited for another hour but nothing lit up on his screen. No tailor, no Cowan young, no yellowtail, no jewfish and certainly no giant turtles. Disheartened, he up-anchored and turned his boat for home.

Aubrey tried again on the quarter moon once the weather had settled, catching the high tide on three consecutive nights, all to no avail. He stayed home for the next four nights because the high tides occurred on the fringes of daylight hours and common sense suggested that the turtles were nocturnal. If they were diurnal, someone somewhere would have seen them.

He went out to the ripple strip on the nights leading up to and past the full moon, and saw indications of jewfish, tailor and bream passing by, but at no stage did he see anything that suggested the return of his turtles. Aubrey had to consider the possibility that the turtles had been in transit, that Broken Bay was a stopover on their migratory route and they'd just rested up for a day or two. It sickened him to think that he'd have to wait a full year for another chance at a sighting. By then he really would be yesterday's news, out of work and scratching around for whatever crumbs he could glean consulting or relieving sick or absent colleagues.

One flicker of hope remained. Perhaps, just perhaps, the turtles would return on the next new moon. If that happened, he had to be prepared and certain of gathering evidence. But what kind of evidence? Aubrey finally accepted what he'd always known: only one kind of evidence would suffice. He recalled the grace of the giant creatures as they glided effortlessly through the water despite their enormous bulk, and the playful way they'd tugged at his fins. He was well aware that, if they'd wanted to, either of the turtles could have crushed his foot and ground it to pulp. But neither had; instead, they had touched him with their gentleness.

Aubrey abruptly dismissed the sentimental thought that the turtles had somehow 'accepted' him. The Archelon was the most primitive living creature on earth and its brain was capable of no more than coordinating the functions necessary for survival. The turtles hadn't 'accepted' him, they'd simply identified him as not being a threat, and the nips, far from being gestures of affection, were evidence of curiosity in the same way that babies put things in their mouths. This clinical assessment helped Aubrey overcome his natural distaste for what he had to do next. He believed he had no alternative but to collect a specimen.

Aubrey had ten days before the next new moon to figure out how he was going to kill and recover one of the giant turtles. The turtles' sheer size and the thickness of their carapace put any thoughts of using a spear gun beyond consideration. Even if he managed a lucky shot in the neck, the strike was hardly likely to be fatal and he'd end up being towed around Broken Bay until his air ran out. And even in the unlikely event that his shot proved fatal, there was the matter of the creature's weight. A two-metre leatherback turtle weighed around six hundred kilos, which meant a three-metre Archelon would weigh well over one thousand kilos and a four-metre specimen possibly double that. These were the problems he had to overcome. In the end, his plan was beautifully simple.

When he took students on field trips his primary responsibility was to ensure their safe return. Once, on the edge of a drop-off a few kilometres out from Rabaul, a four-metre tiger shark had speared up from the depths and begun circling his group of divers. Its state of agitation suggested it was preparing to feed. Aubrey had herded the students safely back to the dive boat, putting himself between them and the shark. The tiger shark was only five metres away and projecting its jaw forward for the bite when Aubrey was hauled from the water. The experience had unnerved him. From that day on, whenever he took students on dives where an encounter with big sharks was a possibility, he took a powerhead with him.

The powerhead was a two-point-three-metre-long metal pole with a .303 calibre bullet in its tip. Decades earlier, following a fatal shark attack in Sydney Harbour, overzealous divers had all but wiped out the harbour's population of grey nurse sharks by driving the powerhead down on their heads, which in turn pushed the bullet against a firing pin. The bullet simply had to penetrate the cartilage around the shark's brain and the resultant explosion of metal and gases did the rest. Ultimately powerheads were banned but not before the docile, bottom-feeding grey nurses, which had not been implicated in any of the attacks, had been largely exterminated. Aubrey had a permit for his powerhead and planned to use it to kill his innocent, unsuspecting Archelon.

It was never going to be easy to get a good strike on the skull of one of the turtles, one sufficiently solid to ensure that the bullet impacted hard enough on the strike pin to fire, but Aubrey believed he'd figured out how to do it. He planned to hold the powerhead parallel with his legs and strike when he felt one of the turtles tug at his fin. There were risks — that the powerhead would hit his foot or ricochet off the turtle's skull onto the carapace where the bullet would do nothing except scare the turtles off for ever — but he figured he'd have at least a second to work out where the turtle's skull was in relation to its jaws. At night he practised with the disarmed powerhead, imagining the feel of the beak and the position of the head, and rehearsed the short, sharp downward thrust so that it became not only instinctive but carried every ounce of his strength.

The second part of his plan was a little easier, but relied entirely on achieving an effective strike and the virtual instant death of the turtle. Aubrey had seen film of sharks in their dying throes swim away up to fifty metres or more after they'd been hit, despite the fact that their brains had turned to mush. He couldn't allow the same thing to happen to his turtle. Given the limited visibility and the depth of the trough, even a giant turtle could be easily lost and, once on the bottom, soon covered in silt. His plan was to follow the stricken turtle all the way down and attach a line to it with an inflatable buoy. Having fixed the location of the dead turtle, he would return the following morning on a boat used to service moorings, attach a heavy line to the turtle and use the powerful mooring winch to haul it up from the bottom. But everything hung on his ability to deliver the fatal blow, which was why he practised.

Over the last few days leading up to the new moon, Aubrey worked hard on his lectures in an attempt to divert his attention from what promised to be the defining moment of his life and to calm his increasingly tense nerves. Sometimes at night his anxiety became unbearable as all the variables scrolled through his mind. So much could go wrong. What if the turtles failed to show? What if their brief appearance really had been the result of a migratory stopover? What if he missed with the powerhead? What if he failed to strike with enough force to push the bullet back hard enough against the firing pin? What if he only wounded the creature? What if it crawled ashore to die and someone else found it? His whole career was balanced atop a pyramid of 'what ifs', any one of which could bring his hopes crashing down.

When a cold front developed in the Australian Bight and hit Adelaide with winds of near tropical ferocity, Aubrey feared that all his careful planning would also be blown away. He spent hours on his computer studying the Bureau of Meteorology's satellite weather maps. Two days before the new moon, the front began to veer south towards Bass Strait and Tasmania. Aubrey breathed a mighty sigh of relief and decided not to wait for the new moon. He would go that night.

High tide was not until 10.40 pm but Aubrey was in position over the ripple strip and ready to roll by 9.00 pm. The night was reasonably light despite the fact that the moon was in its last crescent, and the nor-easterly wind, which had reached fifteen knots in the midafternoon, had died away to occasional zephyrs. The conditions were as good as Aubrey could hope for and almost a repeat of the month prior. He sat with his eyes glued to his fish finder, expecting at any moment to see the red splotch he was waiting for. By 10.40 pm, when tide and river hung in balance, Aubrey was almost hyperventilating. There had been one false start that sent his pulse rate rocketing when a tightly packed school of whitebait had passed beneath his boat and another when a large fish, possibly a shark, had moved on upriver. By eleven he was beginning to accept that the turtles would not show and by eleven thirty he was convinced. But there was too much at stake to ignore the possibility that the turtles might turn up late so he stayed put, staring at the screen of the fish finder for another hour. Only then did he accept that his Archelon were not coming. Deflated and disappointed he turned for home, consoling himself that the new moon was still two nights away.

The tide peaked at 11.07 the following night and Aubrey maintained his vigil from nine thirty until 1.00 am. There were two more false alarms as more schools of whitebait drifted downstream but no sign of the turtles. Aubrey took heart that he hadn't been anywhere near as tense as on the previous night, but it was faint consolation. He was beginning to accept the very real prospect that his Archelon would not return at all.

The following day Aubrey phoned the university to tell them he had food poisoning and would be unable to deliver his lecture. The truth was, he wanted to rest and prepare himself for the new moon. When he wasn't trying to relax by watching TV, he filled in his time checking and rechecking his equipment and practising the fatal thrust. Nevertheless, when he once more boarded the Bertram he was filled with apprehension.

The cold front had been good to him and had veered away south and east to give New Zealand a pasting. As he motored down Pittwater the water was dead calm and gave off a near-perfect reflection of the lights of Palm Beach. At any other time Aubrey would have appreciated the beauty. He motored out wide around West Head before turning southwest, keeping equidistant from both eastern and western shores. As he expected, there were fishing boats anchored over the Flint and Steel reefs and he gave them a wide berth. By the time he'd dropped anchor and played out line from his anchor buoy it had turned ten thirty. He switched off all of his lights except for the anchor light and hoped that none of the fishermen over the Flint and Steel would be so disappointed with their catch that they'd come over to see how he was doing, or simply anchor nearby on the suspicion that he had local knowledge.

He turned on his fish finder and began the long wait. At eleven he armed his powerhead and at eleven thirty, with thirty-four minutes still to go before high tide, fitted the tanks on his back and his weight belt around his waist. He thought about pouring himself a coffee but worried that he'd only throw it back up. His fish finder picked up signals from fish but he ignored them, refusing even to speculate on what species they might be. He felt hot in his wetsuit and cursed himself for his eagerness in putting on his tanks and weight belt. It was still only 11.45 pm. He occupied himself by mentally calculating how long he'd have to spend decompressing on the way up according to how long he spent on the bottom at thirty-five metres, even though he had a dive watch that automatically did the calculations for him. It was something to do to take his mind off the variables.

He tried to calculate how long it would take the turtle to sink twenty metres, assuming he managed a fatal shot, and how long it would take to attach the lines inflate the buoy and ascend back to the five-metre mark. He thought of another variable. What if sharks homed in on the dead turtle? The realisation that there'd still be the carapace and whatever flesh remained within, both providing sufficient evidence for further funding, calmed him down. He forced himself to take long, deep breaths.

He glanced at his watch. Midnight. Four minutes to the magic moment when the tide reached full flood, four minutes that could determine whether or not he still had a career. He stared hard at the screen of the fish finder. It was disappointingly devoid of any signs of life.

'Forget it,' he said softly. He cursed his stupidity in allowing his hopes to build up, in believing that he really could snatch a last-minute reprieve. Things just didn't happen that way for him. He was becoming increasingly convinced that his sighting of the Archelon had been a once-in-a-lifetime fluke, an event contrived to torment him by a capricious God, when his screen lit up. There were three of them and they were surfacing. They were back!

Aubrey pulled on his fins, spat into his face mask and rinsed it, pulled it down over his face, jammed his regulator into his mouth and picked up his torch and powerhead.

Bluh!

Bluh! Bluh!

Suddenly Aubrey forgot his nervousness and became the expert he professed to be. He knew exactly what he had to do and set about doing it. He descended to five metres and began to revolve slowly, shining his torch up and down as he'd done previously. For some reason there was less sediment in the water, giving him at least another metre to a metre and a half of visibility. He glimpsed the shadowy form of one of the giants descending and knew that others were doing the same all around him. He continued to revolve hoping that his movement and the movement of his light would attract one of them to him. He tucked his light under his armpit, positioned the powerhead and took hold of the shaft with both hands.

Something brushed the underside of his fins and he only just managed to check his reflexive strike with the powerhead. What could he have hit other than the carapace? He forced himself to calm down and think clearly. All of his hopes could have come undone at that moment. Another turtle glided in front of him, turning its bald head and fixing him with its beady eyes. It was massive with a head the size of an outboard motor. Aubrey wondered how he could possibly miss such a large target and simultaneously wondered how his .303 bullet could possibly penetrate such a mass of bone.

A turtle took hold of his right fin.

Aubrey struck thirty centimetres to the right of his foot, struck with all his strength, felt the powerhead crunch down on something hard and unyielding and the recoil as the bullet fired, heard the muffled explosion and the unnerving sound of the turtle's scream.

The turtle's scream?

Even before he'd pulled his foot free and turned his light onto the stricken creature, he realised what a terrible thing he'd done. He let go of the powerhead as if it were something repugnant.

The turtle was still screaming, harshly, the sound now duller and more like a roar. It began to spiral down to the depths, its flippers twitching powerlessly. Aubrey followed. He hated what he'd done, *what he'd had to do*, but still he followed the stream of blood flowing from the turtle's shattered skull. He had a job to do and now there was no choice but to see it through. He knew he'd get over his revulsion given time and the professional adulation that would follow.

He recoiled sharply as a giant turtle cut in front of him,

interrupting his descent, and watched in amazement as turtles came from all directions to the aid of the dying Archelon. Even in the grainy, diffused light of his torch Aubrey could clearly see what the turtles were trying to do. They gently clamped their beaks around the victim's flippers, positioned themselves under its belly and together began to lift it slowly back towards the surface so it could breathe. Aubrey was in no doubt that they were trying to save its life. Other turtles circled, their distress obvious in the agitated way they swam. But it was all too late and their efforts were in vain.

Aubrey's strike had not missed its target. The stricken turtle's head lolled from side to side, paused momentarily upright as if taking one final look at the members of its clan, then closed its eyes for the last time. A single bubble of air emerged from its beak. The turtles ceased their ascent.

Aubrey hovered above them. If it had been possible to apologise for what he'd done, he would have, unhesitatingly. The herpetologist in him watched in absolute fascination. What he'd witnessed was clear evidence of a community working together to assist a stricken member, but the Archelon's primitive brain was not supposed to be capable of any such action, collective or otherwise. He was well aware that modern turtles were reasonably intelligent in that they responded to training and could learn routines, but these giant turtles were demonstrating a higher level of intelligence altogether. And, disturbingly from a personal point of view, they appeared to be exhibiting emotions: distress, sorrow, anxiety, affection. Aubrey abruptly dismissed the latter as a clear case of anthropomorphism brought on by his own regrets. Attributing human characteristics was reading far too much into the turtles' responses.

The turtles slowly and reluctantly turned back towards the sea bottom, dragging the dead Archelon with them. Aubrey followed at a respectful distant but made sure his specimen was always within the range of his torch. He checked his pressure gauge as the turtles descended through twenty-five metres, thirty metres and finally reached the bottom at thirty-five metres, giving Aubrey his first look at the peculiar ripple strip that had originally attracted his attention to this spot. It was only then that he realised the significance of the ripple strip and how it was formed.

It was an Archelon cemetery.

It was also a treasure-trove of fossils and the reason why no turtle fossils had been found in Australia even though it had always been supposed that turtles from the Cretaceous era would have touched on Australian shores. This monumental discovery alone would re-establish his reputation and standing. He cursed himself for not investigating the ripple strip first. If he had, he would have found all the evidence he needed to prove the existence of Archelon turtles and killing one would not have been necessary.

He looked on in wonder as the turtles began the process of burying the deceased. They placed Aubrey's specimen belly down at the end of the last ripple and deposited sand and silt over it with their flippers. Aubrey lost sight of the turtles as the water clouded over. He checked his watch. There was a limit to how long he could remain at this depth and still have enough air to decompress near the surface. Another variable that could bring him undone. But suddenly he felt the ebb tide begin to flow and soon the silted water started to stream away from the site in a cloudy plume. Everything appeared to be working in his favour. All he had to do was wait until the turtles had finished the task of burial, uncover one of his specimen's flippers and attach a line to it.

In fact the turtles quit when they'd only partially buried the carapace, leaving nature to cover the rest in sand and silt washed down by the Hawkesbury River. Again, the forces seemed to be on his side. He waited patiently, hovering above the burial mound until the last of the turtles completed its duties and swam slowly away. What he didn't need was an inadvertent collision with one of the giants as he descended to attach his rope and secure for ever his place in the history of zoological science.

A turtle took his right fin gently in its beak.

Aubrey's initial reaction was to interpret it as an act of forgiveness but he soon dismissed the thought as foolish sentimentality. The Archelon's primitive brain lacked the ability to associate him with the demise of its brother. This turtle was simply doing what the others had done: it was demonstrating its curiosity.

A second turtle gently took his left fin in its beak. Aubrey smiled. If ever there was a creature that deserved the sobriquet of 'gentle giant' it surely was the Archelon. He reached down and gently patted the head of the turtle holding his right foot and began to withdraw his fin from its beak. To his surprise the turtle's grip seemed to tighten. Aubrey wasn't alarmed because the creature showed not the slightest sign of aggression. He patted the head of the turtle holding his left foot and tried to withdraw his left fin but it also tightened its grip.

Aubrey was confused. This wasn't playfulness or simple curiosity. There seemed to be something deliberate behind their actions, a motive. He became even more convinced as the turtles slowly descended, dragging him with them. Frightened now, he tried to jerk his feet free. Neither budged a millimetre. When they pulled him down to the bottom and sat him alongside the carapace of their dead brother, Aubrey began to panic. He kicked out and to his relief his feet came free. He decided he'd surface and return to attach the line once all the turtles had gone. Just as he was about to push off, a massive flipper crashed across his face, knocking his regulator out of his mouth, dislodging his face mask, sending his torch spinning from his hand and laying him flat on his back. This was the kind of collision Aubrey had feared. His hands groped frantically for his regulator.

The flipper hit him a second time just as he located it, stunning him and sending the regulator spinning from his grasp once more. He searched groggily and unsuccessfully for it, lungs aching for want of oxygen. He tried to push himself up off the bottom but felt a sudden weight land on his chest.

Sand. A flipperful of sand!

Aubrey no longer had any doubt about the turtles' intentions. His desperate hands finally found his regulator and he hit the purge button as he pulled it towards his mouth. Too late. Another mass of sand landed on his head and shoulders, burying them. More sand covered his belly, his legs, his arms. Aubrey couldn't move. Couldn't breathe.

Couldn't . . .

A last bubble of air escaped from his mouth.

Fat Boy and the Professor

Fat Boy was easy to dislike.

The first time I saw him I wanted to pick him up by the scruff of his neck and beat some decency into him. I wanted to tell him a few facts of life and how easily the world could do without spoilt, selfish, vindictive little pricks like him. I didn't, of course. You don't do that sort of thing when the parents are loitering nearby.

We were standing on Naviti Lau's one and only jetty waiting for the resort game-fishing boat to unload and motor out to its mooring so we could bring our boat in. I didn't take any notice of Fat Boy and the Professor at first. They were just two kids, ten or eleven years old, larking about. The Professor had just finished videoing the morning's catch. Fat Boy's father and his friend had caught two wahoo on the troll up Lighthouse Reef. Both fish were around twenty-five kilos and they would have been fun to catch if they'd been using ten- or fifteen-kilo gear. Looking at the rods in the rod holders and those being hosed down with fresh water by the Fijian crew, they'd fished with nothing lighter than twenty-five kilos. The best thing about catching wahoo is their first blistering run. There's probably no faster fish in the ocean. But the shock of hooking up on a trolled lure against a heavy drag probably knocked half the fight out of them. I felt sorry for the fish.

Fat Boy's father and his friend were boasting about their catch to my friend and host, Damian, in their broad Californian accents. Damian was being gracious though he was probably every bit as aggrieved as I by the use of such overpowering force on the hapless wahoo. There was nothing to brag about. I turned my attention to the kids. Apparently Fat Boy's dad had also caught a barracuda on the way in. Now I hate barracuda, hate the way they smell and the look and feel of them. When we catch barracuda we do everything we can to avoid bringing them on board the boat, which usually involves hanging over the side and risking being bitten or, in extreme cases, losing a finger while trying to unhook the lure. Barracuda have teeth like dogs and take no prisoners. I guess Fat Boy didn't like barracuda either because he was playing football with the one his father had caught. It flapped helplessly. I may not like barracuda but they do have a place in the scheme of things and I think they deserve better than to be kicked to death by some punk of a kid in overpriced sneakers. As I said, Fat Boy was easy to dislike.

I turned my attention to the Professor. Now here was a kid I could warm to. He was short, thin and bespectacled, with lenses that made his eyes seem as big as oysters. He had the look of someone who did nothing without thinking it through. He was crouched over, a light spinning rod on the planking in front of him, tying a snap swivel onto the line, the very picture of concentration. I watched as he pulled the line tight, tested the knot and clipped on a small metal lure. Clearly he intended to try to catch the trevally or small barracuda that hung around the piles. The moment he stood up and started walking towards the end of the jetty, Fat Boy snatched the rod from his hands.

'That's my rod,' said Fat Boy.

'No, it's not,' said the Professor. 'Yours is the red one.'

There was another spinning rod laid carelessly on the planking behind Fat Boy, just waiting for someone to stand on it and snap it in half.

'It's mine now,' said Fat Boy. 'Anyway, they're both my dad's.'

The Professor silently accepted the injustice and turned his attention to the second rod. The line was hopelessly tangled and the tangles had been wound around the reel. Only an idiot or someone truly thoughtless and spoilt would do a thing like that. I looked at Fat Boy and had no need to look further.

As the Professor set about repairing the damage, Fat Boy attempted to cast. He hadn't bothered to wind the lure up to the tip of the rod and it swung dangerously on about a metre of free line. I was about to say something when Fat Boy let fly. The lure whipped up and caught the sleeve of the Professor's shirt. The kid cried out in shock. The lure could have ripped across his face and scarred him for life, sent his glasses flying to the next island or, worse, plucked out an eye. It was a miracle he wasn't hurt. I stood transfixed by the suddenness of this near disaster.

'Get out of my way!' snarled Fat Boy. He kept jerking the line trying to dislodge the lure. Every time he pulled, the Professor's arm shot up in the air in a fascist salute. 'Dad! DAD!!! Look what he's done!'

'What's going on here?' said Fat Boy's dad. He took hold of the lure and began trying to unhook it from the Professor's sleeve. The Professor was shaking.

'Hurry up!' said Fat Boy.

'Hold still,' said Fat Boy's dad to the Professor. 'What were you thinking of, Anthony? You know you shouldn't stand behind people when they're casting.'

So the Professor's real name was Anthony. Anthony and, I bet, never Tony. I preferred the name I'd given him. It suited him better.

'God damn, I'm just gonna have to cut this hook out.' Fat Boy's dad looked up. 'Anyone got a knife? Somebody bring me a knife.'

'Let me see it,' I said. Over my fifty years of fishing I'd removed hooks from kids' fingers, feet and ears; from the backsides of anglers foolish enough to sit on their tackle; and from every item of clothing you care to name. The sleeve of the Professor's Billabong shirt was a piece of cake.

'You might tell young Zane Grey to wind the lure up to the tip of his rod before he attempts to cast again,' I said. 'Then accidents like this can be avoided.'

Did Fat Boy's dad take offence? Not a bit.

'That's a good idea,' he said. 'Hey, Maurice, wind your lure up to the tip of your rod before you cast. You'll get more distance.'

So Fat Boy was called Maurice. I think my name fitted him better too.

Fat Boy sullenly did as instructed. His cast went all of four metres.

'Fishing sucks,' he said.

'You okay?' I said to the Professor.

'Yes, thank you,' he said. He turned his magnified blue eyes onto me. I looked closely into them to see what he was thinking, but the Professor seemed to have anticipated that. If there had been hurt, pain or even a sense of injustice in his eyes, he had got rid of it. His eyes said nothing and that disturbed me more than anything. Ten-year-old boys shouldn't have to hide their feelings like that.

'Need help to untangle the line?' I said.

'I can do it,' he said. 'I've had to do it heaps of times.'

I bet he had.

Fat Boy left his rod lying on the end of the jetty and sloped off to watch the Fijians cut up the barracuda. The Professor sat back on his heels and concentrated on untangling the line from Fat Boy's reel. No two kids had ever polarised me more on the basis of one brief encounter. I loathed Fat Boy and everything about him and I wasn't very proud of the fact. That only made matters worse. On the other hand, I couldn't help feeling for the Professor. I'd thought the concept of whipping boys was long gone and was stunned to realise it just came in a different disguise. The Professor was Fat Boy's whipping boy, no doubt about it. I knew he would finish untangling the line, pick up both rods, both tackle boxes and the video camera and load them onto Marvin's four-wheel-drive Toyota. I also knew Fat Boy would not lift a finger to help.

Marvin was Fat Boy's dad. He introduced himself after I'd freed the lure. Now there was a name that fitted. It turned out that Loud-Mouth Marvin and his friend, 'Call me Cord' Cordell, had been nobodies prior to the tech boom. Both had started companies that amounted to nothing more than a couple of nerds with electronic boxes and ideas that seemed hot at the time. They'd taken their companies public and watched as the price of the stock soared beyond any reasonable or even unreasonable assessment of the companies' true worth. Naturally, they'd both sold out at the right time and made enough money to buy everything they ever wanted or needed, except manners and common courtesy. Both had traded in their wives for new, younger, high-maintenance versions with enhanced breasts, bleached hair and the brains of Barbie dolls.

'Good luck, guys,' called Marvin, as Damian and I finally pulled away from the jetty to do a bit of fishing ourselves. 'Bottle of champagne says you won't beat our wahoo.'

The Professor had finally finished untangling the line and was winding up the slack. I wished we could have taken him out with us.

'Nice guys,' I said to Damian.

'Well, that's the problem when you have a house on a small island,' said Damian. 'You can't avoid your neighbours.'

'Pity.'

'Marvin wants to come out with us. It's about the fifth time he's asked. I can't put him off much longer without being rude.'

'Just Marvin?'

'What do you think?'

'I think you should be rude.'

By the time we'd cleared the channel the wind had come up, which put any thoughts of a run up Lighthouse Reef out of the question. Instead we motored slowly around to the lee of the island looking for scad and rainbow runners. We put out lures with barbless hooks on ten-kilo lines and set a light drag. The idea was not to catch fish on the troll but to use the lures to alert us to the presence of the fish we were after. As soon as we got a strike we cast out tiny bibbed lures on our three-kilo gear.

When you fish that light over coral you're asking for trouble, but the scad and rainbow runners were only between one and two kilos. Nevertheless, they could put up one heck of a fight and the shallow water over the reef tipped the odds in their favour.

We caught a few scad to smoke and kept two rainbow runners for sashimi when, wouldn't you know it, line started to scream off my reel. I thought I'd caught a passing torpedo. Damian spun the boat around and took off after the fish while I did my best to get back some line. The rod and reel was one I used for tailor and bream back home in Sydney. A one-and-a-half-kilo tailor could take off ten metres of line with ease. My problem was the tiny reel only took around one hundred metres of three-kilo line and the fish I'd hooked into would have eaten a one-and-a-half-kilo tailor for breakfast and come back for more.

Line fizzed off the reel and I actually saw the knot tying the line to the spool before the boat had got up enough speed to gain on the fish. I managed about three winds before the fish took the line back. I saw the knot on five more occasions, each time putting us within three or four metres of losing the battle. Fortunately a fish can't outrun a fast boat for ever and we hot-dogged back half of my line. Now I could use the drag and the spring on the rod to tire the fish. It still took off on blistering runs that had Damian spinning the boat on its axis and setting off in pursuit, but the runs were getting shorter and less frequent. I had to admire Damian's skill. He seemed to anticipate the fish's every move. At times like this, the skipper is due as much credit as the angler for catching the fish, sometimes even more.

I glanced at Damian and the smile on his face told me he was enjoying the fight as much as me. We still didn't know what had taken the lure, only that we had no right to even think we could land it on such light gear. In the open ocean maybe, but we were metres from a reef and continually having to duck outcrops of coral. The fish was tiring but so was I. Veins stood out like twisted cord on my rod arm and the muscles began to cramp from the effort of keeping the rod tip up.

'Keep winding,' said Damian.

As if I'd stop.

The fish swung away from the reef and following it took us out of the lee into the stiff sou-easterly. Now we had to battle the wind and rising sea as well as the fish. I took the tops of green waves flush on my face as we backed up on the fish.

'Keep winding,' urged Damian.

Only death by drowning could stop me winding and, as another green wave enveloped me, I had to consider the possibility. I wound and wound and the fish took back less and less line. We were winning.

'I can see it,' said Damian.

That was encouraging. My arms ached and my eyes burned from the saltwater spray. The boat was pitching and rolling so badly that just staying upright took almost all my remaining energy. But Damian could see the fish. The end was in sight. Of course, seeing the fish and actually landing it were two totally different matters. Two important factors in

fighting big fish with under-gunned tackle are the spring of
the rod and the stretch of the line. Clearly, the shorter the line
becomes as it is wound in, the less stretch there is and the less
margin for error. To be honest, we expected to lose the fish at
this point. We had no double and no heavy-duty trace.

'We'll get one shot at it,' said Damian. He was standing
alongside me with the gaff in his hands. The boat was just
drifting before the wind. I nodded. One shot — if we were
lucky.

'I think it's a *walu*,' said Damian, his surprise obvious.

'*Walu?*' I said. I envisaged the fifteen- and twenty-kilo
monsters we'd caught most evenings in the deepwater
channel between the reefs. I had one of those on my line?
How could anyone catch a Spanish mackerel on such flimsy
tackle and over a reef? I wanted that fish more than any other
I'd ever caught, as proof of an amazing achievement, of our
prowess and for our joint bragging rights.

The fish came up alongside the boat and rolled onto its
side exhausted. Why wouldn't it be? I was. The fight had
lasted almost half an hour.

'Steady,' said Damian.

He gaffed the fish effortlessly, as though our boat was
sitting in the middle of a duck pond instead of a raging sea.

'*Walu*,' he said. 'Can you believe it? A small *walu*.'

Small? He was right. It was a small *walu*, probably no more
than eight or nine kilos. On the scale of things it didn't
amount to much until you took into consideration the
pathetic three-kilo gear we'd caught it on, the proximity of
the reef and the final stages of the fight when we'd had to
battle the wind and chop. All things considered it was a hell
of an achievement. We shrieked and high-fived and carried

on like a couple of kids. That tussle epitomised why we loved fishing. Fish didn't have to be the heaviest or the longest, just the greatest challenge.

We turned the boat around and returned triumphantly to the jetty. Fat Boy and the Professor were back trying to catch the trevally and baby barracuda. The Professor had on a clean shirt. They reeled in their lines so we could tie up.

'What did you catch?' asked Fat Boy.

We showed him our pride and joy.

'That all?' said Fat Boy. 'You ought to ask my dad to take you fishing.'

The wind kept up all night and through the following day. It's nice to fish every day when you're on holiday and surrounded by water that offers the very real possibility of catching something memorable. But it's not essential to go fishing, especially when you've experienced a bit of magic the day before. We went snorkelling with our wives instead, to a sheltered beach where coral trout occasionally visited, big parrotfish nuzzled up to coral and small black-tipped reef sharks kept things interesting. The women loved snorkelling there because they could surround themselves in beautiful, multi-coloured tropical fish in less than a metre of water. My wife, Pru, was always more comfortable when her feet could touch bottom. She and Jenny, Damian's wife, also found the odd collectable shell: nautilus, trochus and kauri shells as well as others with long, elegant finger-like spines. The reef sharks looked on but never came close enough to cause concern.

A golf course ran along the back of the beach like a lush green carpet and the course architects had thoughtfully planted shade trees where beach met grass. The trees not only provided shade and colour but protection from mishit golf balls. A cooler containing a bottle of Bombay gin, two bottles of tonic, two lemons and more ice than we could possibly need made our little piece of paradise perfect.

Sometimes doing nothing beats doing anything else and this was one of those occasions. The women were deep in magazines but Damian and I were both sitting back, letting the sun warm our bodies after our swim, gin and tonics in hand and with as little as possible passing through our minds. I'd once practised meditation and I have to say we were fast approaching a similar state, not so much meditation as profound, utterly pointless daydreaming. When Marvin roared up in his Toyota it was a rude intrusion from another world. We struggled to believe that his arrival had anything to do with us. But of course it did.

'Anthony's missing,' he said. 'I need your dinghy.'

'What's happened?' said Damian.

'He talked Maurice into taking him diving over the reef. Out there.' He pointed to the reef way out in front of the bay. 'He swam away from the dinghy and Maurice almost got swamped looking for him.'

'Where's Maurice?' I said. I almost said, where's Fat Boy.

'He came back and raised the alarm.'

'What!' I said. I couldn't believe what I was hearing. 'He left Anthony out there?' I thought of the wind, the chop, the coral and the sharks.

'That's why I need your dinghy. Ours is swamped. I need to go look for him.'

'We'll go,' said Damian.

Some things were already evident. The Professor couldn't persuade Fat Boy to do anything. The dynamics of their relationship just didn't allow for that. Secondly, the Professor was far too cautious to swim away from the dinghy in open water. Thirdly, Fat Boy was lying through his teeth. As a consequence of all the above, the Professor was in more trouble than he'd ever been in his short life. That is, if he was still alive.

Damian and I jumped aboard the tray of the Toyota and roared off towards the jetty. There was no way on earth that Damian would lend Marvin his dinghy. The man was a fool on land and a disaster on water. He'd shear the prop off on the reef inside five minutes and then we'd have two problems.

Damian grabbed his fuel tank from his locker in the boathouse and connected it up to the outboard.

'You stay here,' I said to Marvin. 'Go get Maurice. We need him to show us where he took Anthony.'

'He was cold and wet,' said Marvin. 'I got one of the Fijians to take him up home.'

The Professor was fighting for survival out on the reef and Marvin sent Fat Boy, the only person who knew where the boy might be, home because he was cold and wet.

'Where did he say they went?'

'Out front of the beach, he said.'

I dimly recalled seeing a dinghy way out over the shallow part of the reef. I'd figured it was one of the Fijians collecting shellfish for dinner or spearing painted crayfish. Either way, I'd assumed it was someone who knew what they were doing. It never occurred to me that it was two reckless boys.

'I think I know where,' I said to Damian.

He engaged gear and we took off, leaving Marvin standing on the shore.

'You know the marker out past Homestead Point?' I shouted.

Damian nodded. Of course he did. He was the owner and I the visitor.

'Start there and work north once we're in line with the beach.'

You have no idea how big an expanse of water can be until you start looking for something or someone. We were out of the main force of the wind but there was enough of a blow eddying around the island to put a chop on the water and lift spray off the top of the waves. Damian slowed and tilted the leg of the outboard as high as he could. Most of the reef was between two and five metres deep but parts rose up to within forty-five centimetres of the surface. With the dinghy bucking like an untrained colt on the chop, it was all but impossible to gauge the depth of the water.

'See anything?' asked Damian.

I shook my head. I tried to stand but gave that up immediately. It was far too rough. Part of me feared that the Professor was already drowned but another part recalled how deliberate he'd been untangling the line on the jetty. There was a kid who thought about things and was very calculating in what he did. But what would he do?

'Turn off the motor,' I said.

Damian hit the kill button.

'What's up?'

'I think we've a better chance of hearing him than seeing him,' I said. 'He's a bright kid, bright enough to find a shallow part of the reef and hang on.'

So we drifted and listened, drifted and listened, knowing the further downwind we went the more chance we had of hearing him if he called out. As the dinghy swung in the breeze I could see the beach where minutes before my only concern had been to finish my gin and tonic before the ice melted. It's funny how quickly things turn around.

'Help!'

Damian and I heard the Professor at the same time. We'd heard him, now we had to work out where his voice was coming from.

'Over here!'

'There!' I said.

'There!' said Damian.

We were pointing in different directions.

'Over here!'

The kid's voice grew fainter the further we drifted. Damian pull-started the outboard and we slowly zigzagged back upwind. Twice we bottomed out on the coral only to drift back free again. Damian killed the motor.

'Over here!'

The Professor's voice was louder, clearer, and Damian and I both pointed in roughly the same direction. That was encouraging. I wanted to call out to the kid, to tell him to keep his chin up, but I knew I'd get nowhere shouting into the wind and, besides, the Professor had probably already worked that much out for himself.

Damian cut the motor again.

'Over here!'

This time we heard the Professor loud enough to get a clear bearing.

'I think I know where he is,' said Damian. 'He's not drifting which means he's hanging onto something. The only thing I know of around here is a pole the Fijians have concreted into the coral to mark a hole in the reef. It's more of a stick actually.'

Damian took bearings off Homestead Point and slowly motored forward.

'There he is!'

I looked where Damian was pointing but the wind and spray still blinded me and I struggled to make out the Professor's head and shoulders. He was exactly where Damian had hoped he would be, clinging to the pole. If we hadn't thought to look there, we never would have seen him. The kid had kept his wits about him and his wits had kept him from being swept away.

'Tell him not to come to us,' said Damian. 'We'll come to him.'

I passed on Damian's instruction but needn't have bothered. In clinging to the pole the Professor was clinging to life itself. Nothing could make him let go until he was in the safe hands of his rescuers. As Damian gently nudged the dinghy up to the pole I reached over, grabbed the Professor and hauled him aboard.

Despite the relatively warm water and the tropical sun, the wind had played on his wet skin and chilled him to the bone. His lips were blue and he shivered uncontrollably in my arms. I wrapped him in my towel, eased off his face mask and held him as tightly as I could. This time his eyes hid nothing. The kid had been scared almost to death. He was still sobbing against my chest when we tied up at the jetty.

'You got him!' said Marvin. His friend, Cord, and the two Barbies had joined him at the jetty. I still held the boy, reluctant to hand him over.

'Hey, buddy, you had us worried,' said Cord.

Not half as worried as they should have been.

'What happened?' said Marvin.

'Maurice left me there!' said the Professor. Even now, after all he'd been through, there was still disbelief in his voice. 'He just drove off and left me there!' The disbelief was now tinged with accusation.

'Now don't go saying things like that, Anthony,' said Marvin. 'That's not nice. Maurice told me what happened. You swam away from the boat.'

'No! That's not what happened. He left me there — he left me!'

'I think we should talk about this later,' said Cord.

'And I think you should listen to him,' I said. 'I've been out there. Nobody swims away from a boat in those conditions.'

'He shouldn't have gone out there in the first place,' said one of the Barbies, who I assumed was Fat Boy's mother. Maybe that was Fat Boy's problem. As a baby he'd been breastfed silicone. 'You shouldn't have talked Maurice into taking you.'

'I didn't,' protested the Professor. 'He was the one who wanted to go. I didn't. He made me go with him. He made me.'

'That's not what Maurice says,' said Marvin. He wagged his finger playfully in the Professor's face, suggesting the boy's lie was transparent.

'He did!'

Marvin tried to take the Professor out of my arms but the boy refused to let go of me. But he had to let go some time. He had no choice.

'I have to put you down,' I said.

The Professor looked at me despondently and I could see that he had already accepted the inevitable. He was the whipping boy and it was time to be whipped. He was the repository of all blame. I smiled encouragingly as I set him down on the jetty, frail, shivering and still wrapped in my towel. I wondered how short-sighted he was without his glasses. I hoped he was very short-sighted. My emotions were swinging between pity and cold anger. I didn't want him to see either.

'It's pretty obvious what really happened,' said Damian.

We were having lunch on the terrace of Damian and Jenny's idyllic holiday home, on the high part of the island above Homestead Point. The house was protected from the wind and a trap for the sun, which lent a sense of unreality to the drama that had just played out on the reef below.

'Fat Boy probably didn't let out enough rope on the reef anchor. My guess is that he was first back into the dinghy when the wind picked up. He probably took a couple of waves over the bow and panicked.'

'So he just drove off and left the Professor in the water?' said Jenny.

'Looks like it,' said Damian.

I loved the way my names for the boys had caught on.

'Can you imagine how that poor boy must have felt when he saw the dinghy leave?' said Pru.

'It must have been horrible,' said Damian.

'The worst part is that lying tub of lard is going to get away with it,' I said. 'Fat Boy can do no wrong. I can't imagine how he and the Professor ever became friends.'

'They only met once before coming here,' said Jenny. 'Apparently Fat Boy's mother and the Professor's mother go to the same gym in Santa Barbara. The Professor's mother and father are going through a messy divorce and they thought it would be good for him to get away. Coming on holiday as Fat Boy's playmate probably seemed like a good idea.'

'Great idea,' I said. 'First he gets stranded out on the reef. Then he gets hung for Fat Boy's crimes.'

'*Badi*,' said Damian.

We all looked at him.

'Up until the mid-nineteenth century in India, a poor man could secure the future of his family by accepting payment to be hanged in place of a convicted rich man. The Hindi word for the practice is *badi*.'

Damian never ceased to amaze me. He was always coming up with stuff like that.

It was midafternoon, that magical time when the type on the pages of the book you're reading begins to swim and your eyes give up the burdensome task of remaining open. All four of us were asleep or on the brink when the phone rang. I wondered who would weaken first and answer it. Jenny groaned as she rose. She wasn't gone long.

'Good news and bad news,' she said. 'That was Marvin. We've been invited over for drinks before dinner. A thankyou for rescuing the Professor.'

'Dear God,' I said. I couldn't think of anything worse, though in truth I wasn't trying really hard.

'The good news is that you'll get to see their house. We had dinner there with the last owner. He's a major Hollywood producer and he used to lend his house to his friends. He had interesting friends — Tom Hanks, Michelle

Pfeiffer, Uma Thurman and Tom and Nicole before they split. God knows who else. The house is utterly amazing, just the sort of place you'd expect movie stars to hang out in.'

'Great,' said Pru. 'I'd love to see it.'

'I think it's a ploy to pressure me into taking them fishing,' said Damian. 'They don't give a toss about the kid.'

Damian was right, as usual.

'So how about it?' said Marvin. 'How about we go fishing in your boat tomorrow morning? Weather forecast is good.'

'Great idea,' said Damian, managing to sound faultlessly sincere.

I tuned out while they discussed the detail. Jenny had said the house was fantastic and it was. It sat on the ridge of a headland, surrounded on three sides by the sea thirty metres below. The architect had obviously been to Bali and been influenced by the homes he'd seen there. The floors were multi-level and built with dark timber while magnificent heavy wooden beams supported the cathedral ceilings. The deck area, which was cantilevered out over the edge of the cliff, was the length and half the width of a basketball court. Greenery and the lack of permanent walls made it hard to know where the outside began and the inside ended. Changes in floor level and imaginatively shaped tanks of tropical fish were used to divide areas off, to separate the dining area from the living room, for instance, and the area where the kids could watch their videos and play with the iMac. It was beautifully done.

The bedrooms were in separate buildings connected to the living area by long wooden walkways which were roofed over but otherwise open to the lush surrounding gardens.

During the tour I'd slipped back to lie momentarily on the bed in the main bedroom. Uma Thurman had slept there some months earlier and, well, I'd always had a thing for her.

The bathrooms were interesting in that they had both an inside and an outside shower. The outside showers were partly walled in and strategically placed hibiscus provided at least an illusion of privacy. Why surround a shower with walls when there's no one to peep? I had to hand it to the architects. Their touches were thoughtful and they'd used a magnificent site splendidly.

Jenny and Pru were in deep conversation with the Barbies. It turned out I'd done the silicone twins an injustice. Both had graduated from good colleges, one with a serious law degree and the other with an MBA. Both had brains and a solid knowledge and appreciation of the arts. It was only in the more mundane areas like parenting that they were found wanting. I guess it just wasn't a subject they were interested in.

The Professor seemed to have recovered from his scare and was transferring video footage onto the iMac. I looked around for Fat Boy but couldn't see him anywhere. He was out of sight and soon to be out of mind, and that was just fine by me.

'So, six o'clock then,' I heard Damian say. 'At the jetty.'

I could tell by his tone of voice that he was anxious to get away. Here's a contradiction for you. We were guests of people who had an indecent amount of money, in a home once frequented by the famous, and what were we drinking? They called it champagne but it was Mitchell Lane sparkling white, the cheapest and, some might say, the least appealing wine of its kind produced in Australia. They'd probably been sent the same list of wines the store in Suva had sent us and, not recognising any names, bought on the basis of price alone. The upsetting thing was that the fizzy plonk was all they offered us to drink. No beer, no spirits, no cheap but endearing red. Even worse, they raved about the Mitchell Lane, constantly congratulating themselves on the bargain they'd got.

'I've pissed better wine than that,' said Damian on the way home.

His observations weren't always erudite.

Marvin didn't have a game boat but any time he wanted to go fishing he could hire the resort game boat, which he did most of the time. But along the way he'd heard stories of fish Damian had caught and become envious. The fact is, Damian fished longer, harder and more skilfully than anyone else and reaped the appropriate rewards. Basically Marvin wanted to cash in on all of Damian's knowledge and experience. We were ready for him and 'Call me Cord' when they showed up at the jetty. We weren't ready for Fat Boy and the Professor as well.

'You don't mind if I bring the boys?' said Marvin.

'Not at all,' said Damian. 'The more the merrier.'

I don't know how Damian kept a straight face.

'I told the boys how good you are,' said Marvin. 'Promised them both a big fish.'

Damian didn't respond, a clear indication to anyone with a modicum of sensitivity that he was not amused. I helped load their bags aboard which seemed to contain mostly Pringles, chocolate bars and soft drinks. There wasn't a hint of a lure or any other fishing equipment. Clearly we were meant to provide it.

We set off up Lighthouse Reef, trolling the right lures on the right weight lines at the right speed. Marvin and Cord settled down alongside Damian and began discussing the Dow Jones and the Nasdac and which stocks had done what overnight. Both Damian and I have investments but the last thing we want to do on a fishy sea on a bright Fijian morning is talk about them or even think about them. I stayed aft, watching the rods and keeping an eye on the boys.

The Professor was playing with his video camera. When we motored past Marvin's house, which looked just as amazing from out at sea, he pointed the camera at it and filmed it. I wished I'd brought my camera because the sun had only just lit upon the house, gilding the roof and windows and turning the surrounding greenery bright emerald. I looked to see if Fat Boy had noticed. He was slumped back on a cabin seat stuffing his face full of crisps.

Game fishing can get pretty boring while you're waiting for a strike. For Damian and me it's normally a period of companionable silence as we scan the ocean for birds or interesting splashes. It's time out to appreciate the good fortune that allows us to be there. For Marvin and Cord it was an opportunity to talk tech stocks and boast of killings. For Fat Boy it was one long opportunity to whine.

'When are we going to catch a fish?

'Fishing sucks.

'When are we going home?'

The Professor just played with his video camera.

We got our first strike an hour and a half out. It coincided with one of the few times Fat Boy got up off his fat arse and he just happened to be passing the rod when the fish hit. Despite being told not to touch the rods, he pulled it out of the rod holder. I hadn't even had time to get to my feet. Just what Fat Boy intended to do with the rod from that point on was as much a mystery to him as it was to the rest of us. He wasn't wearing a belt and it was immediately clear that in any tug-of-war the fish would win hands down. There was a mighty splash out behind the boat as the fish realised it was in trouble.

'Marlin!' screamed Damian. Like a good skipper he was watching the fish, not what was happening below.

A marlin, for God's sake! Here we were, hooked up on a marlin, a rare occurrence around Naviti Lau, and Fat Boy had hold of the rod. It was hard to think of a worse scenario. I raced across the deck to grab the rod from him. My intentions were those of any fisherman: secure the rod, keep the tip up and the line taut until somebody managed to put a belt on. I don't know what sort of fish Fat Boy had caught before but he hadn't a clue. The fish pulled the rod tip down so that the rod was parallel to the sea and Fat Boy dragged hard up against the transom. He screamed as both his feet lifted off the deck. The next logical step was that the fish would pull him overboard. Dear God, could we be so lucky? That thought must have occurred to Fat Boy about the same time it occurred to me. He let go of the rod and its thousand-dollar reel.

This sequence of events takes longer to describe than it did to happen. Probably only three or four seconds had passed from the moment the fish struck. Even so, I was only centimetres away from Fat Boy when he let go. Less than a tenth of a second away. Fat Boy was as aware as I was that help was at hand. But would he hang on? No. He saw me coming and still he let the rod go, almost threw it away, just as

I reached him. That was the last thing I'd expected. We had a marlin on, for God's sake. I made a desperate lunge for the rod but didn't get close.

I pushed Fat Boy away, more vigorously than was probably necessary, and he obliged by taking a tumble which would have cracked any deck less sturdy. I used the security line clipped onto the reel to haul in the rod, hoping against hope that the marlin was still hooked. Some hope. It was long gone and probably still laughing. At least we'd got the rod back which was something, although the reel would have to be stripped right down to its smallest parts and soaked in oil.

'What happened?' said Damian.

I told him.

'Oh my God!' said Marvin. 'You mean Maurice could have been pulled overboard?'

'With any luck,' I said softly.

'What?' said Cord.

'I said it was lucky he fell backwards.'

I couldn't believe Marvin. There was no 'sorry about the rod', no 'sorry about the reel', no 'sorry my ignorant, selfish slob of a son caused you to lose your fish'. None of that was a consideration. Fat Boy was still lying bum down on the deck looking at me in wary disbelief. I think I'd given him more of a shock than the marlin had. I noticed the Professor was still videoing. It suddenly occurred to me that he might have videoed the whole thing, including my vindictive treatment of Fat Boy. If he had, it didn't matter. The Professor was smiling and that was something I hadn't seen before.

After that morning's fishing trip we managed to avoid Marvin, the boys and the Barbies for another two days. Then we had the misfortune to have them turn up on Homestead Beach the same morning we were there. If it hadn't been such a glorious day and if the water hadn't been so clear, we would probably have found an excuse to leave them to it. But we stayed and, while Homestead Beach is a good three hundred metres long and only ten metres of it were occupied, they decided to set up right alongside us.

The smiles froze on Pru's and Jenny's faces. Damian decided that the article he was reading on servicing expensive game reels was the most compelling story he'd ever encountered. I took on the responsibility of engaging with our uninvited guests. I passed some time in polite conversation with Marvin and Cord before wandering over to the Professor and asking him to come snorkelling with me. I'd noticed that he seemed more isolated and withdrawn than usual. He nodded and bent to pick up his face mask and flippers, but not before I'd had a chance to look into his magnified eyes. He no longer made any effort to hide his feelings. What I saw there shook me to the core. There was a sense of defeat, bewilderment and hurt that had him on the knife-edge of tears. I wanted to throw my arms around him but we walked down the beach and into the water instead.

If his video camera had worked underwater I think the Professor would have been as happy as it was possible to be. We spent an hour and a half together, duck-diving, peering under coral heads and swimming from reef to reef. I could hear him exclaiming through his snorkel as we got buzzed by reef sharks up to a metre long, encountered a manta ray about one and half metres across, and made the acquaintance of giant parrotfish, briefly a grand trevally and as many different kinds of tropical fish as there were grains of sand on the beach. As it happened, it turned out that tropical fish were the problem.

I'd just towelled down and settled back with a deserved gin and tonic when Marvin dropped his bombshell. The Professor had wandered off up the beach by himself to video shells.

'We're sending Anthony home tomorrow,' said Marvin.

'What?' I said. I was peripherally aware of Damian lowering his magazine.

'I don't know,' said Marvin. 'We try and do our best by him but we just can't deal with him any more.'

'What's the problem?' asked Damian.

'Oh, lots of things. You know, swimming away from the dinghy that time they went out snorkelling. Kid could have got himself killed and, my God, what would we have told his parents?'

I couldn't believe what I was hearing. I guess Damian, Jenny and Pru couldn't either because a deathly silence had descended.

'The tropical fish were the last straw.'

'What happened?' I asked.

'We couldn't figure out why they started dying on us. It turned out Anthony had been urinating into the tanks.'

'I don't believe that for a second,' I said, probably more forcefully than was polite.

'Oh, he did it all right,' cut in Cord.

'How did you find out?' I asked. 'I mean, did you see him do it?'

'No,' said Marvin. 'But Maurice did.'

I felt so bad about what had happened to the Professor that I offered to drive him out to the airstrip in Damian's Suzuki. I lied and told Marvin that I had to meet the plane anyway, that it was bringing us more supplies. Even so, I didn't expect Marvin to agree; after all, they had a duty of care to see the Professor safely aboard.

'Hey, that's downright neighbourly of you,' said Marvin. 'You hear that?' he said to his silicone soul mate. She was downright appreciative too.

That night I put pen to paper and wrote a letter to the Professor's mother outlining what I believed had really transpired and the injustice of the way her son had been treated. I told the others what I'd done and they each added a footnote and their signature. None of us could bear the thought of the Professor arriving home in disgrace.

The next morning I collected the Professor and his bags and drove him out to the airstrip. While we were waiting for the plane I handed him the letter and told him what was in it. He stared at it for a few moments and then his eyes lit up, more brightly than I'd thought possible, and even seemed to dance.

'I really appreciate this,' he said. 'The fact that you all signed it. That makes it really special. But it wasn't necessary.'

Wasn't necessary?

He reached into his bag and extracted a DVD. His magnified eyes watched me expectantly and lit up again when he saw comprehension dawn in mine. Suddenly it all came together. The video camera and the iMac. Doubtless the kid was a whiz on iMovie.

'You take it,' he said, handing the disc to me.

'You sure?' I said.

'I don't need it now,' he said. 'Not now that I have this.' He held up my letter as though it was a trophy, before carefully zipping it into a side pocket of his bag.

'I'm sorry you have to go,' I said.

'I'm not,' he said. 'Not any more.'

Jenny rang Marvin and told him the Professor had given me a DVD of some of the footage he'd taken with his video camera and could we watch it on their iMac? She sweetened the pill by saying we'd bring a couple of bottles of Veuve Clicquot and some sushi. Marvin thought that was a great idea. Clearly he was just smart enough to know that a fifty-dollar-a-bottle Veuve might have the edge over a four-dollar-a-bottle Mitchell Lane. So we found ourselves back at their place, sipping and supping while we watched the sun go down in a blaze of glory. Fat Boy was moping around suspiciously.

'He's missing his little friend,' said Marvin's Barbie.

'That reminds me,' I said. 'The disc.'

We all rose and wandered over to the iMac. I passed the DVD to Fat Boy.

'Stick around,' I said. 'With any luck you might be in the movie.'

I think that was the point when Fat Boy realised this was one movie he didn't want to be in. He wasn't wrong.

The movie opened innocently enough on a close-up of a hibiscus bloom, but then slowly pulled back to reveal Fat Boy on tiptoe peering through the bush.

'Isn't that cute?' said Marvin's Barbie.

'Hey, that's our outside shower!' said Cord's Barbie. She obviously didn't think it was cute at all. 'He's peeping at us in the shower!'

'No!' said Marvin.

Yes, said the footage.

There were lots more scenes of Fat Boy peeping into showers and into the guest bedroom midafternoon, when Cord and his Barbie might just have been enjoying a bit of horizontal dancing. By the sharp intakes of breath alongside me, I guessed that thought had also crossed their minds. There was Fat Boy, albeit silhouetted, peeing into the fish tanks and Fat Boy dribbling spit into glasses of beer. I was both grateful and relieved that they'd offered us nothing but Mitchell Lane the previous visit. If Fat Boy had been my son I would have turned off the DVD there and then and dealt with its contents in private, one on one, with my hands around the evil little brat's throat. But I think his parents were too stunned by the revelations to react. And there was something awfully compelling about watching. The Professor had done a good job of editing and kept scenes short. I couldn't help wanting to know what other horrors would be revealed. But then the scenes changed to footage obviously taken while the camera was concealed in a bag. It showed Fat Boy slumped on his bed.

'Why did you drive off in the dinghy and leave me?' said the Professor off-camera. 'I could have drowned.'

Fat Boy's face curled in a smug grin. 'But you didn't drown.'

'But I could have. Why did you leave me like that knowing I could drown?'

'I told you to hurry up,' snarled Fat Boy. 'I warned you. I told you I was cold.'

'But you didn't give me a chance to swim back to the dinghy.'

'I told you I was cold! If you wanted to come back with me you should have been quicker.'

It was at this stage that I reached over and stopped the DVD.

'I'm sorry,' I said. 'I had no idea.'

'Revenge is a dish best served cold,' said Damian on the way home.

'He didn't make the DVD for revenge,' I said. 'He made it for his mother. I think he knew all along that the holiday would end badly. It was only when I handed him the letter that he realised the opportunity for revenge and gave me the DVD. He knew I'd find a way to use it.'

'Smart boy,' said Pru.

I thought of the Professor and the way his big blue eyes had lit up when he'd passed me the DVD. I couldn't help looking up at the night sky as I got out of the Suzuki. Somewhere high above the Pacific the Professor was sitting in an aeroplane. I bet his eyes were still dancing.

Second Best

If you were a good darts player and you threw a dart at a map of the United States of America, there's every chance your dart would land somewhere close to Salina, Kansas. Salina is about where the bulls-eye would be and about as far from the ocean as you can get in mainland USA.

People from Nebraska and the Dakotas might point to the Gulf of Mexico and claim they are further from the ocean than Kansas, but these states are all within a day's drive of the Great Lakes and, as far as Salina-born-and-bred businessman Karl B. Reinburger II was concerned, this invalidated their claim.

His father had taken him to Racine, Wisconsin, on the shores of Lake Michigan when Karl II was just ten years old. He'd stood on the shore and gazed out, fully expecting to see the other side of the lake. When he didn't, and saw only an endless expanse of water, he was convinced his father had made some kind of mistake and taken him to the shores of the Atlantic Ocean instead. It took a lot to persuade him otherwise. He went home convinced that lakes the size of an ocean should be called an ocean so young people from the

Midwest plains didn't get confused. He regarded the Great Lakes as oceans from that day forth.

Karl B. Reinburger II was named after his father who thought it was neat to pass his name on to his first-born son and suggested his son did likewise. If he'd hoped to establish a family tradition he was destined to be disappointed. Karl had two sons among his four children, neither of whom he named Karl. It wasn't that Karl II disliked his name, it was just that the appendage — 'the second' — seemed to set the tone for his life.

Like everyone else, Karl II wanted to be a winner but his father's whim took on the form of prophecy. Right through school, Karl always came second in his class to a girl called Gretchen, who was a straight-A student and universally regarded as the smartest kid Salina had ever produced. People thought they were doing the right thing by Karl when they clapped him on the back and told him he was the second-smartest kid Salina had ever produced, but that wasn't what Karl wanted to hear.

When he played little league baseball, his team was beaten in the final three years in a row.

When he played little athletics, it was Karl's bad luck to come up against a kid with wings on his feet. In any other year he might have been champion, but his father's whim decreed that he run second.

Karl thought about switching to basketball but he was too short. He thought about switching to gridiron but he was too thin. Not even being the second-fastest kid of his age could get him on the team.

By the time he enrolled in the University of Kansas he was tired of coming second but soon discovered that coming second in Salina was a whole lot better than anything he could expect at college. While other kids played around and got drunk, Karl applied himself and worked as hard as he knew how. His application almost took him to the top.

He became vice-president of the debating club, deputy editor of the college magazine and came runner-up in a competition to write a new song for the college gridiron team. He married the girl who came second in a poll to choose the leader of the cheer squad.

Karl II left college with a business degree, which earned him the only job going in his home town at the time: manager of the second-largest privately owned market in Salina. Calling the business a market flattered it. In reality it was just a general store that had got a bit above itself. The market was on the slide, but nothing Karl said or did could convince the ageing owner to change his outmoded methods of doing business.

When the business began to fail, the owner tried to sell it but no one was interested in a business going nowhere in a town headed in the same direction. There was some talk of pulling the building down and putting in a gas station, but even that fell through. The owner was on the point of closing the door for ever when Karl offered to buy the business and pay for it over time. The owner thought Karl was on a hiding to nothing, but, faced with the possibility of an income stream over the probability of carrying an empty building, he accepted Karl's proposal.

That was the turning point for Karl and the business.

People came to see if the newly named Karl's Mart was any better than the old market and weren't surprised to discover it was. They all knew Karl II was the second-smartest kid Salina had ever produced and that he was a worker. They expected nothing less of him. His business expanded into the building next door and became a real market, where customers could find pretty much everything they wanted at a reasonable price. Karl was lean and hungry and nothing in his lifestyle gave rise to suspicions that he was living high on the hog at their expense, so the people supported him. Midwest folks are like that.

No one was surprised when Karl's Marts started appearing in Junction City, Great Bend, Dodge City and Garden City. Karl knew what Midwest folks wanted and gave it to them. He expanded into Wichita, the second-biggest city in Kansas, and Lincoln, the second-biggest city in Nebraska.

'The Wal-Marts and K-Marts have the biggest cities wrapped up,' Karl liked to say. 'Best not to tangle with them.'

No one was surprised when Karl's Marts became the second-largest chain of privately owned stores in the Midwest, and no one was surprised when, at the age of sixty, Karl decided to hand over the day-to-day management of the business to his equally hard-working children.

What surprised everyone who knew him was his decision to take up fishing. What really surprised them, more than they cared to admit, was his decision to take up ocean fishing, given Kansas's geographic position and the fact the nearest Karl had ever been to any ocean was his one and only trip to Lake Michigan. But Karl had found a way to right the injustice that had blighted his life.

His Salina store had once carried a complete collection of Zane Grey's fishing stories, leather-bound editions from The Derrydale Press. Not surprisingly, they weren't a hit in landlocked Kansas. When they didn't sell he'd taken them home to read and they had opened his mind to a world as far removed from Salina as he imagined any place could be. More importantly, they opened up the possibility of shrugging off the curse that had shackled him all his life. Zane Grey showed Karl II how he could become Karl the Champion.

Second to none.

Numero uno.

El toppo doggo.

Until Karl II read Zane Grey's fishing adventures, it had never occurred to him that it was possible for a Midwestern storeowner to be number one in anything, let alone a world record holder. But that was the wonderful thing about game fishing: ordinary people, as opposed to professional athletes, could win tournaments, ordinary people could become world record holders. Thin, short and unathletic, Karl was about as ordinary as anyone could be.

Karl read and reread the six books in the Zane Grey series until the pages became dog-eared. He wanted to discuss his favourite books, *Tales of Swordfish and Tuna* and *Tales of the Angler's Eldorado*, and talk about his ambitions but who was there to talk to? Saltwater game fishing wasn't the sort of thing that got discussed in Salina and, besides, his customers might think he was getting a bit above himself. Midwestern folks didn't take kindly to that and he had his stores to consider. So he kept his dreams to himself and read his books at night after he'd finished doing his accounts.

Some time later his wife went on a trip to Kansas City and brought him home a copy of *The Old Man and the Sea*. He read it and reread it until he could almost recite every word. Yes, he sympathised with the old man and shared his pain and disappointment, but what encouraged him, what excited him beyond measure, was the fact that the old man, with the most meagre of resources, had caught such a magnificent fish — a trophy winner and a possible world record. If the old man could do it, so could he, and his resources would be anything but meagre. He'd made up his mind to fish the Caribbean and the Gulf of Mexico until his wife went on a second trip to Kansas City and brought home a copy of John Steinbeck's *The Log from the Sea of Cortez*.

Steinbeck's descriptions of his boat, the *Western Flyer*, sitting in a sea surrounded by thousands of jumping swordfish, thousands of acrobatic porpoises, stampeding schools of dorado and lazy pods of grey whales, filled Karl's imagination to bursting. This wasn't fiction. This was real. These were observations made with scientific detachment. He used the internet and logged onto *Amigos de Baja* and made fishing friends on the web. Some backed up Steinbeck and claimed to have seen the waters off Buena Vista on the south-eastern coast of the Baja Peninsula boiling with leaping marlin. Karl closed his eyes and tried to imagine the wonder of it all.

Everyone has something they want to see before they die. For some it's something as simple as the Grand Canyon, for others it is earth from space. Karl just wanted to see what Steinbeck saw. He thought about the Sea of Cortez every day while he waited to turn sixty.

Karl didn't just race off and buy a boat. He did his homework with regard to the kind of conditions he was likely to experience, the kind of fish he wanted to catch and the kind of comforts he needed. Typically, he wanted to provide for the times his wife would accompany him and when he'd play host to each of his children and their families. He settled on a thirty-year-old Elliott Sportsfisher, an elegant, handcrafted cruiser fifty-nine feet in length. The flying bridge was well equipped and big enough to accommodate the permanent crew of two. Below, there was a well-equipped galley, a lounge/dining room/day area with glass doors that opened wide to the rear deck, a stateroom with a queen-sized bed and a cabin with four bunk beds. Below decks amidships there were a pair of freezers, generators, a battery of water purifiers and as much storage room as he could ever need. Beneath the stern deck there were twin generators and two mighty diesels. There was no question that the Elliott was luxurious but it was luxury without excess, and age had imbued it with a sense of efficiency and practicality. In many ways it was a reflection of its new owner.

The Elliott was called *Billfisher II* when Karl bought it. Karl was happy with the Billfisher part but had the ship chandler paint out the II before he took delivery. Coming second or being second had no part in his new life. *Billfisher* was a lovely old lady with a top speed of seventeen knots stripped down and with near-empty tanks. In fishing trim with full tanks, thirteen knots was closer to the mark. It was painfully slow compared to the modern game boats with their planing hulls, but Karl was in no hurry to go anywhere. He had all the time in the world.

Karl hired a crew out of San Diego to run *Billfisher* down the west coast of the Baja Peninsula to Cabo San Lucas. His friends on the internet had advised him to take on a Mexican crew and even lined up a skipper for him, twenty-four-year-old Gerardo, and a twenty-two-year-old deckhand called

Jose. Both of them had grown up on game boats. Karl was
suspicious of their youth and probable lack of experience.
With his American crew looking on, he made Gerardo and
Jose take *Billfisher* in and out of dock three times with a stiff
sou-wester on their beam. They did so with ease and a sense
of bewilderment. They couldn't comprehend why Karl had
even asked them to demonstrate their skill once, let alone
three times. Game boats were all they'd ever known.

'These kids are good,' said his American skipper
grudgingly. What he was really saying was that they were
excellent.

Satisfied that both boat and crew were sound, Karl set about
enjoying his semiretirement. He spent between two and
three weeks of every month during the fishing season
learning how to fish, flying back to Salina between trips to
oversee the running of his chain of markets.

It took Karl all of his first season to get the hang of fishing.
Considering the pride they took in their ability to catch
marlin, Gerardo and Jose were commendably patient in
teaching their new *patrón* how to reel in, how to keep the
fish's head turned towards the boat, how to keep tension on
the line and how to make the rod do the work. Karl wasn't
their first greenhorn *gringo* but they'd never had one quite so
green before. Karl knew nothing. He'd never tied a hook on
a line, never caught a fish. But he applied himself to learning
as he'd done to everything else important in his life and
worked hard at getting better.

Gerardo thought he'd begin teaching Karl the ropes by
trolling for skipjack. What could be easier? But Karl managed
to make a hash of hauling in the two- and three-kilo fish that

queued to impale themselves on his lures. He managed to break two nine-kilo rods, lose as many fish as he caught and hook-up his shirt, his trousers, his hat and, on one memorable occasion, a substantial portion of his backside. Gerardo and Jose looked on in despair. But Karl's enthusiasm and determination grew with every fish he caught and every night he took to his bed as excited and as happy as a child.

Meanwhile, Gerardo and Jose mournfully watched the sailfish, striped marlin and blue marlin glide by in easy casting distance and prayed for the day when their *patrón* would be capable of catching one.

Karl gradually worked his way up from small skipjack to big skipjack and then to the hard-charging dorado. When he hooked his first dorado, Karl could not believe how ferociously it fought, or how fast it could run or how beautiful it looked when it tail-walked with all its colours aglow. He could not believe how a fish that barely topped eight kilos could leave him so exhausted. What would a marlin be like, he wondered. He thought of the two- and three-hundred-kilo blues that roamed the Sea of Cortez and found it hard to believe that anyone managed to catch them.

By the end of the season, Karl was regularly pulling in dorado over twenty kilos and had caught a forty-two-kilo yellowfin tuna. His technique had improved dramatically but he still had a long way to go. He still had to learn to tie knots, tie a double and cast live bait. He still had to learn how to fight the fish, to short stroke and not to waste his strength fighting the spring of the rod, but he was growing in competence.

At the beginning of the Mexican summer, Karl arranged for Gerardo and Jose to take *Billfisher* north to San Diego to avoid the hurricane season while he flew home to Salina. When Gerardo took Karl to the airport at La Paz, the skipper took his hand.

'*Patrón*,' he said, 'remember what you have learned. When you come back we will catch marlin. Striped and blue. *Rayado* first, then *azul*. I promise you.'

Marlin rayado. Marlin azul. Karl rolled the magic words around in his mouth and savoured them all the way back to Salina.

Karl caught his first marlin in the first week of his return to the Sea of Cortez, but it wasn't the first fish he caught. Fearing the worst, Gerardo made his *patrón* do a refresher course and took Karl to the fishiest place he had ever seen.

'What is this place?' Karl asked.

'*Arrecife de la Foca*,' said Gerardo.

'What's that in English?'

'Seal Rock,' said Gerardo.

'Why did I ask?' said Karl.

Seal Rock was the perfect place to hone his skills. It sat alone, no more than twenty metres around, in a seemingly empty sea, an insignificant sentinel rising from the deep. But Seal Rock was anything but insignificant to the sea life that surrounded it. Seals and sea lions crowded every inch of the rock while the waters around it teemed with fish and the air screeched with whirling, diving sea birds.

Gerardo made Karl bait his own hook with live *caballitos* and cast the small fish into the swirling masses of skipjack. He cast ten times and landed ten fish. Gerardo was impressed, unaware that his *patrón* had spent hours every day practising casting on the lawn behind his house.

He attached a sinker to Karl's line and sent it plummeting down to a rock shelf ten metres below. Karl hooked up immediately and, after a brutal arm wrestle during which he fought the fish perfectly, landed a twenty-three-kilo yellowtail. Gerardo was impressed, unaware that his *patrón* had fitted a harness to his pet labrador, attached a line to the harness, and spent most of the off-season practising reeling in his dog while his grandchildren offered it inducements to run in the opposite direction.

Karl fished to the point of exhaustion, releasing all his catch save for the yellowtail and half a dozen snapper. He lost no fish, broke no line and worked his rod confidently and expertly. The transformation of their *patrón* was so great, Gerardo and Jose believed they were witnessing a miracle. What they were really witnessing was Karl's determination.

'Tomorrow, *patrón*, we go after the marlin,' said Gerardo.

The following day they made the run down from La Paz to Buena Vista, trolling out wide around the island of Cerralvo, but no billfish so much as looked at their lures. Neither did any other fish. Karl wondered if they'd headed south too soon.

'Tomorrow we fish the eighty-eight,' said Gerardo. 'Ask me tomorrow if we have come too soon.'

'The eighty-eight?'

'*Si, patrón*, the eighty-eight.' Gerardo opened his charts and pointed to an underwater mountain. 'Eighty-eight fathoms. The water around it is between two and four hundred fathoms. This is where we will fish tomorrow, this is where you will catch your marlin.'

Karl looked at all the other game boats anchored off the beach at Buena Vista and felt his excitement build. There had to be sixty of them and they had to be there for a reason. If he was early so were they, and they were too many to all be wrong.

Billfisher was the first boat to haul anchor in the morning but not the first out to the eighty-eight. For three hours, Karl watched the big planing game boats roar past him followed by the local hire boats filled with holidaying *gringos* and *chilangos*, the not-always-loved residents of Mexico City.

'Don't worry, *patrón*,' said Gerardo. 'Their lures will only raise the fish for us. The more there are of them, the more fish there will be for us.'

Karl knew there was truth in what his skipper said, otherwise tackle shops would not sell rattlers and teasers designed to bring fish to the surface. All the same, as he watched boat after boat speed past them, he wondered how there could possibly be any fish left for him.

'Look, *patrón*,' said Gerardo. 'Porpoises.'

Karl had seen porpoises before but none doing what these porpoises were doing. As though bored by their normal games, they were racing each other upside down, hurdling waves belly up. They wore grins on their faces as if aware of the silliness of what they were doing and Karl couldn't help but smile back. A little further on they encountered spinner dolphins competing with one another to see how many rotations they could do before they crashed back into the water.

'Is this normal for here?' asked Karl.

'They are playing because they have eaten,' said Gerardo. 'This is a good sign. It means there is plenty of bait fish.'

It was another thirty minutes before they reached the rise and put out their lures. Karl counted more than forty other game boats plying the same eighteen-kilometre strip of water and guessed there were more further south that he couldn't see. He was wondering what sort of chance he stood in the face of such competition when a striped marlin cleared the water not fifty metres to starboard of them.

'The boat next to us has hooked up,' said Gerardo.

'Two more over this side,' said Jose.

Wherever Karl looked, striped marlin were soaring out of the water, shaking their heads desperately as they tried to throw the hook. He checked his own lures but they failed to attract attention.

'Marlin, marlin!' screamed Gerardo, pointing to a spot on the surface just seven metres off the bow.

Karl stood transfixed. All there was to see was the tip of a marlin's crescent tail beating slowly back and forth. The fish seemed totally unaware of the presence of the boat.

'Quick, *patrón*!' screamed Gerardo, slipping the boat into neutral, but Karl was too overawed to move.

A line flicked out dropping a live *caballito* right in front of the marlin's bill.

'*Patrón, patrón,* take the rod,' screamed Jose.

Almost immediately, line began stripping off the reel.

'*Patrón, patrón*!'

Karl snapped out of his trance and grabbed the rod.

'Count to five, *patrón*, then set the drag and strike hard.'

Karl swung into action. How many times before had this scenario played out when they were chasing dorado? How many times before practice makes perfect? But butterflies swarmed in his belly, his heart leapt into his throat and his

hands shook uncontrollably as he took the rod and set the
butt into the gimbal of his game belt. This was the real thing
and no amount of practice had prepared him for the thrill of
his first marlin.

'Three,' he counted.

'Four.' He set his feet.

'Five.' He pushed the drag up against the stops, felt the
weight on his line and struck.

And struck again!

Karl nearly lost the battle there and then when the
panicked fish launched itself clear of the water barely ten
metres from him. Stunned, he let the fish pull down his rod
so that all the strain was placed directly onto the reel.

'Lift, *patrón*, lift!' screamed Gerardo.

Karl lifted, grateful that his error hadn't cost him his fish.
The rod bent over hard as the marlin continued its dash for
freedom. He let it run, counting the jumps. Eight ... nine ..
. ten ... eleven ... Eleven jumps in a row!

'It is a trophy fish, *patrón*,' cried Gerardo gleefully.

Trophy fish? A smile spread across Karl's anxious face that
not even dynamite could have dislodged. His first marlin was
a trophy fish. A trophy fish! He settled down to the fight.

'Short stroke,' instructed Gerardo.

'Not too fast.

'Keep the tip up.

'Very nice, *patrón*, very nice.'

Karl knew he was making mistakes, knew he was fighting
the spring of the rod and was all too aware of his impatience.
But this was his first marlin and a trophy fish. And what a fish!

'When he lifts out of the water you must pull hard,'
shouted Gerardo.

Karl pulled hard.

'In the water he is strong,' said Gerardo. 'In the air he is weak.'

Weak was not a word Karl would have used to describe this fish. It fought magnificently, ferociously, spectacularly. But after twenty minutes of throwing itself about the ocean, the marlin began to weaken and Karl managed to claim back some of his line.

'Wind, *patrón*,' shouted Gerardo as he began to back the boat up to the fish.

Karl wound.

'*Patrón*, you want to take this fish?' asked Gerardo.

Karl stared at his marlin as it flashed colour back at him. After his wife on their wedding day and his kids as they entered the world, his marlin was the most wonderful, magnificent thing he had ever seen. His choice was easy.

'No,' he said.

'It's okay to take your first,' said Gerardo. 'Most people do.'

'There'll be others,' said Karl.

'But this is a trophy fish, *patrón*.'

'We're not in a competition,' said Karl. 'There's no trophy to win.'

'You want Jose to let it go?'

'Is it a world record?' asked Karl.

'No, but it is a good fish for thirty-pound line,' said Gerardo.

'Not good enough,' said Karl. 'Let it go.'

Once Jose had hold of the trace, Karl lowered the tip of his rod.

'Your camera, *patrón*,' said Gerardo.

Jose cut the fish free but held onto its bill, gently towing it so that the water passing through its gills could re-oxygenate the marlin's blood and help it recover. Karl took shot after shot while the fish lay quietly on its side, its big black eye staring up at him, assessing him as though preparing for their next encounter. Then, with a single beat of its tail, it wrested free of Jose's hand and spiralled away to the depths.

'Congratulations, *patrón*, your first marlin,' said Gerardo. 'It will go and sit on the bottom for a day or two while it recovers its strength. Next time we meet this fish it will be even bigger and stronger.'

Karl high-fived both his skipper and his deckhand as was the custom, but his head was too saturated with images of his magnificent fish to do much more than go through the motions. Catching his first marlin had exceeded all his expectations. Catching a trophy fish first-up was a bonus beyond his wildest dreams.

'How big?' he said eventually.

'Ninety, maybe one hundred kilos. A good fish, *patrón*.'

Ninety, maybe one hundred kilos. On thirty-pound line. Karl offered silent thanks to Zane Grey for introducing him to this wonderful world. Ever since he'd first made contact with game fishermen on the internet, his cyber friends had talked about being bitten by the fishing bug. Karl had been bitten but he'd never imagined that the bite could be so sweet. Yet even then, even at his moment of triumph, he knew sweeter moments lay ahead — when his trophy fish actually earned him trophies, and the trophies proclaimed Karl II number one.

Karl caught four more striped marlin that day but none came close to the size of his first. It didn't matter. Marlin were marlin and these were the first marlin he'd ever caught. Along the way he also caught two dorado, both of which topped twenty-five kilos and made handsome fillets for his freezer. The icing on the cake occurred when Karl realised he'd seen what Steinbeck had seen on his expedition aboard the *Western Flyer*. He'd seen cavorting porpoises and leaping marlin fill the seas from horizon to horizon. There was hardly a moment when there hadn't been a striped marlin soaring through the air. A spotted whale shark, the first Karl had ever seen, also chose this day to pass gracefully beneath their bow and, fifty metres astern, a mako shark had honoured them with a rare appearance. It had broached, executed a perfect barrel roll and crashed back into the sea. Karl could not remember a more exciting day in his entire life.

When they anchored back off the beach at Buena Vista, Gerardo talked about cooking some dorado fillets for dinner, but Karl wanted more. Though by no means a drinking man, he felt the need to party, to sink a few margaritas and extend the magic of the day. Karl the conservative, God-fearing, Midwestern storeowner wanted nothing less than to go ashore and celebrate like a sailor.

Captain Pete and his fishing buddy, Low Gear Joe, were feeling no pain when Karl, Gerardo and Jose walked through the batwing doors into Tio Pepe's Cantina and Bar. Captain Pete had seen Karl around various marinas but had never spoken to him except to exchange greetings or updates on the weather or the whereabouts of fish. But something made Captain Pete call out to him and wave him and his crew over to his table. Maybe at that instant he realised what was on Karl's mind and wanted to ride his wave with him. Maybe it was the smile welded to Karl's face, the smile of a man who'd caught his first marlin. Maybe it was the fact that he and Low

Gear Joe were on their third margarita and well down the straight towards a fourth. Or maybe it was just their destiny to meet.

Whatever.

Captain Pete called Karl over. And in the shuffle of chairs and the scrape of tables being pushed together, nobody suspected for a moment that, as a result of this happy and chance meeting, Karl would stagger back to his boat a man irrevocably committed to an impossible mission.

Karl told Captain Pete and Low Gear Joe about his first marlin and of course they celebrated his success. Because Karl was not normally a drinker, it didn't take many margaritas to loosen his lips and for him to admit to his quest to win a fishing tournament.

'It's a pity you weren't fishing a tournament today,' said Low Gear Joe generously. 'It sounds like your fish would have won.'

'Trophy fish for sure,' confirmed Gerardo.

'We caught nine marlin today,' said Captain Pete, 'but none in the class of yours.'

Karl glowed and not just because of the alcohol he'd consumed.

'What we've got to do, my man,' continued Captain Pete, 'is find you a tournament while you're still running hot.'

Yes, Karl thought smugly, that was exactly what he was doing. Running hot.

'When's Cabo San Lucas?' said Captain Pete. 'The Gold Cup?'

'Months away,' said Low Gear Joe.

'What about Bisbee's?'

'Month after.'

'Puerto Vallarta?'

'November.'

Karl's spirits sank as, one by one, each opportunity disappeared into the distance.

'I know,' said Captain Pete triumphantly, 'Ixtapa!'

'Next year,' said Low Gear Joe morosely.

'There must be a tournament somewhere about now,' said Captain Pete.

'Barra de Navidad,' said Gerardo. 'The Calima Tequila Tourneo de Pesca. In three weeks.'

'Ha!' said Captain Pete contemptuously.

'Forget it!' said Low Gear Joe.

'Why?' said Karl. 'I'm running hot.'

'Not hot enough for the Calima,' said Captain Pete and laughed. 'Some people confuse the Calima with the Barra de Navidad Tourneo de Pesca in January, but it's a different tournament.'

'The Calima,' said Low Gear Joe. 'Man wants to fish the Calima? Jesus!'

'What's wrong with it?' said Karl.

'Forget it,' said Captain Pete. He called their waiter over. 'Tell the chef we're hot to trot, ready to roll, eager for action.'

'What?' said their waiter.

'Please inform the chef that we're ready to eat,' said Low Gear Joe. 'Keep my steak rare and the Captain's fish plain.'

'What about the Calima Tequila?' said Karl, but no one took any notice. The subject had moved on.

'What about the Calima?'

The question had been burning in Karl's febrile brain all through dinner, all through the stories and the countless bottles of Negra Modelo, Low Gear Joe's beer of choice.

'Only mugs fish the Calima,' said Captain Pete.

'Why?' said Karl.

'Because only mugs enter tournaments to come second,' said Low Gear Joe.

It would be wrong to suggest that Karl sobered up at that moment. That was physiologically impossible, but certainly he felt as though somebody had dumped a bucket of cold water over his head.

'Second?' he said weakly.

'Best a *gringo* can hope for,' said Captain Pete. 'Far as I know, no *gringo* has ever won the Calima.'

'They've caught the biggest fish,' said Low Gear Joe. 'But that's usually the problem.'

'But why? If they've caught the biggest fish?' persisted Karl.

'Don't ask,' said Captain Pete. 'We came second with a two-hundred-and-sixty-two-kilo blue marlin. It was at least fifty kilos bigger than anything anyone else caught. And I use the word "second" loosely.'

'Loosely?' said Karl.

'We were disqualified,' said Low Gear Joe. 'Thrown out on a technicality. If you're a *gringo* and you catch a big fish, you get disqualified.'

'But isn't that the whole point of the tournament?' said Karl.

'That's what we thought,' said Captain Pete.

'So what went wrong?' said Karl.

'Don't ask,' said Captain Pete. 'It doesn't matter what went wrong. If what went wrong hadn't gone wrong something else would've. Right, Joe?'

'Right on.'

'Ask anyone,' said Captain Pete. 'Anyone who has tried.'

'I'm asking you,' said Karl.

'Do me a favour. Don't ask,' said Captain Pete.

'More Negras!' called Low Gear Joe. 'And make sure they're cold.'

'But, *senor*,' said the waiter. 'You are drinking them faster than we can cool them.'

'How about that?' said Low Gear Joe. 'Got any cold Pacifico?'

'*Si.*'

'Better here than in the fridge.'

'*Si, senor.*'

'I'm going to win the Calima,' said Karl suddenly.

'Forget it,' said Captain Pete. 'Wait for Cabo.'

'The captain's right. Don't waste your time even thinking about it,' said Low Gear Joe.

'I'm running hot and I'm going to win the Calima,' persisted Karl.

'No *gringo* wins the Calima,' said Captain Pete. 'Haven't you been listening? No *gringo* wins the Calima! Never has, never will. If you want to come second to a bunch of *pangeros* in their pissy, narrow-gutted *pangas*, you go ahead. But you're going to come second.'

'No!' said Karl fiercely. So fiercely, in fact, his new friends were momentarily in danger of sobering up. 'I've listened to you, now you listen to me. I'm going to win. Whatever it takes, I'm going to win. I'm never coming second again in my life.'

Three weeks later Karl stood dockside at Barra de Navidad, one of fifty-four contestants, waiting for a wooden chip with his entry number and the signal which would begin the five-day event. Of the fifty-four boats taking part, only ten belonged to *gringos*, six to wealthy *chilangos* and the remaining thirty-eight to *pangeros*. While the odds favoured the local fishermen numerically, Karl couldn't see how the *pangeros'* slim, outboard-powered open boats could possibly compete with his *Billfisher* with her high tower, fish finders, radar, GPS video plotter and water temperature sensors. The *pangas* were rarely longer than seven metres, offered their crew of two no shelter or protection from sun, wind or rain and carried no equipment. Only a handful even bothered to carry a radio or a compass, despite the fact that they often fished up to eighty kilometres from shore. The *pangeros* were hard men who trusted their lives to their ability to read the weather and trusted their livelihood to their ability to guess where fish would be. Bad weather, mishaps and the price of fuel ensured they never did much more than keep their families housed, fed and clothed in the most basic fashion. Winning the tournament offered their only way of getting ahead, short of running drugs across to the Baja Peninsula. Karl figured the only thing they had in their favour was local knowledge and patience.

But even so.

The organisers must also have thought the locals were too disadvantaged so, to even things up, they ruled that no boat could use more than three rods, which was all the *pangas* could fish at one time.

But even so.

Karl turned his attention to the *chilangos*. Their boats and equipment were flashy and doubtless expensive, but Karl saw his rivals from Mexico City as soft, beneficiaries of wealth they'd played little part in amassing. To him they were big boys playing with their big toys and Karl doubted any of them would finish the day sober. The other *gringos* were not unlike himself: eager, earnest and probably a touch inexperienced. Nevertheless, Karl fancied his chances. Even on the run over from Buena Vista to Barra de Navidad on the eastern shore of the Sea of Cortez, he'd managed to hook-up to three blue marlin and bring two up onto the double. The biggest had run close to two hundred kilos and he'd caught it just fifty kilometres short of port. There was no doubt about it. He was running hot.

So was the water. Blue marlin like the water temperature to be at least twenty-seven degrees Celsius and on their way across from Buena Vista, Gerardo had found a current from the south running at twenty-eight degrees. That was where they'd caught their big blue. That was where they were heading as soon as they were given the wooden paddle with their number.

Karl glanced over at the prizes while last-minute instructions were delivered in Spanish. First prize for the biggest blue marlin was an immaculate Chevrolet pick-up, with a V8 motor, lowered suspension, tandem rear wheels and at least two dozen Calima Tequila logos bedecking its brilliant red paintwork. It was precisely the sort of vehicle Karl had avoided owning or even being seen in throughout his entire Midwestern life. The prize meant nothing to him, only winning the tournament. However, Gerardo had fallen in love with the truck and Karl had promised to give it to him once they'd won.

First prize for the biggest sailfish was a one-hundred-and-fifty-horsepower four-stroke Honda outboard. Gerardo had also fallen in love with that even though he had no boat to attach it to. First prizes for the biggest yellowfin tuna and biggest dorado were both seventy-horsepower Yamaha outboards. Gerardo was generous enough to suggest that Jose might like one of the Yamahas.

'I give it to my father,' said Jose. 'The motor on his *panga* is old.'

All their dreams and plans were predicated on winning and, as Karl completed his sweep of the opposition and prizes, he thought he had as good a chance of winning as anybody. And a better chance than most.

The first dent in Karl's confidence came when the *pangeros* were given their wooden paddles the instant the instructions were completed in Spanish. He watched them race for their *pangas* and speed off down the channel while he and the rest of the *gringos* gritted their teeth and waited for the rules to be read to them in English. The *pangeros* had been gone half an hour before *Billfisher* even made it out into the channel leading to the open sea. Maybe this was what Captain Pete was trying to warn him about, thought Karl angrily.

'Most of the *pangeros* have gone northwest or west,' said Gerardo. 'I think we should head southwest.'

'What about him?' Karl pointed to a *panga* which had latched onto them and hung off about four hundred metres astern on the port side.

'Maybe he thinks we know something,' said Gerardo. 'Maybe he wants to share the benefit of our equipment.'

'Maybe,' said Karl, not convinced. The *panga* gave him a bad feeling.

They motored for three hours at close to maximum speed until they picked up the warm current from the south.

They'd trolled lures behind them but Karl hadn't expected a hit. Gerardo had convinced him that if there were blue marlin about they'd be in the warm current. Blue marlin were the only fish that interested him. Blue marlin were the biggest fish and earned the biggest prize. Anything else was, well, secondary.

'*Ballena!*' screamed Jose suddenly, from high in the tower. A torrent of Spanish followed.

'What?' said Karl. 'What's happening?'

'Whale,' said Gerardo.

'What do we want with a whale?' said Karl.

'It is a dead whale, *patrón*,' said Gerardo, setting course for it.

'What do we want with a dead whale?' said Karl.

'Dorado and marlin, *patrón*, they gather beneath dead whales. Look, our friend has seen it now.'

Karl spun around to see the *panga* that had been tracking them zoom past, cranking every knot out of its oversized outboard.

'Damn!' said Karl. Maybe this was the sort of thing Captain Pete had tried to warn him about.

'Get your belt on, *patrón*,' said Gerardo. 'Watch what Jose does and cast your *caballito* as close to the whale as you can.'

'What about our friend?'

'If he gets in the way I will accidentally run him over.'

Karl looked for the smile on Gerardo's face but saw no trace of humour. He dropped down the steps from the flying bridge and out onto the rear deck. Jose had already threaded hooks through the cheeks of two bait fish. They were swimming nervously in the bait tank.

'God help us,' said Karl. They were still one hundred metres from the whale when the wind brought the smell of decay to them. Jose screwed up his face and smiled.

'Look,' said Karl. Both men in the *panga* had hooked up.

'Don't worry,' called Gerardo. 'We will take the other side, upwind.'

Karl waited impatiently as Gerardo put *Billfisher* in position. Suddenly his big boat no longer seemed such an advantage. The *panga* was much faster, more manoeuvrable and had virtually no windage.

'Cast, *patrón*!' screamed Gerardo.

Karl set his feet, took a moment to feel the weight of the fish on the heavy fifty-pound rod and cast. All the hours of practice in the backyard of his home in Salina paid off in that one cast. His *caballito* landed within a metre of the dead whale's flanks and immediately wished it was anywhere else. It panicked, and in panicking became a magnet for every predator nearby. Jose's fish was still flying through the air when Karl's bait was swallowed. Line stripped off his freewheeling spool.

'One,' counted Karl.

'Two, three, four, five, six!'

He set the drag and struck hard and struck again, the heavy rod high above his head. The shock when the hook set made Karl think he'd hooked into a high-speed interstate truck. The rod arched and line crackled off the reel at an outrageous rate. Was he running hot or what? Yes, he was running hot!

'Got to be a blue!' he cried ecstatically.

'Maybe, *patrón*,' said Gerardo.

'Keep the tip up.

'Short stroke.

'Not too quick.'

Karl corrected his stance and concentrated on making the rod do the work. But for every metre of line he recovered the fish took ten.

'It has to be a blue!' said Karl.

'Maybe,' said Gerardo. 'Jose is on a dorado.'

'Don't let it get in the way of my blue,' said Karl.

He fought his marlin, dimly aware of Jose battling his dorado alongside him, finally taking it on the trace and sinking the gaff. For the life of him he couldn't understand why his skipper and deckie were messing around with a dorado while he had a marlin on, and a probable trophy fish at that.

His fish angled away from the dead whale as though blaming it for its predicament. Gerardo pursued it, keeping it at a right angle to the boat, turning so that the fish lay dead astern when it ceased its run.

'Wind, *patrón*,' called Gerardo as he began to back up. 'This is a tournament. We can't take all day.'

Karl wound furiously.

'What if it's green when we try to gaff it?' he asked.

'That's my problem,' said Gerardo.

Karl glanced at Jose alongside and found him holding a heavy wooden club. Suddenly the prospect of an angry green marlin didn't seem quite as frightening.

'Hey, what are they doing?' said Karl.

The *panga,* which had been following them, had taken up station one hundred and fifty metres astern and the occupants were observing his battle with the marlin.

'Tell them to piss off,' said Karl.

'It's a free country,' said Gerardo.

Karl's marlin suddenly broke clear of the water and his shoulders slumped. Unbelievably, his blue marlin was only a dorado.

'Damn,' he said, and thumped his reel hand against the transom.

'What are you doing, *patrón*?' screamed Gerardo. 'It's a trophy fish! A trophy fish, *patrón*! Wind! Wind!'

Trophy fish? Karl returned to his task with renewed vigour. For the first time the prospect of winning more than the main category dawned on him. That would be something to tell Captain Pete and Low Gear Joe. They didn't think he could win one category. Karl wound like a madman, now determined to win every category. That would show them. That would really show them. Alongside him Jose had put down his club in favour of his gaff. He had a smile on his face as though the seventy-horsepower Yamaha was already his.

'Steady!' said Gerardo.

Once Jose had the dorado on the trace, Gerardo left the controls, grabbed the gaff and helped Jose boat the fish.

'Look at the size of it!' said Gerardo. 'I have never seen dorado this big before.'

While they stood admiring their catch, they missed seeing the skipper of the *panga* pick up his microphone and send details of their catch back to the marina. With their radio away in the flying bridge, they also missed hearing it. Karl didn't realise it at the time, but that was another advantage the smaller *pangas* had over his fifty-nine-footer. Jammed in their tiny cockpit, the *pangeros* missed nothing.

Gerardo mounted the tower so he could check the water around the whale. He saw plenty of dorado and what he was sure was a big wahoo, but no sign at all of marlin. Certain that they wouldn't catch a bigger dorado than they had already, they motored away, following the warm current with three lures out for the elusive blue marlin. The *panga* tagged along behind.

Karl caught two sailfish and a wahoo before Gerardo turned *Billfisher* for home to meet the five o'clock deadline for weigh-in. Neither of the sailfish was big enough to justify keeping and Jose released them. He filleted the wahoo and put one of the fillets in the fridge for dinner. Once it was clear they were headed back to the marina, their escort powered away ahead of them.

As they entered the channel leading into the Laguna de Navidad, Gerardo pulled alongside the organising committee's *panga* where Jose exchanged their wooden paddle for a red disc, which signified that they'd returned inside the allotted time. They'd listened to the radio all the way in and, as far as they could tell, only one blue marlin had been captured, a modest fish around one hundred and twenty kilos. Someone had caught a good-sized sailfish around fifty-five kilos but nobody had sounded particularly excited about catching dorado.

As his dorado was hauled up to the scales, Karl was confident that his fish would set a mark that would not be beaten. From the reaction of the other game fishermen and *pangeros*, they seemed to agree. He could tell that they were in awe of the sheer size of his fish. A cheer went up as the pointer on the scales spun around to forty-four point three kilos. Karl accepted congratulatory handshakes from other *gringo* fishermen and *chilangos*. Smiling Mexican girls with outrageously dyed yellow hair and wearing the sponsor's

T-shirts surrounded him for publicity photos. Karl's chest swelled with pride. If this was what being a winner was like, he wanted more of it.

Other fish were hauled up to the scales but none made the impact of his magnificent dorado. Just as darkness loomed and fishermen and crews alike were falling victim to the sponsor's generous donation of free tequila, a local fisherman presented another dorado to be weighed. It was big, but even in the poor light Karl could see that his fish was bigger.

'*Patrón*, something is wrong,' hissed Gerardo. 'That fish has no colour. That fish has been dead for days.'

Karl looked on in disbelief as the pointer on the scales spun around to forty-five kilos, point seven of a kilo heavier than his fish. How could that be? The dorado was clearly smaller than his. *Pangeros* raced to congratulate the lucky fisherman and the golden-haired girls found a new hero to be photographed with.

'Look, *patrón*, look at its belly,' said Gerardo indignantly. 'See how it overhangs? They have stuffed it full of lead weights. I am going to take a close look at it. I bet they have sewn up its lips so the weights don't fall out.'

But Gerardo couldn't take a closer look. The *pangero*s closed ranks so tightly around the fish that he struggled to find a way past them. By the time he made it to the scales the dorado had been taken down and removed.

'I'm going to protest,' said Karl. 'This is outrageous.'

He made his way angrily to the committee table.

'That dorado is ineligible,' he said. 'Look at its colour. Anyone can see that it has been dead for days.'

'*Senor*, unfortunately not everyone has a fine boat like yours,' said the official. 'When you catch a fine fish, you can take it on board and keep it under shelter so the sun does not suck all the water from its body. *Pangeros* are not so fortunate. Their *pangas* are small and have no shade. When the sun sucked the water out of this fish it also sucked out the colour.'

'Nonsense,' said Karl. 'Wet burlap. The *pangeros* cover their fish in wet burlap to protect them from the sun. Anyway, that dorado was noticeably smaller than mine. And if the sun had sucked out all its water, as you say, then it would have weighed much less.'

'Maybe this fish had just had a meal of *caballitos*,' said the official. 'Maybe his belly was full. Who knows why one fish weighs more than another?'

'I want that fish opened up and the contents of its belly examined,' said Karl. He had to work hard to keep his voice calm in the face of the official's deliberate obstruction, but his anger was building dangerously. 'I insist.'

'Unfortunately the fish has gone,' said the official. 'As organisers we reserve the right to keep the biggest fish and sell it to offset costs. That fish has already been sold.'

'It will still be here somewhere on the marina,' insisted Karl. 'There hasn't been time to take it away.'

'So what?' said the official. 'The fish is no longer ours to cut open. It is sold. Now, if you have no more questions, I would like to get on with my duties.'

To Karl's astonishment the official rose from behind the committee table and walked away. Now he understood what Captain Pete had tried to warn him about.

'It's blatant cheating,' said Karl into his cell phone. 'That *pangero* cheated and the committee went along with him. They deliberately turned a blind eye.'

'That's what they do,' said Captain Pete sympathetically. He was anchored in Bahia de Los Muertos, still fishing the rise south of Cerralvo.

'If they allow stuff like that, how can I possibly win?' said Karl.

'You can't,' said Captain Pete. 'No *gringo* can.'

'But it's dishonest.'

'That's what it is.'

'They can't get away with it.'

'They can and they do.'

'Not this time,' said Karl. 'Somehow I'm going to get even.'

'To do that you'll have to beat them at their own game,' said Captain Pete.

'I don't cheat,' said Karl.

'That's too bad,' said Captain Pete.

The following morning was a re-run of the first. Once again the committee contrived to give the *pangeros* a good half-hour's start. Gerardo set a course due southwest to pick up the warm current. Despite being robbed of a certain trophy for best dorado, Karl felt optimistic. When somebody caught a big marlin the word spread, and it would be difficult for a *pangero* to have caught one prior to the start of the tournament and to have stored it in a freezer. Even if the *pangero* managed to sneak a big marlin ashore, where would he find a freezer big enough to store it? And how would he defrost it? Fish the size of a big blue would take days to thaw out and, by then, not even the committee could ignore the smell. As for loading a fish with lead weights, Karl doubted anyone would try that trick again.

Marlin attracted too much attention and were the subject of too many photographs; no one could get away with sewing a marlin's mouth shut.

The *panga* moved into position astern of them before they'd covered ten kilometres.

'Why us?' said Karl.

'I asked around,' said Gerardo. 'A *panga* followed all the *gringo* boats.'

'But why?'

'It's a big ocean, *patrón*. Maybe they think big boats raise big fish.'

'Crumbs from a rich man's table.'

'Something like that.'

But Karl wasn't convinced. The *panga* seemed to spend as much time watching them as fishing. He shrugged. What could he do?

They caught their first blue right on the stroke of eleven, brought it up to the double, but Gerardo ruled it smaller than fish that had already been weighed. They released it. Within ten minutes, the *panga* behind them hooked up on a blue roughly the same size and kept it.

'This is a good sign, *patrón*,' said Gerardo. 'There has to be a big blue around here somewhere.'

And there was.

It struck just as Karl was thinking of making a turkey burger for lunch. It hit like a runaway bus and absolutely monstered the lure. By the time Karl got the rod out of the holder and into his game belt, the marlin had stripped off one hundred and fifty metres of line. By the time Jose had strapped him into his shoulder harness, it had stripped off another seventy metres. It leaped and thrashed and smashed the surface of the sea. Karl had never seen a more powerful fish and certainly never caught one.

He checked his stance as the fish tore off more line and mentally rehearsed how he was going to fight it. Short strokes. Fight the fish not the rod. Wind only when there is line to be gained. Don't wind against the drag. Raise the tip with his body, not with his arms. And don't panic. He had no doubt about the calibre of the fish he was up against and he didn't need Gerardo to tell him it was a trophy fish and likely tournament winner.

'It's a trophy fish, *patrón*!' Gerardo told him anyway. 'This is my Chevrolet truck,' he added, reminding Karl of his promise.

Gerardo backed up on the marlin and Karl wound furiously. But any line he recovered was soon reclaimed. The marlin went deep and turned its bulk sideways against the pull of the line. For twenty minutes, Karl tried everything he knew to gain line and failed.

'I can't lift it,' said Karl.

'Maybe the fish is foul-hooked,' said Jose.

'No, it is just playing hard. It wants to see if we are as patient as it is,' said Gerardo.

'I want to see if it's as tired as I am,' said Karl.

It was an hour before Karl began recovering line in any worthwhile quantity and retaining it. Gerardo seemed to anticipate the fish's every move and edged the boat nearer. All the while Karl recovered line. The fish surfaced about fifty metres astern. It still lifted its head and shoulders out of the water and thrashed it into boiling white foam, but it was clearly tiring.

'It seems a pity to take it,' said Karl. 'It's magnificent.'

'It's why we're here,' said Gerardo.

Fifteen minutes later, Jose had it on the wire. Five minutes later it was dead, clubbed to death by Gerardo. It took all three of them to haul the dead fish up onto the swim platform. Its head hung over one end, its tail the other.

'This is a serious fish, *patrón*,' said Gerardo. 'That's more than two hundred and fifty kilos. Maybe closer to three hundred. This fish will win the tournament, no doubt about it.'

Karl stared at the big fish. Already its colours were fading. This was a fish to match those he'd seen photographed in Zane Grey's books. He heard a sudden splash nearby and looked up. The *panga* had closed to less than fifteen metres and both men on board were taking a good hard look at his marlin.

'Look and weep,' shouted Karl, and turned his back on them.

'Now we go back,' said Gerardo. 'It's already two o'clock and we are at least two and a half hours from the marina. We don't want to miss the five o'clock deadline.'

They left the *panga* still ploughing that same fertile stretch of water as they set course for home. Karl felt like celebrating but was wary about celebrating too soon. The painful events of the previous day were still fresh in his mind. But how could the committee deprive him of his rights this time? It was almost inconceivable that anyone had a bigger marlin or anything comparable, deep-frozen or otherwise.

The wind swung around offshore, slowing them down with a short steep sea they had no option but to take head-on. Karl watched the minutes tick by. For the first time he regretted not buying a more modern boat with a planing hull. That would have given them another hour of fishing and still got them home on time. But Karl needn't have worried. Gerardo brought *Billfisher* alongside the committee *panga* with ten minutes to spare.

'Congratulations, *senor*,' said the official as he handed Karl his red chip. 'That is a fine fish.'

'Thank you,' said Karl. He was heartened by the committeeman's warm response. Maybe the organisers were feeling guilty about the previous night's skulduggery.

There were two more committeemen among the small crowd waiting at the dock as Gerardo backed *Billfisher* into its bay. People began clapping as soon as they saw the size of Karl's blue.

'May we come aboard?' asked one of the officials.

'Of course,' said Karl. He thought they also wanted to offer their congratulations. He held out his hand to help them step over his fish.

'That is a fine fish,' said the first official.

'A very fine fish,' confirmed the second.

'May we look below?' said the first official.

'Of course,' said Karl, anxious to oblige.

'What is this?' said the first official, pointing to the rods and reels stored on racks in the forward compartment.

'They're the rods we're not using,' said Karl. 'We're aware of the rules. We know we're only allowed to fish three rods.'

'But that is not the rule,' said the second official, shaking his head. 'The rule states boats are only allowed to *carry* three rods.'

'At the briefing you said "use three rods".'

'Perhaps an error of translation or maybe you did not hear correctly. Read the rules,' said the first official. 'The rules clearly state boats may only carry three rods.'

'Every game boat here carries more than three rods,' protested Karl.

'We can't answer for the mistakes of others,' said the second official. 'We recommend boats store their extra rods.'

'But there's nowhere to store them,' said Karl.

'You could store them in the hotel,' said the first official, waving vaguely towards the Grand Bay Hotel which occupied the slopes around the marina in a white-and-terracotta imitation of an Italian fishing village.

'At five hundred dollars a day?' said Karl incredulously. 'Twenty-five hundred dollars for the five days of the tournament. For fishing rods? You've got to be joking!'

'I'm sorry, *senor*, but the rules are the rules,' said the second official. 'The rules are clear on this. Boats may only carry three rods.'

'But we're only fishing three rods.'

'But you are carrying more than three,' said the first official. 'That is against the rules. I regret that we have no choice but to disqualify your fish.'

'Wait a minute,' said Karl. 'You can't disqualify us. We only used three rods! We obeyed the rules to the letter. I am not a cheat and I won't be treated like one.'

But the committeemen were no longer interested in talking to him. They'd said what they had to say and achieved what they'd set out to achieve.

'Two hundred and eighty-eight kilos,' said Karl into his cell phone. 'That's what it weighed.'

'Like I keep telling you, my man,' said Captain Pete sympathetically, 'they'll always find some way to get you.'

'There's a guy with a one-hundred-and-seventy-foot motor yacht on the outer moorings who has offered to store our rods for the remaining three days.'

'You're going to keep fishing?' said Captain Pete. 'After everything they've done to you?'

'What else can they do to me?' said Karl.

'They'll find something,' said Captain Pete. 'They always do.'

The following day, Gerardo managed to squeeze fourteen knots out of the diesels as they went in search of the warm current. It had moved another twelve kilometres further west, costing Karl more valuable fishing time. Once again he regretted buying the Elliott. As much as he loved *Billfisher*, it had taken them three hours to reach the current while a boat with a planing hull, like Captain Pete's Salthouse 62, would have taken little over two. Allowing three hours for the return trip, he had just four hours of fishing time. He glanced over to the *panga,* which had once again stationed itself off their stern. Even that could cover the distance in half the time it took *Billfisher.*

For two hours their lures swam unmolested in a flat, lifeless sea. There were no sea lions, no porpoises, no whales — nothing to ripple the water or give them hope that life was lurking beneath the surface. They searched the horizon fruitlessly for diving birds. There was nothing to encourage hope or lift their spirits. Just when it seemed Karl's hot run had finally come to an end, a big blue hit the nearest lure.

Karl leaped to his feet and grabbed the rod. He held the tip high as Jose clipped him into the shoulder harness, and waited for the marlin to complete its first blistering run. It threw itself out of the water, somersaulting and shaking its head from side to side as it tried to dislodge the hook.

'It's a good fish, *patrón*,' confirmed Gerardo from the flying bridge. 'Not as big as yesterday but big enough.'

Karl watched the line fizz off his reel. The fish felt big, indisputably big. He leaned backwards, hard against the pull of the rod, hoping to turn the marlin's head towards the boat. He would have crashed onto the deck if Jose hadn't been standing behind him and caught him. The lack of bend in the rod confirmed his fears.

'Wind, *patrón*!' screamed Gerardo. 'Maybe he is swimming towards us.'

Karl wound like a man possessed in the slim hope that Gerardo was right. But he could feel nothing. Not even the weight of the lure.

'Relax. It's gone,' said Gerardo.

Karl pulled in the rest of the line up to the double. As Jose reached over to retrieve the rest of the line, the lack of trace and lure made it obvious what had happened.

Karl's shoulders slumped and he glared up at Gerardo.

'For heaven's sake! Haven't I got enough to contend with? If you can't tie knots properly we may as well give up now and go home!' He slammed the rod into the rod holder and stormed inside to cool off and drown his disappointment in a Coke. Gerardo and Jose watched him go, stony-faced.

It took Karl an hour to cool off sufficiently to apologise.

'I'm sorry,' he said.

'I was hot and upset.

'Could even have been one of my knots that broke.'

'*Patrón*,' said Gerardo, 'I am not perfect but I always do my best. Please don't shout at me like that. It feels like someone is sticking hot needles in my ears.'

Karl apologised for shouting.

That evening they checked into the marina with nothing to trouble the weigh-master or the committee.

'We've all had that happen,' said Captain Pete sympathetically.

'In the middle of a tournament?' said Karl.

'It's a pain any time,' said Captain Pete. 'What are you going to do?'

'Hang in,' said Karl. 'We've still got two days.'

'Keep in touch,' said Captain Pete and hung up.

'Sailfish weather,' said Gerardo.

'*Pez vela*,' echoed Jose. 'Sailfish.'

Overhead, pale, thin clouds diluted the tropical blue of the sky while fresh breezes from the northwest put white caps on the tops of waves. Karl put down his book and closed his eyes. *Pez vela*, sailfish — by whatever name it wasn't what he wanted to hear. Only blue marlin, *marlin azul*, would do. Nothing less.

Wheeling birds and distant splashes alerted them to the fact that they were closing in on the warm current.

'Sailfish, *patrón*,' said Gerardo. 'Look at them! They are going crazy.'

In a reprise of the wonderful day on the rise south of Cerralvo when the striped marlin had decided to spend the day free jumping, sailfish rose vertically like so many silver missiles almost everywhere Karl looked. It was the sort of scene he'd dreamed of back in Salina, but with the deadline for catching a trophy marlin looming, he could only look on with a sense of frustration.

'Sometimes, *patrón*, we cannot catch the fish we want. Sometimes we have to catch the fish that are there. Today is our chance to win the Honda outboard. There is no shame in winning the Honda outboard. Winning is winning.'

But it wasn't winning the big one. Karl slipped on his game belt in preparation, wishing he could feel more enthusiastic.

'Get with it!' he said softly, berating himself. Five weeks earlier, he'd never even caught a billfish. Now he was behaving like a prima donna over the type and size. He wanted a blue marlin but had to settle for a sailfish. Five weeks earlier, a sailfish — *any* sailfish — represented the thrill of a lifetime. Chastened, he determined to do as Gerardo suggested and catch what was there to be caught. Moreover, he resolved to enjoy it.

The first sailfish would have been fun on a twenty-pound rod, but on a fifty it was a one-sided contest. This was the rod that two days before had brought in two hundred and eighty-eight kilos of angry blue marlin. It was hardly troubled by a twenty-seven-kilo sail. He brought it in quickly to minimise the stress on the fish.

The second sailfish was a respectable thirty-five kilos and fought above its weight. On a twenty-pound rod it would have been an epic battle. The third sailfish struck right on the stroke of two o'clock, the limit of their fishing time.

'This is the one, *patrón*, this is the one!' The pitch of Gerardo's voice eliminated all doubt.

Could it be? Karl decided to fight the fish without the benefit of the shoulder harness.

'Wind when he jumps,' said Gerardo.

Karl didn't need telling. He concentrated as hard as he could, reacting to the feel of the rod, playing the fish as he'd been taught. He didn't look up at the fish as it threw itself about the ocean, didn't look to see how big it was, didn't look to see if it really was the one, as Gerardo had claimed. Could he be that lucky? In the space of four days, he'd caught a trophy dorado and a championship-sized blue marlin. He was running hot but could he really nail a third trophy fish so soon? In his heart he was prepared to accept that winning the sailfish section might be the best he could now do. Maybe it wasn't the main prize but it was a first prize and, given that this was his first tournament, perhaps it was enough.

'Concentrate, *patrón*!' admonished Gerardo. 'You want to lose this fish?'

Karl glanced up at his skipper to acknowledge the reprimand. A fish isn't caught until it's boated, and a competition isn't won until the trophy is awarded. He accepted he was getting ahead of himself. For the first time, he stole a glance at his sailfish as Gerardo backed up towards it. Its size took him by surprise. It was big enough to be a good stripey, certainly bigger than many of the striped marlin he'd caught off Cerralvo.

'Easy, *patrón*, easy.'

Karl guided the fish gently towards him as Jose prepared to take the double.

'Good fish, *patrón*,' said Gerardo as he sank the gaff home. 'This is bigger than any sailfish caught so far. This is at least seventy kilos.'

The sound of the *panga* coming close to inspect their catch made Karl glance at his watch. Two twenty-five. Even going flat out, it would be lineball whether they made it back to the committee *panga* and collected their red disc in time.

'I'm taking the helm,' he said, climbed the steps up to the flying bridge and turned *Billfisher* for home. Gerardo and Jose were still hosing down the sailfish and clearing the deck when the twin diesels hit maximum revs.

'Are we going to make it?' asked Karl, once Gerardo had taken over the controls.

'I think so, *patrón*,' said Gerardo.

'We'd better,' said Karl.

He went aft to tell Jose to keep hosing down the fish to minimise dehydration. He wanted his sailfish weighing as close to its landed weight as possible. He made himself a sandwich but threw half away uneaten. He poured himself a beer and tipped half down the sink. This was his last chance and there was no getting away from it. He had been extraordinarily lucky. Under normal circumstances and in any other tournament he would have weighed in the biggest fish in two categories and be favourite for the prizes. He was about to weigh in a third. Captain Pete had told him about fishermen who went years without winning a tournament or even any of the lesser categories. Yes, he had been lucky, and yes, he still had a day to go. But luck like he'd enjoyed didn't last. All his hopes for winning a prize resided in the sailfish lying on the stern deck. Provided they got back to the marina in time.

'How are we doing?' he asked Gerardo for the umpteenth time.

'It will be close, *patrón*, it will be close.'

The radar image showed the coastline around Barra de Navidad and a stream of boats heading towards it. Karl looked at his watch.

'Damn it!' he said.

'We'll make it, *patrón*. Trust me.'

Karl went and lay down on the day bed but could neither concentrate on reading nor sleep. He checked his watch. Four fifteen. He climbed back up to the flying bridge. Both throttles were as far forward as they could go. He could hear the fuel being sucked into the cylinders and tried not to think of the fuel bill. Ahead of him, the coastline began to resolve in definite features.

'It's closer than it looks,' said Gerardo. 'In sailfish weather things always look further away than they are because of the gloom. If there were no clouds you would see how close we are.'

Karl looked but was unconvinced.

'We will make it, *patrón*. I know now we will make it. By five minutes at least. Trust me.'

'This is our last chance,' said Karl.

'No,' said Gerardo. 'We still have tomorrow.'

'We've ridden our luck,' said Karl. 'I kinda think our luck is about ridden out.'

'There,' said Gerardo, pointing to a blip on the radar. 'There is the committee *panga*. And look, *patrón*, there are still two boats behind us.'

'Maybe they don't have fish to weigh in,' said Karl.

He checked his watch and tried to judge the distance from the channel leading into the marina. They had twelve minutes in hand. How many kilometres did they still have to travel and how quickly would they cover them at fourteen and a quarter knots? Karl gave up on the maths. He could clearly see the committee *panga* through his binoculars.

'Are we going to make it?'

'*Si, patrón.* With minutes to spare. Trust me.'

'I'll go below and get the paddle ready to exchange for the disc.'

'Good idea, *patrón*. And *patrón*? Don't worry.'

At seven minutes to five, Gerardo began to throttle back. Even in an emergency he was thinking of the motors. Karl wanted to shout up to Gerardo to tell him to get the disc first then run down the motors in the bay, but held his breath. Sometimes you had to trust people and he had to trust Gerardo not to do anything foolish now. He strode onto the stern deck and peered forward along the side of the boat. A *pangero* was just leaving the committee *panga*. He checked his watch again. Five to five. The committee *panga* was less than two hundred metres away. They were going to make it. He began to smile as the twin diesels throttled further back.

He checked the ship's clock. Four minutes to five. His watch. Again. Four minutes to five. The clock on his VCR. Four minutes to five. They were going to make it with two whole minutes to spare.

'No!'

Karl heard Gerardo's anguished cry and stiffened. What now? He heard *Billfisher*'s horn blast. What was happening? Were they running over somebody? Had somebody cut in front of them?

'Bastards!' Gerardo sounded distraught.

'The committee *panga* saw us coming and packed up early,' said Karl. 'We would have made it with two minutes to spare.'

'Typical,' said Captain Pete.

'We couldn't chase them because they'd disqualify us for speeding in the channel.'

'They'll get you, one way or the other.'

'It's that damned *panga*,' said Karl. 'They must radio back our catch to give the committee time to figure out how to cheat us.'

'That'd be right,' said Captain Pete. 'Sort of thing they'd do.'

'I should have listened to you back in Buena Vista.'

'Yeah, well . . . but look on the bright side. You've caught some fabulous fish, the kind of fish any fisherman would give his right arm to catch.'

'True,' said Karl.

'Anywhere else, you'd be tournament champion.'

'True.'

'You just picked the wrong tournament. In the Calima, it's always *pangeros* first, *gringos* second.'

Karl closed his eyes and gritted his teeth at the sound of the hated word.

'There's still tomorrow,' he said.

Karl set out on the last day of the tournament with few expectations. He'd done everything right but had been shamelessly cheated out of his just rewards and, worse, he'd been treated as though he was a cheat. The whole experience offended him deeply and was an affront to his conservative Midwestern values.

'There's still tomorrow,' he'd said to Captain Pete. But what did that mean? Even if by some miracle he caught another championship marlin, the committee would find a way to deny him. He stared morosely at the *panga* tagging along behind.

Gerardo found a pod of porpoises with yellowfin tuna feeding just metres ahead of the pod, but Karl wasn't interested in yellowfin. Jose spotted dorado stampeding across their bows in hot pursuit of flying fish. Karl still wasn't interested. He wanted blue marlin. Sometimes you have to fish for what you want, not what is there.

The *panga* left them to pursue the dorado but was back shadowing them within forty minutes. Karl didn't care. It was perfectly clear what the *pangero's* mission was and any fish he caught were merely a bonus.

Karl was down but his gloom was not infectious.

'Lots of bait fish,' said Gerardo.

'Good water temperature. Over twenty-eight degrees.

'This is good marlin weather, *patrón*.'

Karl was mystified by their good spirits. The organisers had robbed Gerardo of his dream truck and Jose of a new outboard motor to give to his father. Yet they behaved as if they hadn't a care in the world. As long as he lived he didn't think he'd ever really understand Mexicans.

At noon he made sandwiches and coffee for himself and his crew.

'*Patrón*, I have a feeling here in my belly that we are going to catch a marlin.'

'That's hunger,' said Karl.

'No, *patrón*, I think we are going to catch a marlin. I feel it.'

'And I feel like another coffee.' Karl went below and lay down on the day bed. He didn't feel like another coffee and he didn't feel like fishing. He just felt down, cheated and defeated. He felt exactly the same way he'd felt as a kid back in Salina when he'd come second in class, second in athletics and second in everything else he'd had a mind to try.

'Damn it!' he said. He leaped to his feet and strode onto the stern deck. The heat and brightness of the sun hit him like a blow to the head, waking him up, reminding him of who he was and where he was. What did it matter? What did any of it matter? It was just a dumb tournament nobody had any regard for. So what if he was cheated? There were other tournaments, fair tournaments. He let the sun burn through his T-shirt and counted his blessings. The sky was clear dazzling blue and the sea a picture. He was on his own boat, doing what he loved doing in the Sea of Cortez, a place he'd dreamed about. Any moment a marlin could take a lure. How many people back in Salina would willingly change places with him? A smile began to spread over his face as he gazed back down *Billfisher*'s wake, and froze the instant it formed. He saw the flash of colour by the closest lure, the unmistakeable electric, fluorescent glow of an excited marlin. He saw the tip of its tail rise and cut through the waves, saw the head break free of the water and the bill slash down upon the lure.

'Marlin!' he screamed.

But the sound of the ratchet as line tore off the reel had already alerted Gerardo and Jose.

Karl grabbed his game belt, jammed the butt of the rod into the gimbal and pushed the drag up against the stops. Against all odds he'd been given one last chance to snatch victory. He only carried three rods and there was plenty of time to get back to the channel and exchange his paddle for a red disc. If the fish was big enough, he was in with a definite chance. Two hundred and two point four kilos, that was the weight he had to beat.

'Is it big enough?' he shouted up to Gerardo.

'Close, *patrón*,' said Gerardo. 'I think it will be very close. I think at least two hundred kilos.'

Karl settled down to the hard work of fighting his fish, heartened by the fact that his skipper consistently under-called the weight of fish so that he wouldn't be disappointed when the fish was weighed.

'Look at him jump!' said Gerardo. 'Nine jumps in a row.'

Just as Karl started to apply pressure to the fish, he heard an explosion and saw a sheet of flame rise in the air about three hundred metres away.

'*Patrón*! *Patrón*! The *panga* has blown up!'

'Blown up?'

'Yes, *patrón*. The *pangeros* have been thrown into the water.'

To his credit, Karl didn't hesitate. He turned to Jose.

'Cut the line.'

Billfisher heeled over hard as Gerardo turned towards the stricken *panga*, which was ablaze from stem to stern. Karl waited for Gerardo to throttle back before joining Jose on the swim platform. One of the *pangeros* was semiconscious and being supported by the other. These were men who had played a key role in cheating him, yet Karl only saw two blackened and scorched human beings in desperate need of help. He managed to bring the semiconscious man aboard before Gerardo elbowed him aside and took over.

'We've got to get this man to hospital as soon as possible,' said Karl. When he examined the other, it was clear that he wasn't in much better condition. 'They both need a doctor, and soon.'

'I'll radio for help,' said Gerardo. 'If we take them back, it will take too long.'

'Did they tell you what happened?'

'We all know what happened, *patrón*. Their fuel tank exploded, that is what happened. Maybe they had a leak in the fuel line, who knows? It is a risk all *pangeros* take. They all smoke.'

Gerardo disappeared up the ladder to the flying bridge. Karl heard him sending out a distress call in Spanish. He stared helplessly at the stricken men. The burns were red and raw on the men's legs and arms and on the sides of their faces exposed to the first flash. All their hair and eyebrows had been burned off and they had the dazed and distant look of people in pain.

'Jose, ask them if I can get anything for them.'

'Water, *patrón*, they ask for water.'

Karl brought them water and all his aspirin, and rigged up a temporary canvas cover to give them some shade. He also brought out a saucepan filled with water and gently encouraged one of the men to rest his badly burnt hand in it.

'Tell him to keep his hand in the water. Water is the best thing for it. Okay?'

The man did as Karl asked, grateful for the consideration.

'They thank you, *patrón*, for rescuing them,' said Jose. 'They say they are sorry they caused you to lose your fish.'

My fish, thought Karl. He'd forgotten all about his marlin. What did a fish matter when men's lives were in danger?

'Tell them it doesn't matter about the fish. The fish is not important. Tell them I'm sorry they are hurt and I'm sorry about their boat.' Karl turned and climbed the ladder to join Gerardo.

'The *pangero*'s brother is nearby in another *panga*. He is coming to fetch them. He can get back to Barra in one hour, maybe one hour and a quarter.'

Karl remained on the flying bridge as the injured were transferred into the *panga*. The brother looked up and waved to him in salute as he pulled away.

'What now?' said Karl to Gerardo. 'The day is a disaster. We may as well go back in.'

'The brother is very grateful to you for rescuing these men,' said Gerardo cagily. 'He is sorry about your marlin. He suggests we keep fishing.'

'What?'

Gerardo set course due north and gazed steadfastly ahead.

'He has given me directions, *patrón*.' Gerardo dialled a bearing on the autopilot but still refused to look at Karl.

'What directions?'

'Like I said, *patrón*, the brother is very grateful. Those men could have died.'

'What directions?'

Gerardo sighed. 'You don't want to know, *patrón*. The brother is a longliner. I have heard of *pescadores* cheating this way.'

'I don't follow you,' said Karl, but he was beginning to.

'It is justice, *patrón*. It's like Captain Pete said. Sometimes if you want to win, you have to beat the committee at their own game.'

'You mean cheat.'

'No, *patrón*, not cheat. Bend the rules. Maybe we don't win the way we would like to win, but even God knows we deserve to win.'

They found the marker buoy exactly where it should be and began tracking along the longline, checking it as they went. The marlin was all but drowned and killing it was an act of mercy. Provided no one else had caught a big blue that day, they had the winner. A little further along they came across a string of tuna. Gerardo and Jose selected the biggest. It was dead when they hauled it aboard.

'Let's go,' said Karl.

'But, *patrón*, there is sailfish and dorado further along. The brother told us.'

'Go!' said Karl, but for once Gerardo and Jose ignored him. They knew what they were doing and they knew what was fair. The sailfish was also dead when they hauled it aboard.

'These fish were not all caught on this line, *patrón*. See? Two hook marks. They keep the fish here and sell them to the highest bidder. Maybe *chilango*, maybe *pangero*.'

Karl studied the marlin stretched out on the swim platform. It was big, big enough to win, but not as big as the one he'd had disqualified. It was the same with the sailfish. The tuna was compensation for his disqualified dorado.

'Okay, *patrón*?' said Gerardo.

Agreeing went against everything he'd been brought up believing in. It went against everything he'd taught his kids.

'Let's do it,' he said.

'We won,' said Karl.

'*You what?*' said Captain Pete. His surprise was so great Karl had to move the phone away from his ear.

'Biggest blue marlin, biggest sailfish and biggest tuna and there wasn't a damn thing the committee could do about it.'

'*You won three categories? In the Calima?*'

Karl told Captain Pete everything that had happened.

'Love it!' said Captain Pete. 'And you gave those cheats a dose of their own medicine. My man, you've just become a legend. I can't wait to tell Low Gear Joe. Hell, I'm going to tell every *gringo* I know!'

'The funny thing is, everybody knew where our fish had come from. The *pangeros* knew, the *chilangos*, the other *gringos* and even the committee. But we were heroes, you see? We'd cut off a trophy fish to save the lives of those men. I think there would have been a riot if the committee had disqualified us this time.'

'It just keeps getting better,' said Captain Pete.

'I gave the Honda outboard to the *pangero* who lost his boat. That brought the house down.'

'Genius, pure genius,' said Captain Pete. 'What about the Chev truck?'

'Gerardo has the truck. I've never seen a happier man.'

'And the Yamaha?'

'Jose is giving it to his father.'

'So you're left with nothing?'

'Way it is,' said Karl in his broadest Midwestern drawl. 'But I'm kinda used to coming second.'

Men in White

The day Gregan stopped wearing white shoes the best part of his wardrobe became redundant. His favourite sports trousers remained on their hangers along with his array of white and off-white linen jackets and all the Ralph Lauren shirts that went so well with them. They'd been the clothes that had singled him out from the pack, signalled his success and signified his occupation. He'd worn them with pride and swagger even after they'd become a symbol — especially the white shoes — of brashness, duplicity and environmental vandalism. Gregan saw himself as a man who made people's dreams come true and regarded his wealth and success as just reward. He was astonished to discover that the rest of the world saw him differently. They saw a man for whom no complimentary adjective could be found. They saw a rapacious Queensland property developer.

Gregan was proud of the fact that he was one of the original few who'd helped make the Gold Coast, especially Surfers Paradise, what it is today. He liked nothing better than to drive guests and prospects up the coast from Tweed Heads to Southport, pointing out along the way all the glass-and-concrete towers he'd had a hand in developing. But the ride didn't stop when he ran out of beach. Oh, no.

Gregan also liked to regard himself as a visionary. When waterfront blocks became scarce and too expensive, he decided to create more. People want waterfronts, he argued, not necessarily beachfronts. So he turned his back on the ocean and attacked the mangrove flats and wetlands behind Surfers. It didn't matter that the flats were vital little ecosystems, providing food and lodging for fish, crabs, prawns and a whole catalogue of water fowl. He dredged and bulldozed until the mangrove flats were no more and in their place built a series of canals and spurs with newly paved and sewered circuits and cul-de-sacs, upon which people could build their outsized waterfront dream homes. The result was monumental testimony to what men in white could do.

At 4.22 am on Friday, 18 January 2000, all the crabs, prawns, calamari, oysters and beer Gregan had consumed over the course of what his associates liked to regard as working lunches took their revenge. A sizeable piece of plaque broke away from the wall of his vena cava and caused a partial blockage leading to the right atrium of his heart. Gregan might have died in the moments that followed if he hadn't exchanged his wife of thirty years for another twenty-nine years his junior. She frequented gyms and was strong enough to get him out of his bed and into his car, and drive him to hospital at a speed normally associated with the Indy Grand Prix. (Gregan was also a vocal supporter of the car races that took over the streets of Surfers once a year.) More plaque detached as he was stretchered into Emergency. Gregan had another shot at dying and would have succeeded if the cardiac arrest team hadn't jolted him back to life.

For Gregan, this near life-ending event was life changing. While he'd never actually considered himself immortal, he did tend to put death in the same category as poverty, disease and retirement — things that affected other people but not him. The realisation that, despite his wealth and success, he had no firmer grasp on life than lesser mortals cut to his very soul. After all he'd done for people, he believed he deserved better.

'You have to reduce your stress levels,' said his cardiologist, so Gregan did what days earlier had been unthinkable, even unimaginable. At the age of fifty-nine, at the height of his success, he retired. Colleagues, competitors and councillors alike treated him to so many farewell lunches he was as busy as he'd ever been. Then the lunches stopped and, for the first time in as long as he could remember, Gregan had time on his hands.

Lots of time.

Days, weeks and endless months of time.

The fact was, he'd been so busy wheeling and dealing there'd been no time for anything else, with the result that retirement left him with nothing.

Nothing.

No reason to get out of bed, nothing to do, nowhere to go and nothing to boast about or even talk about. Whenever he rang his old mates to organise a lunch, they were always too busy arranging to bulldoze more countryside or erect more glass-and-concrete towers. Even worse, when lunches were organised, his mates forgot to ring him. Unfortunately for Gregan, he'd dropped off their radar. He was no longer a player and no longer part of the game. He was irrelevant. The complete lack of stress caused him more stress than he'd ever endured dealing with banks and councils.

'What can I do?' he asked his cardiologist.

'Go play golf,' the doctor replied. 'That's what people who retire do.'

'Can't stand golf,' said Gregan. 'Where's the excitement?'

'Then do what I do.'

'What's that?'

'I fish,' said the cardiologist.

'Fish?' said Gregan. As far as he was concerned, fish was something he ate when there were no crabs, calamari or prawns.

'Why not?' said the cardiologist. 'After all, you live on the water. You've got fish at the end of your backyard.'

And he did. When he'd completed his first canal development, Gregan had kept the three best blocks for himself. They were adjoining and sat at the very tip of the most sought-after spur he'd built from the mud and sand dug up by the dredges. He needed three blocks to accommodate the mansion, swimming pool and jetty he subsequently built.

'How do I learn to fish?' said Gregan.

'You take lessons,' said the cardiologist. 'You learn how to cast a fly.'

'A fly?'

'Real fishermen are fly fishermen,' said the cardiologist. 'You want something to occupy your time? Believe me, nothing will occupy your time more. Becoming an expert fly fisherman will take all the time you've got left.'

Gregan never did anything by halves. He found fly fishermen on the net who were only too happy to advise him on which rods, reels, lines, tippets and flies to buy. He hired a fly-fishing guide to teach him how to cast and took two-hour lessons every morning. He set aside a room in his anything-but-humble home and installed a bench, rotating fly dryer and vice for tying his own flies. He read every magazine about saltwater fly fishing he could get his hands on. And he practised his casts.

He practised with an eight-weight, a ten-weight and a twelve-weight until he felt competent no matter which rod was in his hand. He practised in the rain and in the wind. His teacher taught him the art of double hauling so that he could land his fly on any given spot even when the westerlies were blowing hard and right into his face. Only two things were missing.

Fish.

And excitement.

When he'd destroyed the mangroves Gregan had also taken away any reason for fish to hang around. Oh, there were mullet and toadfish and sometimes a lost school of tailor, but good fighting fish and table fish were rare. His young wife, who did her best to encourage him in his new pursuit, stopped enquiring if he'd caught anything. Then one day, for no reason anyone could think of, a one-point-five-kilo flathead decided to swim up into the canals. Its visit coincided with Gregan's morning tuition. Whatever the flathead was expecting to find, Gregan's beautifully presented red prawn fly must have come as an irresistible surprise. It bit the fly like it hadn't eaten for weeks and got a far bigger surprise than it had bargained for.

With no previous experience, Gregan didn't know what had hit him. His eight-weight Loomis rod bent under the impact and it was all he could do to hang on and scream. Fortunately his fishing guide was able to tell him what to do and how to do it. Nevertheless, Gregan's heart beat as madly as it had the day he'd made his first sale: a two-bedroom unit with a spectacular ocean view that got built out within six months of his buyers moving in. He followed instructions and lived the fishing videos he'd been watching. He couldn't believe that something as easy as stripping and winding line back onto his reel could suddenly become so complicated simply by the addition of a one-point-five-kilo fish. He made many mistakes but finally the guide slipped a net under his catch.

'Well hooked,' said the guide.

The flathead was well hooked. But nowhere near as well hooked as Gregan.

He cleared his walk-in wardrobe of all the trappings of his previous trade: his white Bally shoes, linen trousers and jackets, his Ralph Lauren shirts and his drawers of white socks. He packed them all up and deposited them in a St Vincent de Paul clothing bin. He restocked his wardrobe with the trappings of his new hobby: shirts, trousers and jackets in soft camouflage tones of grey, green and brown that bristled with pockets and places to put things and hang things off. Only the gold chain and gold Rolex remained as stark testimony to the fact that Gregan the committed fly fisher had once been Gregan the property developer.

Over the next few months, his guide took him out onto Moreton Bay where he caught more flathead and added tailor, salmon, whiting and bream to his list of conquests. Once he'd grown in both competence and confidence, his guide took him onto a sandbar in Hervey Bay where, standing in thigh-deep water with his rod tucked up in his armpit and double stripping for all he was worth, he caught his first grand trevally. At a tad under six kilos, it was hardly a trophy grand trevally, but it was still far and away the biggest and hardest-fighting fish Gregan had caught. When he released the fish he stood transfixed with the look of a man who'd just discovered Christmas.

Suddenly he realised that all the ads for overseas fishing adventures he'd glossed over in the saltwater fly fishing magazines were actually aimed at him. The big three — bonefish, tarpon and permit — weren't just fish other people caught but fish he could catch. He read every ad in every magazine and was stunned by the number of places he wanted to go that he'd never even heard of. He took his ambitions with him when he went to see his cardiologist.

'I don't know which of the big three to do first,' he said. 'Bonefish in the Turks and Caicos Islands, tarpon in the Florida Keys or permit in Belize.'

'Sounds wonderful,' said his cardiologist. 'But aren't you overlooking something?'

'What?'

'Trout.'

'Trout?'

'Tasmanian trout.'

'But they're freshwater fish.'

'And they're the ultimate,' said the cardiologist. 'Until you've learned to catch trout on a fly, you can't really call yourself a fly fisherman.'

'What do you mean?' said Gregan indignantly. 'Are you saying I don't know my stuff?'

'Blood pressure,' warned the cardiologist. 'Just lie back while I do this ECG and I'll tell you about trout fishing.'

He told Gregan how catching trout was only one part of the attraction. He told him about sharp, clear mountain air, crystal water and the beauty of the wilderness. He told him about lakes in the morning when the surface is as flat as glass, of snow-capped peaks perfectly mirrored, of waters so still you can see the ripple of a trout rise two hundred metres away. He told him about stalking trout up rivers running with the clearest, freshest water he'd ever seen, of the difficulty of casting beneath overhanging trees, of the joy and elation of seeing a backhand cast into the wind land right by the nose of a hungry brown. He told him about the value of observation and of matching flies to the insects the trout were feeding on. He told him about epic struggles with trout in rapids and in shallow lakes and how there was no sight in the world to match that of a leaping rainbow. He also lied and told Gregan that God didn't count days spent trout fishing against his allocation.

The cardiologist didn't ask Gregan if he'd infected him with his enthusiasm. He didn't need to. He could tell by looking at the print-out from the ECG.

When Gregan first set eyes on Highland Waters in Tasmania's Central Highlands, he couldn't help but mentally revert to his whites. The place reeked of potential for development. He could picture gleaming glass towers dotted around the perimeter of the lake, taking the place of the celery-top pines, eucalypts and myrtle. He envisioned long jetties for mooring boats and for casting a fly, a marina or two, and a gravel walkway right around the perimeter of the lake. Of course he'd have to bulldoze a few trees and a few hectares of heath and bracken to put down a decent lawn for the walkway to bisect, but the result would be magnificent. He pictured white ducks and little girls with long blonde hair feeding them. He had difficulty pulling back from his vision to remember that perhaps it wasn't the kind of magnificence trout fishermen were attracted to. He closed his eyes and reopened them, this time trying to see Highland Waters through his cardiologist's eyes. It took a moment to adjust, but he finally had to admit his doctor had a point.

Even so, the lodges were an extravagant waste of prime real estate, barely rising two storeys and designed to merge into their surroundings rather than announce their presence. They were single dwellings, sitting on plots big enough to build six good-sized mini-lodges, each with a water view. Again he had to remember that wasn't necessarily what trout fishermen wanted. His cardiologist had also spoken about solitude and communing with nature, listening to the many different kinds of birds and watching wallabies graze. It required considerable mental adjustment for a man who'd made a fortune evicting and dispossessing countless herons, waders and water fowl, but Gregan was prepared to give it a try if it would make him a better trout fisherman. A particularly handsome lodge caught his eye.

'Whose lodge is that over there?' he asked Peter, his guide for the week.

'It belongs to a Sydney man, Bob Horrocks.'

'What does he do for a crust?'

'He's an ex-advertising man. By all accounts, a very successful one.'

'An advertising man? You mean that place is owned by an ex-advertising man?' Gregan was incredulous. He'd met many advertising men and thought he had a lot in common with them. They worked hard and played hard, loved good food and wine, drove flash cars, were entertaining company and, like him, lived by their wits. He could accept that cardiologists, doctors, dentists, barristers, bank managers and accountants might be attracted to Highland Waters, but an advertising man?

'We get quite a few advertising people down here,' said his guide. 'Had a party of six just a week ago.'

Gregan was intrigued. He'd thought he was blazing a trail. He turned to gaze across the lake where there were no lodges and the sun was preparing to dip below the eucalypts. There was a stillness in the air, a silence and a sharpness. He heard the strangest birdcall, which surprised him; he wasn't accustomed to listening to birdcalls. Way out in front of him, ripples began to radiate from a spot where the surface of the water had been punctured. He felt himself smile but had no idea why.

'The trout are a bonus,' said Peter softly.

Gregan continued to scan the lake, looking for overhanging trees, wondering whether he'd be obliged to make a backhand double haul cast into the wind, a skill he was still working on. How satisfying would that be, especially if he hooked up? Gregan wanted to be a real fly fisherman more than he'd ever wanted anything.

'Come on,' said Peter. 'We've got all day tomorrow to see what you're made of.'

Gregan was in his waders and thigh deep in water long before the morning sun lit upon the surface of the lake. The calmness and stillness all around him was in marked contrast to his racing pulse and keen expectations.

'Just remember,' said Peter quietly, 'in still water if you can see the trout, the trout can see you. You have a good action. Just stay relaxed, let your cast come nice and easy and cast where I tell you.'

Gregan scanned the water trying his best to stay calm, looking for movement that might betray the presence of a trout. He wore the Costa Del Mar polaroid sunglasses he'd sent to the States for, after reading an article that claimed they were the first choice of America's leading fishing guides. Peter, who was standing alongside him, wore polaroids he'd picked up in a pharmacy in Launceston, but he was still first to spot a trout.

'There,' he said.

'Where?' said Gregan.

'Two o'clock, fifteen metres.'

'Where?' Gregan looked where the guide was pointing, expecting to see the shape of a fish beneath the surface, but in the dawn light the water was impenetrable.

'Don't look for the fish, look for the wake.'

Suddenly Gregan could see it, now that he knew what to look for. The trout was head up, zigzagging slowly by. Gregan's pulse rate shot up as he began to pull line off his reel.

'Easy,' said Peter. 'Stay relaxed.'

Gregan tried to relax. His back cast was a little shaky and his line a little short for the cast he needed to make. He drew off more line and cast. Despite his nervousness and the tension that turned his normally smooth action into a series of stuttering movements, he landed his fly spot on target, fifteen centimetres from the trout's nose. He braced himself for the explosion that would follow. The trout ignored his offering entirely.

'Nice work,' said Peter. 'But nice work doesn't always bring a reward. We might look at changing your fly. Swap the red tag for a caenid.'

'Damn it,' said Gregan. 'That was a perfect cast.' He watched as the trout slowly swam past. 'Let me have another crack at it.'

'Your call,' said Peter. 'But it isn't eating what you're offering. If it was, we wouldn't be having this conversation.'

Gregan reeled in his line.

'Try this caenid,' said Peter.

Three more trout passed by within range and Gregan did a creditable job of landing his fly in close proximity to their noses each time, but to no avail.

'When does it get exciting?' said Gregan.

'They're easier to catch when they're feeding on scud,' said Peter.

'I thought scud were missiles.'

'These scud are shrimp-like crustaceans that inhabit weed beds,' said Peter. 'Now, pay attention. One o'clock heading straight towards us. About twenty metres.'

Gregan's first cast landed short. He cast again, feeding more line, and dropped his fly forty centimetres from the trout's nose.

'Let it sit, let it sit . . .' said Peter.

Peter didn't have to comment any further. Gregan's fly disappeared in an explosion of water.

'What's it doing?' shrieked Gregan.

'Jumping,' said the guide. 'Keep the tension on your rod.'

Gregan had caught tailor that jumped a bit and one time a native salmon had kicked up a bit of a fuss, but mostly the fish he'd caught had stayed well within their element and their fight had been dogged and, in some ways, predictable. But there was nothing at all predictable about his trout. It went ballistic, somersaulting and cartwheeling out of the water. When it ran, it ran with arrogance rather than desperation, as though it knew the angler was new to the sport and their attachment to each other only temporary. It changed direction unexpectedly and began a blistering run back towards him.

Gregan could see what was happening but couldn't strip his line fast enough. When the trout veered off and exploded clear of the water, Gregan suspected he was in trouble. The tippet probably made a bit of a ping when it snapped but he never heard it. When the trout threw in another two jumps for good measure, Gregan thought it was still hooked. The realisation that it wasn't left him bitterly disappointed.

'Few fly fishermen net their first trout,' said Peter. 'Particularly a trout as good as that one.'

'How big?' said Gregan. He couldn't drag his eyes away from the spot on the water where his trout had disappeared.

'Maybe three kilos,' said Peter. 'Maybe a touch under. But it fought well above its weight. Come on, let's take a break and have breakfast.'

Gregan took a last look around. The air was dead still and had a brittle clarity. He could make out individual leaves on individual branches hundreds of metres away. The lake was as unruffled as a sheet of glass. It was a scene of unbroken tranquillity. It was hard to believe that so much excitement and mayhem lurked mere centimetres below the surface.

Through the course of the day, Gregan caught and released two browns and kept a two-point-five-kilo rainbow for the pan. Peter called it a triploid. Gregan thought his guide was just referring to the fact that it was the third fish he caught. He ended the day on a high that even exceeded the one he'd experienced when the council had granted him approval to build his first tower, despite the fact that it breached just about every rule, restriction and guideline in their building code. He drank more Cascade that night than his cardiologist would recommend and went to bed thanking Peter profusely.

'How was your client?' Peter's wife asked when she finally got him on his own.

'More enthusiastic than skilled and really eager to learn. I mean, really eager. He listens to what I have to say and does exactly as I tell him. I have to watch what I say because he absorbs everything.'

'I can always tell when you've got a good one because you come home happy,' said his wife.

'All my clients give me pleasure,' said Peter.

'Some when they arrive, others when they leave,' said his wife. She'd heard it all before.

'A rainbow triploid is the fish equivalent of a capon,' said Peter. He and Gregan were enjoying a leisurely lunch of chicken salad and celebrating Gregan's capture of a four-kilo rainbow triploid. It was the only trout they'd caught all morning and its size and the fight it had put up more than compensated for earlier disappointments. 'They're deliberately made sterile so that they grow bigger faster.'

'But why make them sterile?' said Gregan. 'I thought you'd want fish like that to breed.'

'Three reasons,' said Peter. 'Triploids make big, strong fighting fish and that's what we all want. Secondly, we don't want them to breed. They breed a month after brown trout and use the same breeding grounds to lay their eggs. Their activity disturbs the eggs of the brown trout and they even feed on them. So if we want both brown trout and rainbow trout to grow big and prosper, we have to have sterile rainbows.'

'But how can rainbows prosper if they can't breed?' said Gregan.

'We buy fingerlings and restock,' said Peter. 'The third reason is purely commercial. Highland Waters isn't the only lake around here. There are hundreds and all of them have trout and many have their own resident guides. The fact is, big fish attract more fishermen and as a professional guide I need to compete and make a living. The bigger and more plentiful the trout are, the more work I get. And there's also the question of land.'

'Land?' This was something Gregan understood.

'There are still a few blocks left to sell. You wouldn't be interested, would you? I could put you onto Ian Walters. He's a local builder. Does a great job. He did the Horrocks house.'

'Maybe,' said Gregan. His heart was screaming 'yes', but his brain was urging caution. The funny thing was, he'd never bought a house from anyone before and had never bought property except on a scale for development. He'd always argued that by the time individual blocks and single dwellings came on the market, the real money had already been made — and he was often the bloke who'd made it. To his white-shoe way of thinking, no matter how much he paid for a block of land at Highland Waters, he'd end up paying far too much. But the seeds of ownership had been sown and they'd fallen on fertile soil. Gregan knew he'd have to figure out a way of doing something about it.

'Before I leap in at the deep end,' he said. 'Tell me about some of these other lakes.'

Gregan sat out on his terrace in sunny Surfers, a lager glass filled with light beer in one hand, his mobile in the other and a teledex on the heavy glass table in front of him. He was wearing plain multi-pocketed shorts and a Patagonia multi-pocketed shirt in an exquisite shade of drab green. He had olive all-terrain walking sandals on his feet. Although in perfect trout camouflage, he was definitely in white Bally slip-on mode. He began working his way through the names of every advertising man he knew. As he did so, he couldn't help comparing his surroundings with those of the Central Highlands. They had nothing in common yet he found beauty in both.

His own home was ruthlessly modern: all angles, white paint and hanging walls of tinted glass. He liked the overall look of it and the interior, which was twentieth-century classic American in a Spence & Lyda/Herman Miller sort of way. There wasn't a wall that didn't boast a Geoffrey Smart, Brett Whiteley or Arthur Boyd, except those in his study, which were adorned with pictures of glass towers and developments. In truth, he'd wanted something a little grander, something *Gone With the Wind*-ish, antebellum South with proud white columns, but his wife had been resolutely opposed.

'The world doesn't need another Tara,' she said.

All the same Gregan couldn't help feeling a little envious when he looked across the water at the replica French château and, two metres away from it on the adjacent block, a replica Tuscan villa with a most delightful Balinese garden. He decided it was the classic look that he liked and stored his preference away for possible application in Tasmania.

'Owen!' said Gregan. 'Mate! How're ya going? I haven't heard a peep out of you since I rang to tell you how much I liked the brochure you did for me.' Gregan kept the patter up before slipping in the key question. 'Been trout fishing down Tassie lately? No? I thought you were a keen trout fisherman. You're not? Never mind, we've still got to do lunch some time. I'll call you.'

He made four similar calls before he finally struck gold. Not only had his old mate Richo been trout fishing in Tasmania, he was considering buying a property there. Richo had sold his agency to an American advertising conglomerate for a potful of money and was just three months short of completing his service contract.

'What are you going to do then?' asked Gregan. 'Retire? Mate, you're far too young to do that and you can't spend every day fishing. I know, I've tried. You've got to have something else going to keep the mind active and the juices flowing. I've had an idea that'll not only make us a decent buck but enable us to chase bloody big rainbows for the rest of our lives. Interested?'

Of course he was.

Gregan flew Richo up from Sydney and took him to his favourite restaurant where the Moreton Bay bugs were exceptional and the mud crabs came from Sandy Bay and were the size of dinner plates.

'I've identified two lakes near Bronte Park with potential,' said Gregan. 'Including the surrounding land, one is fourteen hectares and the other eighteen. Both are fed by streams with gravel beds which are ideal for breeding.'

'Interesting,' said Richo. 'But what's the hook? What's the marketing edge? Why would anyone buy and build on our land in preference, say, to Highland Waters?'

'Bigger, stronger fish,' said Gregan. 'Potentially world-record fish. Done right, I reckon our lake could attract fly fishermen from all over the world. In fact, that's what I'm counting on.'

'If these lakes have world-record trout in them, why haven't they already been developed?'

'They haven't got world-record fish in them,' said Gregan smugly. 'Not yet, they haven't, but they will have.'

'Go on.'

'Tell me, Richo, what do you know about triploids?'

'I've heard of them, of course, even caught a few, but I haven't a clue what they are.'

'I've made some enquiries,' said Gregan. 'Triploid rainbows are trout with an extra set of chromosomes. Normal trout are diploids, which is to say they have two sets of chromosomes, one from each parent. Trout eggs also have two sets of chromosomes from their mother, which means that they have to "cast off" a set to accommodate their dad's chromosomes when they're fertilised. If you treat newly fertilised trout eggs to block the "casting off" of a set of chromosomes, you end up with triploids. Because tripoids are sterile, they don't lose the energy normal trout put into breeding and so maintain their condition and growth rate. They grow bigger and stronger faster.'

'Okay,' said Richo. 'But I still don't see our advantage. Triploids already exist in other lakes.'

'True,' said Gregan. 'But if trout can be manipulated to become triploids, who's to say that's where manipulation ends? I've spoken to people in universities and made contacts on the net. Theoretically, there is no reason why growth genes can't also be manipulated to make trout grow even faster, and no reason why the triggers that limit growth can't be delayed or disabled.'

'You're talking genetic engineering.'

'That's what I'm doing.'

'Forget it, Gregan. It took teams of scientists working with the latest, fastest computers years to identify the human genome. It would take just as long to identify a trout's.'

'Not necessarily.'

'What do you mean?'

'This is the good part,' said Gregan. 'The web turned up this guy in Sydney, a bloke called Everton Sweet. He's a genetic engineer with a thing about fish. He's way-out weird and as boring as flat beer, but he thinks he can give us what we want for half a mill.'

'Five hundred thousand dollars?'

'Yeah. What do you reckon?'

'My car cost more than that.'

'The first thing we have to do is make sure Everton can deliver and squeeze some kind of time frame out of him,' said Gregan. They'd finished lunch and were lingering over a fifty-year-old Para port. 'Once that's in the bag, we can approach the two guys who've optioned the eighteen-hectare property.'

'What two guys?' said Richo.

'Two guides,' said Gregan. 'Brothers. The Hydro released the land and they optioned it with a view to building a fishing lodge, thereby guaranteeing themselves a steady stream of clients. They're pushovers, literally babes in the wood. They're grossly under-capitalised and haven't a clue about marketing. When they read our proposal they'll think they've died and gone to heaven. We'll get the property for a song.'

'So it all comes down to a mad scientist with a thing about fish?'

'Yes, but we have to be careful,' said Gregan. 'It's not a big jump from genetically modified fish to Frankenstein fish. If word ever gets out about what we're doing we could be in trouble. Fly fishermen are nature freaks and won't be happy. They could boycott us and deny us world records.'

'Bloody tree huggers,' said Richo.

'How big do you want these trout to grow?' asked Everton Sweet.

'Thirty kilos would just about double the current world record,' said Gregan. 'But forty kilos has a nicer ring to it.'

'It's possible,' said Everton. 'But have you thought about how you'll support a colony of forty-kilo trout in one small lake?'

'What do you mean?' said Gregan.

'Have you any idea how much a forty-kilo trout would need to eat?'

'No,' said Gregan.

'Can you imagine how many insects a forty-kilo trout would need to eat in a day, how many galaxia, how many scud, how many tadpoles, how many frogs, how many dragonfly larvae?'

'No,' said Gregan.

'Can you imagine how much food a colony of forty-kilo trout would consume? Can you imagine how quickly they'd clean out the lake's entire food source? Nature isn't stupid, you know. There's a pretty good reason why trout only grow so big.'

'Thirty kilos is sounding pretty good,' said Gregan.

'Twenty-five kilos sounds even better,' said Everton. 'Your fish will be magnificent. We just have to make sure they're not too magnificent.'

Gregan did some quick calculating. Twenty-five kilos was roughly fifty-three pounds, more than enough to break every world record and get rich American pulses racing.

'Can you make twenty-five-kilo trout?'

'Brown, rainbow or brook?'

'Rainbow.'

'Hmmm . . .' said the man who could make broccoli taste like chocolate and pork taste like beef. 'Genetic engineering isn't rocket science. Oh no, it's much more complicated than that. Yes, I can do it but it's going to take time.'

'How much time?' said Gregan.

'A year,' said Everton. 'So long as nothing happens to me in the meantime, ha-ha.'

'I've got the land,' said Gregan. 'And the guides have begun stocking the lake with triploid fingerlings.'

'Why triploids?' asked Richo. 'Why bother?'

'Assuming we get our GM trout in twelve months, it could still take them three or four years to reach record size. The triploids will reach a good size in two.'

'Can't we just wait?'

'Out of the question,' said Gregan. 'We've got to get the business up and running. The bank will only release money in stages and they'll want to see some evidence of the project working along the way.'

'Okay. What do you want me to do?'

'Dress up the proposal and get going with the marketing and advertising. Have you come up with a name yet?'

'Yeah,' said Richo. 'Wuthering Heights.'

'What?' said Gregan.

'Wuthering Heights. You said it was near Bronte Park, right?'

'What's that got to do with it?'

'Bronte? *Wuthering Heights*? No? Ah, forget it. Of course I've got a name.' Richo drew in a deep breath. Naming was often the trickiest part of a marketing program and often the most critical. 'You know I don't like names for the sake of names or logos for the sake of logos.'

'I've heard this speech before,' said Gregan.

'A name should reflect what it represents,' said Richo doggedly.

'So what is it?'

'Big Trout Lake,' said Richo.

'On the money,' said Gregan.

'Home of Big Trout Lodge.'

'How do you do it?' said Gregan admiringly. 'We could have a giant fibreglass trout over the entrance.'

'Don't push it,' said Richo.

Gregan was back on his home turf, metaphorically speaking, wheeling, dealing and selling his dream. He flew his architect and surveyors down to Big Trout Lake so that his plans could begin to take on substance. He needed substance to show the banks.

'I want something classical,' he told his architect.

'Classical?' said the architect.

'Classic North American.'

'Classic? North American?'

'Yeah, you know, classic north shore Lake Tahoe. Think Incline Village. Think money, dark timber, big fireplaces, big rooms, stuffed trout and deer heads, high ceilings and steeply pitched roofs.'

'Good choice,' said the architect. 'Sort of Heidi meets William Randolph Hearst.'

'I want Big Trout Lodge to be top dollar. I want Huka Lodge in New Zealand to feel like a weekender in Woop Woop by comparison. Give me twenty bedrooms with ensuites and jacuzzis. Big dining room, coffee shop, tackle shop, souvenir shop and newsagent/pharmacy store. Oh, and a boutique for wives. Better have a games room with snooker table and fly-tying facilities, gym and heated indoor pool. Maybe a sauna too. And lots of views, okay?'

'Easy,' said the architect. 'How many floors?'

'No more than four,' said Gregan. 'And I want the lodge to be the hub of the wheel. Know what I mean?'

'Sure.'

'And do me indicative drawings of eight private lodges, all Incline Village style. Put them on big blocks. If people want to buy into Big Trout Lake it's going to cost them. They're going to have to spend at least seven hundred and fifty grand on building their lodge or they can go elsewhere. I don't want riffraff. Only rich people deserve the world's biggest trout and they don't come cheap.'

Gregan turned to the surveyor.

'I need the whole property surveyed, lake and all. I want an accurate model made. I want models of Big Trout Lodge and the private lodges. I want people with no imagination at all to be able to look at this and see exactly what they're getting for their bank's millions. Okay?'

'No worries,' said the surveyor.

'You've got six months,' said Gregan.

'Need twelve,' said the architect.

'Nine it is,' said Gregan.

Next Gregan met with the two fishing guides, Dan and Dave. He was paying them not to fish Big Trout Lake and to make sure nobody else did either. But there were exceptions.

'I'm bringing two guys from the bank down next week. I want you to take them out on the lake and I want both of them to catch a big trout. We do have some big trout here?'

'Sure do,' said Dan. 'Big browns.'

'But do you know where to find them?'

'Sure do,' said Dave. He gave Dan a knowing look.

'Guaranteed?'

'Sure thing,' said Dan. He returned Dave's knowing look. They stood there grinning like a couple of idiots.

'What am I missing?' said Gregan.

'Fishing guides have always got to know where to find fish,' said Dave. 'So good ones take precautions.'

'What precautions?'

'Phosphates,' said Dan and grinned.

'Phosphates?' said Gregan.

'You know,' said Dave.

'No, I don't,' said Gregan.

'It's simple,' said Dan. 'We put phosphates down in certain parts of the lake so the weed grows thick there. Where the weed grows we get scud.'

'Lots of scud,' said Dave.

'And where you get lots of scud, you get lots of trout,' said Dan.

It was Gregan's turn to grin. The brothers were men after his own heart.

'So you know where to take my guys from the bank?'

'Sure do,' said Dan.

'And you guarantee they'll each catch a big fish?'

'Sure do,' said Dave.

'Glad to hear it,' said Gregan. His voice turned cold. 'I like you boys and, you know what, I'd sure hate to lose you.'

One of the things Gregan had always prided himself on was his ability to keep his projects on schedule.

'Banks want certainty,' he liked to say. 'Projects that run on schedule translate to repayments being made on schedule.'

Nine months into the project he had his model of Big Trout Lake and completed plans for Big Trout Lodge. His bankers were impressed. Gregan was back in business and his business had always been good.

Three months later, bulldozers and earthmovers began clearing the site for Big Trout Lodge and laying the foundations. Gregan's bankers were thrilled. Clearly the master had lost none of his touch.

About the same time as the first celery-tops toppled over, Gregan called in on Everton Sweet to see when he could take delivery of his genetically modified rainbow trout fingerlings. He'd rung the scientist every three months to check on progress and Everton had given him no cause for concern. In fact, Everton had impressed him with his enthusiasm and obvious delight at the way the project was going.

'Hi,' said Gregan as he was ushered into Everton's office. 'How are my fish doing?'

'They're doing very well,' said Everton. 'They will be magnificent fish.'

'Great. Are they ready for release?'

'Not exactly,' said Everton.

'What do you mean?' said Gregan. 'You said it would only take a year and the year's up.'

'Ah, yes,' said Everton. 'I did say that. A year, unless … unless something happened to me in the meantime.'

'So?' said Gregan.

'Something happened.'

'What?'

'Something happened to me in the meantime.'

'What?'

'Cancer, actually, in the brain.'

'Cancer!' Gregan felt the blood drain from his face and his heart skip a beat. 'How bad?'

'Incurable. That is, unless I come up with a cure myself.'

'What about my fish?' Gregan showed the same level of sympathy and concern as Everton's adoring wife.

'Backburner, I'm afraid. I know it sounds selfish but finding a cure has become something of a priority.'

'Can't you give my fish to someone else to do?'

'I've done that already. Young Lothar. He's quite brilliant and capable of enormous leaps. Unfortunately he rather likes the constraints of correct scientific procedure and is inclined to take small steps instead.'

'How long?' said Gregan.

'Ninety per cent of the work is done,' said Everton.

'How long?'

'Of course, that was me doing it.'

'How long?'

'If it was me? Six weeks.'

'And Lothar?'

'Six months, maybe. More probably a year.'

A year! Gregan thought of his schedule and the effect of a year's delay on his precious bankers.

'Damn it!' he shouted. 'I haven't got a year! I've only got a couple of months.'

'I know exactly how you feel,' said Everton sympathetically.

'We're history!' said Gregan. 'Finished! The whole thing's cactus because that nutter went and got brain cancer.'

'Hold it,' said Richo. They were sitting in Lucio's in Paddington, and the crabs they were eating were blue swimmers over linguini. It was exactly the kind of subtle dish that Gregan had no time for. The jumbo prawns they'd ordered to follow were barbecued in their shells. Gregan didn't have much time for that, either.

'Hold what?' said Gregan.

'You said the fish were ninety per cent ready.'

'Yeah, and ten per cent, or one year, unready.'

'Well, I don't know about you, Gregan, but ninety per cent sounds pretty good to me. I know one hundred per cent sounds better, but, under the circumstances, ninety per cent sounds good enough.'

Gregan's fork stopped en route to his mouth.

'What does ninety per cent ready mean, anyway?' said Richo. 'Instead of growing to twenty-five kilos they'll only grow to twenty-two and a half? That's still one hell of a big fish. It's still a world record.'

'You know something? You're right,' said Gregan. 'But how many ninety per cent-ready fish have they got and how can we get hold of them?'

Gregan took a dislike to Lothar the moment they met. The young man had peach fluff on his upper lip in a vain attempt to grow a moustache and look older. Even worse, he was pedantic and dismissive of Gregan's problems.

'These things take time,' said Lothar. 'Ideally we should grow out a few fish from this batch to discover exactly when they stop growing. Everton thinks the triggers will cut in at around twenty-five kilos, but they could just as easily cut in at thirty kilos.'

'It's only five kilos, for Christ's sake,' said Gregan.

'Those five kilos could be the difference between success and failure,' said Lothar patiently. 'Think about it. Your lake may be able to sustain twenty-five-kilo fish but thirty-kilo fish are another matter altogether. The worst-case scenario is that the growth inhibitors won't cut in at all.'

'How long will it take to grow out the fish?' asked Gregan.

'With the growth accelerants, eighteen months to two years.'

'Two years! That's out of the question.'

'That's good practice,' said Lothar, unperturbed.

'What are you going to do?' asked Gregan.

'I think it's safer to err under than over,' said the young scientist primly. 'I think I'll make another batch with growth inhibitors that activate earlier.'

'What are you going to do with these?' Gregan eyed the hundred or so fingerlings in the tank.

'Waste disposer.'

'What! You mean you're going to put my fish down your waste disposer?' Gregan couldn't believe his ears.

'Me? God, no,' said Lothar. 'That's what people like Murray are for.' Murray was a laboratory assistant twice the young scientist's age.

'Well, you've got to do what you've got to do,' said Gregan. 'I won't hold you up any longer.'

'Let me show you out,' said Lothar.

'No need,' said Gregan. He turned on his most engaging smile. 'That's what people like Murray are for.'

It took less than thirty seconds for Gregan to do the deal. He needed fish. Murray needed money. The lab assistant promised to deliver the fish that night.

Gregan flew down to Tasmania the following day and quietly released his trout into Big Trout Lake. It was a glorious day but he knew sudden death was ever present. One hundred fingerlings didn't amount to much, given that they had to survive the predations of bigger trout, birds and competition from fingerling browns and triploids. But Gregan believed enough would survive. Oh yes, enough would survive to become trophies. They would mature right on schedule.

There are always problems building in a wilderness: problems getting materials and supplies, problems getting tradesmen and problems keeping them. Like a true professional, Gregan had factored in the delays. He thought it would have taken him twelve months to build Big Trout Lodge in Surfers so he allowed an extra nine months to build it in the Central Highlands. Eighteen months in, his estimate had proved accurate. The biggest problem he faced was hanging onto tradesmen, especially during the bleak Central Highlands' winter.

Many tradesmen were attracted to the job and prepared to put up with the isolation by the prospect of doing some fly fishing. They were somewhat peeved to learn that fishing in the lake was strictly forbidden on pain of instant dismissal and so they often didn't stay long. Nevertheless, while they were there they kept their eye out for trout rising, and when they saw the extraordinary size of the trout they weren't allowed to catch, felt even more cheated. Fearing that some of the tradesmen might succumb to temptation, Dave and Dan mounted around-the-clock surveillance and confirmed what the builders had seen. The trout really were enormous. As tradesmen came and went, word of the big trout in Big Trout Lake began to spread.

While Gregan kept a watchful eye on the final fit-out, Richo went about organising the trout-fishing media event of the year. He identified the twenty most influential trout-fishing magazines and television programs in Australia, the United States and Great Britain and invited their editors plus partners to the grand opening of Big Trout Lake. He did deals with travel agents, airlines and tour operators. He provided first-class air tickets, five-star hotels on stopovers, and limousines to ferry them from the airport to Big Trout Lake. The package was as lavish as Richo could make it, but that wasn't what won him one hundred per cent acceptance. What caught the editors' eyes was his promise: he guaranteed that everyone would catch the biggest trout they'd ever caught and promised that one of them would break the world record. How could they resist?

Two months before Big Trout Lake was due to open, that promise was the lead story in every major trout-fishing magazine and program. The story even made the major dailies and, in some instances, the TV news. Before a single fish had been caught, there wasn't a serious fly fisherman in Australia, the United States or Great Britain who wasn't desperate to fish Big Trout Lake.

'Are you absolutely sure we can deliver on these promises?' Richo asked Gregan when they met to review progress. 'We're going to look pretty stupid if we can't.'

'Absolutely sure, unless the guides are lying to us,' said Gregan. 'They claim to have seen trout as long as their arms.'

'Yeah, but have they caught any?'

'You know they're not allowed to fish,' said Gregan. 'But it's not just Dan and Dave who've seen the fish, the builders have as well. You remember the chippie with the kelpie?'

'The dog that likes to retrieve sticks?'

'That's the one. Apparently the mutt just lives for it. He's in and out of the water a dozen times a day and loves it.'

'So?'

'So last week one of the blokes throws a stick right out into the lake and the kelpie sets off after it. Halfway out it does a high-speed U-turn and paddles like crazy for the shore. The builders swear there were a couple of monster trout circling it the whole way in. Now the dog won't go near the water.'

'Trout chasing a dog? Give me a break.'

'A break is what I had in mind,' said Gregan. 'The first suites have been fitted out and we've begun hiring and training staff. I think we should go down this weekend and test out our investment.'

The sun was ready to dip below the eucalypts when Dave led Gregan out into the shallows on the western shore, which were already in shade. Fifty metres away to his left, Dan was doing the same for Richo.

'See that swirl at eleven o'clock?' said Dave.

'I see it,' said Gregan. He stripped line off his reel and lined up the target seventeen metres away. He rocked back and forth as his instructor had taught him as he fed out more line.

'Just relax,' said Dave.

Gregan was relaxed. He was as confident and relaxed as any man certain of his own cleverness could be. He cast and watched his fly sail through the air and land smack on target. He barely had time to gather in the excess line when his fly was hit by what felt like a runaway train. Despite the fact that he was using an eight-weight with an unsporting three-point-five kilo tippet, he felt hopelessly under-gunned. Line screamed off his reel and he was powerless to prevent it.

'Bloody hell!' said Dave. 'What have you got there?'

Richo and Dan stopped what they were doing to watch.

'Put some pressure on him,' said Dave.

'I've got pressure on him!' said Gregan.

'Then give him more pressure! Jam him up! You're running out of line!'

Gregan grabbed hold of the last metre of his line and held on tight. His rod doubled over, then sprang back to the vertical. The line hung limp from the tip.

'Damn!' said Gregan. For a moment his disappointment outweighed his delight in confirming the presence in his lake of trout that would not only break the world record but shatter it. He turned to Dave with a rueful smile. 'Got any more good advice?'

'Yeah,' said Dave. 'Next time use a twelve-weight with a nine-kilo tippet.'

Gregan smiled and his smile broadened when he noticed Richo cast. Almost immediately his rod doubled over.

'How long do you give him?' he asked Dave. 'Fifteen seconds? Twenty?'

'Dunno,' said Dave. 'By the look of things, his fish isn't as big as yours.'

The guide was right. Richo wasn't just holding on helplessly but fighting his fish. As Gregan watched, the lake in front of him shattered into a million brilliant shards. The trout cleared the surface by more than a metre.

'Triploid!' said Dave. 'And a bloody monster at that.'

Gregan smiled to himself. He was happy to have Dave believe the monster rainbow was a triploid. The fish jumped again, and again, and again. But each time it jumped, Richo regained line.

'Look at the size of that thing!' said Dave. 'It's got to go close to the record.'

'It's going back,' said Gregan. 'Record or no record.' He felt like a proud father. His dream, his vision, his scheme was coming to fruition.

It took ten minutes for Richo's fish to tire enough for him to think seriously about netting it.

'Net,' he said.

'No way,' said Dan. 'You concentrate on getting the bugger in. I'll net it.'

Richo was happy to comply. He knew when he had his hands full.

'Here it comes,' he said.

'Get ready . . .

'Get ready . . .'

'Bloody hell!' said Dan.

'Bloody hell!' said Dave.

Gregan just watched open-mouthed. For a moment he thought he was back on the sandbar in Hervey Bay when a shark had come screaming in and made off with a trevally he was fighting.

Richo stood stunned with just the head of his enormous trout dangling from the end of his rod. Whatever had taken the rest of it had created a wake that had washed up over his knees and flooded his thigh-high waders.

'Jesus Christ!' said Dan, wide-eyed with awe. 'What kind of trout cuts a world record in half with a single bite?'

'How big do you reckon it was?' said Gregan when they were back at Big Trout Lodge and had swallowed a few beers to clear their minds.

'I've caught a forty-kilo bluefin tuna,' said Dan. 'It wasn't any bigger than the trout that took Richo's.'

'Did you get a clear look at it?' said Gregan. He wanted to know, wanted to be sure.

'No, he didn't,' said Richo. 'I was as close as he was. There was far too much disturbance on the water. That thing threw a wake like a surfacing submarine. It could have been twenty kilos or thirty or forty. There's no way of knowing. In truth, all I saw was its head, its wide-open mouth and bloody big teeth. It was big but I couldn't put a weight to it.'

'Do you agree with that, Dan?'

'I guess so. I got a sense of the size of the fish rather than a good look. But I've fished for trout all my life and I don't think I've ever seen anything half as big.'

'I reckon the fish it swallowed was a world record,' said Dave. 'I got a good look at that one. So I'd have to say thirty kilos is looking good.'

'Ever seen a twenty?' said Richo.

'All we can agree on is that it was big,' said Gregan. 'Bloody big. And I want you all to agree on something else. I don't want anybody to breathe a word of what happened to anyone else. Not to your mothers, wives or girlfriends. Not a dickybird, not to anyone. Okay?'

'No worries,' said Dan. 'Who'd believe us?'

Gregan had always imagined that his first night in Big Trout Lodge would be cause for celebration, and he and Richo had celebrated long after the brothers had taken their leave to try out the staff quarters. They sampled the champagne the editors would be drinking, the sauvignon blanc, the pinot noir and the botrytis riesling. Richo grew more pleased with what they'd achieved as the night wore on, but Gregan grew increasingly uneasy. He kept his disquiet to himself and took it with him to bed.

As he lay awake in the darkness he couldn't help recalling snippets of conversation with Everton and the boy wonder, Lothar. They whirled around in his head and refused to go away.

'*Your fish will be magnificent. We just have to make sure they're not too magnificent,*' Everton had said the very first time they met.

'*They should grow out in eighteen months to two years,*' Lothar had said. Well, the two years were nearly up. Gregan took some comfort from that.

'*The growth inhibitors may not cut in at all.*' That was also something the boy wonder had said. Gregan thought of the monster in the lake and shuddered. But then he remembered that Everton had created the fish in his lake, not Lothar, and Everton had thought that they'd peak at twenty-five kilos. Everton was a famous genetic engineer and Lothar was, well, just a know-all kid with peach fuzz on his face. Gregan decided to back Everton. Nevertheless he slept uneasily.

Three weeks later Gregan returned to the lake to make sure everything would be ready in time for the grand opening. He was more concerned with the work that hadn't been done than with the monster that might or might not be lurking in the lake. It was only at Dan and Dave's insistence that he agreed to go fishing in the morning. As they walked out into the pre-dawn stillness, Gregan remarked on how quiet it was.

'You noticed it, too,' said Dan.

'What?' said Gregan.

'No frogs,' said Dave.

'What do you mean, no frogs?' said Gregan.

'There are no frogs,' said Dan. 'Something's happened to all the frogs.'

Suddenly Gregan's blood turned cold and it had nothing to do with the morning chill.

'Something strange is going on,' said Dave. 'There are no frogs, no tadpoles and no galaxia.'

'And now we've got big brown trout acting like they're spooked or something,' said Dan.

'What do you mean?' said Gregan. He felt faint.

'We'll show you,' said Dave.

'Notice anything else strange?' said Dan.

'What?' said Gregan.

'There are ducks on all the lakes around here, but none on this lake. Don't you think that's kind of weird?'

'Maybe there's something in the water they don't like,' said Gregan weakly.

'Maybe there's something in the water that likes them,' said Dan. 'Want to think about that?'

'Look!' said Dave suddenly.

They'd walked along the bank to where an old eucalypt had fallen and deposited most of its upper storey in the lake. Gregan saw a monster brown lurking in among the branches, in water so shallow the tip of its tail broke the surface.

'And there,' said Dan. 'And there!'

Wherever Dave and Dan pointed there were big brown trout. Some even had part of their backs out of the water.

'You can walk right up to them and they won't budge from their hiding place unless you actually touch them. Even then they don't go far.' Dave tiptoed into the water to demonstrate. The trout darted away at his touch but not very far. It hovered nervously in knee-deep water.

'We've got browns here as big as the best from Lake Pedder and they're scared stiff. They're more frightened of whatever chased them in there than they are of us,' said Dan. 'Reckon we know what that might be.'

'What?' said Gregan. He couldn't meet the brothers' eyes.

'That monster trout that cut your friend's record trout in half,' said Dan.

'Has to be,' said Dave. 'It must be some kind of mutant triploid.'

Mutant triploid? The brothers thought his GM trout was a mutant triploid. That was fine by him but it still didn't solve his problem. If the monster trout ate all the food in the lake and all the surviving browns and triploids, there'd be nothing in the lake when the world's press arrived. So much for his promises of world records! The future swam before his eyes and he didn't like the look of it one bit. No fish. No fame and glory. No guests for his hotel. Just public ridicule and, worse, a financial catastrophe.

'What are we going to do?' he said.

'We're going to have to catch it,' said Dan. 'And catch it now.'

'Maybe we can catch it and release it again the day before the media arrive,' said Gregan hopefully.

'If we catch that mutant the best thing we can do is put a bullet in it,' said Dave.

'Two bullets,' said Dan.

'But can we catch it?' said Gregan.

'I took the precaution of bringing a fifty-pound game rod. It's back at the lodge,' said Dave. 'Mind if I go get it?'

'Fifty-pound?' said Gregan.

'We're not catching this fish for sport,' said Dan.

'I know that,' said Gregan. 'But are you sure fifty pounds will be strong enough?'

As Dave set off for the rod Gregan turned to watch the brown trout among the dead branches. He noticed a couple of rainbow triploids also hiding in the shallows.

'It's a pity we're not holding the opening now,' said Gregan. 'That mutant triploid would keep the entire trout world talking about us for years.'

'No one would ever break that record, that's for sure,' said Dan.

'Any idea where we're going to find it?'

'It's hungry,' said Dan. 'Reckon it'll find us.'

When Dave returned, they moved on from the fallen tree and away from any known snags.

'This is one of my saltwater poppers,' said Dave. He tied the shocking pink lure onto his line with a perfection loop. 'It's got a very aggressive action. Probably scare the daylights out of every fish in the lake except the one we're after.' He pulled his game belt out of his bag and offered it to Gregan.

'It's all yours,' said Gregan. He didn't want to let on that he'd never so much as touched any rod that wasn't a fly rod. He noticed that Dave had also brought a heavy-duty game gaff with him. The boys weren't taking any chances.

'Here goes,' said Dave. He cast long out into the lake and retrieved as fast as he could wind.

'Are you sure you're not overdoing it?' asked Gregan. The lure skipped and darted and dived and kicked up a rooster tail.

'Maybe,' said Dan.

They watched as Dave sent the lure flying a second time. Halfway in, the fish struck.

'Bloody hell!' said Dan in awe.

Dave held on as the giant trout rose from the water and tail-walked away from them for twenty metres before crashing back beneath the surface. Then Dave's problems really began. It took off for the far side of the lake.

'Bloody hell!' said Dave as he watched the line fizz off his Penn International. One hundred metres went, then two without the fish showing any sign of slowing.

'You're going to have to increase the drag,' said Dan.

'It's up to twenty now,' said Dave. 'Can't risk any more.'

The line continued to fizz off. Then, without warning, it slowed.

'Gotcha!' said Dave. He began the hard work of regaining his line, short stroking like he did when he was fighting bluefin. The trout set off in an arc, turning sideways to the line, making Dave fight for every centimetre.

'My God,' said Gregan breathlessly. 'Why couldn't it have waited for the opening?'

'There'd be no fish left in the lake by the opening,' said Dan. 'And once it had eaten everything there was to eat, it would probably die itself.'

'I'm going to have it mounted,' said Gregan suddenly. 'I'll hang it over the reception desk. I might put a hidden camera there, too, to catch the look on those editors' faces when they check in. Show the tape on the night of the farewell dinner.'

'Maybe that's not such a great idea,' said Dan. 'After all, you did promise one of them would catch the world record. There's no fish going to beat this one.'

'We can say we found it floating belly up one day,' said Gregan. 'Say we kept it as an example of the size of fish this lake has to offer.'

'You're the boss,' said Dan.

'Damn right,' said Gregan. 'Just catch that fish.'

They turned their attention back to Dave. His forehead was beaded in sweat and the muscles in his arms were as pumped as a weightlifter's. He still had a hundred metres of line to get back. Every time he gained a couple of winds the fish took it back.

'Bloody thing's turned sideways on me,' grunted Dave. 'I'm not getting anywhere with it.'

'I'll take over,' said Dan. He took the game belt off Dave and fitted it around his waist. When he was satisfied, he took the rod and pushed the drag up a couple of notches.

'What the hell are you doing?' said Dave.

But Dan ignored him. He started short stroking and winding, short stroking and winding, until he'd turned the fish's head. The fight resumed in earnest. The fish darted one way and then another, ducked, dived and threw itself recklessly out of the water.

'Bloody hell!' said Dan.

'We should have fished heavier,' said Gregan. 'For Christ's sake, don't let it break the line.'

Dan continued to put pressure on the fish, aided by the extra drag. Slowly, bit by bit, he regained line. In desperation the fish resorted to its earlier tactics and turned side-on. It was a manoeuvre that wore down the fisherman while giving the fish time to recover. But Dan was determined not to allow the fish to get away with the tactic a second time.

He pumped the rod hard, methodically and resolutely, and once again managed to turn the fish's head. This time the monster was slow to react and Dan grabbed back valuable metres. They could now see it in the shallow water just thirty metres away, shaking its head from side to side, trying to turn away but unable to gain the necessary line.

'It's spent,' said Dave. 'Ease off the drag.'

'No way,' said Dan. 'It could be foxing.'

As if on cue, the giant fish suddenly kicked into life and swam hard at them.

'Wind!' screamed Dave.

Dan wound. He didn't need telling. Any slack in the line

when the trout changed direction would bring an abrupt end to the tussle.

'Lighten the drag!' screamed Dave.

Instead Dan wound more furiously and backed away from the water's edge in short skipping steps. The fish turned. The rod dipped as though someone was deliberately trying to snap off the tip. But the line held. Dan wound his way to the water's edge. The fish was now just fifteen metres away and beginning to wallow.

'Get the gaff,' said Dan.

'Ease off the drag,' said Dave.

'Already done that,' said Dan.

'And I've got the gaff,' said Dave. The fish glided towards them like an in-bound space shuttle, out of fuel and engines shut down.

Dan held the rod tip high and eased the fish towards shore.

'Shoulder,' said Dan.

'No worries,' said Dave.

'Hurry up!' said Gregan. He could have learned a lot by watching the two professionals in action but he only had eyes for the giant fish. It was a monster. Its back and tail were already out of the water yet it was still out of range of the gaff.

'Easy,' said Dave.

'No worries,' said Dan.

'Easy . . .'

Dave buried the tuna gaff deep into the trout's massive shoulder and with Gregan's help dragged the struggling fish up onto the bank.

'Got 'im!' screamed Gregan. 'We're back in business!'

The fish — *his* fish! — was magnificent. This was no Frankenstein fish but a superb XXOS example of a rainbow trout, perfectly proportioned and perfectly coloured. If he'd had a camera he would have taken a photo to show to Everton Sweet, if the scientist was still alive. Who wouldn't be proud of such a fish?

'What a freak,' said Dave. He made no effort to remove the gaff even though the trout had ceased to struggle.

'What a brute,' said Dan.

'What a shame,' said Gregan. Now that they'd caught his fish and saved the launch of the lodge he could begin to think of happier scenarios. 'Just imagine if one of the editors had caught it. Would Big Trout Lake be on the world map or what?'

'Just be glad we got the bastard,' said Dave. 'What do you reckon, Dan? Thirty-five kilos?'

'And some,' said Dan. 'Trout have no right growing this big. I can't begin to imagine the damage this fish has done. All the food it must have eaten. All the galaxia, scud, frogs and hundreds of trout. I guess those browns and the normal triploids can come out of hiding now and get on with the business of fattening up.'

A duck landed on the lake as though sensing it was now safe to do so.

'Maybe,' said Dave. He'd taken a few steps towards the fallen gum to check on the status of the browns hiding among its branches. 'So far they haven't moved.'

'Give them time,' said Dan. 'And give me a hand with this.'

Dan took off his jacket and rolled the monster fish in it, making sure the fins were pressed flat against the fish's body.

'The taxidermist will love me for this,' he said. 'However, my wife may take an opposing view.'

Gregan laughed. He could already imagine the sensation the giant trout would cause mounted behind the reception desk.

His partner Richo had scoffed at the suggestion of a giant fibreglass trout. Now he had something infinitely better. He turned to watch the sun clear the eucalypts and alight on a lake untroubled except by the silent paddling of the lone duck.

'The beginning of another successful day,' he said.

The duck rose on its haunches, flapping its wings as though desperate to take flight. The water around it exploded. It was snapped up as if it was no more than a well-presented nymph.

'God help us!' said Dan. 'There's another one!'

Gregan watched the ever-widening ripples in horror. He went weak at the knees and had to grab hold of a tree branch for support. How many giant fish were there still in the lake? His whole project was headed down the gurgler and he was powerless to do anything about it.

Gregan and the two brothers discussed the problem over breakfast.

'We're going to have to catch it,' said Dan. 'As soon as we finish eating.'

'How do we know there's not a third or a fourth?' said Dave. 'Or a fifth or a sixth?'

'It doesn't matter how many of those mutants there are,' said Dan grimly. 'We've just got to keep fishing until there are no more left.'

'How can we be sure we've caught them all?' said Dave. 'If one's just dined on a couple of those big browns it might not eat again for days.'

'Well, what do you suggest?' said Dan. 'The whole future of this lake depends on us catching those mutants and catching them quickly.'

The brothers fell silent as they chewed on their toast and searched their minds for solutions. None beckoned.

'What do you think, boss?' said Dave.

'I think we're tackling this problem the wrong way,' said Gregan eventually. 'Tell me, you boys ever wear white shoes?'

Gregan looked a little out of place in his white linen suit and white shoes as he made the farewell address at the farewell dinner of what had been the most amazing event the magazine editors had ever attended. In truth, it didn't matter what Gregan wore. He could have dressed in a clown suit or a full-length ball gown and it wouldn't have changed a thing. Gregan had delivered on his promise. The editors had all caught their biggest trout and one of them had set the new world record. They were ecstatic, overwhelmed and eager to splash their stories all over their magazines. Television coverage had already ensured that Big Trout Lake would become the most famous trout-fishing lake in the world.

'Don't forget to tell your readers Big Trout Lodge opens for business in three weeks,' said Gregan. 'And tell them to come prepared.'

He sat down as happy as he'd been when he'd bought two magnificent Queenslanders in a cul-de-sac at the southern end of Surfers and replaced them with a thirty-two-storey block of apartments. At certain times in the afternoon, the shadow stretched more than three hundred metres down the beach. He thought back to the day when the first editors had arrived and how they'd openly ridiculed the enormous XXOS trout mounted on the wall behind the reception desk, how they'd laughed at it and called it a fake. Well, they were all believers now, disciples even, anxious to go forth and spread the word.

He looked across the room to where his bankers sat, their faces flushed with wine and their association with yet another success. He saw Dan and Dave propped up by their wives and enjoying more fame and attention than they'd entertained in their most febrile dreams. And there was his young wife, dazzlingly beautiful as always, being videoed with the editor of *American Trout and Stream*. Brilliant explosions lit the night sky beyond the windows and he rose to look over his lake, where the fireworks were reflected in all their splendour, and where the last of his trout, his wonderful, magnificent, world-famous, world-record trout, were dying.

He couldn't help smiling.

Gregan let his thoughts slide back to the despairing breakfast with Dan and Dave three weeks earlier. He remembered their conversation word for word.

'You know what?' he said to the brothers. 'Maybe we shouldn't try to catch these mutant fish.'

'What?' said Dan.

'The problem is not that they want to eat everything in the lake, but that we're not giving them any option.'

'What do you mean?' said Dave.

'Maybe we should feed them instead.'

'Feed them?' said Dan.

'Yeah,' said Gregan. 'Then they won't eat the other trout. Tell me, what do they feed the salmon in the salmon farms down on the Derwent?'

'Pellets,' said Dave.

'I want two truckloads. How soon can you get them here?'

'Tomorrow morning,' said Dan. 'We've got a cousin who works for the supplier.'

The following day they loaded the largest of their boats with sacks of pellets and motored out into the middle of the lake.

'Okay,' said Gregan. 'Start shovelling.'

Within minutes the surface began to boil with giant trout homing in on the handout. They bumped the boat so hard in their eagerness to feed that the boys had to sit down to prevent it from tipping over.

'Bloody hell!' said Dan.

'How many do you think there are?' asked Gregan.

'At least a dozen,' said Dave.

'At least twenty,' said Dan.

'Keep shovelling,' said Gregan.

He kept them shovelling until the trouts' bellies could hold no more and the giant fish lost interest.

'Okay,' said Gregan. 'That's half the job done. Now we've got to go in and feed the browns and triploids hiding among the snags.'

Over the following three weeks, Dan and Dave became skilled at assessing how much to feed the giant trout so that they had no need to snack on the browns and triploids, and how much to feed the browns and triploids so that they didn't grow too fat and lazy. Three days before the editors arrived, they stopped feeding the browns and triploids.

'I want them hungry and eager when the first fly hits the water,' said Gregan. 'I want them venturing out for food.'

'What about the mutants?' said Dan.

'Feed them right up to the eve of the launch,' said Gregan. 'And feed them well. I need three days to give everyone a chance to catch a big brown or a triploid before the mutants start feeling hungry again. On the fourth and fifth day, I want them smashing every bit of tackle in the lake. Okay?'

For three days the magazine editors caught huge browns that regularly topped seven kilos and triploids that topped five. A lucky few caught browns over twelve kilos and the editor of *International Fly Fisher* took the world record with a brown that weighed in at seventeen point five kilos. While obviously delighted with their catches, they still derided the monstrous trout mounted on the wall behind the reception desk. Then, on the fourth day, they caught fish heads as Gregan's monsters woke up hungry and discovered there were no more free handouts. No one ridiculed the trout behind reception after that.

Everyone lost fish to Gregan's monsters and everyone succeeded in hooking up on them. Not surprisingly, none of the editors managed to land one on their flimsy gear. Gregan had promised they'd catch their biggest trout but hadn't guaranteed that they'd land them. Nevertheless, everyone had a monster story to tell, which was exactly what Gregan wanted.

'What now?'

Gregan turned away from the fireworks and his reverie to find that his partner, Richo, had ghosted up alongside him.

'We enjoy our success,' said Gregan.

'However short-lived,' said Richo. 'We both know there'll be no trout left alive in the lake by this time tomorrow.'

'With any luck,' said Gregan.

'But how can we run a successful trout-fishing resort if there are no trout in the lake?'

'There'll be trout in the lake.'

'How?'

'Remember I told you there were two lakes?'

'Yes.'

'I put a deposit on the other one three weeks ago. The banks are falling over themselves to finance the rest. It's full of nice big browns and triploids. In a week's time, when I'm certain that all the trout here are dead, I'm going to start transferring them over. In the meantime, I've found someone who can begin restocking the lake with galaxia, scud and tadpoles.'

'Brilliant,' said Richo. 'But what about world records? The trout in our lake will be no bigger than anyone else's.'

'Of course they'll be bigger,' said Gregan. 'Of course there'll be world records. I spoke to Lothar, the boy wonder, just this morning. He's growing out our new crop of trout. He says they're coming along nicely.'

'I've got to hand it to you,' said Richo admiringly. 'I don't know how you do it.'

'This was nothing,' said Gregan. He put his arm around his partner and led him back to his table. 'Did I ever tell you about the time I built a block of condos on a sacred site?'

Not Good Fish for Man to Eat

Adrian Tremaine was an adulterer.

He was neither ashamed of the fact nor boastful. He simply regarded his affairs as his right, part of the trappings of success, a fair reward for his hard work and the gambles he'd taken building his thriving business. He'd been a senior funds manager until a number of killings in the tech boom had provided him with the capital to launch out on his own. He took his best people with him and already his new company had become the darling of investment advisers and other fund managers who shrewdly invested part of their portfolio in his products.

Adrian was rich, but his wealth and power were not his only attractions. Far from it. Nature had gifted him height, presence, good looks and the physique of an athlete. Had he concentrated on sport he could have become a national hero. At various times he'd been tipped to represent Australia at both cricket and rugby. But sport had never been more than a diversion. Becoming a player in the rarefied world of investment was the only game that interested him.

When he chose partners for his liaisons he exercised the same care with which he selected investments. To his credit he didn't prey on the young and innocent, the impressionable junior staff who were easy pickings for a man of his charm, looks and position. His preference was for women of substance who were not only beautiful but ambitious, rising stars who were driven and worked and played as hard as he did. In other words, busy women who wanted what he wanted and also wanted it without complications. He gave them a taste of the high life they could expect when they, too, reached the top: weekends in exotic places, splendid hotels and a whirl of fine restaurants. He gave them gifts and something every woman appreciates — his undivided attention. Adrian had charm to burn, intelligence and conversation, but it was his ability to make his partners feel *chosen* that set him apart from other men. Even Adrian baulked at the word but he could find none that fitted better.

Of course, his wife and family knew nothing about his extra-curricular activities and Adrian went to great lengths to ensure things remained that way. Most of his affairs were conducted offshore or at least interstate. One of his golden rules was, well, *the* golden rule: *Never foul your own nest.* As far as Adrian was concerned there wasn't a woman alive worth the risk.

Until he met Suzanne.

Suzanne was a New Yorker, ambitious and no mere rising star. Her star had already ascended. At thirty-three she was a fixture in the Wall Street firmament, the subject of profiles in many notable publications including the *Wall Street Journal*, the *New York Times* and *Time Magazine*. While some of Adrian's conquests had been all too aware that friendship with him was hardly an impediment to a burgeoning career, there was nothing Adrian could do to brighten Suzanne's star. It already outshone his. His success did not impress her; it was merely the entry price to her circle. The promise of weekends in exotic places, the hotels and restaurants meant nothing to her. They were already part of her life. And just as nature had been kind to Adrian, it had been even kinder to her.

Undoubtedly, among the many reasons the *Wall Street Journal* and the like had been drawn to profile Suzanne was the fact that she didn't look at all like financiers were supposed to look. Her face didn't belong in financial pages but in glamorous magazines. She had it all — perfect features, perfect figure, naturally blonde hair, intelligence, sophistication and impeccable taste.

The instant Adrian laid eyes on her he realised she was his ideal of the perfect woman, the perfect prize and the perfect reward for his labours. When the meeting broke for coffee he immediately singled her out for his very special attention. She waved him off with the casual indifference with which stockmen dispatched flies.

Adrian had a simple policy towards being rebuffed. When he hit on a woman, she either responded favourably or was forgotten. He was a busy man and had no time to waste on pursuit. If the horse ain't willing, he liked to say to his men friends at the squash club, giving it sugar lumps won't change anything. No, you're better off throwing your leg over another horse.

Adrian found other women who were willing but he couldn't forget Suzanne. Suzanne was simply unforgettable. She became the standard by which he judged all other women and without exception they came up wanting. He created new investment products he knew would appeal to her and flew over to New York to present them. Mostly they met in boardrooms but sometimes he contrived to meet her over dinner. But those occasions were the exception. Dinner never led to breakfast and the only thing consummated was another business deal.

Adrian began to despair and his interest in other women waned. He even wondered if, at the age of forty-five, his libido was finally cracking under the pace. But he only had to sit in the same room as Suzanne or speak to her on the phone to realise that his libido was still firing on all cylinders. It simply shared the same focus he did.

Just when all seemed lost, fate intervened. The breakthrough came unexpectedly, at a convention in Hawaii. Adrian had decided to attend the moment he learned that Suzanne was one of the speakers. He finally met up with her at a function the evening after she'd delivered her paper. She was keeping a martini company and smiling at delegates who were obviously thrilled just to be in her proximity, though it was obvious to Adrian that she wasn't quite so thrilled to be in theirs. Her smile when she spotted Adrian was her first genuine smile of the night.

'Get me out of here,' she said.

Adrian found a quiet table in a quiet bar.

'I've just split with my husband,' she said. 'I only agreed to speak here to get away.'

'Get away?' said Adrian.

'Give him time to move out of the apartment. Now I'm stuck here for five more days, God help me,' she said.

'I have a house,' said Adrian. 'On a tiny, private island in Fiji. It's nothing fancy. But it's as far away from anywhere as anyone can get.'

'What are we waiting for?' she said.

Adrian had plenty of time to do some thinking on the plane from Honolulu to Nadi, and plenty of thinking needed to be done. Once he'd overcome his euphoria he had to address his stupidity. He couldn't believe he was taking a woman other than his wife to his holiday home on Naviti Lau. Correction, his *family's* holiday home. It broke his golden rule. Hell, it broke every rule! He wondered what had possessed him but didn't have to look far to find the answer. She was asleep in the seat alongside him. Dear God! One glance confirmed she was worth the risk. But how much of a risk was he taking? As soon as the plane touched down in Nadi he put in an urgent call to the manager of the company that administered Naviti Lau to find out.

'Don't worry,' the manager said. 'You're not Robinson Crusoe. You're not the first homeowner to bring a girlfriend here. The Fijians understand. They know to be discreet.'

'But what about Mary?'

'Ahh . . .' the manager said, 'Mary.'

Chubby, smiling, Seventh-Day Adventist Mary was the woman who looked after his holiday house in his absence and looked after him and his family when they were visiting. His wife and children adored her and the sentiment was reciprocated. She was more like the Fijian member of their family than hired help. When Mary's husband had gone away, they'd helped her raise her two boys, provided shoes, clothes and finally introductions which had resulted in both of them finding work in Suva. Adrian was acutely aware of the embarrassment he would cause Mary. Asking her to turn a blind eye was also asking her to be party to his infidelity, to be disloyal to his wife and family and to act contrary to her church-honed sense of morality.

But damn it!

Suzanne was special.

He refused to be deterred simply to spare the feelings of someone who, at the end of the day, was an employee. Mary, he decided, was simply a problem that had to be managed.

'Have a word with her,' Adrian said to the manager.

'Oh my God,' said Suzanne when she saw the tiny six-seater charter plane that would take them out to the remote island.

'Oh my God,' she said when she saw the narrow grass landing strip and the sheer cliffs that fell away at each end.

'Oh my God,' she said again as she set foot in Adrian's holiday home, but this time with an entirely different inflection. 'Nothing fancy, you said.'

Adrian's house wasn't fancy. It was spectacular, the rare conjunction of functionality and taste. The main building was circular and eighteen metres in diameter, like a large version of an African rondavel. The roof was a towering thatch of palm leaves supported by dark crossbeams and rafters made from the trunks of coconut palms. It sheltered a lounge/dining room, a small toilet and a good-sized kitchen. The walls, floor and dining table were all white polished concrete. There were scatter rugs from the Middle East and deep stuffed sofas and chairs, elegant coffee tables and, on the terrace, the most inviting sun lounges Suzanne had ever seen. There were no windows; instead there was a series of connected glass doors across the front of the building, running fully a third of the circumference. The doors could be pulled back against each other to reveal a lofty, uninterrupted view of the western side of the island, a panorama of palm tops and a sweep of ocean from Ovalau to the south almost to Vanua Levu to the north.

'My God, it's breathtaking,' said Suzanne.

Adrian's pleasure at her reaction was tempered by the appearance of Mary in the corridor leading to the kitchen.

'Helloo ...' Mary said. She was smiling dutifully, but Adrian could see the hurt and reproach in her eyes.

'Mary!' he said. He kissed both her cheeks and gave her his usual hug but she may just as well have been hewn from wood for all the response he got.

'Mary, I'd like you to meet a business colleague,' he said. 'This is Suzanne.'

'Helloo,' said Mary.

'Hi,' said Suzanne with the same lack of interest with which she viewed waiters, bellhops and cab drivers.

'Let me show you around,' said Adrian. 'The bures below are the bedrooms.'

Two pairs of bures separated by a swimming pool nestled among palms on the level below the main building. Each pair had a bedroom at each end with an elegant polished concrete bathroom in between. Each bedroom boasted its own private terrace looking out over the ocean. As befits a holiday home for the rich and privileged, the architects had made sure there was no need for curtains or blinds.

'Two bedrooms for the family and two for guests,' said Adrian.

'What am I?' asked Suzanne.

'A special guest,' said Adrian hurriedly. 'Special guests qualify as family.'

His spirits sank when he discovered Mary had made up both rooms in the family unit. While Suzanne had suggested escaping to Naviti Lau there'd been no discussion of sleeping arrangements. He'd just assumed they'd sleep together. At that moment Adrian realised he could have flown all the way down from Hawaii for nothing. He closed his eyes expecting her to say, 'Which room is mine?'

'Which has the bigger bed?' she asked instead.

'This one,' said Adrian cautiously.

'Should do us nicely,' she said. 'Now why don't you get our bags and mix up a couple of margaritas while I shower.'

Adrian danced back up the steps to the main building.

Adrian opened the fridge door, grabbed the bottle of margarita mix and glanced quickly over the shelves. They groaned with food and cans of Fiji Bitter. He smiled. Mary may not like the circumstances of his visit but they didn't appear to have affected the way she did her job.

'Lots of beer,' he said.

'Yes,' said Mary.

'Lots of fish.'

'Yes.'

There were two plates of fish, each covered by cling wrap. One had the large pieces of fillet he was accustomed to, cut from big fish like tuna, Spanish mackerel and wahoo. Beneath it, the second plate held six or seven small fish, none more than thirty centimetres long. This puzzled Adrian because, while he liked fish, he hated fish-bones. He didn't eat small fish for that reason and stared at them with distaste.

'What's for dinner?' he asked.

'*Walu*,' said Mary. 'Spanish mackerel. I buy from Mika.' Mika was the boat boy who looked after the boats in the lagoon and sometimes took him fishing. 'Caught fresh this morning.'

'Well done,' said Adrian, relieved that he wouldn't have the embarrassment of pulling small bones out of his teeth in front of Suzanne. It dawned on him that the small fish were probably Mary's. Fijians preferred their fish small.

'First I make you sashimi to eat with your drinks.'

'Thank you,' said Adrian, genuinely surprised. He hadn't expected Mary to be quite so obliging. 'That's very thoughtful.'

'Make special for you and Miss Suzanne,' said Mary.

Adrian and Suzanne were lounging on recliners watching the setting sun dip over the distant island of Ovalau, their second frozen margaritas in hand, when Mary brought out the sashimi.

'Oh my God,' said Suzanne.

Adrian couldn't help smiling as Mary placed the plate between them. She'd arranged the pieces of sashimi in the outline of a sunfish, as his wife had taught her, with two tiny bowls of soy sauce laced with wasabi in the middle. He passed Suzanne a pair of chopsticks.

'My God,' said Suzanne. She took another piece. 'This fish is superb. Delicious! I don't know that I've ever tasted better.'

'I don't know that I have, either,' said Adrian. And he meant it. The slivers of fish were sweet, tender and subtle in flavour. He looked at Mary in a new light. Maybe the manager was right. Maybe Fijians, Mary included, were more understanding than he'd expected. 'Well done, well done,' he said. 'What kind of fish is this?'

'Fiji fish,' said Mary noncommittally. She retreated to the kitchen.

By the time Mary brought them their dinner they were openly flirting.

'*Walu*,' said Mary. 'Cook rare on garlic mash potatoes with green beans and salad.'

'Mary, you really are a treasure,' said Suzanne.

Again Adrian had to smile. His wife had taught Mary how to bake fish so that it was just cooked through and how to make garlic mash. Clearly she'd taught Mary well. With the green beans and salad it was exactly the sort of meal Suzanne liked. He topped up Suzanne's wine and they clinked glasses.

'*Bon appetit*,' he said.

Mary stayed only long enough to clear away the dishes and bring them coffee, before retiring to her bure. Her bure had not been included in the tour Adrian had given Suzanne. It was on another level below the bedrooms, tucked away out of sight beneath a giant fig tree. Suzanne wasn't the kind to show interest in employee accommodation.

'Seems I have you all to myself,' said Adrian.

'Indeed,' said Suzanne. The candlelight was in her eyes but that wasn't what made them glitter. He'd seen that look many times before. Adrian had no doubt that the most unforgettable night of his life lay ahead of him.

'I can't understand it,' said Adrian. He was both bewildered and embarrassed. 'I've heard of this sort of thing happening but it's the first time it has ever happened to me.'

'First time it has ever happened to me too,' said Suzanne. 'I promise you that.' She was not amused. 'I usually have the opposite effect on men.'

Disappointment hung like a curtain between them.

'I'm sorry,' said Adrian.

'So am I. Maybe you shouldn't have had so much to drink.'

'I can drink three times that amount without problems,' said Adrian hotly. Humiliation had replaced his feelings of bewilderment, and humiliation was not a sensation he was accustomed to or enjoyed.

'Whatever,' said Suzanne and yawned.

'A dawnbreaker,' said Adrian. 'I promise you, when the sun comes up, so will I. Ever since I was a teenager it's been a race to see which rises first.'

'I'll look forward to it,' said Suzanne.

But the sun rose all on its own.

Adrian spent the morning apologising.

'Don't worry about it,' Suzanne said.

'It happens,' she said.

But nothing she said made Adrian feel any better.

'Come on, I'll drive you around the island,' he said, seeking distraction.

He took her to Nautilus Beach where storms often brought nautilus shells up from the depths and deposited them on the beach, but the only shells they found were either cracked or broken. He took her Lawedua Cove where the beautiful white lawedua birds nested, but they'd all gone searching for fish far out to sea. He took her to Chieftain's Leap where they could look up the length of the island to the distant lighthouse marking a channel through the reef.

'What's that?' said Suzanne suddenly, startled by a rustling in the bushes.

'Deer,' said Adrian. 'Someone thought it would be a good idea to introduce deer to the island to control the undergrowth.'

Three does and a fawn stepped tentatively into the clearing.

'How cute,' said Suzanne.

'Actually they're a bloody nuisance,' said Adrian. 'They're the reason all the properties have fences and gates. They eat everything: plants, shrubs, vegetables. Even our precious roses.'

'My, you are a ray of sunshine,' said Suzanne.

Once again Adrian found himself apologising.

Mary had made them a salad for lunch but it was too hot to do anything more than pick at it. They sat reading in the shade on the terrace where they enjoyed the benefit of the slight breeze until it died away.

'It'll be cooler on the beach,' said Adrian. 'Come on, I'll take you snorkelling.'

Snorkelling at Homestead Beach was always spectacular but on this day it was more spectacular than most. Permit up to six kilos grazed on oysters within metres of the shore. Well-disciplined schools of trevally swam past, turning and diving with perfect synchronisation. Spiky gossamer-finned lionfish nosed gently around the holes in the coral, sharing their habitat with parrotfish and leatherjackets of every colour and size. And the usual suspects, the myriad small, riotously coloured coral dwellers, surrounded them, taking care to remain just — and only just — out of reach.

Even more spectacular, from Adrian's point of view, was the beautiful woman swimming alongside him. The previous night when they'd lain in bed together, her skin glowing by the soft light of the candles arranged along the shelf behind the bed, he'd been totally besotted, unable to imagine any woman more exquisite or desirable. That had only added to his frustration and confusion. Yet, if anything, Suzanne looked even more gorgeous in her tiny bikini, with the sun on the water dappling her skin. He stopped breathing every time she glided beneath him in pursuit of a fish that had caught her attention. He could not take his eyes off her. His face mask and the crystal-clear tropical water magnified her, accentuating her curves, exaggerating her perfection. He forgot about his failure and the disaster of the previous night. Before long he began to feel a familiar tingling in his loins.

'Hallelujah!' he said into his snorkel.

'I think we should go straight home,' said Adrian.

'Oh?' said Suzanne. She'd only just picked up her towel to dry herself.

'Unfinished business.'

'Oh!' she said again. The reason for urgency had become obvious. 'Welcome back.'

'A quick shower,' said Adrian in the Suzuki four-wheel drive as they headed up the road. 'Then a lie-down before dinner.'

'Why does the shower have to be quick?' asked Suzanne.

Adrian laughed. It was the easy, joyful laugh of a man for whom all burdens had been lifted, the laugh of a man on a promise.

'It doesn't,' he said. 'We can take as long as we like.'

* * *

Adrian hoped Mary wasn't watching as he jumped out of the little Suzuki to open the gate. No one could mistake his intentions. He drove in, parked and raced back to close the gate. Suzanne could hardly stop laughing.

'Patience,' she said. 'All good things come to those who wait.'

'Damn it, I've waited long enough.'

To avoid Mary, he led Suzanne around the side of the main building to the steps leading down to the bures. They were like teenagers in their eagerness.

Bugger the shower, thought Adrian. He decided to head straight to bed where he intended to make up for lost time with the most urgent, energetic, frenetic lovemaking of his life. Then he saw the movement in the garden.

'Oh no!' he cried. 'Not now!'

'What's the matter?' said Suzanne.

'Deer,' said Adrian.

'Leave them be,' she said.

'Can't,' he said. He knew exactly how much damage deer could do in just a matter of minutes. He also knew that it would take him at least half an hour to chase the deer out and repair the fence, even with Mary's help.

'You go ahead and shower,' he said miserably.

Suzanne stared at him in disbelief before turning her back on him and storming off.

It took Adrian and Mary more than half an hour to chase off the deer and repair the fence. By the time he caught up with Suzanne she'd showered, changed for dinner and returned to the main building. She was reading a copy of *Stock Watch* when he joined her.

'I'm sorry,' he said.

She ignored him.

'Margarita?'

She'd made her own.

'It's not a cancellation,' he said. 'Only a temporary delay.'

'Wanna bet?' said Suzanne icily.

Adrian made her another margarita and it helped.

'Mary's making us more sashimi,' said Adrian.

The sashimi helped even more.

When Mary brought them Thai fishcakes Suzanne actually smiled for the first time that evening.

'Thai fishcakes,' she said. 'I adore them.'

'Make special for you and Mr Adrian,' said Mary solemnly.

'If you like them so much, have one of mine as well,' said Adrian.

'Thank you,' said Suzanne.

'Thai green chicken curry to follow,' cut in Mary quickly. She clearly disapproved of Adrian sharing his fishcakes.

'In that case I'll just have what I've been given,' said Suzanne. 'I adore green chicken curry.'

'Am I forgiven?' asked Adrian, once Mary had returned to the kitchen.

'Almost,' said Suzanne. 'But I'm expecting big things from you tonight.'

'So am I,' said Adrian. 'So am I.'

* * *

'This is getting beyond a joke,' said Suzanne.

They lay side by side with nothing covering them except the mosquito net hanging from the frame above the bed.

'I don't understand it,' said Adrian miserably. 'I can't believe this is happening to me.'

'I can't believe what's not happening to me.'

'I'm sorry.'

'Maybe it's my fault,' said Suzanne. 'Maybe there's something about my body that turns you off.'

'Are you kidding?' said Adrian. 'You are the perfect woman. Your body is everything men dream of. Your body would give a snowman an erection.'

'Maybe you'd better get me a snowman,' said Suzanne.

Something suspiciously like contempt had crept into her voice, adding to his humiliation.

Once again Adrian pinned all his hopes on a dawnbreaker but once again the sun rose alone. For Suzanne it was the last straw.

When she asked him to arrange a charter to fly her back to Nadi, Adrian didn't object. After all, what could he say to placate her? What guarantees could he give? Instead he booked a light plane and also rescheduled her onward flight back to Hawaii. Conversation was desultory on the drive out to the airstrip. When the light plane raced down the grass runway and took off over the indigo sea, Adrian felt a sense of relief overcome his shame and disappointment. He'd never suffered such humiliation before in his life and was relieved that he wouldn't have to endure more.

He didn't drive straight home. He wanted to give Mary time to clean up and remove any trace of Suzanne. He wanted no reminders of his failure. Instead he drove down to the lagoon, parked his Suzuki and walked disconsolately onto the jetty. A slight breeze ruffled the water in the lagoon but not enough to obscure the dark shapes of trevally cruising by. He thought he was alone until he noticed the boat boy, Mika, fishing with a handline from a small boat tied alongside. As he watched, Mika pulled in a small brownish-green fish and dropped it into the live-bait tank by his feet. The fish joined four or five others just like it.

'Your dinner?' said Adrian.

'Noo . . . not dinner,' said Mika. He looked up guiltily.

'Sashimi?'

'Noo . . . not sashimi.'

'No?' said Adrian. 'Why not?'

'Dis fish not good fish for man to eat.'

'What do you mean?' asked Adrian irritably.

'*Ujimate* fish,' said Mika uncomfortably.

'What?' said Adrian. He never could get the hang of Fijian. He had no ear for the language. It had too many vowels.

'*Ujimate*,' repeated Mika.

'Does it have an English name?'

'Yes.' Mika clearly wished it hadn't.

'What is the English name?'

Mika was prepared to look anywhere except at Adrian, his guilt and complicity inescapable.

'Come on!' said Adrian.

'Him call deadwillyfish.'

'Deadwillyfish?' said Adrian. 'Dead-willy-fish!' He looked more closely at the fish in the tank, recognised them as the same kind of fish he'd seen on a plate under cling wrap in his refrigerator. 'Dead-willy-fish?' he repeated weakly. He closed his eyes. At last he understood what Mary had meant when she'd said, 'Make special for you and Miss Suzanne.'

Footnote: The deadwillyfish exists. The Fijian name for it is *ujimate*: *uji* is slang for penis and *mate* means dead. It is also known by a somewhat more polite name, *ulumate*; *ulu* being the Fijian word for head. *Ujimate* are brown in colour and rarely exceed thirty to forty centimetres. When they're not intended to be used as live bait, their heads are cut off so men know not to eat them. Women, apparently, can eat them with impunity. Spanish mackerel or *walu* treat them as a favoured staple and appear to suffer no ill effects, but then again how would you know?

The Peppermint Pom

Terry looked at the rotating cowl atop his stainless-steel chimney and thought lubricating it would be a cinch, the sort of thing any chartered accountant could do. He'd bought the squeeze bottle of graphite he'd been told to use and borrowed his neighbour's extension ladder. A wiser man might have waited for a calm day, but the deep-throated moaning and groaning of the cowl swinging in the wind had been driving his wife spare. She'd made him promise to fix it before he went fishing. He hoped a squeeze of graphite would silence both the cowl and his wife.

When he lifted off the cowl he was surprised at how light it was. When a sudden gust came up and blew him off the roof he was surprised how something so small could catch so much wind. When he hit the ground he was surprised how much it hurt.

'Barry,' he gasped into his mobile phone, 'I've had an accident. I won't be able to go. Sorry.' He had just enough time to make a second call for an ambulance before he lost consciousness.

'Terry's a non-starter,' said Big Barry to Carlton. Like Terry, they were also chartered accountants but with different specialisations: Big Barry worked in insolvency while Carlton was a tax adviser. 'He fell off his roof.'

'What on earth was he doing up there?' said Carlton.

'Nothing he was good at.'

Carlton smiled into the phone. Accountants weren't supposed to have a sense of humour but this was the way he and his mates carried on. Nothing was so serious that they couldn't find a laugh in it.

'Anything break his fall?' said Carlton, picturing Terry's home and the height of the roof.

'Only the ground,' said Big Barry.

This time Carlton laughed out loud.

'Poor bugger,' he said. 'How is he?'

'Broke his leg.'

'Ouch.'

'In two places.'

'Ouch, ouch.'

'He rang me before he rang the ambulance.'

'At least he understood the gravity of the situation.'

This time it was Big Barry's turn to laugh.

'I'll tell him what you said when I see him tonight,' said Big Barry. 'He's in Royal North Shore. But, mate, it's time to get serious. He was our last reserve. His broken leg leaves us a man short.'

Every two years the boys abandoned jobs, families and their normal sense of responsibility and went away fishing together. This time Big Barry had been the organiser and he'd arranged a barramundi fishing expedition to Maningrida, way up at the Top End in the wilds of Arnhemland. He'd spent hours on the internet talking to barramundi fishermen before settling on Maningrida. According to his research, the Liverpool and Blyth rivers were loaded with the best saltwater barra fishing in the country. Normally Maningrida fished three anglers to a boat but Big Barry had been advised that fishing in pairs was the way to go. The boys had agreed to pay an extra five hundred dollars each for the privilege. There was one drawback to Maningrida, however, and for a while it had been something of a sticking point. Maningrida was on Aboriginal land and there were tough penalties for anyone caught taking alcohol there. It took a lot of convincing by Big Barry before the others were persuaded that the quality of the fishing justified the abstinence. They couldn't imagine sitting around in the evening without a beer, scotch or glass of red. It was the sort of sacrifice none of them had ever envisaged making, especially on one of their fishing trips.

Maningrida could only accommodate six more guests so Big Barry signed up five of his mates and sent off their deposits. To be safe, he also lined up three reserves because he knew from past experience that someone always dropped out.

Russell, a divisional manager with a manufacturing conglomerate, was the first to withdraw. His company decided to take over a competitor and Russell was put in charge of the project. It was exactly the sort of opportunity he'd been hoping for to give him a leg up the corporate ladder.

'Man's lost all sense of perspective and priority,' said Carlton, even though he'd sent Russell a bottle of champagne along with his congratulations. 'It'll bring him more money, more prestige and more job satisfaction. But he'll have nothing to go with his chips.'

Yanni, their token Greek, took Russell's place. Yanni was a partner in an import company that brought in specialty foods from Europe. He'd been bitterly disappointed when he was balloted out of the original six.

Then Neal, a marketing director, had to drop out to attend the birth of his first child. The boys had a field day over that.

'You're out of your mind,' Big Barry told him. 'You can always have another kid.'

'You could have dozens,' said Carlton. 'Now that you've worked out what to do.'

Mick, a software sales manager, took Neal's place. Mick wasn't a natural fisherman but made up for the deficiency with sheer enthusiasm.

Then Steve, a corporate lawyer, had a routine colonoscopy that revealed a cancerous growth needing immediate surgery.

'Gruesome,' said Carlton. 'Can't they wait a couple of weeks?'

'First question I asked,' said Steve. 'They said if I wait a couple of weeks I could die.'

'Tough decision,' said Big Barry.

Terry, the roof diver, took Steve's place and promptly landed them in their predicament.

The five survivors met over a beer at the Newport Arms to discuss their problem.

'The thing is, we're committed,' said Big Barry. 'We have to pay for six even if only five of us go. We'll save a bit on airfares but it's still another seven hundred dollars each.'

'The tech wreck hasn't exactly left me flush,' said Mick. 'I'm not sure I can afford the extra.'

'It's a big ask,' said Graham, who was the oldest and retired.

'Big ask, maybe, but you've got the big answers,' said Carlton. 'You could buy and sell the lot of us.'

'Who'd want to?' said Graham.

'Does anyone know anyone else who'd like to come with us?' said Big Barry. 'Graham?'

'I've tried a few blokes but they need more notice.'

'Same here,' said Carlton.

'Come on. Somebody must know someone,' said Big Barry.

'Well . . .' said Yanni hesitantly. 'I met this bloke at a dinner party who reckons he's mother-shipped on the *Iron Lady* up in Buckingham Bay.'

'I looked into that,' said Big Barry.

'Said he'd also fished the Arafura Swamp.'

'Lucky man,' said Big Barry. 'I looked at both those options. They're lineball with Maningrida.'

'He actually said that if anyone dropped out he'd love to go.'

The boys all turned and looked at Yanni as if he'd just materialised from another dimension. They couldn't understand why he hadn't volunteered this information earlier so they could get on with some serious drinking and the kind of facetious exchanges that kept them entertained.

'So what are you waiting for?' said Big Barry. 'Written instructions?'

'Could be an invitation to disaster,' said Yanni. 'Remember the golden rule. Never go away fishing with someone you don't know well enough to lend your car to.'

'I thought it was wife,' said Carlton.

'No, car,' said Mick. 'We upped the stakes last meeting.'

'What's he like?' said Big Barry impatiently. He wanted business settled so he could relax.

'Can't say for sure. We'd both had more than a few. He seemed all right. For a Pom.'

'For a Pom?' said Mick.

'A Pom that sucks peppermints. When he reached into his pocket for his car keys, rolls of peppermints went everywhere.'

'At least he doesn't suck his teeth,' said Graham charitably.

'Not to invite him just because he's a Pom smacks of discrimination,' said Big Barry after the fifth round of beer. 'After all, we're talking seven hundred bucks a head here.'

'Are all his limbs intact?' asked Carlton. 'Does he wander about on his roof?'

'I think you should give him a call,' said Big Barry.

'Okay,' said Yanni. 'But don't blame me if he turns out to be a jerk.'

'What's his name?' said Big Barry.

'Neville.'

The boys sat back and thought of all the Nevilles they knew, as if that might give them some inkling of what to expect, but nobody actually knew any.

'Had a mate once who had a dog called Neville,' said Carlton eventually. 'Goofy-looking thing but a brilliant ratter.'

'In that case Neville will probably do fine,' said Big Barry.

When the light plane that flew them from Darwin to Maningrida touched down, the boys could hardly hide their excitement. The Liverpool River looked as fishy as all hell. Not too murky and with just the right amount of water flowing.

'Not the prettiest place,' said Neville, sucking on a peppermint. 'Bit of a dump compared to Buckingham Bay.'

The boys paid Neville no attention and carted their bags and gear over to the accommodation. It looked good. The tents were high and spacious, protected from both sun and rain by generous flysheets, and were erected over timber floors. The toilets, which they queued to use, were clean and not at all on the nose. The boys were impressed.

'Not exactly the Hilton,' said Neville. 'I was expecting better. Even Millingimby in the Arafura Swamp has hardstand accommodation. Only the toilets and bathrooms were under canvas.'

'The rooms are clean and dry and the beds look comfortable,' said Mick cheerily. 'They'll do me.'

'I've put all our names in the hat,' said Big Barry. 'Neville, since you're the new bloke, why don't you draw a name out first to see who you're sharing with.'

'Be my luck to get someone who snores,' said Neville.

When they gathered beneath the awnings in the dining area, they found their table side by side with two others, which were already occupied. There was another party of six and one of eight. The boys returned greetings and sat down, figuring there'd be plenty of time to socialise with the others later.

'We're in luck,' said Carlton. 'There are two women on the far table.'

'I took a look at them,' said Big Barry. 'We're in luck; they're with someone else.'

'Uncalled for and ungracious,' said Graham. 'I bet they look great after half a dozen beers.'

'There is no beer,' said Big Barry.

'Then we're in trouble,' said Graham.

Everyone laughed except Neville.

'It's easy to be cruel,' he said. 'Not always so easy to apologise afterwards.'

The boys stared at Neville in disbelief. There was nothing intentionally sexist or personal in their comments; it was just the sort of meaningless banter men carry on with when they're off on their own and determined not to act their age. For once they were lost for a comeback.

That night they had steaks for dinner, which had come in on the plane that had brought them to Maningrida. As the meal progressed, the boys' good humour returned.

'This is one of the most tender steaks I've had in ages,' said Big Barry.

'Got me,' said Yanni. 'I think the cook must bake the whole sirloin in the oven for an hour or so at low temperature before he cuts it up and sears it on the barbie. It's the only way to get steak an even pink all the way through.'

'I reckon the cook's a genius,' said Carlton. 'Getting steak to taste this good way out here.'

'I don't know what you're all going on about,' said Neville. 'It's just steak. You can get that any day anywhere. I think the least a place like this can do is serve fresh fish.'

The boys didn't say as much that night but they began to get a very bad feeling about Neville.

Neville had been paired with Mick and at breakfast the boys decided the arrangement would extend to the boats for the first day's fishing.

'What size fish can we expect?' said Neville to Jack, the guide they'd been allocated.

'Average size is three to six kilos,' said Jack. He was an easygoing Territorian, small and wiry, with a love of fishing matched by an equal desire to please. 'A good fish is ten kilos.'

'You call that good?' said Neville. 'In the Arafura Swamp we called that ordinary.'

'Ten kilos will do me,' said Mick.

'We sometimes get them up to fifteen,' said the guide. 'Occasionally bigger from the billabong. Now let's check your gear.'

'I'm already rigged,' said Neville. 'Six kilo with ten-kilo trace.'

'You might find that a bit light for here,' said Jack, trying to be helpful. 'Too many mangroves and paperbarks. Too many snags. You could find yourself losing a lot of lures.'

'What do you recommend?' said Neville.

'Ten-kilo Gelspun with a twenty-kilo trace usually does the business.'

'Why don't we just use dynamite?' said Neville.

Neville wasn't happy. He sucked furiously on his peppermints.

'Gelspun cuts through knots,' he said.

'Then you have to tie a new bimini twist,' he complained.

'And an Albright knot.

'And a perfection loop.

'All takes valuable fishing time.'

By the time Mick had lent Neville some ten-kilo Gelspun and he'd re-rigged, the others had already gone off in their boats.

'Typical,' said Neville. 'They take the best spots and we get what's left.'

Some guides react to fishermen who whinge by taking them where they know the fish aren't so they've really got something to whinge about. Jack did exactly the opposite.

He thought that once he'd put Neville on the end of a good barra, everything would change. He'd seen it happen before. Barra worked wonders on people; worked better than grog, drugs or a good woman. Jack decided to take them straight upriver to a rock bar he knew where big barra lurked. He figured it would only take one good fish to put a smile on Neville's face that would last all day. There was another consideration too. Jack liked Mick, liked his type. He picked him for the kind who only ever sees the upside of things and delights in everything good that comes their way.

When they reached the rock bar, Jack could see by the way the water swirled and by its clarity that big barra would be hovering on the downriver side, waiting to gobble up anything smaller than themselves that had the misfortune to drift past.

'Let your lure settle before you start to retrieve,' said Jack. 'Then hang on.'

Mick hooked a nice five-kilo fish with his first cast. He shouted for joy as his fish broke the surface and went absolutely ballistic. His enthusiasm brought a smile to Jack's face.

Neville offered neither encouragement nor congratulations. All he said was, 'Use my Bogagrips. Barramundi gill cases are sharper than broken bottles. I don't want my day ending early because you've ripped your hands open.'

Mick used the device to hold his fish by the bottom lip while he unhooked his lure.

Neville cast and retrieved, cast and retrieved, but couldn't buy a strike. 'Bloody typical,' he said. 'I'm on the wrong side of the boat.'

'Try another lure,' said Jack. 'Mick's using a B 52.'

Neville crushed the barbs on the B 52's triple hooks — as all the boys did — to make it easier to release the fish after it had been netted and weighed. He hooked up first cast. Jack thought that would make him happier but it didn't.

'It's only a tiddler,' said Neville. 'Hardly know it's on. I get almost as much fight from the lure.' His fish ran to six kilos, a kilo heavier than Mick's.

'What a beauty!' said Mick. He took a photo of it before Neville returned it to the water. 'Your luck's in.'

'I don't count fish under ten kilos,' said Neville. 'Certainly don't waste film on them.'

Jack listened to the exchange, gritted his teeth and resolved to try harder. He took them up gutters onto the flood plains where the run-off streamed down through clumps of mangroves.

'What's that beautiful palm?' said Mick.

'That,' said Jack, 'is a geebung, one of our rarest. Beautiful things. You only find them in a few places here and in New Guinea. They take thirty years to grow, then flower and die.'

'It's magic,' said Mick, lining up his camera for a photo.

'It's in the way of my cast,' said Neville.

They caught another six barra around the geebung palm before the crocodiles came to investigate.

'Bloody typical,' said Neville. 'We find the fish then the crocs find us.'

'Stop and have a drink while I sort this out,' said Jack. 'You've got to keep up the liquids out here.' He pushed an esky towards them. 'Plenty of water in there.'

'You need more than water,' said Neville. He pulled a bottle of Powerade out of his tackle box and swallowed half a dozen mouthfuls. 'You need electrolytes.'

'Good idea,' said Mick. 'Give me a shot of that.'

'I don't share bottles,' said Neville. 'Herpes, hepatitis C, meningitis.' He put the bottle back in his tackle box, slipped a peppermint into his mouth and began sucking on it noisily.

'You missed out blackwater fever,' said Mick amiably. 'And AIDS.' His smile vanished when he saw Jack pick up a rifle.

'Hey! I thought crocodiles were protected.'

'They are,' said Jack. 'The rifle's for emergencies. I'm just moving it out of the way. Ah! Here's what I'm looking for.' Jack pulled a bag of marbles and a catapult from a storage box. 'Strictly speaking, this isn't allowed either.' He lined up a crocodile and let fly. The marble zinged off the croc's head with a resounding crack. The croc raced away. Jack fired marbles at one croc after another until he'd scared them all off. Mick laughed so hard water spilled from the bottle he was holding.

'They'll be back,' said Jack. 'But it should give us time to catch another couple of fish.'

'Be my luck to catch something big just as they return,' said Neville.

Neville hooked into a monster. It hurled its whole body clear of the water so they could see how big it was. It was magnificent, the sort of fish that addicted people to barra fishing for life; the sort of fish that could bring a smile to the face of a marble statue; the sort of barra every fisherman dreamed of catching. A crocodile took it as it landed.

'What did I tell you?' said Neville. He took another swig of Powerade and sucked angrily on a peppermint.

Big Barry and Carlton were first back to the camp. They wore smiles almost too wide to photograph. They'd caught thirty-two barras between them including one that ran to twelve kilos. They couldn't speak highly enough of their guide.

Graham and Yanni came in next and it was the same story. They'd caught thirty-five barras, one a touch over eleven kilos and, as a bonus, four two-kilo fingermark bream for dinner. They made no secret of the fact they thought their guide was a champion.

'That guy can put you onto any fish you want,' said Graham. 'If I'd asked, I reckon he could have put us onto a mermaid.'

'So why didn't you ask?' said Carlton.

'What would I do with a mermaid?' said Graham. 'How do you scale them? How do you fillet them?'

The boys were still playing silly buggers when Mick and Neville came in. Incredibly, there wasn't a smile to be seen.

'How'd you go?' asked Big Barry tentatively.

'Had better days,' said Neville.

'What did you get?' asked Carlton.

'Forty-two if you count them all,' said Neville.

'Forty-two?' said Big Barry. 'You caught forty-two?'

'Only four over ten kilos,' said Neville. 'Only four that mattered.'

'You got four over ten kilos?' said Graham.

'Biggest landed was only fourteen kilos,' said Neville.

'Fourteen kilos?' said Yanni. 'You caught a fourteen-kilo barra?'

'That was a tiddler,' said Neville. 'The biggest got taken by a croc. Bloody typical. I said that would happen.'

No one noticed Jack clean out the boat and walk away to join the other guides without saying a word. No one noticed

Mick unload his gear and walk away to have a shower without saying a word, either.

'I need a drink,' said Mick. 'No, better make that a dozen. Call the bloody plane and put me on it. I've never needed a drink more in my life.'

'He can't be that bad,' said Carlton.

'We're going to have to do something about him,' said Mick. 'He never lets up. Never. Not for a moment. I should have been having the time of my life; instead all I could think of was getting back.'

'He wasn't like that at the dinner party,' said Yanni.

'Well, he is now,' said Mick mournfully. 'Better hide my razor in case I decide to slash my wrists.'

'What fantastic fish,' said Big Barry over dinner. 'You know, I think it's worth coming up here just to eat fingermark bream.'

'Got me,' said Yanni. 'I think the cook must just sear both sides then put the fillets in a hot oven for a few minutes. See how evenly cooked they are all the way through? You can only get that using an oven.'

'Exquisite,' said Carlton. 'I don't care how the cook does it, I'm just glad that he does.'

'I'll pass your comments on to the cook,' said Jack. 'He appreciates feedback.'

'Salt and fried fat,' said Neville. 'That's all you're tasting.'

'What?' said Jack. The boys all stopped eating to look at Neville, clearly embarrassed and not believing what they'd heard.

'Could be any fish,' said Neville. 'It's overcooked and oversalted. Could be eating fish fingers.'

'Fish fingers,' said Jack faintly.

'You pass that on to the cook as well,' said Neville.

'What are we going to do?' said Big Barry after Neville had packed it in for the night. 'The man's a nightmare.'

'He wasn't like this at the dinner party,' said Yanni.

'So you keep saying,' said Mick.

'Boys!' said Graham quickly. 'Our problem is with Neville, not with each other. Right?'

'What the hell can we do?' said Yanni. 'I was afraid this would happen. Maybe he's a different bloke when he's got a few drinks in him. Maybe we should try and smuggle a bottle in.'

'Not an option,' said Jack. 'Unless you want to risk a compulsory gaol sentence and fine.'

'Pity. I know I'd feel better if I'd had a few,' said Mick morosely. 'What the hell are we going to do?'

'I'll take him tomorrow and give you a break,' said Big Barry. 'Maybe I can bring him around.'

'Take your own Powerade,' said Mick. 'He doesn't share.'

'Powerade?' said Big Barry.

'You'll see,' said Mick. He looked up as the cook arrived with a pot of coffee and a tray of cups.

'Any chance of Irish?' asked Mick.

'None at all,' said the cook. He placed the tray on the table and let his tall, angular frame sink down onto a chair. 'Had a problem with the grog once, that's why I work here.'

'Then we'll be grateful for what we've got,' said Graham.

'No worries,' said the cook. 'By the way, thanks for the comments about the fish. Jack passed them on. I do use the oven and it's nice to have my efforts appreciated.'

'Did Jack also . . . ?' asked Big Barry tentatively.

'Fish fingers,' said the cook.

'Sorry about him,' said Carlton.

'I bet they slapped his mother when he was born,' said the cook.

The next day Big Barry changed places with Mick and Jack handed over to his fellow guide Murray. Muzza had been raised on Melville Island and had fished for barra all his life. He could find fish when no one else could and he could pretty well guarantee to put an angler onto something special. Muzza was a legend. His fellow guides reckoned that he was just the man to put a smile on Neville's face. If he couldn't, no one could.

'Where to?' said Neville.

'I know a couple of deep holes on the flood plains where the barra have grown big and fat on frogs,' said Muzza. 'I was keeping them for myself.'

'That'd be right,' said Neville. 'Keep them for yourself and screw the paying customer.'

Carlton and Mick were first back. They'd gone up past Three Ways to the billabong where the water was fresh. They'd topped the magic fifty with three barra over ten kilos, one a tad under thirteen. Mick had also caught his first saratoga in the fresh and half a dozen mangrove jack on the way home, which he'd kept for dinner. Mick was ecstatic. It didn't matter that Carlton had caught more barra than him or that he'd caught the biggest. Mick had had the best day's fishing ever.

Yanni and Graham were next home. They'd had trouble all

day with crocodiles but still managed more than forty fish, one of which was over ten kilos.

'Graham hooked up on a croc as big as he is,' said Yanni. 'Bugger wanted to bring it into the boat.'

'Had my best Elton Chrome in its mouth,' said Graham, as if that explained everything. His mates started laughing.

'He wanted me to hold the croc with the Bogagrips,' said Yanni. 'A one-point-eight-metre crocodile with Bogagrips. The bugger was serious.'

'I had my rifle ready,' said Jack.

'What? To shoot the croc?' said Carlton.

'No. To shoot Graham. Stupid bugger.'

The boys were in a great mood as the boat carrying Big Barry and Neville swung into sight.

'Hope for our sake they had a good day,' said Mick.

'Hope for our sake Neville had a good day,' said Carlton.

'Hope for our sake he had a fabulous day,' said Yanni.

The laughter and wisecracking died like a guttering candle.

When Big Barry stepped off the boat with his rods and gear and walked off without a word, the boys feared the worst. When they turned to Muzza he ignored them, put his head down and started cleaning the boat.

'How'd you go?' asked Mick tentatively.

'Done better,' said Neville.

'We boated fifty fish before lunch,' said Big Barry to his mates while Neville was taking a shower. 'Know what? That bugger still wasn't happy. Claimed he caught a hundred before lunch in the Arafura Swamp. He caught a beauty. Went fourteen kilos. He complained that a fish that long would have run over seventeen in the swamp.'

'He complained about a fourteen-kilo fish?' said Carlton incredulously.

'Then it was too hot,' said Big Barry.

'Then there were too many crocs.

'Then too many mosquitoes.

'Then he ran out of his bloody Powerade.

'Keep an eye on me tonight, boys,' said Big Barry, 'in case I borrow Jack's rifle and turn it on myself.'

'He can't be that bad,' said Yanni defensively. 'Nobody could be that bad.'

'You'll find out tomorrow,' said Big Barry. 'Tomorrow he's all yours.'

'Barry, you're going to have to sort out that mate of yours,' said Jack as soon as Big Barry arrived for dinner. He nodded towards Neville who was on the opposite side of the tent, depressing people from one of the other fishing groups. 'None of the guides want to go fishing with him. I'm facing a mutiny here.'

'None of us wants to go fishing with him, either,' said Big Barry. 'I'm facing a revolt of my own.'

'He's your responsibility,' said Jack. 'Up to you to sort him.'

'Gee, thanks,' said Big Barry. He would have killed for a scotch, though in truth he needed a whole bottle. His spirits sank as one of the fishermen from the other group made a beeline towards him as soon as Jack moved off.

'G'day,' said the fisherman. 'I'm Grant.'

'Anything to do with Grant's Whisky?' said Big Barry.

'No, unfortunately.'

'Pity,' said Big Barry. He introduced himself and shook hands. 'What can I do for you?'

'That mate of yours,' said Grant. 'We were having a good time until he decided to honour us with his presence.'

'Know the feeling,' said Big Barry sympathetically.

'Is he always like that?'

'As far as I know.'

'We've got Shirley, she's the one at the end of the table. She's got a voice that makes an angle grinder sound like easy listening, but she's nothing compared to your mate. Hasn't he got anything good to say about anything?'

'Not that I know of,' said Big Barry.

'Can't you do something about him?' asked Grant.

'Like what?'

'I don't know. He's your responsibility not mine.'

'Gee, thanks,' said Big Barry.

Big Barry's mood improved markedly over dinner. He loved his food and appreciated food done well. Good food had a way of taking his mind off things it didn't particularly want to deal with.

'You know,' he said, 'I think these mangrove jack taste even better than the fingermark.'

'Got me,' said Yanni. 'Mick and I had a look in the kitchen. They've got gas cylinders but, even so, the conditions are hardly ideal. I think the cook's a bloody genius to do as well as he does. I've had mangrove jack before but I'm not sure I've ever had better.'

'It's exquisite,' said Carlton. 'Especially with the lime butter sauce.'

'I'll pass your comments on to the cook,' said Jack.

'You guys are too easily pleased,' said Neville. He pushed his dinner away half-eaten.

'What now?' said Jack.

'What lives in water drowns in sauce,' said Neville. 'You should pass that on to the cook as well.'

'No beer, no wine, no whisky,' said Neville as they sat around over coffee. 'No conversation worth staying up for either. Think I'll go to bed and read.'

'You do that,' said Big Barry.

The boys waited in silence until the light went on in Neville's tent.

'I can't take five more days of this,' said Big Barry. 'This isn't how I planned things.'

'We've all had as much of him as we can take,' chipped in Jack.

'Muzza was sensational today,' said Big Barry. 'No offence to you, Jack, but your mate was really hot. He found us fish, good fish, everywhere we went but it still wasn't good enough for Neville. According to the Peppermint Pom, your six-metre boats are no good. They only use three-point-three-metre boats in Buckingham Bay, and they can get closer in to the shore, fish further up the gutters, get in under the mangroves. You know, we caught ninety-two fish all told and the bugger still wasn't happy.'

'For heaven's sake, why not?' said Mick.

'Only eight were worth counting, only eight were worth photographing, only eight were over ten kilos. Of course we would have caught more in the afternoon but the Gelspun cut through his trace. He had to tie a new bimini twist, a new Albright and a new perfection loop. Lost good fishing time.'

'Doesn't he ever let up?' asked Grant who'd wandered over from his table. 'Even Shirley shuts down from time to time.'

'No,' said Big Barry. 'He's like rust. He never lets up. Not for one second.'

'Jack, what do you do when you get a customer like him?' asked Yanni. 'You must have some way of dealing with blokes like Neville otherwise you'd go mad.'

'He's a tough one,' said Jack. 'But there's a trick we've pulled in the past. Might get rid of him.'

The boys listened carefully as Jack explained what they had to do. They started to grin and finally to laugh. They suddenly felt good. This was how they were supposed to feel. This was the way all their other trips had been.

'Nice to see you taking your responsibilities seriously,' said Grant.

'You feel all right,' said Mick to Neville as they got up for breakfast.

'Terrific. Why?'

'Just look a bit pale,' said Mick.

'Pale?' said Neville.

'Yeah, like one of your peppermints.'

'I feel okay,' said Neville.

'What happened to you?' said Big Barry as Neville sat down to breakfast.

'Nothing. Why?' said Neville.

'You don't look well,' said Big Barry.

'Looked okay in the bathroom mirror,' said Neville.

'Morning, everyone,' said Yanni. He turned to Neville. 'Jesus! What have you done?'

'What do you mean?' said Neville.

'You look like a candidate for a cremation,' said Yanni.

'That's what I said,' said Big Barry. 'He doesn't look good.'

'Something might have bitten you,' said Jack. 'There are some pretty strange things up here. Do you feel light-headed?'

'Look, I know what you're doing,' said Neville. 'It's a game you play up here, right?'

'What do you mean?' said Carlton.

'It's a stupid game to make me think I'm sick so that I fly back to Darwin Hospital. You get a laugh, the doctors and nurses get a laugh, and I waste three days trying to get a plane back here. The blokes tried it on in Buckingham Bay and in the Arafura Swamp.'

'I bet they did,' said Big Barry miserably.

Once again Neville's boat was last in.

'How'd you go?' asked Carlton.

'Terrible,' said Neville. 'Waste of time, waste of money, waste of a whole bloody day. Guide couldn't find his own dick in daylight. Hell, he couldn't find it if it was on a piece of string.'

'How many did you catch?' asked Graham.

'Eleven,' said Neville.

'Eleven over ten kilos?' said Mick. He'd had another great day with Big Barry. They'd caught over forty.

'None over ten kilos,' said Neville. 'Not one.' He stormed off to the showers.

The boys turned to Yanni.

'What happened?' said Big Barry.

'Tell them,' said Yanni, turning to Peter who had been their reluctant guide for the day.

'I thought to hell with him,' said Peter. 'The bugger's making everybody's life a misery so I thought I'd turn the tables and really give him something to complain about. Big mistake. I took him among the snags. He lost a dozen lures including his pink Mann Stretch 20.'

'It was his favourite lure,' cut in Yanni. 'The one he caught most of his fish on. Mann doesn't make that pattern any more.'

'Jesus,' said Carlton. 'Does he have a Classic Barra?'

'Lost that as well,' said Peter.

'What did he do?' said Mick.

'You'd think I'd stolen his wife and barbecued his babies,' said Peter. 'He never let up. I couldn't catch a cold. I couldn't find a fish in a fish shop window. I couldn't find my arse with both hands.'

'He said that?' said Big Barry.

'That,' said Peter, 'was just for starters. Halfway through I decided to give up and put the bugger onto as many fish as I could. But it was too late. He'd got to me and by then I couldn't take a trick. I took him to the wrong places at the wrong time. Made a total hash of it. Better tie me up, fellas, before I do something stupid and make a widow of my wife.'

'That,' said Big Barry, 'has to be the best mud crab I've ever eaten.' He pushed his plate to the side and sighed with satisfaction. The pile of empty crab shell was testimony to his enjoyment.

'Got me,' said Yanni. 'Just the right amount of black bean and just enough chilli to lift rather than overwhelm the flavour.'

'Exquisite,' said Carlton. 'A delicate balance for a delicate flavour.'

'I'll pass your comments on to the cook,' said Jack. 'He's proud of his crab.'

'You guys have got to be kidding,' said Neville. 'Obviously you've never had chilli crab in Singapore. Compared to Singapore chilli crab this is as bland as baby food.'

'Baby food?' said Jack. 'Baby food?'

'Jesus Christ, Neville,' said Carlton, as the boys cringed with embarrassment.

'I call things as I see them,' said Neville defiantly. 'Baby food is baby food.'

'Right,' said Jack. 'I'll pass that on to the cook as well.'

They were relieved when Neville again excused himself barely half an hour after dinner and went to bed.

'What did you blokes do to deserve him?' said Grant. He brought a few of his mates over to join the boys around their table.

'More to the point, what are we going to do about him?' said Carlton. 'We've got to do something.'

'I suppose murder is frowned upon up here?' said Graham.

'Afraid so,' said Jack. 'Though if you did want to commit a murder, up here's the perfect place to do it.'

'We found a four-and-a-half-metre saltwater croc sitting on its nest,' said Grant helpfully. 'Put the Peppermint Pom ashore there and they'll never find him. Croc would have him in a hole under the riverbank in five minutes.'

'Bit rough on the croc,' said Big Barry. The boys laughed.

'I know where there are some wild pigs cut off by the floods,' said Jack. 'We could nick the bugger a couple of times with the fishing knife, get him bleeding nicely, then put him ashore there. There wouldn't even be a smell of him left once the pigs had finished with him.'

'We could stake him out and let the mud crabs have him,' said Yanni. 'Apparently they go for the genitals first.'

'Bones,' said Muzza. 'Crabs leave the bones.'

'Plenty of sharks down at the rivermouth,' said Jack. 'They don't leave no bones.'

'What about snakes?' said Carlton.

'Don't see a lot of them,' said Peter. 'When you do, you wish you hadn't. Taipans and king browns don't scare easily.'

'What about malaria and dengue fever?' said Big Barry.

'Both rare,' said Jack. 'And too slow.'

'Don't want anything slow,' said Graham. 'I vote we go with the four-and-a-half-metre croc.'

His mates burst out laughing.

'I'm not joking,' he said.

'I'm serious.'

'I've got him tomorrow.'

The boys laughed even harder. But their laughter choked off the instant Neville burst in on them, wild-eyed and dishevelled.

'What's the matter?' said Big Barry.

'I've been robbed!' said Neville. 'Some bastard's been rifling through my things.' He was almost sobbing.

Jack leaped to his feet.

'You're kidding. We've never had any robberies here. What's missing?'

Neville hesitated, clenching and unclenching his fists impotently.

'Well?' said Jack.

'My Powerade!' said Neville. 'Someone's stolen my Powerade.'

'Your Powerade?' said Jack. 'Who the hell would want your Powerade?'

Carlton started laughing.

'It's no laughing matter,' snapped Neville, but by then the boys were struggling to contain themselves.

'Could be worse,' said Carlton. 'They might have taken your peppermints as well.'

'Wake up, wake up!' said Mick. He shook Neville's shoulder until he opened his eyes. 'So you finally nodded off? You kept me awake half the night with your tossing and turning.'

'Wha . . . ?' said Neville.

'Never mind,' said Mick. 'It's time for breakfast.'

'Breakfast?'

'Yeah, breakfast,' said Mick impatiently. 'You know, where the cook you don't like fries eggs you don't like with bacon you don't like.'

'Wha . . . ?' said Neville again. He tried to sit up but fell back on his pillow.

'Jesus!' said Mick. 'Hell's the matter with you?'

Neville swung his feet to the ground and sat up rubbing his eyes.

'You okay?' said Mick, suddenly concerned. 'You look terrible.'

'Don't start that again,' said Neville weakly.

'Bloody hell,' said Yanni as Neville sat down for breakfast. Everyone else had just about finished. 'If I didn't know better I'd say you were hungover.'

'As if,' said Neville. He knocked his knife onto the ground.

'You look like the brother of one of those crabs we had last night has made a home in your undies,' said Carlton. He reached over and picked up Neville's knife. 'I've never seen anyone more fidgety.'

'You guys don't give in, do you?' said Neville. His lips curled in a snarl.

'Mate, I'm serious,' said Carlton. 'You look like you've got the rigours. If I looked like you I'd check to see if I still had a pulse.'

Neville ignored him, trying hard to suppress a shiver.

The cook dropped a plate of fried eggs and bacon in front of him and a steaming mug of coffee. Neville couldn't hide the shaking of his hands as he tried to take a sip. Hot coffee splashed over the sides and burned his fingers.

'Shit!' he said.

'Do you want to give fishing a miss today?' asked Yanni.

'The only thing wrong with me,' said Neville icily, 'is the company I keep.'

By the time Neville met up with Graham at the boat the others were long gone.

'You took your bloody time,' said Graham.

'Had to re-rig,' said Neville. 'My hands don't seem to want to work this morning.'

'When you two ladies have finished we'll go fishing,' said Jack impatiently. 'I thought we'd go up the creek at Three Ways. All right with you, Neville?'

'Three Ways, Four Ways, Five Way . . . who cares?'

Both Jack and Graham stared at him.

'Most people up here fish for barra,' said Jack cuttingly. 'You're the first bloke I've ever seen cast to a jabiru.' The big black-and-white stork scrabbled away as fast as its long pillar-box red legs could carry it.

'You might catch more fish if you got your lure in the water occasionally,' said Graham. They'd spent half the morning retrieving Neville's lures from the branches of mangroves, pandanus and paperbarks. 'I thought you were supposed to be good.'

'I am good,' said Neville grimly. 'I'm just not myself today.'

'I've seen filleted fingermark bream that look better than you do,' said Jack. 'You sure you don't want me to take you back?'

'I'm fine,' said Neville.

Neville hooked up on a barra pushing eight kilos but played it so ineptly it soon threw the lure.

'If that's the best you can do, you better go back to using barbed hooks,' said Graham.

'Or dynamite,' said Jack.

Neville pretended to ignore them as he cast again.

'Maybe you've got a peppermint deficiency,' said Graham. 'Maybe you're in withdrawal. I notice you haven't been sucking them today.'

'No need,' mumbled Neville. He worked harder on his next fish, a nine-kilo fighter, and managed to net it. He lifted it free of the net with his Bogagrips as he'd done hundreds of times before.

'Watch it!' cried Jack.

'Oh shit!' cried Neville.

'Bloody hell!' cried Graham.

Neville stood over his barra, which had tumbled free of the Bogagrips onto the bottom of the boat. The barra, which had left the water a brilliant metallic silver, was now red with his blood.

'What are you doing back?' said Big Barry as he and Carlton pulled into shore.

'Mission of mercy,' said Graham. He couldn't keep the smile off his face.

'What mission of mercy?' said Big Barry.

'Facilitating the absence of friends,' said Graham.

'Bloody hell!' said Carlton. 'Where's the Peppermint Pom?'

'Darwin,' said Graham. 'Getting his hands sewn back together.'

'You're kidding!' whooped Big Barry. 'What happened?'

'Wait till the others come back,' said Graham. 'I'll tell you all over dinner.'

'He had the Bogagrips in the barra's jaw and he still dropped it?' said Big Barry incredulously.

'Like a hot brick,' said Graham. 'By the way, this is the offending barra that we're eating.'

'Best I've ever tasted,' said Big Barry.

'Got me,' said Yanni.

'Exquisite,' said Carlton. 'And for once I don't think we'll give the cook all the credit. Should have taken a cast off it in honour of the favour it did us.'

'He would have been all right but the stupid bugger tried to grab the barra as it fell,' said Graham. 'Couldn't believe it. The gill case slashed his fingers to the bone.'

'They would,' said Big Barry. 'But he knows his way around barramundi. He knows how sharp the gill case is.'

'He was on another planet,' said Graham. 'Away with the pixies. Had no coordination at all. We offered to bring him back a couple of times.'

'What do you reckon was wrong with him?' asked Big Barry. 'He didn't look good.'

'Dunno,' said Jack. 'Maybe something bit him. What do you reckon, Muzza?'

'Could be anything,' said Muzza.

'They'll probably do tests and find out at the hospital,' said Mick as the cook came to clear away their plates.

'They won't do any tests,' said the cook. 'Up here people like him are a dime a dozen. There's no secret to what he needs.'

'What do you mean?' asked Big Barry.

'Think about it. He wouldn't share his Powerade. He sucked peppermints all day. He disappeared straight after dinner.'

'You're not serious?' said Carlton.

'First the constant bad temper, then the shakes. It wasn't Powerade I took from his room,' said the cook. 'It was the two bottles of Absolut vodka he mixed with it. The imported stuff, one hundred per cent proof. And a half of crème de menthe.'

'I never picked it,' said Mick. 'And I shared a room with him.'

'Sometimes it takes one to know one,' said the chef. 'Now, what's the word on the barramundi?'

'Salt and fried fat,' said Carlton. 'Absolute crap. I've had better wrapped in newspaper.'

His laugh set the tone for the remaining three days.

The Burden of Responsibility

I think I was twelve at the time, which meant it was 1956 and I'd spent two-thirds of my life in New Zealand and could no longer be regarded as a Pommie. At least, that's what I hoped. Both of my older brothers had picked up a Kiwi accent, although nowhere near as broad as mine. Neither had worked quite as hard at it as me. Neither had felt the need as keenly. I played soccer not rugby. Soccer, in a country in which rugby is both religion and sport, and playing it is regarded as an affirmation of national identity. I also belonged to the Church of England, which, as far as my schoolmates were concerned, was further evidence of my Englishness and lack of New Zealandness. That was two strikes against me. I'd managed to persuade my mother, through a mixture of argument, pleading and tears, to stop buying the long-legged, English-style khaki shorts and let me wear grey boxer shorts like all the other kids my age. And I took off my sandals, which my mother made me wear to school, as soon as I was out of sight, tucked them into my schoolbag and proudly walked barefooted like the rest of the kids. You couldn't be a

Kiwi unless you could walk on scorching pavements, on gravel and on prickles and kick a ball around barefooted.

Let me tell you, nobody did more to look and sound like a Kiwi. I could make the local Self-Help store sound like Sowf-Owp, which was the way Maxie, part-Scottish, part-Samoan but one hundred per cent Kiwi, said it. I said 'hooray' for 'goodbye' and referred to strange kids we met down in Grey Lynn Park as 'sonny', which was a put-down. I said 'tramping' while the rest of the English-speaking world said 'hiking', and I said 'really tramping' when I described a car or motorbike exceeding the speed limit. I tried my hardest to be a Kiwi, a pig-islander, and I had to. I had a third strike against me. Unlike every other kid I knew, I liked writing essays; in fact, I liked writing anything. If pushed, my pals could understand why I played soccer because it was the English game and they thought my parents — being English — had probably forced me into it, thereby denying me the right to play rugby. But there was no excuse for liking essays, none at all. That, as much as anything, marked me as different when all I wanted to do was belong.

I lived in Auckland, across the road from Richmond Road School, smack on the border between Ponsonby and Grey Lynn. In those days Ponsonby was not regarded as a nice place to live; in fact, it was one of the poorer suburbs. There were even brothels, two that I knew of, which we used to ride past on our bikes expecting to see something akin to the gates of hell, adorned of course with fallen women in various stages of undress. But all we saw were wooden bungalows much the same as the ones on either side, but with their blinds down. This, apparently, was significant.

For some reason Grey Lynn was considered altogether more salubrious although I never could see any difference in either the houses or the people who lived in them. My mother, however, could and it was important to her. She always told people we lived in Grey Lynn even though, technically, we lived in Ponsonby. The richest people I knew lived in Grey Lynn. Not only were they a two-car family in a suburb where the vast majority of homes had no car at all, both their cars were brand-new Morris Minors. Both of them. For years they were the only people I knew who'd bought a brand-new car and they'd bought two. We had a 1934 four-cylinder Chevrolet which my father used to slip out of gear every time we went downhill so he could save petrol.

I'm telling you this so you can get a feeling for the times. Nobody had much, and most of that was second-hand, yet New Zealand was credited with having the third-highest standard of living in the world. As far as I can remember, most people were pretty happy, probably happier than people are today. For the most part I was happy too, even if there was an essay to write and I stayed home to write it when I should've been making up the numbers in a scratch game of soccer or touch footy. My pals regarded this as an act of treachery, if not outright treason. That's when they called me a 'mummy's boy' or, worst of all, a Pommie. The funny thing is, my pals used to make me read my essays to them as soon as I'd finished them. They really seemed to enjoy them.

I used to make up my stories but that day in 1956, when I was twelve, everything changed. I wrote a personal story, a story about my family and me. The teacher gave us the title of the essay — *The Burden of Responsibility* — and we were expected to write a couple of pages in praise of people like the Prime Minister, Keith Holyoake, who had the burden of running the country, the mayor, who had the burden of running Auckland, the headmaster, who had the burden of running Richmond Road School, the captain of the All Blacks, who had the burden of carrying national pride, or our fathers, who had the burden of keeping a roof over our heads and food on the table. I wrote instead about the burden I carried.

I wasn't born with a fishing rod in my hands because in those days they were a luxury. No, I was born with a fishing line in my hands. The rod came much later. I went fishing whenever I could. I used to catch the trolley bus to town after school and race down Shortland Street to the Admiralty Steps or to the steps alongside the ferry building. Bread didn't get a chance to go stale in our family so I had to nick a couple of slices when Mum wasn't looking to break up and throw into the water to attract the fish. For bait, I made dough.

For years I was small fish's worst nightmare. I was deadly on sprats, piper and *pakiti*, which, thinking back, I suppose was a species of wrasse. There were afternoons when my mother encouraged me to go fishing whether I wanted to or not and I'd come home with twenty or so sprats and piper. They became dinner and I became my mother's hero for the night. She called the sprats 'herrings' and that somehow dignified them and made them more than they were. My father and brothers weren't exactly thrilled because they didn't like having to deal with the bones — and there were millions of them — but the alternative was splitting cauliflower cheese five ways. So at least one night a week we had 'herrings' for tea, just as we had 'pork fillets', which was really tripe in a white sauce accompanied by a mountain of mashed potato.

In my essay I made the point that I had the responsibility of providing at least one meal a week, although I didn't see it as a burden even though some nights I had to hang around until it was almost dark to catch enough fish. When the wind was in the wrong direction it could get really cold down there on the Admiralty Steps.

Once I got a bike, an old back-pedal-brake Rudge, things started to change. I decided I was too old to catch sprats and piper. I saved every penny I could get my hands on. I delivered newspapers, groceries and prescription medicines for the local pharmacy. I mowed lawns even though it was a job I hated and everyone expected me to trim the edges as well with hedge clippers. Mostly I got a shilling for my efforts. Every penny I earned went into the fund to buy a fishing rod and reel so I could go after snapper.

It took a while but I finally managed to buy a split cane rod with a side-cast reel, and enough line, hooks and sinkers. That was when my problems arose. That was when I assumed The Burden of Responsibility.

Real fish, like snapper, required real bait. I couldn't get by any more on two slices of bread and a scone-sized lump of dough. I required real bait and real bait cost money, which I often didn't have. I'd have to ask Mum for money and this put her in a real quandary. Nowadays you'd say she was between a rock and a hard place. She usually had just enough money to buy something for tea and if she gave any money to me for bait she had to gamble that I'd catch enough snapper to feed everybody. How's that for a burden of responsibility? Fishing never comes with a guarantee. Even the best fishermen miss out at times. Yet I'd set off for the breakwater at Mechanics Bay with my rod tied to my crossbar and a shilling's worth of liver in my saddlebag, knowing I had to deliver — or else. I made this point in my essay as well.

Nobody ever fished with greater dedication or earnestness. I nearly wept every time a snapper took my bait and I failed to catch it. But I caught enough on enough occasions to justify my mother's faith in me, although sometimes the fish I brought home were kahawai instead of snapper. Mum made fishcakes with the kahawai, which was the only way we knew to make them palatable. In those days we didn't know that the qualities that make kahawai break up in the pan are precisely what makes them sensational for sashimi. Even if we had known back then, we wouldn't have eaten sashimi anyway. Just the idea of eating raw fish would've made us sick. Besides, anything Japanese was on the nose. Still, kahawai was better than nothing and there were plenty of times nothing was all I caught.

Up until then I'd thought pressure was what occurred when I was trying to score a goal to win or draw a soccer match in the dying seconds, and that wasn't really pressure but tension. Pressure, I now discovered, was what occurs when your mother is depending on you to catch fish for tea and the fish aren't obliging. Pressure is also what occurs when a mother gives her youngest son the tea money in the hope that he'll catch fish. My mum and dad argued on the nights I failed to provide. My dad comes from South Shields in the northeast of England, and meals that consist entirely of cauliflower or macaroni cheese just don't hit the spot. They don't now and they sure didn't then.

To improve my chances and reduce the number of arguments I started consulting the wisest fisherman I knew. His name was Mack, just Mack, and he lived in Brown Street, which ran alongside Richmond Road School. Mack had spent most of his life on Great Barrier Island which all of us kids knew was the best place in the world to catch snapper. Great Barrier lay on the horizon about ninety kilometres east of Auckland, a low dark smudge visible only on really clear days. We all knew about Great Barrier Island but the closest any of us had ever got to it was Waiheke Island, and that wasn't even a quarter of the way there. As far as we were concerned, Great Barrier Island was as unreachable as England. The only way we knew you could get there was by flying in Fred Ladd's Grumman Widgeon flying boat from Mechanics Bay. Flying, for heaven's sake! Flying wasn't even a remote possibility. In those days flying was strictly for the rich and privileged.

Mack had come to Auckland because his wife was sick and needed hospital treatment. I never knew what was wrong with her but she seemed to take an age dying. By the time she died Mack had grown old and couldn't face moving back to Great Barrier and living alone. Besides, he'd had to sell his house there to help buy the one he lived in by the school. All this was irrelevant to me at the time. All that mattered was that Mack had lived on snapper heaven and knew all there was to know about catching them.

I could testify to the fact. One day in the Christmas school holidays he'd taken me out on the *La Rita*, a one-hundred-and-twelve-foot Fairmile charter fishing boat that went way out into the Hauraki Gulf. It wouldn't leave port unless it had at least forty paying customers and I never went out when there were fewer than fifty. Unless it was a really bad day, most people caught more snapper than they wanted, certainly enough to cover the seventeen shillings and sixpence it cost for the trip. There was always a sweep for the biggest, second-biggest and third-biggest snapper. When I went out on the

La Rita with Mack he caught the three biggest snapper. It was never a contest. And he was smart enough to slip the second-biggest snapper into my sugar sack so I could claim the prize for second. (Nobody was allowed to win more than one prize.) Catching the three biggest snapper was typical of Mack. He'd be hauling in big snapper while no one else was getting a bite.

I can't tell you how many times Mack stopped me going fishing because the tides, moon or winds weren't right. When he said go, I rarely missed. But tides don't rise and fall to accommodate school hours so the number of times I went fishing declined dramatically. Often on the nights I didn't go fishing we had liver for tea, which Mum called lamb's fry. Call it whatever you like, only the bacon she fried with it made it edible as far as we kids were concerned. Even Dad started pushing me to go fishing. So I went down to the breakwater when Mack said don't and came home with fish about the same number of times I came home with nothing. Those were the nights we didn't even have lamb's fry and I felt my failure to provide so keenly that I used to slip away to the bedroom after the dishes had been done and try not to cry. I hated letting my mum down. I hated letting Dad down. Never did any burden feel heavier; never did fishing feel less like a sport.

I concluded my essay with both of these points.

A funny thing happened when I read my essay to my pals. They were used to me writing stories that made them laugh or hold their breath with suspense. But this story was different. I think it hit them where they lived, touched nerves and made them think about their own lives. I knew for a fact there were days when some of my pals only had toast for tea.

Or copped a few bruises to take their minds off their rumbling bellies. They never said they liked the story but I could tell that I'd suddenly gone up in their estimation. In telling my story I'd captured something of them. I made them realise that each of us had our own burden of responsibility and were important in our own way.

My teacher, of course, thought he'd finally hit the target after twenty years of casting his pearls before swine. (Well, we were pig-islanders.) He felt vindicated, rewarded and, I swear, he almost broke down. He read my essay out loud to the class. He read it out loud in the staffroom to all his fellow teachers at morning break. He went to the headmaster's office and read it to him. The headmaster read my essay to the entire school at assembly the following morning. I had teachers and kids coming up to me to congratulate me on my essay and talk about it. It was amazing. I could see the wonder in their eyes as they tried to figure out where the hell the story had come from.

Of course I read the story to Mack. My mum wasn't really keen on my going to see Mack because he lived alone and was inclined to drink far more than was good for him. On the other hand she was proud of me going to see him because he lived alone and was obviously lonely. Nevertheless, I could never go to Mack's without telling Mum I was going and how long I'd be. It was years before I understood why, when words like paedophile and 'kiddy-fiddler' reared their ugly heads.

When I read my essay to Mack I expected a pat on the back and a 'good on yer'. After all, Mack played a key role in my essay and it was clear that I thought the sun shone out of his tackle box. I'd been taught to look up at my audience while I was reading and since I knew every word of my essay by heart, I looked up a lot while I was reading to Mack. His smile faded and he seemed to turn grey in front of my eyes. He started to shake. His reaction scared me. I began to wonder if he'd had a heart attack or something. He heard me out, attempted a smile, then got up and walked out into his backyard. I followed him and found him sitting in an old kitchen chair between his tomatoes and his gherkin patch, crouched over, elbows on his knees, head in his hands.

When I asked he said he was all right. I didn't know what else to do so I said I had to go home. He told me to hang on, said he'd be all right in a couple of minutes. I didn't have a clue what was going on.

'I didn't know you was a writer,' he said, which was a lie because I'd told him all about my essays. 'At least, I didn't know you was a good one.'

Mack told me to sit tight while he went and poured himself a beer. The way he was behaving had me worried so I spied on him through his kitchen window. He filled his glass and drank it straight down. His shoulders slumped and he sighed like he was carrying the weight of the world, a burden of responsibility beyond anything I could imagine. I'm ashamed to say it but I couldn't help suddenly thinking there was another essay there, one with which I would wow everyone all over again. There was, but it wasn't the one I expected. Oh, no.

Mack poured himself another beer and turned to walk out to the yard with it. I bolted back to the beer crate I'd been sitting on. In those days beer came in wooden crates as opposed to the cardboard cartons you get nowadays. People usually only bought crates of beer when they were having a party or a celebration. Mack bought his beer in crates all the time, which was how he'd earned his reputation as a drinker and why there was always something for me to sit on.

'Your story reminded me,' said Mack heavily. 'I've got a story, too. Never told a soul, no way. Spent years trying to put it out of my mind.'

I didn't say a word. I just sat there quietly, waiting for him to elaborate. I didn't know at the time that this is a standard technique of reporters. It just seemed the right thing to do. Mack stared at his beer, stared at his hands, stared at his feet, clearly trying to make up his mind whether to tell me or not.

'I got picked up by a submarine,' he said eventually. 'A German submarine. June 1940. Can you believe it, a U-boat, straight out off Medlands Beach?'

It was as though he'd drawn a cork out of a bottle that had been sealed sixteen years earlier. It took a while for the story to realise it had finally been set free and the words came hesitantly, uncertainly. For me it was like slow torture. I knew Medlands Beach was on the southeast coast of Great Barrier Island. There was a map of Great Barrier Island on the wall of the school library and my pals and I knew it by heart. We'd studied it while teachers had tried to teach us about Latvia and Estonia, where the school's newest arrivals — three astonishingly blond kids — had come from. And Mack had been picked up by a German submarine straight out from Medlands Beach. That was — and still is — the most enthralling, amazing, wonderful, stimulating, gob-smacking snippet of information anyone had given me. Imagine how I felt! My mate, Mack, had been picked up by a German submarine.

To put things into perspective, in those days a trip from the North Island to the South Island almost qualified as an overseas adventure. We were twelve hundred miles from Australia, twelve thousand from Britain. When my parents went on a round-the-world trip in 1957 to visit their families in England, it rated a mention in the daily paper. New Zealand was just so far away from everywhere. Even with a war on, you'd have to have said that the chance of being picked up by a German submarine in New Zealand waters was about the same as a Martian spaceship landing on Mt Eden. And yet here was Mack telling me that was precisely what had happened to him.

I had been raised on war stories. I'd been born in London during the Blitz. My father hadn't been allowed to enlist because he made anti-aircraft predictors and the authorities told him he was making a bigger contribution to the war effort doing that than he ever would carrying a rifle. Even so the Luftwaffe nearly got him half a dozen times when they dropped bombs through the roof of the factory where he was working. He ducked under his workbench and that was all that saved him. One time he was riding his bike home from work late at night when a V1 flying bomb ran out of fuel right behind him. It hit less than four hundred yards on up the road. One less cup of kerosene in the V1 and he'd have been a goner. All our English friends had stories like that.

It shouldn't come as any surprise that war movies were my favourite kind. I saw *The Dam Busters* four times. Names like Guy Gibson, who led the raid on the dams along the Ruhr, and Barnes Wallis, who invented the bouncing bombs, were as familiar to me as the names of my classmates. I read every book about World War II that I could get my hands on, knew the names of all the Spitfire fighter aces and the names and silhouettes of every plane in the British and German air forces. I was brought up believing that Churchill and Britain won the war and that Montgomery was a military genius. I was brought up believing that the men of the Merchant Navy were all heroes to the last man, and actually met a visiting sailor who'd been sunk three times by German U-boats. In all my reading about the war and all the movies I'd seen, there was nothing more threatening, more deadly, more fearsome or more calculated to inspire awe than a German submarine. And Mack had been picked up by one.

Holy cow.

'What happened?' I said.

Mack was miles away, lost in thought, with the expression on his face people get when they're recalling unhappy or bitter memories. He gave no indication that he'd heard me. He wasn't even drinking his beer. I sat as still as a shag drying its wings.

'Bloody motor conked out,' he said wearily. 'Some bastard had siphoned the diesel out of my tank. Reckon I know who it was too. Didn't find out till I was on the six-mile reef ready to come home. Jesus Christ, what a mess.'

Bloody? Bastard? Jesus Christ? Mack never swore or blasphemed, certainly not in front of me, but there was no way I was going to cover my ears.

'It was probably about eleven at night. Westerly blowing, not hard but enough to cause a bit of a chop. There was no moon and the night was as black as the lining of a mullet's stomach. I'd got onto a school of good snapper, all the perfect size, between three and four pounds.' Mack took a massive swallow from his glass and retreated back into his thoughts.

I kept up my shag impression while I waited for him to continue.

'Couldn't believe it when the motor conked out. Last bloody thing I expected. Nothing ever went wrong with it. Never thought for a second that I was out of diesel. I'd up-anchored and only gone about a hundred yards when she died. My torch battery was on its last legs and my running lights were no help. I wasn't allowed to use them anyway. The last thing I checked was the dipstick in the tank, and I only did that because I'd checked everything else. By then the westerly had pushed me out another couple of miles and it was too deep to anchor. I threw out my sea anchor to slow the rate of drift and tried to figure out what to do. I hadn't told anyone where I was going because it was a spot I'd found and didn't want to share it. Even with the sea anchor out, I figured I'd be twenty to thirty miles out to sea by morning. I was in a right pickle, let me tell you.

'I suppose I drifted for a couple of hours. The submarine was on the surface but I never saw it coming. In truth, I wasn't looking. The first clue I had was the sound of its diesels and, because of the way the wind was blowing, I never heard them until they were a hundred yards from me. I shone my torch towards the sound. I didn't give much thought as to what kind of boat it was. I just wanted to make sure it saw me and picked me up. Next thing I know I'm pinned in this searchlight. Struth! Talk about going from the sublime to the bloody ridiculous. One second I can't see my bloody hand in front of my face, next I'm staring into the sun. Just as quickly it's dark again. I thought the boat was one of ours, some kind of naval craft or a small coaster. I called out and someone called back. Suddenly there's this dark shape alongside me, and people running around with torches and shouting at me in some foreign language. I hadn't a clue what was going on but I threw them a line anyway. What was I supposed to do?

'The boat turned into the wind so mine lay alongside it. Next thing I know, a rope ladder drops into my boat. Before I get a chance to climb up it, this bloke climbs down. I can see by the light of the torches that he's holding a rifle and, do you know what, it still doesn't dawn on me what's happening. "Am I glad to see you," I say. Instead of shaking my hand he points his bloody rifle at me and starts yelling at me in Kraut. Bloody hell! I didn't know what to do. I thought he was going to shoot me. I looked up to where the blokes with the torches were, hoping someone would sort things out, and that was when I noticed the curved sides of the hull and realised that I was looking up at a submarine; a German submarine. Well, you could've knocked me over with a feather. Someone threw me a stern line and I tied it off.

'I'm standing there with my hands in the air when this officer type climbs down the ladder. Bugger me if he doesn't speak English. He asks me my name and introduces himself. Christian Berger, his name was, and it sounded like he was some kind of lieutenant. He finds my snapper and says, "Do you mind if I take these?" What difference did it make if I minded or not? He was taking them anyway. I told him I'd swap the snapper for some diesel. That got him thinking. He started talking Kraut to someone in the conning tower, then turned to me.

'"No one can know we are here," he said. "So I have a choice. I can shoot you now and sink your boat. Or I can let you drift away for the same result. Or I can take you prisoner." He studied me for about fifteen seconds although it felt longer. "Or I can give you the diesel you want. Are you a man of honour, Mack?" It threw me, him using my name like that, like we was pals. But I could see he was serious and weighing up the decision. I nodded and told him my word was my bond. He took this in. His eyes weren't hard or anything but they were unnerving. They never wavered. "If I give you diesel," he said, "you must give me your word that you will tell nobody about us, about the submarine, for forty-eight hours after you reach the shore. No one must know we are here. No one. Understand?" I nodded. "Do you understand your choices?" I nodded again. "Can I rely on your word?"

'I told him he could and we shook on it. Then he said the strangest thing. "Tell me about your home," he said. So, as briefly as I could, I told him about Great Barrier. I swear he looked envious, or perhaps just wistful. Someone passed down a jerry can. I poured the diesel into my tank and handed the can back. "We are civilised people," the officer said. "I am giving you your life in exchange for your word. Break your word and you put my life and the lives of my comrades in jeopardy. Do you want to kill us?" I told him I didn't. I promised I'd keep my word. I gave him every reassurance I could. I still wasn't convinced they wouldn't blow me out of the water as soon as I'd untied. "Go home," he said and shook my hand again. "But you must go slowly," he added. I think that was his idea of a joke.

'By the time I'd cast off and started my motor they were gone, swallowed up by the night. I drew some comfort from the fact that I'd be equally invisible to them. The horizon had already started to colour up as I headed in and it was half light as I swung around the point back into Medlands. By then I'd had plenty of opportunity to think. I had no doubt about the seriousness of the promise I'd made and its implications. On the one hand, I had a clear duty to report the presence of the submarine; on the other, I'd given my solemn promise that I wouldn't. There was a policeman waiting with my wife and a couple of my mates on the beach. They were about to launch their boat to go out looking for me. One word to the policeman and I knew he'd be straight on the radio back to Auckland and they'd have aircraft up looking for the U-boat within the hour. I couldn't do it. The Germans had done the right thing by me and I was obliged to do the right thing by them.

'Of course, my wife, my mates and the policeman wanted to know what had happened. I told them I'd fallen asleep. They didn't believe me, but was that any less believable than me being picked up by a German submarine? I felt terrible about lying and it probably showed. My mates looked in my boat and saw that I had no fish and, more to the point, no fish boxes either. I saw them looking at each other, puzzled, trying to work out why that would be. They knew something had happened but I also knew they'd never guess what, not in a million years. I made my apologies, pulled my boat up onto the beach, and let the wife drive me home. I am a man of honour who kept his word. But I left that beach feeling like I'd betrayed my country, that I was a traitor.

'The following day the liner *Niagara* was sunk by German mines in the approaches to the Hauraki Gulf. Just inside the Mokes. It took fourteen souls with it when it went down. Fourteen!' Mack buried his head in his hands again and his shoulders heaved suddenly as though he was sobbing. I didn't know where to look.

'They thought it was the work of a German Raider — one of them heavily armed cargo boats — but I knew better. I knew exactly who and what had laid those mines. I felt

responsible for the deaths of those poor souls who went down
with the ship. The next day I climbed up Mt Tataweka and
watched minesweepers working to and fro across the Gulf. It
was too late. The damage had already been done. My forty-
eight hours passed but I still didn't tell anyone about the
submarine. I was too ashamed. I never told anyone about it.
After the war I learned that a troopship had left for Europe
the same day that I saw the U-boat. Some said it was the
Queen Mary. I knew then what had been the U-boat's real
target. That was why it had been sent all the way down to
New Zealand. Just think: my silence could have cost the lives
of thousands of young men. Jesus Christ! Imagine having that
on your conscience. You talk about a burden of responsibility,
young fellow, but put that in your pocket and see how it feels!'
He turned away from me, his eyes brightly rimmed with red.

'I'm sorry,' I said, though I wasn't exactly sure what I was
sorry about. It upset me to see Mack so distressed, but I also
had to consider the possibility that Mack had betrayed his
country, that he'd placed his obligations to the enemy above
his duties to God, King and the entire British Empire. I was
torn between supporting Mack, my friend, and my own
sense of what was right. I felt guilty for thinking Mack
should've told the policeman straightaway. Yet that would
have meant breaking a promise, and you had to be a pretty
poor type to do that. On top of everything was a feeling of
disappointment. Mack had been picked up by a German U-
boat, and I'd expected a *Boy's Own Annual* story with Mack
emerging as a hero. I hadn't expected a moral dilemma. Some
of Mack's guilt settled on me.

I noticed his glass was empty so got up and fetched a
bottle of Lion Red from his cooler. He took it from me

without a word. I could see by his eyes that he was miles away. I sneaked away down the passage, out the front door and home. My mum was a bit anxious because I hadn't come home when I'd said I would. I told her Mack had been telling me fishing stories and that I'd got carried away.

That night we sat around the radio listening to *Take it From Here* with Jimmy Edwards and an episode of *The Day of the Triffids*. I loved John Wyndham stories but couldn't concentrate because my head was full of Mack's story. I couldn't stop thinking about it. I wanted to write it down, but even then I sensed that the story was incomplete and unbalanced. I started thinking of ways to extend it and give it a better ending, one that let Mack off the hook. I didn't want my story to end with Mack a traitor.

A couple of days later, the school broke up for the May holidays and I was free to write Mack's story. But, once again, I had to take up my burden of responsibility. I didn't consult Mack because I didn't know how to face him or what to say. Besides, the high tide was at three o'clock and I knew it was best to fish two hours either side of it. The butcher sold me skirt steak because he was out of liver and claimed it was dynamite bait. I wasn't happy about that. Nevertheless, Mum was counting on me to catch dinner so I set off on my old Rudge bike that had no gears, a back-pedal brake and a front brake on the handlebars. I thought about Mack's story as I pedalled to the breakwater, trying to picture it as a movie and what would have happened next if the story had gone on a bit. It used to annoy my pals went we went to the matinee at the Esquire Cinema because I could nearly always guess what would happen next. They reckoned I ruined the serials for

them. But that skill seemed to desert me as I thought about
Mack's story.

My hopes plummeted when I unwrapped the bait the
butcher had sold me. I couldn't believe it. It was nearly all fat
and everyone knew snapper hate fat. My spirits sank even
further when I started to trim it. I was left with about a third
of the amount of bait I needed. What could I do? I baited my
hooks, cast out as far as I could and hoped for the best.

It's often quite cold in May but this day was an exception.
There were no clouds for the sun to hide behind and the sea
had that flat, oily look it gets when there's no breeze. They were
exactly the sort of conditions Mack always claimed were good
for fishermen but bad for fishing. Once again, it seemed that he
was right. The tide came in but didn't bring any fish with it, at
least none that were tempted by my fatty bait. I left the strips of
meat out there until they turned grey, rebaited and tried again.

A bloke I knew by sight set up on the wharf along from
me. He was using strips of trevally for bait but wasn't having
any more luck than me. I started thinking about Mack's story
and, because of the combination of sun on my back and lack
of activity on my line, got right into it. I remembered how
the German officer had asked about Great Barrier Island and
become wistful as Mack had described it. The 'what ifs' began
to scroll through my mind. The last words the German officer
had spoken were, 'Go home. But you must go slowly.' That
was good, but what if he'd said, 'Go home, Mack. Maybe one
day, when this war is over, we'll meet again.' My heart leaped.
I knew I was onto something. That's what the German
would've said if it had been a movie. My mind raced with
possibilities. Of course! They had to meet up again after the
war. But how? When?

'Want the rest of my bait?'

I jumped. I nearly dropped my fishing rod. I was so deeply immersed in my imagination I hadn't heard the other fisherman come up to me. He'd packed up and was leaving.

'Nothing out there,' he said. 'But if something does come along, I reckon you'll do better with trevally than you will with the meat you're using. What happened to your liver? You usually use liver.'

I thanked him for the trevally and again silently for bringing me back to reality and reminding me of my obligations. I had fish to catch for tea. I had to put Mack's story out of my mind.

My first cast with trevally was productive. I brought in a small snapper. It was undersized but I kept it. I tucked it into the cotton flour bag Mum had given me to put the fish in. I caught another the same size with my next cast and kept it as well. All I needed was another two or three and I could go home and write. But the school the two baby snapper had come from had moved on. It went as dead as a dodo. I changed baits and directed my next cast inshore. I tried to concentrate but I couldn't stop my mind returning to Mack's story and the wonderful options that were opening up. Maybe ten minutes later, while my mind was ablaze with possibilities, something hit my line. My rod doubled over and line fizzed off my reel despite the fact that I'd set a fairly heavy drag. I was late striking because I hadn't been concentrating. And I paid the penalty. The line stopped running out and went limp. I nearly screamed with frustration. It could've been a big snapper, could've been my first kingfish, and I'd missed it through not keeping my mind on the job.

I cast again and wound up the slack as soon as my sinker hit bottom. Bang! Talk about a strike! This time I was ready and hooked up. I knew straightaway that this fish was a good size, the sort you expect to catch way out in the Gulf on the *La Rita*. I was so scared of losing it I didn't dare play it. Against all the rules I tightened the drag and winched it in. The snapper still had plenty of fight in it when I began to lift it out of the water. It wouldn't stop thrashing its tail about. I would've given anything for a gaff but I'd never owned one, and didn't even know if they made them seven foot long — just over two metres by today's reckoning — which was how far I had to lift the fish to get it onto the wharf. The line snapped just as I swung the snapper over the edge of the wharf and, mercifully, the fish's momentum carried it onto the planks. Even so, I had to dive on it to stop it skidding back into the water. I dragged it away from the edge towards my tackle box, grabbed my knife and shoved the blade up through the gills into its brain, the way Mack had taught me. The snapper stopped flapping, but there was no way I could. I was shaking with excitement. The snapper was a good four pounds, a muscular two kilos, what Mack called the perfect size. I was absolutely ecstatic.

I didn't waste time trying to fit it into my flour bag because I realised there had to be a school going past and I fancied my chances of catching another. I re-rigged, cast again and hooked up immediately. Unbelievable, when you think how slowly things had begun. The fish took off on a run that I thought would never end. It headed inshore and I had to walk with it to save line. When it turned, I had to walk back the way I'd come, past my tackle box, right to the far edge of the wharf. I'd thought the four-pounder was big but this was the four-pounder's great-grandfather. This was a Mack special. I had no choice but to play it. I slackened off the drag to make sure the fish had no fight left before I brought it up near the piles. I could afford to be patient because I already had the four-pounder and I was all too aware of the chances I'd taken with that one. So I concentrated on bringing in the fish to the exclusion of everything else. I never gave Mack's story a thought while I was reeling it in, never thought about anything but catching that fish.

When I got it up to the surface where I could get a good look at it, my eyes just about bulged out of my head. It was huge, and I realised my only hope of landing it was to climb down the pilings and somehow lift it from the water with my bare hands. I lowered myself onto one of the crossbeams and lay along it on my belly. It seemed to me the snapper had pretty well fought itself to a standstill and was beginning to wallow in the water. I lifted the tip of my rod so that it lay on its side, and gently drew it towards me. The fish was so big I was almost scared of it. But I could also see my mum's delight, hear my dad's congratulations and feel my brothers' envy. I could also feel Mack's proud hand on my shoulder.

The snapper spread its gill case and I struck. I got my hand inside its gills and lifted. But the moment I felt its weight I knew I was in trouble. The fish was far too heavy and I was lifting left-handed, lying on my belly, balanced on a wet crossbeam. The snapper settled the issue. It kicked convulsively and the gill case cut deep into the fleshy bottom part of my index finger. I let the fish go, heard the line snap, felt the splash and watched my prize snapper spiral away down to the bottom to recover. I was devastated. But worse was to come.

When I climbed back up onto the wharf, my four-pounder was nowhere to be seen. I panicked. Someone had stolen my fish! I couldn't believe the injustice. Tears started forming in my eyes. But then gulls screeched by the covered walkway onto the jetty and I realised immediately what had happened, who the culprits were. I dashed to the walkway and there, to my enormous relief, was my snapper, poised half on and half off the wharf. I dived on it for a second time, just as it was about to topple over. My fish was no longer the beautiful thing I'd pulled from the water. The gulls had pecked at its gut and taken both of its eyes. It looked like a ghost fish.

I decided to pack up. The four-pounder stretched the flour bag to its limits. I tried to hang the bag from my crossbar as I usually did, but the fish was so big it interfered with my pedalling. In the end I wrapped the top of the bag once around the handlebars and clung onto it. It was awkward but I managed. The excitement of catching and losing the big snapper had died away, and I'd got over the fright the gulls had given me. Once again I started thinking about Mack's story and what should happen next. Once again I became engrossed with the possibilities. I'd never tried to develop such a complex story before and my head was spinning.

I was aware of the Ford Prefect coming towards me as I was about to make a right turn but didn't give it another thought. My mind was a giant movie screen with actors trying out dialogue. I automatically moved to the centre of the road and prepared to slow down to let the Ford Prefect pass by. But because I was holding the bag of fish, I only had my little finger left to apply the front brake and I couldn't pull the lever hard enough. I immediately tried to brake by back-pedalling. As I jammed down with my left leg, my right leg came up. The snapper's fins, which had burst through the cotton of the flour bag, impaled themselves in my calf. The pain was instant. In trying to pull my leg free, I pulled down on the handlebars. The next thing I knew I was sprawling on the road. I remember my fish going flying and trying to save my fishing rod. I remember a squeal as the driver of the Ford Prefect hit the brakes and swerved. The wheels missed me but got the fish.

The driver was a young woman and she was shaking like a leaf as she helped me to my feet. She saw blood on my shorts and burst into tears, but that was old blood from the finger the snapper had cut. There was blood on my leg but that was from where the fins had jabbed me. I'd lost a bit of skin off my knees but I was always doing that. I picked my bike up and it seemed all right, picked my rod up and was relieved to find I hadn't broken it. The snapper hadn't fared quite so well. Its brains were splattered all over the road.

The young woman offered to drive me home but there's nowhere on a Ford Prefect to put a bike. I convinced her I was fine and rode off with my scraped knees and flattened fish. I'd put on a brave face but in truth I was distraught. My beautiful fish, my four-pounder, was ruined.

Mum thought otherwise. Sometimes she could amaze me. She washed the fish and made me fillet it and remove the broken bones in the ribs. She made me slice the fillets into chunks. I did the same with the two small snapper. Mum fluffed up the squashed bits with her fingers and cooked the fish pieces in breadcrumbs, as though they were fish fingers, and made chips to go with them. My dad and brothers thought that was the best snapper they'd ever eaten. They never suspected the fish had been mauled by seagulls and then run over by a car.

Mum had saved the day when I thought all was lost, and now I had to do the same for Mack. Unfortunately, I'd promised my pals I'd go down to Grey Lynn Park with them the following morning to play soccer and there was no way I could break my promise. Nowadays kids break promises all the time and think nothing of it. Back then a promise was binding, a test of character to which God was witness. I got stuck into Mack's story after soccer, as soon as I'd washed and changed and had lunch. Everything I'd thought about out on the breakwater and riding home came back to me. I could see the German officer, I could feel Mack's wariness, I could hear the dialogue as though it came straight off the silver screen. For reasons that will become apparent, I don't have a copy of the story I wrote, but this is sort of how the ending went and that's the important part. The dialogue was pure Saturday-afternoon matinee, but the last couple of lines were BBC radio drama. I remember feeling quite proud of them.

It's 1953. Early morning. Mack is launching his boat from Medlands Beach. He feels someone watching him. He turns around and sees a man step out from the shadows of a centuries-old pohutukawa tree. The man has an eye-patch. (An eye-patch! Well, I was only twelve.) And he walks stiffly with an obvious limp.

'Good morning, Mack,' he says. 'It seems we meet again.'

It is only when the man speaks that Mack realises who it is. He is stunned speechless, too shocked to feel revulsion or anger. Here is the man who caused him to betray his country. The German holds out his hand but Mack refuses to take it.

'You!' says Mack finally. 'How dare you come back here! Keeping my promise to you cost the lives of fourteen men.'

'I don't understand,' says the German.

'Your mines. They sank the *Niagara*. Fourteen men went down with her.'

'*Niagara*?'

'Don't pretend you don't know. It sank right in the mouth of the Gulf.'

'I'm not aware of sinking any boat in the Gulf. But even if I did, it was war, Mack, and they were my country's enemies.'

'They were my countrymen,' says Mack bitterly. 'You killed them. I betrayed them.'

'Do you remember my name?' says the German suddenly.

'Of course,' says Mack. 'How could I forget it?'

'Then say it.'

'Christian Berger.'

'That's right,' says the German. 'I am Christian Berger from Germany, you are Mack from New Zealand, and we are no longer enemies.'

'Perhaps not,' says Mack. 'But I can't forgive you for what you made me do.'

'Your promise changed nothing,' says Christian Berger.

'What do you mean?' says Mack.

'If I had decided to shoot you and sink your boat, would that have saved the *Niagara*? If I'd taken you prisoner, would that have saved those men?'

'I don't suppose so,' says Mack reluctantly.

'My priority was to keep the presence of my U-boat a secret. I didn't take you prisoner because there is no room on a U-boat for prisoners. By rights I should have shot you. But when you asked for diesel in exchange for your fish I didn't have the heart to do it. You presented me with another alternative, provided you were a man of honour. Mack, I made a judgement that you were the kind of man I could trust, a man who would keep his word. I gambled with the lives of the fifty men on board my U-boat. I gambled fifty lives to save one life. Your life. Think about that. And you should also consider the fact that there is no certainty that I caused the loss of the fourteen men aboard the *Niagara*.'

'What do you mean?'

'A submarine is an inefficient means of laying mines. There is no room to carry them. The German Navy had two Raiders operating in New Zealand waters in 1940. The *Orion* and the *Komet*. They were equipped to lay mines. We carried a grand total of three, which, I admit, we released. But we were not sent down to New Zealand to lay mines.'

'No, you were sent to sink the troopship. That's right, isn't it?'

'Ahh . . .'

'My silence could've cost the lives of thousands of young men.'

'No, Mack, that is not true. When we found you in your boat we knew it was already too late. We knew the troopship had already sailed and we had no hope of catching up with her. If the troopship hadn't sailed, do you think for one moment we would have let you go?'

Mack is stunned by this revelation.

'So you'd already given up?'

'Yes, we were on our way back to the Atlantic. We needed the forty-eight hours to get clear.'

'And you didn't sink the *Niagara*?'

'No one will ever know, Mack. But what are three mines

against the hundreds laid around the Gulf by the Raiders? The chances that it was one of our mines are very slim.'

Mack slumps against the side of his boat. The German reaches out to steady him.

'Are you all right?'

'Yeah,' says Mack. 'I'm fine. It's just that for the last thirteen years I've been blaming myself for the loss of those men.'

'It was not your fault, Mack.'

'No?'

'No.'

Mack looks ruefully at the German.

'Those fish I gave you, did you enjoy them?'

'The fish? Yes, they were wonderful.'

'How'd you like to come out with me and catch some more?'

'I would love to. I admit I came here hoping you would ask. But I will only come with you on one condition.'

'What's that?'

'You let me pay for the diesel.'

I couldn't write down those last lines fast enough. The moment I finished the story, I raced around the corner to read it to Mack. I found him out in his backyard, on his old chair between the tomatoes and gherkins, having a beer. I pulled up a beer crate and began reading. Mack hung on every word.

'Read it again, son,' he said when I'd finished. 'This time read it more slowly.'

So I read it again. When I'd finished, a smile had spread across Mack's face. His eyes were closed as if picturing every detail.

'Like it?' I asked.

He nodded and opened his eyes. They were shining.

'It's a good story,' he said. He put down his beer and began rubbing his hands together. It was a funny thing to do but I think it meant that he was pleased. He couldn't get the grin off his face. I could tell my story had got to him just as my essay had got to my pals.

'It's better than good,' said Mack. 'It's really good. And you know something? I reckon you've hit on something there. I reckon that's how it could've happened. Yeah, that's how it could've happened.'

'I wrote the story for you,' I said.

Mack's face lit up in the biggest smile I'd ever seen, as though I'd done him the greatest favour.

'You wrote it for me?' He reached across and reverently took the pages from my hand. He held them and stared at them as though they were something really precious. 'Thank you, son,' he said. 'Thank you very much.' He carefully folded the pages and tucked them into his shirt pocket.

I realised then that he'd taken my words literally and that I'd never see my story again unless I wrote another copy. But looking at Mack and seeing the happiness I'd brought him, I knew I never would. It was Mack's story and Mack was entitled to keep it. As much as I wanted to read it to my mother and my pals, I realised I'd read it to the only person who really mattered. Mack's burden of responsibility had been lifted.

I was only twelve years old but I was as proud as I'd ever be.

Educating Pinky

It was one of those Mexican mornings when dogs disappeared, when you could drive through any one of a hundred dry, dusty villages and not hear a single bark; when old trucks refused to start on principle and, if they did, would only overheat anyway. It was under these dead trucks, in the dark cool beneath the oil- and dust-coated undersides, that the missing dogs could be found, lying motionless on their sides, tongues lolling, tolerating the flies that crawled into ears and nostrils because it was too hot to object.

It was no less hot in the marina at La Paz where Captain Pete waited for his drunken, suffering and, doubtless, abjectly apologetic crew to return from a night off. The sun had bludgeoned the water around the quay to stillness and the mirror-flat surface amplified both glare and heat. There wasn't even a suggestion of a breeze, nothing to cause ripples or bring relief, and no hint of the storm that had kept them in port for the past four days. The bait fish, which lived in the marina and found sanctuary in the weeds and barnacles beneath the floating arms of the pen, had also disappeared, forsaking their refuge for the cooler waters down deeper where they ran the risk of being swallowed by marauding *pargo*. One by one, the fish in the live-bait tank attached to the outer arm of the pen gave up and switched to backstroke. Captain Pete was not amused. He scooped up one of the dead fish and tossed it towards a pelican sheltering in the shadow cast by his boat. Being a pelican in Mexico was a highly competitive occupation and normally the bird would have seized greedily upon the offering. This time it swallowed the fish reluctantly as though doing a favour.

The boys' non-appearance disappointed Captain Pete even though he knew better. He accepted that, no matter how much time he spent in Mexico, he would never understand the way Mexicans think and had given up trying. His skipper, XR, was as conscientious and loyal as a man could be, and his deckie, Chuy (rhymes with coo-ee), had been chosen because he possessed the same qualities. Captain Pete knew without question that both XR and Chuy would do anything he asked of them. So when the boys gave him their assurances that they would be back by dawn, ready and capable of beginning the six-hundred-kilometre crossing to Puerto Vallarta on the west coast of mainland Mexico, he had believed them and granted them shore leave on that basis. Their assurances and promises were made in good faith and they had insisted they valued their jobs too highly to put them in jeopardy. Captain Pete never doubted that. But that was then and this was now, and between the two points in time a hot night of passion and tequila had intervened. This was also the second time in three weeks that the boys had failed to return before the scheduled departure time. The captain had dismissed their earlier transgression as a product of their youth and natural exuberance, but the repeat performance following so closely on the first spoke of a pattern and a wilful disregard for authority.

Captain Pete occupied his time and attempted to dissipate his frustration and disappointment by rigging up a makeshift awning over the rear deck of his Salthouse 62. Already it was too hot to walk over in bare feet. There was no real reason for the awning because there was no reason for him to step outside of the air-conditioned cabin, other than that he was too irritated to sit still. He checked his watch. Again. By rights they should be fifty kilometres out to sea, making the most of the conditions, out in the open in a breeze or creating one of their own with their passage.

He glanced along the quay but there was still no sign of his boys. Calling them 'boys' was a term of affection because neither was a boy any more. XR was twenty-six and Chuy was twenty-four. But they was a his boys and he didn't want to dismiss them because he'd grown both fond and protective of them, and he knew they'd be very difficult to replace. He paid them well and treated them well, which made their transgression even harder to understand. It was a question of respect and trust. But in the back of his mind was the advice he'd been given when he'd first brought a boat down to the Sea of Cortez.

'This is Mexico,' a gritty old sea-dog from Fort Lauderdale had told him. 'Different rules apply. Down here, intention has a looser affiliation with action. To get by you need patience and tolerance by the bucketful. Don't try for understanding or you'll only get confused.' The old man had sailed into the Sea of Cortez thirty years earlier, come to terms with the place and never left.

There were other issues preying on the captain's mind, which he'd hoped to negate with an early departure. If the conditions were good for him, they were also good for the *pangeros* who ran drugs over to the Baja Peninsula, and for the Armada de Mexico — the Mexican Navy — which was out on patrol trying to intercept them. Sometimes the *pangeros* transferred their illicit cargo from their long but basic open boats to high-speed offshore cruisers, mostly Cigarette, Danzi and Fountain boats, which ran the drugs straight up the west coast of the Baja to California. Captain Pete didn't want *For Pete's Sake*, his Salthouse 62, mistaken for one of them. On occasions the Mexican Navy had been particularly heavy-handed in their treatment of *gringos* in game boats, and many an owner had sweated a week or two in a Mexican gaol while misunderstandings were resolved. Captain Pete sympathised with the navy and the difficulties of their job, but nonetheless he was anxious to avoid any entanglements.

He decided to put on a video. Just the thought of putting on a video brought the first faint smile of the day to his face. The boys loved videos. Captain Pete reckoned they could hear the whir of the take-up mechanism from a kilometre away. Sometimes the lure of the video proved even stronger than a come-on from the sweet-faced *chicas* who worked in the hotels around the marinas. If anything could get the boys back it was the video. The captain wished he'd thought to put it on earlier. He was about to go inside when he heard the quay security door open. He looked up, fully expecting to see the boys, and saw armed sailors instead. He groaned and ducked quickly inside his cabin, hoping he hadn't been noticed.

It wasn't unusual for naval officers to inspect and search boats on marinas, though it had never happened to him before. They searched for drugs, but also for places quantities of drugs could be hidden: secret storage areas behind false panelling, between bulkheads and in the gaps between the inner and outer skins. The penalty for having a boat capable of concealing drugs was almost as great as being caught in possession of drugs. Captain Pete thought of all the supplies he had on board and the prospect of opening every box and container, and hoped that the naval detail would pass him by.

His spirits, already low, sank further when he heard the firm knock on his cabin door. He cursed XR and Chuy and thought of ways to punish them as he slowly made his way aft to greet his visitors. No videos, not for a month. That, he decided, would be a fitting punishment, one which would hurt the boys and which no power on earth could prevent him from enforcing.

'*Buenos dias, senor*,' said the lieutenant. '*Americano*?'

'Australian,' said Captain Pete. 'American resident. Please, come in out of the heat.' Why not invite them in, thought the captain, why not be courteous? They were going to board him anyway. The lieutenant introduced himself but made no mention of the three ratings accompanying him.

'You have a very beautiful boat,' said the lieutenant, taking in the detail of the timber panelling and trim, the carpet and furnishings. 'Like a *hacienda*, like a beautiful house. American?'

'Kiwi,' said Captain Pete. 'It's a New Zealand boat.'

'Very beautiful. It is so good in here, so cool. So hot outside.'

'Can I offer you refreshments?' said Captain Pete. 'Coke?' He regretted saying 'coke' the instant the word left his lips.

'Not Coke,' said the lieutenant.

'Beer?'

'I see you have some tequila. Very fine tequila.'

'With ice?' Captain Pete took his bottle of fifty-year-old Grandfather tequila down from the rack, half-filled two tumblers with ice and poured a ten-dollar shot into each. He wasn't sure whether the lieutenant was a connoisseur of tequila or simply an opportunist but either way he couldn't afford not to be generous.

'*Salud*!' said the lieutenant.

'*Salud*!'

Captain Pete watched as the lieutenant first sniffed his glass before reverently taking a sip. Seeing the lieutenant afford his tequila the respect it was due made the captain feel better. At least it was appreciated.

'You are leaving La Paz this morning?'

'Yes. For Puerto Vallarta then south to Ixtapa and Zihuatenejo. Provided my crew sober up long enough to remember and put down their *chicas*.'

The lieutenant liked that and translated for his underlings. They all smiled. They understood *chicas* and the necessity of occasionally going AWOL. They liked the fact that the *gringo* understood, too, though technically Captain Pete was Australian and therefore not a *gringo*.

'Please, now my men will search your boat. It is our duty.'

Captain Pete noticed that the tequila had vanished from the lieutenant's glass. When had that happened? He topped it up immediately.

'This is very fine tequila,' said the lieutenant. 'Will you accompany me while I look around your boat?'

'Sure.'

The lieutenant ordered his men out of the stateroom so he could appreciate it at his leisure. He did the same in the guestrooms. His men could not get out of the lieutenant's way fast enough.

'You are a rich man,' said the lieutenant.

'Rich enough, I guess.'

'One time we found the walls of a boat like this boat jammed full of twenty-dollar bills, American twenty-dollar bills, counterfeit American twenty-dollar bills. They were printed here in Mexico. Did you get rich carrying counterfeit American twenty-dollar bills?'

'I wouldn't know what counterfeit bills looked like.'

'They look just like real bills.'

Of course they did. The captain made a mental note not to try any further levity.

'Do you carry drugs?' asked the lieutenant.

'Drugs? No,' said Captain Pete. 'Not now, not in the past and not in the future. They get in the way of fishing.'

'Fishing.' The lieutenant opened the rod locker and looked over the businesslike array of rods, turned to his men and ordered them back onto the quay. He put his empty glass down delicately on the dining table. 'Thank you for your hospitality and good luck with the fishing.'

Captain Pete saw the officer to the door and out onto the quay. When he finally returned to the cabin and closed the door behind him he became aware that his shirt was soaked with sweat that had nothing to do with the heat of the sun. He'd got off lightly and knew it. If the lieutenant had been so inclined he could have forced him to unload the boat and let them strip it bare. He knew of boats that had been impounded on suspicion of being used in drug-running or simply because the officer in charge was having a bad day. He poured himself another ten-dollar shot of tequila to settle himself down, knowing full well he'd pay for it later once the boys got back and they put to sea.

'I hope you've got a good excuse.'

It was eleven o'clock and the captain's relief at having the boys back, safe though worse for wear, had tempered his anger. Whatever they'd been doing they'd obviously had all the pleasure they could handle. They looked exhausted.

'It's not our fault, *patrón*,' said XR. He could barely keep his bloodshot eyes open.

'Then whose fault is it?'

'The cow, *patrón*. It is the fault of the cow.'

Captain Pete knew better than to believe a word XR said but was irresistibly drawn to hear him out. XR's excuses often lacked credibility but never originality.

'I take it the cow was the *chica*'s mother?'

'No, the cow was a cow. I decided to drive down to Cabo to see my wife and so Chuy could see his girlfriend.'

'I thought Chuy's girlfriend lived in La Paz?'

'Not that girlfriend, *patrón*. The sister of my cousin's boyfriend.' He held his hands in front of his chest as if supporting huge breasts. 'That girlfriend.'

'Of course.'

'On the way back a cow walk out in front of my car. It is a miracle, *patrón*, a miracle I did not hit it. It is a miracle I am not standing here dead.'

XR only had two speeds and surviving a drive with him was the real miracle.

'So you didn't hit the cow.'

'No, *patrón.*'

'So not hitting the cow made you late?'

'Yes, *patrón*. Because we did not hit the cow, we ended up in the desert. Sand up to our axles, *patrón.*'

'I see.'

'We had to wait for the *campesino* to bring his truck and pull us out. The truck did not want to start. On days like this, *patrón*, it is a known fact that old trucks do not want to start.'

'Okay, okay,' said Captain Pete. He'd heard enough. 'We leave in half an hour. You and Chuy take a shower. You reek of booze and cheap perfume, the same cheap perfume Chuy's La Paz girlfriend wears. It doesn't go well with bullshit.'

'*Si, patrón.* Though I am sad you don't believe me. I tell you the truth.'

'Mexican truth.'

'*Si, patrón.* Mexican truth.' XR started laughing.

Captain Pete decided to take down the temporary shade while the boys showered. In an hour they would clear Isla del Espiritu Santo and the Bay of La Paz. The boys would apologise and repay his forgiveness with a hundred small kindnesses. That was the Mexican way. Then everything that had happened that morning would be forgotten.

Captain Pete took the helm once Espiritu Santo had dropped astern so the boys could finally get some sleep. Dots on his radar revealed the presence of large vessels and occasionally he glimpsed the threatening grey silhouettes of the Armada on the horizon. The important thing, he knew, was to do nothing that might arouse interest and set a course gun-barrel straight for Mazatlan. From Mazatlan they could troll down the line of the drop-off to Puerto Vallarta. In the sluggish sea, with four thousand litres of fuel and one thousand litres of water aboard, *For Pete's Sake* cruised easily at twenty knots. Twenty knots was comfortable, economical and fast enough without attracting attention.

Having ascertained there was no traffic on an intersecting course, he let the boat run on autopilot and went down to the galley to make himself a turkey burger. As an afterthought he left out four buns and four pieces of turkey to thaw. If past patterns were anything to go by, the boys would sleep for two hours, awake ravenous and eat, sleep for another two hours, eat, and so on until they'd recovered. He took Carl Hiaasen's latest novel back up onto the bridge with him. He needed a good laugh.

Captain Pete was a third of the way through his book and doing one of his periodic checks for *pangas* and whales when XR spoke.

'Look, *patrón*, ahead to the left.'

Captain Pete looked where XR was pointing. All he saw was a slight disturbance on the surface, the sort caused by bait fish.

'Packages, *patrón*.'

'Packages?' Captain Pete focused his binoculars on the disturbance and sure enough saw something that looked like the tips of packages. It never ceased to amaze him how Mexicans could be fast asleep one second, then wake the instant before something happened. Sometimes it was the moment before a whale broached in their path, or a marlin jumped, but whatever it was, their instinct or sixth sense made sure they rarely missed it.

'Slow down, *patrón*, I think we should take a look.'

'Okay. Where's Chuy?'

'He's gone downstairs to get the gaff ready.'

The captain shook his head. The boys' instincts were obviously unaffected either by excesses of tequila or sleep deprivation.

'I think a *panga* has sunk, *patrón*,' said XR worriedly. 'Maybe it tried to outrun the storm, hit a big wave and sank.'

'What are you saying?'

'Marijuana, *patrón*. I think those packages are marijuana.'

'If it's marijuana we're not stopping.'

'But, *patrón*. Maybe the *pangero* is clinging onto the packages.'

'Okay. Tell Chuy we're stopping but we're not stopping to pick anything up.'

The bales were now clearly visible less than fifty metres off the port bow. Captain Pete had never seen bales of marijuana before but they looked exactly as he'd imagined they would look.

'But, *patrón*, it might also be cash.'

'Cash?' The captain recalled his conversation with the lieutenant.

'Someone has to bring back the cash. We assume the *panga* was heading west with drugs but who's to say it wasn't heading back east with cash?'

Or west with counterfeit greenbacks.

Captain Pete throttled back. In the conditions, drawing alongside the bales was a piece of cake.

'Any sign of the *pangero*?'

'No, *patrón*. There is no one clinging to the packages.'

Captain Pete slipped the engines out of gear. Though quietly anxious to see what the bales contained, he walked slowly aft with XR, pretending to show no more than a passing interest. By the time they'd joined Chuy at the stern, the deckie had already cut through the canvas and plastic liner of the nearest bale and had brought a couple of plastic-wrapped packages on board.

'Chuy! What are you doing?' XR reached down to Chuy's feet and grabbed the packages.

Chuy looked baffled. He thought he was only doing his job.

'*Drogas*! We never bring *drogas* aboard!' XR held both packages at arm's length over the side.

'I look inside,' protested Chuy. 'You say maybe dollar.'

'Let him look,' said Captain Pete.

Chuy took one of the packages and split it open with his knife.

'Marijuana,' said Captain Pete. 'Okay, ditch it and let's get out of here.'

Chuy threw both packages over the side.

'Look how much, *patrón*, do you know how much this is worth?'

'Yeah, the rest of my life in a Mexican gaol. Yours, too, XR. Now let's get moving.'

'I'm not arguing with you, *patrón*. Maybe this is a trap, maybe the Armada is watching us on their radar.'

'Tell Chuy to wash his hands. I don't want him patting any sniffer dogs.'

The sun was less than a hand's width from the horizon when Captain Pete returned to the bridge and engaged gear. He checked the radar image on his video plotter. The naval vessels were still at the outer range of his radar and none appeared to have changed course to intercept them. He breathed a sigh of relief. The bales of marijuana had slipped behind. God only knew what the boys got up to in port but he knew they had enough sense not to bring any marijuana on board, ever. Captain Pete found his thoughts drifting eastwards towards the unseen shore. Somewhere over there, a desperate family was in mourning for a lost *pangero*, or a mother was grieving the loss of a wayward son. That was worth remembering too.

The following morning Chuy retied traces, sharpened hooks and cleaned out the tackle drawers. The boys were eager to begin fishing along the line of the drop-off but Captain Pete was just as eager to press on south. Somewhere behind them, XR's Ford was on the ferry from La Paz to Mazatlan where the father of XR's cousin's boyfriend would take delivery and drive it down to Barra de Navidad. Another of XR's extended family and retinue of friends had been teed up to drive it down from Barra to the marina at Ixtapa. There was always someone who wanted to be where they needed the car. How XR knew who wanted to be where and who to contact was a total mystery to the captain. He just accepted that was the way things worked in Mexico and left the arrangements to XR. Captain Pete needed the car in Ixtapa so he could pick up his wife, Peggy, who was flying in for some fishing but mostly to spend some time with him. Captain Pete was fortunate that Peggy liked Mexico and was also a keen fisherman.

They spent the night in Puerto Vallarta where they refuelled and took on water, then fished all the way down to Barra de Navidad for one blue marlin and a wahoo. More bait fish showed up on the fish finder the further south they went and, just as importantly, fewer ships of the Armada de Mexico appeared on their radar. Captain Pete had not been able to put the marijuana out of his mind even though he knew he had nothing to fear.

They spent the night at Barra de Navidad before leaving at first light for the four-hundred-kilometre last leg of their journey. They took their time and fished, knowing they weren't due to take up a berth in the marina at Ixtapa until the following day. They caught three yellowfin tuna, including one that ran over one hundred kilos and held them up for more than two hours. Captain Pete didn't mind. He was in his element. Nothing cleared the mind faster than an extended arm wrestle with a raging yellowfin. When they finally cruised up the channel into the marina they were surprised to find it full to capacity. When Captain Pete and XR reported to the marina office they were even more surprised to discover their pen had been given to someone else.

'You were expected four days ago, *senor*,' said the manager. 'What was I supposed to do?'

'But, my man, I rang to say we were delayed by the storm,' said Captain Pete. 'I called from La Paz to tell you. I rang again from Puerto Vallarta.'

'You did not speak to me, *senor*,' said the manager.

'No, I spoke to a *senorita* — what was her name? Mina or Mimi.'

'Maybe you speak to Mirla.'

'That's it, Mirla.'

'You should have spoken to me, *senor*.'

'You weren't around so I spoke to Mirla. She said she'd tell you and that everything was okay.'

'But everything is not okay, *senor*. Mirla had no right to tell you everything is okay when you can see for yourself that everything is not okay.'

'But she took my reservation.'

'But you have no reservation.'

'But I made a reservation.'

'But you have no reservation.'

'XR, maybe I'm not making myself clear. Could you please explain to the manager in Spanish that I made a reservation with Mirla.'

'He knows that, *patrón*, but there is no reservation. Maybe you should have spoken to the manager, then we would have a reservation.'

The captain sighed. This was a road he'd been down many times before. Patience and tolerance, patience and tolerance.

'Could you please ask when we can have a reservation?'

'You can have a reservation in three days' time, *senor*.'

'See? No problem, *patrón*,' said XR. 'We have a reservation in three days' time. How long do we stay?'

'Six weeks,' said Captain Pete. 'But there is a problem. Where do we spend the next three days?'

'You can't stay here,' said the manager. 'You have no reservation.'

'I think we've established that.'

'You want a mooring,' said the manager.

'That'll do it,' said Captain Pete. 'I'll have a mooring.'

'Unfortunately I have no mooring to give you,' said the manager. 'If I had a mooring I would most certainly give it to you.'

'I appreciate that,' said the captain without any obvious trace of sarcasm.

'But my brother's wife's brother has a mooring off the beach at Zihuatenejo which his cousin isn't using.'

'I'll take it.'

'I'll tell my brother,' said the manager. He reached across his desk and shook the captain's hand. 'Next time you talk to me, okay? That way no problems.'

'Okay,' said Captain Pete. 'Thank you. Oh, and when you see Mirla, give her my regards.'

'Okay,' said the manager. Privately he was wondering why the *gringo* wanted to pass on his regards to his cleaner.

'How about that?' said XR on the way back to the boat. 'We have a reservation and now we have a mooring. Our luck is holding, *patrón.*'

The following morning Captain Pete awoke to find the bay bustling with pleasure craft and the beach already alive with people swimming and jogging. Stallholders were setting up in the markets behind the beach. It would have been a glorious morning if he hadn't also awoken to find someone had stolen his tender.

'XR! Do you want to tell me what's going on?'

'*Patrón?*'

'Where's the tender?'

'It's over by that yacht, *patrón.* See? The third yacht past the big pontoon with all the pelicans.'

The bay was so crowded with craft it took Captain Pete a moment or two to work out which yacht XR was pointing at.

'What's it doing over there?'

'It is taking people ashore, *patrón.*'

'I can see that. What I want to know is why.'

'Why? It is taking the people ashore because they want to go ashore. How else are they going to get ashore? They have no tender.'

'So you lent them my tender?'

'No, *patrón*.'

'Then what is it doing over there, XR?'

'Last night you said you want to go ashore, so this morning Chuy and I lowered it into the water.'

'And?'

'Someone took it.'

'You mean someone stole it.'

'No, *patrón*. Not stolen.' XR smiled indulgently as though dealing with a child. 'If the tender was stolen it would be miles away by now, but you can see for yourself that it isn't.'

Captain Pete glanced out of the window and saw his tender heading flat out for the shore with four raggers aboard, driven by a pencil-thin kid with a baseball cap on backwards.

'Jesus Christ, XR, if he doesn't slow down he's going to rip the bottom out of it.'

'Don't worry, *patrón*, Pinky knows what he's doing.'

'Pinky? Who the hell is Pinky?'

'Pinky is Pinky, *patrón*. Look out the window. You can see for yourself who Pinky is.'

'He's a kid with his head on backwards. What I want to know is, what's he doing driving my tender?'

'He is taking people ashore, *patrón*.'

Captain Pete watched as Pinky throttled back and gently skidded the tender into the sand. So much for his fears of the boy ripping the bottom out. The kid was good.

'Now what's he doing?' The captain watched as his tender turned on its axis, leapt up onto the plane and raced away from the beach with its outboard motor revving to the maximum.

'See that Azimut, *patrón*?' XR pointed to a massive new cruiser. 'There are people waiting on the stern for Pinky to take them ashore.'

'Jesus Christ, XR! What's the kid doing? Running a taxi service?'

'Yes, *patrón*. He is running a taxi service to all the boats.'

'You're kidding me.'

'No. Why would I kid you?'

'Why doesn't he use his own boat?'

'Pinky doesn't have a boat.'

'So how does he run a taxi service?'

'He has your boat.'

'Who gave him permission to use my boat?'

'No one gave him permission, *patrón*. Pinky just took it.'

Why? Because he didn't have a boat of his own. Captain Pete gave up in the face of such irrefutable logic. XR had given him all the answers except the one that really mattered, and he hadn't a clue how to phrase the question in a way that didn't begin another circular debate. XR didn't seem at all bothered and the captain had learned from experience that if XR wasn't bothered there was no reason for him to get upset either. Nevertheless, he couldn't help feeling irritated and used. He beat up some yellow-coloured powdered egg whites and made scrambled eggs and tried not to think of sunny yolks, strips of bacon, hash browns and greasy sausages, which had been his morning fare before his heart attack had changed the rules. Now he ate carefully, drank moderately and worked out in gyms and at sea with hand weights and a step machine. He didn't feel like a man in his mid-sixties or like someone who'd dodged a premature exit, and was proud of the fact that he was fitter than most men half his age. He splashed some *salsa picante* into his pan of scrambled egg. This, plus his one dry piece of toast, was part of the price he paid for continued health. Outside, Pinky broadsided his tender beautifully so that it barely nudged the Azimut's swim platform. The kid was good, really good.

Captain Pete showered after breakfast and dressed for shore in shorts and a short-sleeved linen shirt he'd bought from a shop on the Ixtapa marina and had only ever worn once in Peggy's presence. Peggy had a great eye for style and it was fair to say the captain did not share it.

'So tell me, XR, now that Pinky has appropriated our tender, how do we get ashore?'

'No problem, *patrón*.'

XR stepped onto the stern deck, put two fingers in his mouth and whistled. The captain saw his tender execute the sharpest high-speed turn he'd ever witnessed and come hurtling towards them. Pinky's two passengers were still rubbing their necks when the tender nudged gently against the stern. Captain Pete stepped down into the inflatable followed by XR.

'*Hola*, Pinky,' said the captain.

'*Hola*,' said Pinky. He had the widest grin the captain had ever seen. When he opened his mouth, he had the biggest buckteeth the captain had ever seen.

'I want my tender back.'

'*Playa*?' said Pinky, indicating the beach.

'*Muelle*,' said Captain Pete, indicating the quay. 'And I want my tender back.'

Pinky's response was to gun the throttle. In deference to the fact that he was ferrying the owner of the tender, he made straight for the quay instead of the beach.

As soon as Captain Pete saw the barnacle-encrusted piles and steps he knew he'd made the wrong call. No matter how hard Pinky ran the tender up onto the beach, it was preferable to pulling in at the quay. The shells were like razors and the slightest misjudgement would consign them to spending the rest of the day mending punctures. But Pinky made no misjudgements and brought the tender to a spectacular halt, centimetres from the step. The captain stepped gingerly ashore followed by the other two passengers who slipped Pinky some coins. XR followed.

'Now you pay Pinky, *patrón*.'

'Why? It's my boat. Why should I pay to use my own boat?'

'If you don't pay Pinky, *patrón*, he won't pick us up later and take us back out to the boat.'

'The hell he won't.'

'*Patrón*, put yourself in Pinky's position. Why would he take you out to the boat if he knows you won't pay him?'

XR had a point.

'How much?'

'Five pesos.'

He gave Pinky five pesos.

'*Gracias, senor*,' said Pinky and flashed his buckteeth.

'You're a pirate,' said the captain.

Pinky laughed. 'Don't worry, be happy,' he said. He laughed again, slipped the gear into reverse and powered away from the quay.

'XR, you didn't tell me he spoke English.'

'Who? Pinky? No, *patrón*, Pinky doesn't speak English.'

'He does. I heard him.'

'No, *patrón*, that is all the English Pinky knows. He learned it from that plastic fish that sings, you know, Big Mouth Billy Bass.'

Captain Pete paid five pesos to return to his boat and, in response to a plea from XR, another five pesos for Pinky to take Chuy ashore.

'Chuy wants to see his mother, *patrón*.'

'Don't give me that. Chuy's mother lives in San Jose Del Cabo.'

'Not that mother, *patrón*. His mother in Cabo is only the mother who lives with his father. His mother lives here in Zihuat.'

It was only the captain's fascination with Mexican machinations that stopped him from walking away.

'Give me a break, XR. How can Chuy have two mothers? Nobody has two mothers.'

'Lots of people have two mothers, *patrón*, some people even have three.'

Captain Pete groaned. He knew immediately that he'd gone one question too far. He also knew that XR would have his way and that Chuy would have the night ashore. He also knew there was about as much chance of Chuy spending the night with his mother — either of them — as there was of him getting his tender back off Pinky. Chuy had a *chica* in Zihuat and a plastic bag full of prime yellowfin tuna with which to impress her.

'My cousin's number-one girlfriend has three mothers,' said XR, warming to his explanation. 'There is the mother

who lived with her father before she was born, the mother
who lived with her father when she was born, and the
mother who lived with her father after she was born. Her
father was a game-boat skipper, *patrón*, he had women all
around the Sea of Cortez. He was a real mother —'

'Don't say it.'

'What? All I was going to say was he was a real mother of a
fisherman. The best.'

'Tell Chuy to give my best wishes to his mother.'

XR laughed and relayed the captain's blessing in rapid
Spanish.

'*Gracias*, patrón. *Buenas noches.*' Chuy was all dressed in his
neatly pressed best. He also knew the outcome of the
discussion was a foregone conclusion.

'Get out of here, Chuy.'

'You won't regret it, *patrón*,' said XR. 'And *patrón*?'

'What now?'

'Maybe we watch a video tonight?'

'You know, *patrón*, I would like to be called Antoine. I think
Antoine is a good name. A good name for the *chicas*.'

Captain Pete opened one eye. He'd slept through most of
the movie and couldn't remember anything about it other
than that it featured a character called Antoine and XR was
much taken with the name. From time to time XR was
much taken with many names. That was something else that
was in his genes.

He liked to be known as XR but his real name was
Ezzard. His father had named him after the famous boxer,
Ezzard Charles. It was the sort of thing his father did. He'd
named XR's brother Omar after the actor Omar Sharif, his

other brother Dustin after the actor Dustin Hoffman and his sister Sophia after Sophia Loren. God only knew what the siblings would have been called if their father had been inspired by *Planet of the Apes*.

XR also liked to be called Scorpio and The Penetrator — a name inspired by the movie *Terminator*, but more accurately reflective of his exploits ashore. He didn't like being called *El Gordo*, or Fatty, even though the nickname accurately reflected his physique. It was not a good name for the *chicas*. Not like Antoine.

'So, Antoine, did you like the movie?'

'No, *patrón*. It was crazy. I think we should have watched *Snatch*.'

By the captain's count, XR and Chuy had watched *Snatch* at least fifteen times. Chuy didn't speak much English but between them they could recite entire scenes. Chuy wasn't Chuy's real name, either. His real name was Jesus, which contracted to Chucho and then to Chuy. Chuy was comfortable with Chuy and didn't want to change. The captain didn't think it a bit strange that the two Mexicans could recite scenes from an English movie in ripe Cockney accents.

'Tell me about Pinky.'

'Sure, *patrón*, what do you want to know?'

'Why is he called Pinky?'

'*Patrón*, how can you ask this question? You have seen his teeth. You have seen Senor Pinky on TV.'

Senor Pinky was a rabbit on kids' television.

'Okay, I got it,' said Captain Pete. 'What's Pinky's real name?'

'Arturo Fernando, but everyone calls him Pinky except when they call him *El Rapido*.'

'*El Rapido*, huh? The fast one. That fits. How old is he?'

'I don't know, *patrón*. Even Pinky isn't sure but we think that he is twelve.'

'Why isn't he at school?'

'School, *patrón*? Pinky does not go to school.'

'Why not?'

'Pinky doesn't like school.'

'Most kids don't but they still have to go. What do his parents say about him not going to school?'

'Pinky doesn't have parents. He has a mother some place, but not even his mother knows who his father is.'

'So who takes care of him?'

'We all take care of him but mostly Pinky takes care of himself. You'll like Pinky, *patrón*.'

'I'm not going to like him if he keeps borrowing my tender.'

'No problems. Pinky is very democratic. Next time he will borrow someone else's.'

'Has Pinky ever been to school?'

'For two days. I told you, he didn't like it so he didn't go back. They tried to find him in Zihuat to make him go back to school so he got on a boat to Isla Grande. When they look for him at Isla Grande he got on a boat to Acapulco.'

'Can he read and write?'

'Of course not. How can he learn to read and write if he doesn't go to school?'

'How indeed,' said Captain Pete.

When he retired to his cabin his thoughts kept drifting back to the skinny kid in the backwards baseball cap, his infectious grin and improbable buckteeth. Despite the fact that Pinky had commandeered his tender, he couldn't help liking him. By the time he'd cleaned his teeth and completed his stretches, he couldn't help feeling the kid deserved a better chance.

The following day was devoted to preparing the Salthouse for Peggy's arrival. While the boys washed down the boat and wiped away the salt crust that had accumulated during their crossing from La Paz, Captain Pete vacuumed the interior, dusted, polished and took two bags of washing ashore to the laundrette. Pinky ferried him to the quay and the captain had to admit the boy provided an impressive service. On the return trip with the clean laundry, he bought Pinky a chicken *quesadilla* and a Coke, figuring the boy could do with a little fattening up. The mooring was only four hundred metres from the quay and, even travelling at top speed, Pinky managed to dispose of both food and drink during the brief journey. Captain Pete had never seen anybody eat so fast. It distressed him to think how hungry the kid was.

He gave Pinky his five pesos and told him to wait, called to XR who was up for'ard cleaning the railings and asked him to come aft.

'Ask Pinky if he wants to eat with us tonight.'

XR passed on the invitation and Pinky's extravagant smile conveyed his answer. The kid rattled off some Spanish and both he and XR burst out laughing.

'What was all that about?' asked Captain Pete as Pinky roared off to ferry someone else ashore.

'Pinky said it is good you ask him to eat with us tonight. Now he won't have to go to the AA meeting.'

AA meeting? Alcoholics Anonymous? The captain's jaw dropped open. The kid was only twelve years old.

Instinctively he knew there'd be more to the story than was immediately apparent and he was already helplessly hooked on needing to know what. Pinky was dirt poor, but he wasn't a drunk and he certainly didn't earn the money to support a drug habit. More Mexican quicksand beckoned but the captain couldn't leave it alone.

'You're saying Pinky goes to AA meetings?'

'Yes, *patrón*. Often.'

'Why? Does he have a drug problem?'

'No, *patrón*. Pinky doesn't have a drug problem. He doesn't drink and he doesn't do drugs. He just tells them that he does.'

'Why would he do that?' Captain Pete braced himself for the answer. 'Why go to an AA meeting and admit to a problem he doesn't have? It doesn't make sense.'

'Of course it makes sense, *patrón*. He goes for the supper. They always serve supper after a meeting. Pinky says it is the best food in Zihuat.'

That evening Captain Pete took six kilos of yellowfin fillet from the fridge and cut it into steaks. When he spread the steaks over the cutting board it looked as if he was feeding the Armada rather than himself and the three boys. He also measured out four cups of rice even though none of the rice was for himself. His continuing good health also depended on him cutting down on the fast carbs — rice, potato, pasta and bread. He cut up some broccoli and carrots to steam over the rice.

In truth he didn't expect XR, Chuy and Pinky to eat all the fish and rice in one sitting, although experience had taught him never to underestimate the volume of food the boys could put away. Their normal pattern was to each eat enough for three people and then eat whatever was left in snacks throughout the night. They tended to sleep the sleep of the dead but only in two-hour sessions. In between sleeping, they'd chat, watch TV and, of course, raid the fridge. By cooking more food than was necessary, Captain Pete also catered to the midnight snacks. Even so, six kilos of fish and four cups of rice was a mountain of food. Captain Pete was an expert in cooking fish in the electric frypan using Pam, an oil substitute. The boys didn't need more fat in their diet, and once they'd smothered the fish and rice in *salsa picante* certainly didn't miss it.

When Pinky arrived it was obvious he'd showered, slicked his hair down with hair oil and somehow conjured up a clean T-shirt and shorts. XR and Chuy were watching the video of *Snatch* and the poor kid was torn between watching the video and looking at the mountains of food Captain Pete was cooking. In the end it was no competition. The food won hands down.

When Pinky sat down at the table he was ravenous, but also shy and uncertain of the protocol. When both XR and Chuy waited for the *patrón* to serve himself, he did likewise and held back. He watched as XR and Chuy heaped rice onto their plates and topped the rice with two large pieces of tuna. He did exactly the same and waited to be handed the bottle of *salsa picante*. Between them the boys emptied half the bottle. None of them had the slightest idea of the restraint Pinky had shown until XR told him to start eating.

Pinky's inhibitions dissolved instantly. The piece of tuna he put into his mouth would have choked any other mortal but Pinky disposed of it as though it were a mere titbit. Captain

Pete looked on awestruck, his fork frozen halfway to his mouth. He'd never seen anyone's jaws move as fast as Pinky's. They reminded him of one of those machines that grind up and swallow branches and other garden waste. Pinky's Adam's apple bobbed up and down like a champagne cork caught in a jacuzzi. He didn't eat his meal so much as demolish it. Even XR and Chuy looked stunned by the onslaught. Pinky had finished both fish and rice before the captain was even a quarter of the way through his meal and XR and Chuy barely halfway through theirs.

Neither captain nor crew said a word, probably for the same reason. They didn't want to embarrass the boy. XR and Chuy cleared their plates and waited politely while Captain Pete finished his meal. This was one of their conventions. Captain Pete finished and invited the boys to help themselves to seconds while he retired to the stern for a quiet tequila. Watching the boys demolish the remainder of a meal was not something he chose to witness twice.

'XR,' said Captain Pete. 'Tell Pinky to help himself if he's still hungry.'

Pinky's eyes lit up as XR relayed the message. He took the offer literally and, instead of helping himself to another two pieces of fish, dumped all the remaining pieces onto his plate. Captain Pete's jaw dropped in amazement. The kid had already eaten enough for two grown men. Clearly he intended to eat enough for six. But if Pinky thought he was going to get away with this manoeuvre, XR soon put him right. Both XR and Chuy had been forced to compete with their siblings for food when there was precious little on offer.

'Hey!' said XR, and in the rattle of Spanish that followed any misunderstandings were cleared up and the pieces of fish redistributed evenly. XR served the rice to prevent any further misunderstandings. Captain Pete watched the proceedings glassy-eyed. The image he couldn't get out of his mind was of Pinky taking all the remaining fish, all two kilos of it, and Pinky's obvious conviction that he could eat it all plus whatever rice he could get his hands on. The captain didn't just take a glass of tequila out onto the stern deck with him, he took the whole bottle. Some days, one drink just wasn't enough.

Pinky slept on the boat that night. Through occasional partings in the veil of sleep, the captain was aware of the boys' intermittent chatting and the soft sound of their TV turned down low. He was also aware of the pitter-patter of feet on the stairs between decks and the sound of the fridge door opening and closing, opening and closing, opening and closing . . .

Peggy was an excellent traveller. She had the ability to do the red-eye flight down from San Francisco to LA, endure the two-hour stopover and the four-and-a-half-hour flight to Zihuat and arrive looking as fresh as if she'd just fallen out of the pages of *Vogue*. Captain Pete had no hesitation in arranging to eat out after he'd safely moored the Salthouse in the Ixtapa marina and picked Peggy up from the airport. After feeding Pinky the night before, he figured he needed professional help.

Pinky arrived at the marina just before sunset, this time without having showered first, slicked down his hair or changed. He'd come straight from ferrying his last paying passenger from beach to boat. He probably hadn't eaten all day and not had any time off other than the waits between fares.

'So this is Pinky,' said Peggy. She and the captain were sitting out on the stern deck, enjoying the cooler air of evening and a frozen margarita each. When she was hooked onto a fish, Peggy could look very much the tomboy in fishing shorts and shirt, no make-up and a cap chosen for protection rather than style. But she wasn't fishing and, although she'd changed into plain linen trousers and a delicate green Italian T-shirt, she still looked very much the *patrona*.

'Pinky,' said Captain Pete, 'come and meet Miss Peggy.'

But Pinky had already seen Peggy and put her in the same category as all the elegant women he ferried to and from the Azimut and Hatteras cruisers in Zihuat Bay and didn't dare speak to. They were from another world. He busied himself mooring the tender and coiling the loose end of the rope. Tall, matchstick thin and wearing his shy smile, Pinky looked tired, vulnerable and lost.

'He's embarrassed,' said Peggy. 'Let him shower and change before you introduce me.' Whatever Captain Pete had seen in the boy that made him open his heart and his fridge, she saw too. Without knowing how, and regardless of the consequences, she wanted to help him. 'XR, does Pinky have clothes he can change into? Does he need soap or a towel?'

'Pinky has a clean shirt and shorts from last night. I will get him a towel. When we go out you won't recognise him.'

They went to Tia Maria's, Aunt Mary's, because the restaurant specialised in *huachenango*, which was one of the few things on his diet that Captain Pete could get genuinely enthusiastic about. *Huachenango* consisted of a *pargo*, or snapper, which had been split down both sides of its spine and all three pieces — fillets and backbone — coated in

Mexican spices and barbecued. It was hot, spicy and invariably cooked to perfection so that the fish's firm white flesh was still moist while the surfaces exposed to the flame were crisp. The only drawback was the expense. Captain Pete and Peggy decided to begin with fish soup and share a *huachenango* between them. The boys knew enough to order something else.

Pinky studied the menu, which was a total mystery to him because he'd never seen a menu before, never sat in a proper restaurant before and couldn't read anyway. He sat quietly while the boys read out the names of the different dishes. They asked if he needed help but Pinky declined, saying he understood just fine.

His tortillas with a combination of fillings arrived at the same time as Captain Pete and Peggy's fish soup. His seafood soup arrived with XR's and his enchiladas at the same time as Chuy's. Pinky finished all three courses in the time it took the others to complete one course.

The waiter brought Pinky's *pozole*, a soup with refried beans, polenta and pork garnished with jalapenos, radish, oregano and chilli powder, while Peter and Peggy waited for their *huachenango* and the boys for their fried chicken and rice. Pinky finished his *pozole* just as the fish and fried chicken arrived, which was just as well because their waiter needed the table space for Pinky's fried chicken.

Captain Pete had a lot of things to discuss with Peggy and hadn't been paying much attention to what the boys ate but he became suddenly aware of the procession of dishes that had found their way to Pinky.

'XR, what's going on here? How many meals is that Pinky's had?'

'I don't know, *patrón*. Do you count the first course as a meal? A first course is not a meal.'

'To keep things simple, yes.'

'In that case, *patrón*, let me see. I think five meals.'

'Five!'

'Oh hush, Peter,' said Peggy. 'He's a growing boy. Let him finish his chicken in peace.'

'Peggy,' said Captain Pete, 'you have no idea what you're dealing with here.'

Pinky finished his chicken in peace and just in time for the steak.

'Who is that for?' said Captain Pete.

'Pinky,' said XR.

'Don't you think he's had enough?'

'I don't know, *patrón*. I'll ask him.'

Pinky actually stopped eating momentarily during the rapid exchange of Spanish that followed. XR and Chuy burst out laughing.

'What did he say?'

'Pinky didn't know he had to choose from the menu, *patrón*. He thought the menu was just a list of dishes they were going to bring him for dinner. He thought that is what happened in restaurants. He thought he had to eat everything on the list.'

'My God,' said Peggy. 'What if we hadn't stopped him?'

'We'd have to sell the boat to pay for dinner,' said Captain Pete. 'XR, get hold of the waiter and tell him no more dishes.'

'Okay.' XR spoke to the waiter and established that it was already too late to cancel two of the dishes, because they had already been prepared.

'Okay,' said Captain Pete. 'Two more dishes. That's all.'

Pinky ploughed his way through a fried fillet of fish and a dish of boiled chicken and potato. To his credit, he never hesitated with either dish and never slowed down.

'I don't believe it,' said Peggy. She thought Pinky was hysterical. 'He must have worms.'

'Better believe it,' said Captain Pete. The waiter had just given him the bill. 'Pinky's eaten more than the rest of us put together.' He turned to the kid. 'Pinky, you're a bandit and a pirate.'

'*Gracias, senor*,' said Pinky. Captain Pete could have moored all sixty-two feet of his Salthouse in Pinky's wide, bucktoothed smile.

Captain Pete rose shortly after dawn, pulled on his shorts, a battered T-shirt and his joggers. Both he and Peggy were keen to go out fishing but not before he'd fulfilled his obligations to his health by running a few kilometres. He ran out through Ixtapa and up the hill towards Zihuat, turning at the billboard that marked the halfway point in his run. By the time he got back to the marina the sun had well and truly risen and his shirt was drenched with sweat. As he walked the last hundred metres he noticed Pinky out past the Salthouse gazing in obvious awe at another boat. Captain Pete couldn't resist going up to him to see what was so fascinating. His brow furrowed as he drew near.

The boat Pinky was interested in was not the kind of boat Pinky should have anything to do with. It was long and slim like a *panga*, but more than twice the length, and its hull, rather than being homemade, was state-of-the-art. The boat was powered by three of the biggest outboard motors the captain had ever seen, all of which were fitted with competition props. There was a game-fishing chair fitted just forward of the motors and an array of rod holders on a chromium rollbar over the centre console. Captain Pete didn't know who the fishing equipment was intended to fool but couldn't imagine it fooling anyone. The boat would probably cruise at seventy-five knots and had been built for only one purpose.

'*Hola*!' said Pinky.

'*Hola, El Rapido*,' said Captain Pete.

'*El Rapido*,' said Pinky. He pointed to the three outboards. '*Muy rapido*!'

'*Si*,' said Captain Pete.

Pinky pointed to the game chair.

'*Pescadore*.'

'You've got to be kidding. No fisherman, no *pescadore*.' Captain Pete racked his brain for the words to communicate the true purpose of the boat. '*Drogas*,' he said. 'Marijuana.'

'*Drogas*,' said Pinky. '*Si, muy rapido*.'

Captain Pete realised that Pinky had known all along that the boat was used for running drugs, and not just marijuana but probably cocaine. What concerned him was Pinky's fascination with the craft, a fascination bordering on lust. Offered the chance to skipper it, Pinky would not refuse, regardless of what the cargo might be.

'*Malo*!' Captain Pete said vehemently, the Spanish word for 'bad'. He spat into the water to show his disgust. 'Come, we've got to go.'

Pinky dragged himself away reluctantly.

XR wanted to power straight out to the seventy-kilometre mark where the water was deeper and the current warmer, and the captain decided to give XR his head. Peggy wanted a blue marlin and out wide was the most likely place to find one. About twenty minutes out from port, the captain made himself a weak black tea and strolled out onto the rear deck. He found Chuy and Pinky tying doubles.

'Hey, Chuy,' he said, 'when did Pinky learn to tie doubles?'

'We show him last night, boss.'

'You showed him last night?' The captain was impressed. Pinky wasn't just providing an extra set of hands but was at the business end completing the knot. 'Fast learner.'

Later, when he went up onto the bridge, he found Pinky at the helm with XR explaining the autopilot and the video plotter. He stood back quietly and unnoticed, watching as Pinky dialled up changes of course and flipped the radar between short, medium and long range. He watched as Pinky played with the fish finder and pointed out the red patches indicating bait fish. He was even more impressed when XR passed Pinky the handheld GPS unit and the kid figured out how to use it and cross-referenced the numbers on the GPS with the position on the video plotter. The fact that Pinky had no formal education and couldn't read or write didn't appear to be the slightest handicap. The kid was as sharp as a boxful of hooks. Captain Pete realised then what he wanted to do and slipped quietly downstairs to discuss his idea with Peggy.

'I want to send Pinky back to school,' he said.

'But you told me Pinky doesn't like school,' said Peggy.

'He doesn't.'

'So why would he stay in school? What's to stop him running away again?'

'No one's ever given him an incentive to stay, certainly not an incentive that's meaningful to him.'

'Oh?' said Peggy.

'What if I promise to take him on as a permanent crew member if he stays at school for two years and learns to read and write?'

'Oh, Peter, that's a great idea. But where will he live? How will he earn money to keep himself?'

'I've got no idea,' said the captain. 'But I tell you what. I guarantee there's a Mexican solution.'

The captain waited until they'd put out the lines and XR had come downstairs to raid the fridge before telling him his idea. Chuy and Pinky were both up on the bridge keeping a lookout for marlin.

'No problem, *patrón*,' said XR. 'Pinky can stay with my wife. He can go to school at Cabo. I will build another room on my house.'

'If Pinky agrees and stays with your wife, I will pay someone to build another room on your house.'

'It's a deal,' said XR. 'I was planning to build another room anyway.'

The captain smiled. Like most adult Mexican males, XR was always almost ready to build another room. That was the way houses were built in Mexico. As soon as families saved up enough money, they put in foundations. When they saved up some more, they built a room. Then, as more money came along, they built more rooms. Mexico was full of incomplete houses, and even when the owners had as many rooms as they needed, their houses still looked incomplete, with steel reinforcing jutting up out of columns as though awaiting the construction of a second storey. This had baffled Captain Pete for a long time until XR had pointed out that the government levied a completion tax.

'No one pays the completion tax,' said XR. 'Why pay completion tax when you can build on another room for the same money? That's why houses are never completed.' XR's house was awaiting the construction of a third room but XR kept finding other uses for his money.

'Do you think Pinky will like the idea?'

'Maybe, *patrón*. Let's ask him.'

They found Pinky with his eyes glued to the video plotter, avidly following the progress of a dot on the screen. Either the triple-engined drug-runner had left port or another just like it. Captain Pete realised at once that Pinky also knew what the dot represented and kept glancing back to the video plotter while XR spoke to him.

'Pinky is very grateful for your offer,' said XR eventually, 'but he says he wants to think about it.'

'What's to think about?'

'He doesn't like school.'

'Did you tell him I guarantee him a job after two years?'

'Yes, but two years to Pinky seems like a long time.'

'Did you tell him that if he learns to read and write he could skipper a boat like this one day?'

'Sure I told him that.'

Pinky's eyes were fixed firmly on the video plotter. The dot was closing fast.

'Isn't that what he wants?'

'Sure, *patrón*, Pinky wants that.'

But Captain Pete wasn't sure that was what Pinky wanted at all. The kid now had his face glued to the window, paying rapt attention to the boat whizzing past them less than half a kilometre away.

*   *   *

Peter and Peggy accomplished what they set out to achieve by going out to the deep water. Both caught and released blue marlin over one hundred and fifty kilos, and caught two more yellowfin to restock the larder. It was one of those rare days when everything went according to plan. XR let Pinky take the helm when they held the marlin by the bill and retrieved the lures. The kid handled the big boat like a veteran.

On the way home, Peggy decided to take on the responsibility of persuading Pinky to return to school. While Captain Pete and Chuy took turns at the helm, she sat down with Pinky and, with XR as interpreter, showed the kid how to write his name. Pinky was in awe of Peggy and gave her all his shy attention. He wrote his name over and over, filled with amazement and delight at his prowess. Peggy showed him how to write her name and XR's and he loved writing XR's name more than his own. He loved the brevity and the shape of the letters. Gradually and seemingly without any pressure, she sweet-talked Pinky into accepting the captain's offer. He agreed to go to school for two years and agreed to stay with XR's wife at Cabo.

Peggy was jubilant and so was XR, though privately he thought Pinky would have agreed to jump off the boat into the jaws of a shark if Peggy had asked him to. Pinky was probably more than just a tiny bit in love with her. He was overwhelmed that such a fine woman would talk to him and take an interest in him. It was something he'd never expected to happen. Of course he agreed.

When they motored back into the marina they had to pass by the stern of the drug-runner. The look on Pinky's face did not fill Captain Pete with optimism.

* * *

Two weeks later, Peter and Peggy returned to their home in San Francisco, to their business and the normality of everyday life with its myriad obligations and irritations. Peter, who was only ever referred to as Captain Pete in Mexico, sent money down to XR so he could begin work on a room for Pinky. When he spoke to XR on his mobile he was concerned to learn that Pinky had run off.

'Pinky has borrowed somebody's tender and is ferrying people to and from their boats in Zihuat,' said XR.

'Does he come back to eat and sleep?' asked Peter.

'No, *patrón*. He has gone back to living how he always lives.'

'What about school?'

'He says he will come back when you come back.'

'I won't be back down for three weeks.'

'Then Pinky will be back in three weeks, *patrón*. No problem.'

'I hope you're right.'

XR went looking for Pinky the same day Captain Pete arrived back in Zihuatanejo. He found him in the yard of a fisherman, working on a *panga* that had come to the end of its life. But the fishermen were preparing the *panga* for one last high-speed crossing of the Sea of Cortez, with a new outboard motor provided specially for the occasion. Most *pangas* were sunk along with their motors as soon as they were unloaded so there was nothing left for the *Federales* to find. The fisherman was risking everything in the hope that the crossing would earn him enough money to build a new *panga* so he could continue to support his family. Pinky left with XR, but reluctantly.

The captain stayed down in Mexico for two weeks and even did a run up to Puerto Vallarta and back, as much to keep Pinky entertained as to catch fish. One night, while they were transiting between ports, Captain Pete went up to the bridge to relieve XR and found Pinky with his eyes glued to the video plotter, watching tiny dots zip across the sea from near Mazatlan to the Baja Peninsula.

Before returning to San Francisco, Captain Pete gave XR more money and told him to speed up work on Pinky's room.

Things can happen quickly, even in the land of *mañana*, when sufficient inducements are offered. On the way to taking *For Pete's Sake* north to safe harbour in San Diego at the start of the cyclone season, XR took Pinky over to Cabo and enrolled him in school. The timing was perfect as far as Captain Pete was concerned because there was little opportunity for Pinky to run away. Few skippers were prepared to take the risk of crossing the Sea of Cortez when a cyclone could hit with little warning.

He rang XR whenever he knew XR was in Cabo to check on Pinky's progress. He was heartened to learn Pinky was still attending school and had fitted in well with his family. But not all the news was good. Pinky was in a class with kids little more than half his age and often less than half his height. In the shame of his predicament, Pinky alternated between desperation and working twice as hard as anyone else to try and reduce his promised two years' schooling to one. He wanted to honour his obligation to Miss Peggy and

Captain Pete. But inevitably, as so often happens in Mexico, intention and action went separate ways and, one day, Pinky failed to return from school. He'd found a boat crossing the Sea of Cortez to Puerto Vallarta and talked his way on board.

By swapping notes with other boat owners, Captain Pete and XR kept tabs on Pinky's movements and eventually tracked him down running people back and forth to their boats in Acapulco. He was thinner than ever. With lashings of food and kind words they persuaded him to return to school and even crossed back to Cabo for that specific purpose. All the way over, Pinky kept his eye on the video plotter, watching for the high-speed boats that fuelled his fantasies. Consequences didn't figure in these fantasies, just the water rushing beneath the hull, the wind in his hair and the thrill of speed.

Pinky ran away from school for the last time just three weeks after Captain Pete and XR delivered him back to Cabo. Now, whenever the captain and XR cross the Sea of Cortez at night, they can't help watching the fast blue dots on their video plotter and wondering if Pinky has finally realised his dream. At the back of their minds are the bales of marijuana they'd found out at sea and the life that was lost there. Whenever they motor down to Zihuatenejo Captain Pete deliberately moors out in the bay for a night or two in the hope of waking up and finding his tender missing.

The Evil Within

'Mr Wallace! Mr Wallace!'

Six o'clock in the morning and our driver, Charlie, was banging on our door. I think the Sumatran sun does a workout every morning because it's already hot and sweaty before it clears the rim of the hills.

'Mr Wallace!'

Alongside me Abby groaned. We were each pretending to be more asleep than the other. It was dare versus double-dare because whoever answered the door would also have to make tea and probably breakfast as well.

'Mr Wallace!'

The sun was making beautiful patterns in the dark, stark, alien room. Shafts of brilliance had cut between ill-fitting wooden slats and defined themselves in airborne dust, our own laser light show reaching high into the rafters. I hoped the sun had also snuck in under the eaves and was giving the bats hell.

'Mr Wallace!' More urgent.

'He wants you, darling.' Abby's voice, heavy, sleepy and phony as all hell.

'Why not you?' I said, miffed. Our bed consisted of two unsprung mattresses over unyielding floorboards and I hadn't slept well. 'Don't answer,' I said, beating Abby to the obvious. If Charlie had wanted Abby he would have called 'Mrs Wallace'. Bare feet hit wooden floor. Muscles complained. Hands parted the mosquito net. The mattresses were barely ten centimetres thick and packed tight with stuffing.

'Hang on, Charlie. Give the door a rest.'

The thumping stopped. Charlie seemed to sleep most of the day, which was probably why he had no trouble getting up at the crack of dawn. Charlie wasn't Charlie's real name nor was he just a driver. He was our guide, our shepherd, our interpreter, our bodyguard, courtesy of the Research Institute for Food Crops. Truth be told, we were more his than he was anything ours. We were his responsibility and, for our entire sojourn in the Minangkabau highlands of Sumatra, his property. Charlie got whatever sleep he needed curled up in his van.

Theoretically, the door I was about to open was three hundred years old. I figured it must have been replaced once or twice, though certainly not in this century. It had an amusing Hammer Films horror-movie squeak as it opened.

'Mr Wallace —'

'Charlie, we have a deal, okay? You call me John and you call Mrs Wallace, Abby.'

'Yes, John.'

'Thank you.' I was about to close the door and crawl back into bed when I realised there had to be another reason for opening it beyond giving Charlie lessons in familiarity. My mind was as foggy as my eyes were bleary, but finally circuits made connections. 'Charlie, why are you holding my wallet?'

'Tombstone founded it on the road. He see your poto in your passport. He giveded it to me.'

Tombstone was the water-buffalo man, but Tombstone wasn't his real name either. I nicknamed him Tombstone because he was always smiling, scrunching up his old wrinkled-prune face and flashing his pride — his single tombstone-like front tooth. He looked about eighty hard years old, stood no more than a metre and a half tall and wouldn't have weighed thirty kilos in a monsoon with a bellyful of rice. Tombstone spent his life up to his thighs in mud and water-buffalo shit ploughing rice paddies. His buffalo weighed as much as a medium-sized tractor but Tombstone could make it turn on a five-cent piece. I think he could have made it sit up and beg if I'd asked. He was the happiest man I'd ever met and always found something to smile about. I wished I had his talent. At that precise moment I couldn't have cracked a smile if Bob Hope had been standing on my doorstep. I was even immune to the Sumatran sun. It could do nothing about the chill in my veins or the icy hand that had wrapped around my bowels. I could distinctly remember tucking my wallet under my pillow as I lay down to sleep.

'How did my wallet get on the road, Charlie?'

'Maybe someone droppeded it, John.'

'Okay. But who droppeded it?' At the beginning we'd thought it cute the way Charlie kept past-tensing his past tenses. We hadn't realised quite how infectious it could be.

Charlie hesitated, unsure how to ask. 'Maybe you droppeded it?'

'No, Charlie, I didn't droppeded it. I put this wallet under my pillow last night. You understand? Under my pillow.'

'You didn't droppeded it? Then how it get droppeded on the road?'

Indonesia has around three hundred different languages and cultures and you have to be patient in all three hundred of them. I noticed a crowd had gathered. They were all watching to see what happened. You get used to not noticing crowds in Indonesia because crowds always gather. Stop to tie your shoelaces and you'll draw a crowd.

'Charlie, I don't know how it got droppeded on the road. Let me look inside it, please?'

I opened my travel wallet fearing the worst. But there was my passport. There was my Amex card, my Amex traveller's cheques, my Visa card, my gold driving licence, my entry/exit immigration card, various receipts and business cards. Now the test. I unzipped the back of the wallet and didn't even have to count to know that the wad of American dollars and rupiah within was untouched. That brought no joy. It didn't solve the riddle but added to it. Only made things more scary. Who would sneak into our house, steal my wallet but not rob it of its contents? Who was so sure of themselves that they would leave it on the road outside, certain that it would be returned to us? Someone was flaunting his power, sending us a message. But who? And why?

'Charlie, I would like to talk about this later. Okay?' Charlie nodded. All Indonesians are good at talking about things. Before radio and television, talking about things was their principal form of entertainment. Up in Minang country, it still is. 'I'd like to thank Tombstone for returning my wallet. He deserves a reward.'

'Tombstone does not ask for a reward.'

'I insist. How much is fair?'

'One tousand.'

One thousand rupiah was roughly fifty cents US, which meant Tombstone would get twenty-five cents for his honesty. I'd already learnt that go-betweens took a commission, which was always a source of negotiation and dispute with the deemed receiver. Fifty per cent seemed common for a go-between, but basically they kept what they thought they could get away with. I wanted to ensure Tombstone got his 'tousand'.

'Two tousand,' I said, which put me four hundred and ninety-nine dollars ahead of where I might have been, not counting the traveller's cheques. I deliberately handed Charlie two one-thousand rupiah notes, one of which seemed to crawl up his arm and into his shirt pocket of its own accord. I waited until the other had found its way to the little man with the heroic tooth, and accepted his beaming gratitude. One thousand rupiah is a lot of money to a man who drives a buffalo for a living. I closed the door behind me. Its groan seemed to mock, sinister and no longer amusing. I tossed up whether or not to tell Abby before deciding it was just the thing she needed to wake her up.

'You mean somebody came in here and stole your wallet just to let us know that he can come again whenever he likes?'

'Do you have a better explanation?'

Abby sat with her arms around her knees, pulling them hard up against her chest. Any other time she would have looked endearingly waif-like. Instead she just looked scared.

'He could have gone through my things.'

'Yes, and he could have taken our heads off with a *parang*.' I wished I hadn't said that but rifling through a bag of undies didn't strike me as the greatest threat to our wellbeing. Abby hugged her knees more tightly, as though cold. 'Fact is, he did neither.'

We stared at our *nasi goreng*. The cold egg yolks stared balefully back. We didn't normally start the day with chilli fried rice, but corn flakes no longer seemed appropriate. Well, you don't go to Rome and not eat pasta, do you? Besides we could live for a week on the price of a single packet of Kellogg's.

'What are we going to do?'

'I'll speak to Charlie, he'll speak to the village headman and they'll put together a deputation to go over the house and make sure all the shutters and doors close properly. I'm sure they feel as badly as we do. Tonight the entire village will sit around and talk about it.'

'What about the police?'

'Nothing was stolen, no one was hurt. What is our complaint? Besides, nobody around here trusts the police.'

'I don't like it.'

'What's to like?'

Our village, Datar Guguk, was the Minangkabau version of the Cotswolds. In the village proper, almost every house sat on stilts and had the traditional upswept buffalo-horn roof; six-pronged, quite ridiculous but indisputably majestic. Some of the roofs were made of corrugated iron and rusted a fierce, burnt brown, but most were still thatched with sago stalks. Huge, dark Tolkien trees gave shade to the village, which sat like a tropical island in a vivid emerald sea of rice paddies. Everywhere I looked was a postcard. I did three rolls of thirty-five mil on our first day. The sea of rice was why we were there.

Abby and I went for a walk to check on the tilapia and gourami hatcheries while Charlie and the village deputation did as I asked and put catches and latches on shutters and doors. Perhaps our intruder was one of the team.

'Unbelievable,' Abby said and had no need to say more. We had offended no one and had no enemies. We were as welcome as anyone would be who promised to put a sustainable supply of cheap, nourishing protein on the plates of subsistence farmers. I'd made a fifty-thousand-rupiah donation to the mosque building fund, a gesture which had been most appreciated. Everyone went out of their way to be kind and helpful. Everyone smiled at us and we repaid their friendship in many thoughtful ways.

It was easy to think of the Minang as delightful children, because they're such a small people and often react like children. They have no artifice. When they're happy they smile, when they're sad they weep. Yet they are clever and renowned through the archipelago for their managerial and organisational skills. They're also known for their honesty and trustworthiness. But one of them was also our intruder, neither honest nor trustworthy. That was what was so unbelievable.

Home invasions had become a real cause for concern among the expats in Jakarta. Friends of ours had had their home broken into while they were sleeping. She was raped, he was beaten and their four-year-old daughter had a gun pointed at her head to persuade her father to hand over every piece of cash in the house. The persuasion worked. They'd left Indonesia for ever inside twenty-four hours, but still have to live with the memories.

We'd taken comfort from the fact that our little village was a cultural world apart, centuries away from Jakarta in lifestyle and a full day by available transport. It's a staggeringly scenic two hours from Bukittinggi, the Minang capital, and another two hours from Padung. Padung is a further hour by plane from Jakarta. Perhaps it still wasn't far enough.

'Unbelievable,' I said and had no need to say more.

We'd come to the highlands of West Sumatra as part of an international initiative to re-establish the raising of food fish in remote villages. The people of Indonesia had a tradition of raising fish in ponds and rice paddies but, through overpopulation or poverty, the practice had fallen away. Both Abby and I had degrees in aquaculture. One day we'd probably become businesspeople and farm barramundi or trochus and make our fortunes. In the meantime we'd decided to use our degrees to see interesting parts of the world and help the underprivileged. Both of us loved living simply among simple people where life was about as basic as it could get.

Raising fish like gourami, tilapia, carp, milkfish and catfish in rice paddies did more than just add welcome protein to the local diet. Fish fertilised the soil more effectively than commercial products, which the villagers could not afford to buy anyway, and reduced pests by eating leaf-hoppers, stem-borers and aphids. Done properly and without a great deal of effort, rice-fish culture can increase the yields of rice by up to thirty per cent. We oversaw the building of breeding and growing tanks, supplied the fish stock and developed the systems that made the whole thing work. In return, the people made us welcome.

We'd never locked doors or troubled to hide money, passports or cameras. We had no cause to suspect the entire village was anything but honest to a fault. If anyone had asked how we felt as we trudged along the narrow pathways between the paddies, we would have answered, 'Heartbroken'. When dreams perish something dies inside. Truly it does.

'Poto!'

We turned at the shout and the giggles that followed. Two young women were sheltering beneath coconut palms to escape the heat from the late morning sun, their dark faces swathed in cotton wraps, white teeth gleaming and mouths wide in smiles. Taking cover behind them were four naked kids, round bellies and spaghetti-thin arms, all eyes and guilt. One of them had called out and embarrassed them all. But we represented an opportunity too good to pass up. Abby already had the Polaroid camera out and was playing with the focus.

The house we rented was large by Minang standards and rather grand. Every exterior panel was intricately carved and coloured with faded vegetable dyes: red, green, brown and white. And we had it to ourselves. In Minang society, that was an almost undreamed-of luxury and proclaimed us as wealthy indeed. Even the newer houses, little concrete bunkers smaller than a one-car garage, were shared.

We'd had the good fortune to be invited into homes to cool off with iced tea and oversweet cakes, often coloured a sickening blue-green. It didn't matter that we had few words of language in common. All they wanted was for us to enjoy their hospitality. In the beginning we had no idea how to repay their kindness. Then Abby had noticed the absence of pictures of any kind and realised the precious gift we had to offer. 'Potos!'

'Rambutan,' said Abby.

'Rambutan,' replied six voices simultaneously. Abby clicked. She didn't know the word for cheese in the local dialect so used the Bahasa word for lychees. Forget television, radio and jet aircraft. In the highlands of West Sumatra there is no greater technological marvel than a developing Polaroid photograph. Abby took six portraits as the first image slowly materialised, each one a study in awe and expectation. How could we not smile? How could we not join in the fun? How could we not forget — at least for a while — that someone was trying to frighten the crap out of us?

'All fixeded,' said Charlie. His smile was as wide as the gaps between some of the floorboards. According to Charlie, this was a deliberate feature, allowing cool air to waft up into the house. I'd always thought that cool air sank and hot air rose but the system seemed to work nonetheless. Our bedroom, where the gaps were widest, was the coolest room in the house. I couldn't help wonder at the kind of air that wafted up when livestock sheltered beneath.

Charlie took me on a tour of inspection. Some shutters were held closed by a horizontal bar slipped between twine loops. Others had wooden pegs. I could have opened any one of them with a good pocket knife but bit my tongue.

'Okay?'

'Okay. How about a guard out front?'

'Why guard out front? I sleep out front.'

It was true. Charlie did sleep out front, had slept out front every single night. It seemed churlish to point out that his presence there had not proved to be much of a deterrent the previous night.

'Okay,' I said and tried to figure out some convincing reassurance for Abby.

That night I tucked my wallet under my pillow once more. Perhaps it showed a lack of imagination on my part but there weren't exactly a million alternatives. There were no wardrobes or dressing tables in our bedroom, just a couple of chairs and a bench festooned with clothes. I couldn't see the sense in hiding my wallet in a bag when somebody could simply walk off with it. Besides, I figured my new level of alertness would make me more sensitive to any movement beneath my pillow. Somebody could steal from the chairs or from our pockets but I couldn't imagine how anybody could steal from beneath my head. Not twice at any rate. And always assuming they could find a way in past our new security measures.

That night we sat outside with our neighbours, filling in the hours with gossip, Charlie interpreting. I think he was fairly liberal in his translations judging by the laughs he got. They sang songs for us and I strummed and picked and sang songs for them. They loved it when I played Taj Mahal's 'Fishin' Blues', but Abby doing Linda Ronstadt was their favourite. 'Feels like home to me,' she sang.

There was one refrigerator in the entire village, which was used to keep bottled drinks cold. The shop was actually the front room of a house and the power was pirated from power lines that ran overhead. Everywhere I'd been in Indonesia I'd seen villagers stealing power this way.

Abby and I had our bottle of icy comforter, vodka laced with fresh limes and fiery wheels of sliced chilli, and barbecued sweetcorn to gnaw on. The night was pleasant, almost mild, even though the equator was so close we could lean on it. By the time we turned in we felt no pain, weren't the least bit apprehensive or concerned. I did a quick check to ensure that all shutters and doors were secure and felt foolish doing it. We were among friends, weren't we?

'Mr Wallace, Mr Wallace!' Charlie was back at the door. Banging. Overhead Luke Skywalker's laser sword held still, waiting to do battle with Darth Vader's. Abby groaned. I slipped my hand under my pillow. It came up empty.

My turn to groan.

'Who founded it?'

Charlie looked over his shoulder to where Jack Palance and Handlebars rested on an old bicycle that had to have seen service with the Dutch East Indies constabulary.

'Where?'

'Up there, John. One hundred metres past mosque.' Charlie pronounced mosque 'mos-kee'. That usually brought a smile but not this morning.

Handlebars looked at me apologetically. Handlebars was a monkey who climbed coconut palms and harvested green coconuts. He threw them down to Jack Palance — or JP, as he was better known — who collected them in string bags which he hung off his old bike. When the monkey wasn't climbing palms he sat on the handlebars of JP's bike, but that wasn't why I'd nicknamed him Handlebars. He had a moustache that any ex-RAF pilot would be proud of. JP was called JP because he was a dead ringer for Jack Palance, the Hollywood actor. Abby always gave Handlebars a treat. I let her know he'd come to visit and turned back to Charlie.

'Charlie, this is getting beyond a joke.'

'This time he throwded it in the ditch. Passport throwded this way. Wallet throwded that way. Business cards throwded everywhere, John.'

I groaned for the second time that morning. My licence was laminated. No problem. Credit cards ditto. The plastic cover on my traveller's cheques was muddy but the contents had come through unscathed. My cash was still intact in the zipped-up section. My passport, however, had been for a bit of a paddle. My business cards were history. Could have been worse, though. Everything from nightsoil to dead animals flowed through that ditch.

'Hello, Handlebars,' said Abby. She gave him a banana. She also held a piece of papaya behind her back. As if Handlebars couldn't smell it.

'How did he get past you, Charlie, how did he get into the house? How did he steal my wallet?'

'Have you checkeded all the shutters, John?'

Don't you hate obvious questions? I turned back into the house, Charlie hard on my heels. We began in our bedroom, found nothing suspicious, and worked our way through each of the rooms. In every case the bars or pegs were still in place, the twine uncut. Whoever had come in had not entered via any of the shutters or the back door. That left the front door, which Charlie was supposed to be guarding.

'How did he get past you, Charlie?'

'No! Nobody getted past me! I tieded string to door and to my hand.'

I'd wondered about that. The twine was still tied to the door-handle.

'What have you discovered?' Abby had given Handlebars the papaya but the monkey was still expecting more. Abby's voice was brittle with tension.

'It appears that West Sumatran burglars can walk through walls,' I said irritably. 'Either that or they can squeeze through the gaps in the wall and floorboards. Possible, I suppose, but I've never met anyone less than ten centimetres thick before.'

'Maybe there's a trapdoor,' said Abby.

Maybe there's a trapdoor. You have to hand it to Abby, she's the master of the bleeding obvious.

'Charlie,' I said, 'do Minang houses have trapdoors in the floor?'

'Of course,' said Charlie.

'And ladders?'

'Of course.'

'Charlie, did you make sure the trapdoors were locked?'

'No, John. But I think good idea. We fix them too.'

Indonesians are very literal people. I remembered telling Charlie and the deputation from the village to make sure all the shutters and doors were securely fastened from the inside. I never once mentioned anything about trapdoors. Of course it was inconceivable to them that Abby and I didn't know about the trapdoors. Everyone knew about trapdoors. But I didn't mention them so they didn't fasten them. Rule one in Indonesia: cover all your bases. If you want the right answer, you have to ask the right question.

'He's holding out for a toffee,' I said to Abby.

Handlebars loved Macintosh's toffees. He drooled at the prospect. Handlebars always looked mildly bored with proceedings until there were toffees in the offing. JP didn't like us giving Handlebars toffees because he considered them far too great a luxury to be wasted on a monkey; better we wasted them on him. Abby compromised with a toffee each.

'I think the mystery is solved, Charlie. Could you fasten the trapdoors and take the ladder away, please?'

'Right away, John.'

'Hang on.' I held out two one-thousand-rupiah notes. 'For JP. Tell him thank you. And tell him we'd like to buy two green coconuts this evening.'

JP smiled his tough gunslinger smile and graciously accepted his reward. One thousand rupiahs is a lot of money to a coconut-harvesting team. One works for peanuts and the other for not much more.

'Paradise regained.'

Abby sniggered. She liked literary allusions. When we'd dabbled with dope we'd toyed with the poets. Milton and Coleridge were two favourites. More than anything, she was enjoying the feeling of relief. We both were. Bloody trapdoors! I must say the tour of inspection with Charlie had spooked me. Every closed, untouched shutter had filled me with dread and liquefied the contents of my bowels. How had the bastard got in? What kind of psycho were we dealing with? I'd actually started wondering whether the house was haunted. How else to explain the inexplicable?

Trust Abby to think of trapdoors. There again, I never was very good at lateral thinking.

*   *   *

'God, this is beautiful.'

God, she was right. Charlie had driven us down to Lake Sinkarak near Padangpanjang so we could check on progress at a commercial Nile tilapia farm we were nursing into production. Our greatest concern was the security of the breeding and growing tanks. Nile tilapia are omnivores and predators, and would literally have the indigenous species for breakfast if they broke out into the waterways. But in truth, the real reason for our trip was to have some time to chill out and Lake Sinkarak was the ideal place to do it.

We'd picked up half a dozen bottles of Bintang beer on the way down and swallowed four of them. We lay flat on our backs, floating on top of the warm, comforting water, our faces, bellies and legs smeared white with blockout. We roasted like two well-basted ducks adrift in warm gravy. Paradise regained in spades. Charlie was asleep in the van to save himself the inconvenience of having to sleep at night. He'd promised to stay awake and guard the front door after we'd gone to bed.

We'd driven down to the lake via Payakumbuh and Batusankar. The only reason for telling you this is so you'll understand why I gave everyone nicknames. To the untrained ear, Bahasa sounds like an empty jerry can rolling down a flight of wooden steps, or a convoy of jeeps backfiring. Unfortunately, the local Minang and Batak dialects aren't much better and I have trouble with all of them. So rather than call people by names I mispronounced, I gave them nicknames. It began as a bit of fun but then caught on. Everyone we renamed seemed to feel a bit special. Everyone wanted a nickname.

We arrived back in the village just before sundown and sat out on the steps to watch our friends straggle in from the fields. We sat, sipped our voddies and said a cheery *'Salamat sore!'* to everyone who passed by. Good evening! Good evening! And it was. Not a cloud in the sky and none hovering over us. Women set aside their looms, stretched cramped limbs and rubbed sore eyes. Tombstone wandered past with his freshly washed water buffalo, man and beast as inseparable as best friends. He treated us to his dazzling smile. Women walked arm in arm and nobody accused them of being lesbians. Men sometimes held hands but that didn't mean they were gay. The Minang are just touchy-feely people and more than normally affectionate. Abby and I were proud to be in their company. Then JP and Handlebars pedalled up and dropped off our green coconuts. JP refused to let me pay for them. They accepted a toffee each.

Yes, paradise was well and truly regained.

'Mr Wallace! Mr Wallace!'

Pitch black. The air electric. The thumping on the door incessant. I couldn't see my hand in front of my face. I reached under my pillow. Skin touched leather. So why was Charlie so excited? Cold sweat. Bowels I couldn't trust. I reached over to Abby's side of the bed.

'Mr Wallace! Mr Wallace!'

Abby sat up. Bolt upright. Silhouetted in a blinding moment of blue. Mosquito net billowing.

'It's still there.' I didn't wait for the question.

'I'm coming with you,' she said. She felt around, found the torch, shone it into every corner of the room and up into the high arch of the roof. We made our way to the door, opened it. The house shook, rattled and . . .

And Charlie stood there with Abby's Polaroid.

He looked like he'd seen a ghost.

Hammer Films could not have set the scene better. Three-hundred-year-old house. Violent electric storm. Three terrified mortals clutching scalding-hot tea around a flickering kerosene lamp, far from home and rational explanations. Charlie was more frightened than us, but then he had more reason to be. He was convinced he'd seen the spectral figure of one of the old-time Minangkabau gods. And the god wasn't happy.

'He throwded lightning,' said Charlie. 'He throwded lightning at me!'

Poor Charlie. He was unsure who to pray to. He was nominally Islamic though his commitment was perhaps a touch casual. Like most Minangkabau, particularly those who still tilled the fields in isolated communities, he hadn't completely abandoned the old gods, a legacy from ancient Indian and Javan overlords. If you've ever witnessed a performance of the Ramayana or a *kecak* dance you'll have some idea of the sort of demons whirling around inside his head.

'He wasn't much of a shot,' I said. But Charlie wasn't listening. Abby had eyes like an owl's. I wondered how long she could go without blinking. We sat wrapped in blankets. Whether the cold was external or internal didn't matter.

'Are you certain you left your camera in your bag?'

'Absolutely.'

'You didn't drop it taking a shot of Shirley Temple?'

Shirley Temple was a gorgeous little tot who lived next door. We'd tried to take her photo for weeks but she was too shy. Abby had finally succeeded.

'Give me a break,' said Abby. 'I put it on top of my bag by the bed. I even checked to see if it needed new film.'

Whenever we went out Abby threw one of those little backpacks over her shoulders. She carried a bottle of mineral water, tissues, toffees, wallet, camera, sunscreen and lippy in it. And mangosteens, which I adored, and rambutans, which she adored. She always left her bag right by her bed. This wasn't sloppiness on her part. Like I said before, there weren't an awful lot of places to put things.

'So somebody somehow found their way into our bedroom, despite the fact that all the shutters, doors and trapdoors are still securely fastened, stole your camera and then dropped it for Charlie to find. Where's the sense in that?'

'Spirit god,' said Charlie. His dark face was quite pale, green-tinged, sort of verdigris. 'Throwded lightning. Droppeded camera.'

I was hoping Abby would come up with one of her statements of the bleeding obvious. I was drifting closer and closer towards Charlie's explanation for lack of any other.

'Interesting,' said Abby.

Good old Abby. Knew she'd come through.

'The camera's open. I'm certain I'd closed it.'

Abby's Polaroid was one of those that folded flat into itself, which made it ideal for travelling. But when Charlie had given it back it was open. Abby and I looked at each other. That could explain the lightning.

'Charlie,' said Abby, 'did the spirit god drop the camera before or after it throwded lightning at you?'

'Before! No, after! I don't know.'

'The question is,' said Abby, 'did it accidentally take a picture of itself when it set off the flash? I've only got one shot left. I'm sure I had two.' Abby gave me her don't-be-a-wimp look.

'Shot in the dark,' I said, borrowed her torch and opened the door. If I'd had my nerves reasonably under control, the door squeak set them off again. It had the same effect on me as fingernails on a blackboard. Where was Lon Chaney? Where was Vincent Price? Outside, waiting for me of course. With an axe in each hand. My hair was standing on end and I couldn't blame the static-charged air or the wind. What if Charlie was right? What if the ancient gods still presided over this primitive country? Animism is alive and well in West Sumatra. I admit I hadn't got very deeply into Minang folklore and legend, but all the gods I'd encountered in other parts of Indonesia seemed to have spilled a heap of blood on their way to the top. Warrior gods were all the go here.

There was a three-metre corridor between our house and our neighbour's, or, more accurately, a corridor between the carved pillars that both houses rested upon. Think of a lane between under-building car parks and you've got the picture. The ground was worn bare by animals, playing kids and foot traffic. Three scrubby fig-like trees and the odd weed were all that grew there. But there were still plenty of shadows, sinister dark places, moving and flickering in the wind. Abby expected me to look under the house, the darkest, most sinister place of all. Forget it! Sumatran tigers are also alive and well and still roam the forests just north of Bukittinggi. Perhaps one had strolled south.

'Got it.'

I'd figured my chances of finding a Polaroid photo in the middle of the darkest of nights with a high wind blowing were somewhere between laughable and non-existent. But the wind had jammed it up against some palings of the house next door where they'd once tried to box in the undersides. Other rubbish had also caught there — plastic and foil wrappers. It's amazing the detail you can pick up in the brief instant of a lightning flash. I grabbed the Polaroid and raced back inside. Well, I'd found what I was looking for. Why be brave unnecessarily?

'Oh shit,' said Abby.

Charlie just gasped, buried his head in his hands and whimpered.

I didn't know what to say. A wise man would have checked the photo first. Unfortunately wisdom had surrendered to fear. The focus was hopeless and the image badly blurred. But the eyes that stared back at us from the photo weren't any we recognised.

They weren't even human.

Charlie didn't want to go back outside and sleep in his van so we made him up a bed on the wooden bench in the main room. He went straight to sleep which seemed a bit unjust. After all, they were his demons not ours. Abby claimed she never slept a wink but she did. I was witness to it. I was witness to every lightning flash, every trick of wind and light, every squeaking bat, every errant mosquito, every scurrying mouse in the thatch, every erratic beat of my heart.

I have a good Bachelor of Science degree. I don't believe in ghosts or demons. And I don't believe my eyes closed for more than a second in total throughout the rest of that interminable night. I tried to find some rational explanation. At best, someone was having a huge laugh at our expense. Perhaps the whole village was in on it. Perhaps we were the local sport and substitute for soap operas. Perhaps there was another secret entrance to the house, a secret shared by everyone except us. But that explanation didn't sit very well. Charlie wasn't pretending to be scared out of his wits. And the photo wasn't pretending to be anything other than what it was. Photos can lie, but this one seemed determined to tell the truth. It was the stumbling block. I could reason around a lot of things but kept coming up empty whenever I thought of the photo.

There were no laser shafts of light to herald the dawn, just a growing grey sullenness. The surrounding hills buried their heads in cloud. The air was as thick as soup. I knew that, as the day progressed, the sun would burn off the low clouds, but who knew what sat above them? More clouds or a misty tropical blue? I opened shutters to let in some air and light. The effort raised a sweat. But the way the day was developing, blinking would raise a sweat. Tropical heat and high humidity could bring a water buffalo to its knees.

When I heard Charlie get up and leave, probably to wander down to the river to do his ablutions, I woke Abby with a cup of tea and told her we were going to Bukittinggi.

Time to call the cops.

Charlie disagreed.

'This not police business, John,' he said.

'Then whose business is it?'

'*Wali negari.*'

'Wally who?'

'Headman.'

'Oh, that wally. And what exactly is he going to do that he didn't do before?'

'Before he shutted up house so man not get in.'

'And now?'

'Now he got to open house so demon get out.'

If this worked I could see I'd have to revise my opinions regarding the existence of ghosts. I wasn't sure I wanted the exorcism to work. I thought I'd rather believe ghosts didn't exist than have the headman prove that they did. In my heart I still believed the presence of a couple of gun-toting cops would be a whole lot more effective.

'Can't we just go to Bukittinggi?' asked Abby once Charlie had left to find the headman.

'We no longer have a driver.'

Instead we went to visit our friend with the refrigerator and downed a couple of Cokes. Amazing, isn't it? There we were in the wilds of Sumatra, tormented by demons left over from the Majapahit empire, one of whom was into self-portraits, sipping the Coca-Cola Corporation's fine product. If the Coke Corp were missionaries the whole world would be Christian.

We ordered another Coke each while we waited for the ghost-busters to arrive. The shopkeeper was all smiles. We were very good for business. He'd once tried to buy Abby's Polaroid. He could see there was more money in 'potos' than cold drinks. When he learned how much the film cost he changed his mind.

Soon people began to leave their fields, looms and anvils. Obviously there was nothing like a good exorcism to liven up a boring day. Working the fields was backbreaking. Likewise working metal in the forges. But the people I most felt sorry for were the women weaving the intricate *songket* cloths with silk and fine threads of gold and silver. I was told it took years to produce a single cloth no more than a metre long. The women worked indoors where it was cool and the light was atrocious. They traded their eyesight for their exquisite creations.

'Hello, Handlebars.'

Abby rose to meet her friend. The monkey looked up at her expectantly. JP had come back from gathering coconuts for the exorcism. He called to some kids playing nearby and instructed them to look after Handlebars. Abby waited until JP had run off to join the swelling throng before letting the kids get on with their game. She had Handlebars' whole and undivided attention. She didn't need any help to look after him. She had toffees.

It took about four hours for everybody to wash and get into the appropriate costumes. Somebody had started practising with drums.

'They're going to drum our demon out of town,' I said, but Abby wasn't listening. Facetiousness, she says, is one of my less endearing traits.

Chickens squawked and something about the pitch suggested that one or more of them had come to the end of its career. I couldn't help wondering how all this fitted in with Islam. Clearly it didn't. I half-expected to see the mullah raging at the gathering with a raised stick. I made a mental note to ask Charlie about it, though I felt sure he'd see no contradiction. Animism still had its place.

By the time they'd all assembled and begun the ceremony, Abby and I were well into the chilli voddies. Somewhere up above, the sun was over the yardarm and someone once told me that alcohol thinned the blood. It needed thinning. There was no escaping the heat and humidity. The shopkeeper had let us make our own ice cubes with mineral water and sold them back to us. They didn't last five minutes in the glass.

Abby kept giving hers to Handlebars, who alternated between wiping them over his arms, his chest and his bottom before returning them to his mouth. Abby was laughing. I wanted to throw up. Handlebars was so tame and placid it was hard to believe he was from the same species of monkey we saw playing in the forests. Look but don't touch is the rule with them. One bite and it's straight on the plane to hospital in Singapore, followed by more jabs than a junkie ever dreamed of.

About a hundred people filed into our house, shouting and chanting. Perhaps they'd forgotten it was built on stilts, overlooked the fact that it was three hundred years old. I got my camera ready, expecting it to fall in a heap. Obviously the exorcism worked by filling the house with people until there was simply no room left for the demon. Throw in the drumming and what spirit wouldn't get the hell out of there? They opened all the doors and shutters and held what I assumed was the Minang version of a disco without the spinning lights. Then they all filed out again as pleased as punch.

'Poor devil didn't have a ghost of a chance,' I said, but Abby wasn't listening. Bad puns don't endear me to her either.

Charlie came trotting up the road, a bandanna around his head but otherwise bare to the waist. He was wearing a borrowed sarong.

'All fixeded,' he said.

'Great.'

'Now will you drive us to Bukittinggi?' Abby had less faith in exorcisms than I had.

'No Bukittinggi,' said Charlie. He made the final syllable last four bars, a sure sign of disapproval. 'All fixeded. No Bukittinggeeeeee. No policemensssssss. Bad mens. You see. Now we feast.'

There's a wonderful system that operates throughout Indonesia. When the people want favours from the gods they make sacrifices and offerings to them. Animals, fruit, vegetables. The gods have first crack at the goodies, then the faithful get to eat the leftovers. Surprise, surprise, there's always a lot left over.

'Charlie,' I said, 'if our visitor comes again tonight I'm going to feed your balls to Handlebars.'

Charlie smiled unconvincingly.

'On satay sticks, Charlie.'

He definitely winced.

'Are you sure you don't want to take us to Bukittinggi?'

'No Bukitinggi. All fixeded.'

JP came back for Handlebars. He looked very important and pleased with himself. JP had led the procession into our house. He must have been top dog in the ranks of animists.

'Thank you, JP,' I said. 'Charlie, how much do we owe him?'

'Not owe JP anything. Pay *wali negari*. You give me twenty tousand.'

'I give you nothing. I pay headman. Ten tousand.'

'Okay, ten tousand.'

'Five tousand now. Five tousand in the morning if our visitor stays away.'

'No, John. You oppend headman.' The Minang have a lot of trouble with 'f's. 'Send demon back.'

I gave Charlie ten thousand so the headman wouldn't be offended, but did it in full view of JP. *'Wali negari,'* I said and pointed to the cash.

'Wali negari,' said JP and never took his eyes off Charlie. Charlie left miffed.

Late afternoon Abby convinced Charlie to take us up to the top of the hill overlooking our valley where she hoped to find some kind of cooling breeze. We let the village kids come with us for a ride. Fourteen managed to squeeze into the back of the van. I had another on my knee. Abby had Shirley Temple. We promised to be back in time for the main feast.

Abby was right. There was a breeze and it rippled through the rice in the terraces. A boy was bringing home a string of ducks along a paddy wall. We counted twenty-two, all in single file, marching with purpose and funnier than anything Disney ever did. I wondered if Tombstone ploughed these narrow steep rice terraces. If so, how did he get his lumbering mate in and out? Another of life's mysteries.

We detoured on the way home to buy ice-creams and win for ever the hearts and minds of our entourage. But our homecoming was not how it should have been. We weren't glad to be back in picturesque Datar Guguk. Somewhere along the way paradise had lost its gloss.

We weren't looking forward to another night in that house.

'Cup of tea?'

Abby hovered over me. She was wearing a T-shirt and knickers. The hairs on her arms were like threads of finest silk. Silver on gold. She was smiling. I closed my eyes to give them more time to adjust. The bedroom was flooded with sunlight.

'What time is it?'

'Just after eight.'

Abby had opened all the shutters and pulled back the mosquito net. Some people say there's nothing like a good sleep to clear the head. I'd slept for eight hours solid and mine felt stuffed with the same material that filled our mattresses. The tea scalded. Abby was clanging away in the next room making breakfast. Probably a *mee goreng* seasoned with TNT and napalm. Abby had decided she preferred noodles to rice first thing. One theory suggests that if you have a lot of chillies for breakfast you're less affected by the heat of the day. My wallet made a familiar lump under my pillow, the one welcome lump among the many. Abby's bag was undisturbed. My Nikon slept on blissfully behind its lens cap. If our nocturnal visitor had called he'd left empty-handed. He probably hadn't come at all. Perhaps he'd gone for ever. So where did that leave us? I finished my tea, pulled on shorts and a T-shirt.

I sat down at the table and waited until Abby joined me. The *mee goreng* could have lifted paint. Hell! It could've melted steel.

'Very good,' I said.

'You'll appreciate it later.'

It seemed we were both in good humour but how deep did the feelings run?

'Well,' I said, 'I suppose now we should believe in ghouls, ghosts and demons.'

'Don't knock it if it works.'

'So what are we going to do? Hang garlic off the doors and windows and crosses around our necks for the rest of our lives?'

'Don't be silly.'

'It's not me being silly.'

Abby has this infuriating ability to withdraw and regroup when argument and reason turn against her. Her lips retreat to a thin red line, at least as stubborn as Victorian soldiers confronting the heathen hordes. She becomes ice cold and as calm as a pond at dawn. Impenetrably calm. Swan-like. Ritual required that I break the silence or Little Miss Injured Innocence would ignore me all day.

'Abby, we don't believe in ghosts. We're rational, well-educated human beings. We don't believe that a ghost took my wallet or your camera, nor do we believe that one hundred or one thousand drum-beating Minangs can drive a ghost that doesn't exist out of our house.'

'Do you have a better explanation?'

'Perhaps someone is using us to reinforce ancient beliefs and turn people away from Islam and back to their roots. Maybe there are Minangkabau traditionalists who want to preserve Minang culture and customs, some kind of nationalist group. The village people are easily swayed. Maybe they saw us as a chance to demonstrate the power of the old ways.'

'So how did our Che Guevara get in?'

She had me there. I'd searched for secret entrances and found nothing.

'And what about the photo?'

I had to concede the photo was still a major sticking point.

'There are more things in heaven and earth, Horatio . . .'

We'd both studied Shakespeare at school and quoted and misquoted him in equal measure. It was her gentle way of letting me know that there was a distinct possibility I didn't know everything.

'The *mee goreng's* too oily,' I said. I had to say something.

'All fixeded,' said Charlie. He wore a smile like a Cadillac grille. 'I tolded you.'

'Yes, Charlie, you tolded us.' Abby gestured towards me. 'Some people just need more convincing than others.'

'You don't believe me, John?'

'Jury's still out.'

Charlie looked disappointed which made all our spectators also look disappointed. Abby frowned at me, the one dark cloud on a glorious tropical morning. Birds sang and the gourami growing in the pond rose to snap up insects, grateful to have survived the previous night's festivities, not to have been netted, steamed and served beneath a dynamite *padung* sauce. Only Sad Sack clothed in his Billabong shorts, Mambo shirt and university education soured the day. Nobody could understand why I was less than overjoyed. I punched Charlie's arm lightly and laughed. Everyone cracked up. Obviously I really was overjoyed and grateful. I'd just been teasing Charlie.

We gave Charlie the day off and set out on bicycles along the tracks between the paddies to visit the neighbouring villages. We passed JP and Handlebars. JP gave us the broadest of smiles. Perhaps more than anyone, he would have got the credit for exorcising our ghost. He'd led the procession. Was his smile one of triumph at his success or the satisfied grin of a con man who'd tricked an entire village? Was JP the local keeper of Minang culture? Was he entirely animist or had he adopted Islam? I returned his smile and made a mental note to check with Charlie.

But what about Charlie? I didn't see him ducking out four times a day to pray. He was as proud of his Minang heritage as anyone. He couldn't wait to get back into traditional costume and join the conga line that discoed through our house. Was he one of them? And what about the headman? Apparently Sherlock Holmes used a seven per cent cocaine-tobacco mix to clarify his mind and help solve his cases. He would have needed pure cocaine to solve this one. How would he explain the photo?

The nearest village was famous for its spider web-like silverware. Abby haggled ruthlessly for silver brooches and rings, usually settling for a fair price plus 'poto'. We weren't the first Westerners to visit the Minangkabau nor would we be the last. Abby is normally extremely generous but didn't want to upset the local economy or spoil things for those who followed. She matched the silversmiths' patience and struck agreement while I did what we were being paid to do.

One of the biggest problems in developing rice-fish farming in remote areas was the cost and availability of fish fingerlings. Abby and I set up hatcheries and trained locals to operate them. While Abby haggled, I showed the locals how to milk eggs from the mouths of tilapia and transfer the eggs to the hatching tanks.

Sometimes our work can be very rewarding and this was one of those occasions. While tilapia was a new fish to the men of this village, there was little I could teach them about carp or gourami. As soon as they'd realised they would have a regular supply of fingerlings, they'd dug fish refuges in all the paddies and used the soil they removed to build up the paddy walls. They built ponds and introduced fish into their nightsoil disposal tanks. This was international aid at its best.

But despite everything, my mind was elsewhere. After a couple of hours I decided to join Abby and play tourist. I watched the silversmiths at work, in awe of their skill and patience, and marvelled at the beautiful *songket* cloths the village women were weaving. If I lived for ever I'd never acquire the artistry they displayed. I'd happily have settled for their patience.

At another village we watched a new house being built to the same pattern as the one we rented, to the same design laid down by an architect hundreds of years earlier. So what did that tell me? Minang craft and culture were still alive and thriving. Did they really need a contrived stunt to ensure their survival?

I cycled home depressed and blind to the beauty surrounding us. Abby made me stop while she took a picture of the sunset. The sun sat jammed between the hilltops and low clouds. Dust and smoke from village fires had created a haze which filtered and refracted the rays. Golden fingers reached over fiery ridges and touched lightly on palm tops and roofs. A man and his water buffalo trudged home by a flooded crimson paddy. Gourami made circles in the water snapping up insects. God affirmed His glory. I know this because Abby captured it all on film. My thoughts were on other matters at the time.

'Peels lie comb toomey.'

I wanted to go to bed. My strumming felt half a beat behind and my fingers couldn't have picked fruit let alone

notes. But our neighbours had requested Abby doing Linda
Ronstadt. We'd sung the song so often they'd learned the
words of the chorus.

'Peels lie comb toomey,' they sang. 'Feels like I'm on my
way back where I belong,' sang Abby when she reached the
bit they didn't know. I usually joined in the chorus too, but I
didn't have it in me. I wanted bed. Maybe I'd had too much
sleep. Maybe the straw or horsehair or kapok, whatever they
stuffed our mattresses with, had permanently infiltrated my
brain. I didn't believe in ghosts. I didn't believe in spirit gods.
I didn't believe in exorcisms. I didn't believe there was a
Minang cultural conspiracy either. I wanted bed. Dreamless
sleep. Maybe the flash of insight that often strikes on the cusp
of consciousness.

'Mr Wallace! Mr Wallace!'

Our 6 am alarm. The voice was shrill and the thumping on
the door manic. Urgent. Even desperate. I didn't know why,
but I felt oddly reassured.

'Where was it, Charlie?'

'Iceman founded it.'

Iceman was the shopkeeper who plundered Indonesia's
electricity grid to power his fridge. He'd heard about the
one-thousand-rupiah bounty and patiently awaited his due.

'Outside mos-kee.'

It didn't make any sense. If Minang nationalists even
existed and if they wanted to make a point, they would
hardly be so blatant. Islam isn't noted for its tolerance of
thieves. I took Abby's little backpack from Charlie and tried
to remember what should be in it.

'Everything throwded,' said Charlie.

Abby's passport. Her lippy. Sunscreen. Her Christmas present Calvin Klein shades. She'd cleaned most of her stuff out of her bag when we'd returned from our bike ride. Taken out her purchases and the fruit we hadn't eaten. The leftover mineral water. Her Polaroid. Only Abby could say if anything was missing. Her purse? No, that was on the table as well.

Abby's hands shook when I handed her the bag. I think she wanted to believe in ghosts because the alternative was even more unacceptable. She could handle ghosts but not some grubby little man who watched her while she slept and took things as a calling card. What else had he done? What did he do that we didn't know about? I wasn't proud of some of the thoughts that crept into my mind, but fortunately I kept them to myself. Abby fought back tears and tried to be thorough.

'Nothing missing,' she said, but she was wrong. Something was missing. Something so obvious we were totally blind to it.

'*Wali negari,*' said Charlie.

I had to admire his optimism. Charlie was nothing if not a tryer.

'Bukittinggeeeeee,' I said. 'Policemenssssss.'

The police were patient and unsmiling. In fact, I think they did very well to keep the smiles off their faces. Maybe Charlie managed to communicate the seriousness with which we regarded the matter.

'Nothing stolen?' they asked repeatedly.

'Nobody hurt?'

Clearly they couldn't understand why we were making such a fuss. Money changed hands, which substantially improved their comprehension. A few notes managed to crawl their way into Charlie's top pocket. I could hardly believe his audacity. The police seemed not to notice, or if they did, they accepted it as his rightful commission.

It normally took us around two hours to reach our village from Bukittinggi. With the police escort we did it in an hour and a half, eating the dust from the police Toyota Landcruiser right to our front door. Even then they didn't turn off the flashing lights or the siren. Our neighbours gathered in sullen, resentful silence, keeping their distance as if to avoid being tarnished by the event. JP and Handlebars rode past without looking at us. Nobody would meet our eyes. Policemens weren't welcome in Datar Guguk and it wasn't hard to see why.

There's something about uniforms that strip Indonesians of everything that's likeable about them. Friendly, generous people become officious and intimidating, if not downright threatening. When I think of Indonesian policemen and soldiers I automatically think of the Javanese. For centuries the Javanese have positioned themselves as the dominant race and used arms to reinforce this presumption. I found it hard to reconcile the gentle people we were living among with the atrocities that had occurred in East Timor and Irian Jaya. I had allowed myself to believe that all Indonesian soldiers were Javanese even though I knew that to be nonsense. Every Indonesian island contributed men to the armed forces. Our gun-toting policemen were undoubtedly Minangkabau.

The officer withdrew his pistol and pushed open the door. Just what he thought he'd find inside was beyond me. His minions stood guard outside in their dark green trousers, paler green shirts, white belts, black holsters, Top Gun sunglasses and no suggestion of a smile. I think the intention was to warn off our intruder. If so, they certainly knew their stuff. When the officer called to us to follow him inside even I hesitated.

Of course he'd found nothing. He just wanted to negotiate his fee for house calls away from prying eyes. That way he wouldn't be seen to be corrupt and he could give his minions a less-than-fair share. No wonder his men weren't smiling.

They left us and paid a call on the headman. We could hear the shouting from where we were. Obviously I'd paid enough for the police to stamp their authority and warn the village into line. I don't think their zeal made us any friends. When I rejoined Abby outside I could see from the reproachful way our neighbours looked at me that I was to blame for the indignity inflicted on them. I could see it would take more than a bit of Linda Ronstadt and a few 'potos' to repair the damage.

The police left at dusk, lights flashing, siren wailing, alerting the surrounding villages to the wrongdoing of Datar Guguk, proclaiming their shame. Even Abby, who'd wanted police involvement from the start, seemed to think I'd been a bit heavy-handed. I shrugged my shoulders in sympathy, but inside I secretly disagreed. Drums might scare off ghosts but there's nothing like a police siren and a show of force to frighten off an intruder.

That evening I sat on the front steps and played guitar. I played for myself, a blues grab bag of Taj Mahal and Eric Clapton. I was dimly aware of dark faces gathering, and of Abby moving among them sharing our replenished stock of toffees. I guess I was aware of the appreciative murmurs after every tricky lick and show-off riff but pretended not to be.

They were a smart audience. There's not a lot you can teach the Minangkabau about music. In the end I gave in and played their song so they could join in.

'Peels lie comb toomey, peels lie comb toomey . . .'

And I sang along, popping my 'p's, trying to keep the smile out of my voice. All forgiven? I thought so. Somebody barbecued corn and the Iceman fetched my voddy. JP brought me two green coconuts and laughed when I mixed coconut milk with the spirit. It tasted fine.

I think I scared Abby when I moved furniture over the trapdoors, and tied empty bottles to the doors and shutters so that they'd clink together if disturbed. I thought of setting up a kerosene lamp on a chair, a night-light for the nervous, but the kero lamp that doesn't smell hasn't yet been invented. Instead I placed my torch under my pillow alongside my wallet. Our neighbours may have forgiven us for bringing in the police but they hadn't forgotten. When a policeman taps you on the shoulder in Indonesia you forgo the right to call a lawyer, not that any of our neighbours would have had or even known a lawyer. But they understood tyranny and they understood power. They understood exactly what would happen the day they fell foul of the police. But a deterrent is only that and what I wanted was impregnable defence. What if it wasn't over? What if the warning had been ignored? What if our intruder called again? We'd raised the stakes. The question was, how would he react to that?

Abby's eyes opened wider when she saw the crudely hewn and broken axe handle alongside my mattress. I'd found it lying under the house. In truth it wasn't much of an axe handle.

But it was a hell of a nightstick.

Abby could sleep standing up. I think she could sleep hanging by her thumbs. Her lumpy mattress had proved no impediment. But she heaved and sighed and plumped up her pillow, seemingly taking for ever to succumb. I lay and listened, eyes useless in the Stygian dark. Mice skittered in the thatch. Bats squeaked. Somewhere nearby an animal snuffled. The voddies leaned heavily on my eyelids. Something happens to determination in the wee small hours. Will weakens, intentions waver. Stygian darkness? There was a word to play with, an escapee from my education on the run in Sumatra. Darkness from Hades, scene-setter for our demon, our evil within. My hand reached out to touch my nightstick, my piece of reassurance tailor-made to deliver us from evil and those who trespassed against us. My hand touched something else.

Something living.

I screamed, gripped the hand that gripped mine and instantly regretted doing so. Whatever had hold of me was immensely strong, inhumanly strong, and pulled me downwards, trying to drag me through the gap in the floorboards.

Abby levitated in the darkness beside me, wailing with fear. From below came a screeching unlike anything I'd ever heard. A foul, breath-snapping stench of pestilence rose like fumes from hell. And me utterly helpless, pinned to the floor, my elbow jammed hard against the gap in the floorboards, my lower arm feeling like it was going to part company with the rest of me.

'Get the bloody torch! Get Charlie!'

Never give people a choice of actions in critical circumstances. Abby hesitated, unsure which to do first, her fear paralysing. Oh God! Nails scored my wrist and the impossible vice-like grip intensified. *It*, whatever *it* was, screeched its frustration, screamed its fury, spat defiance.

'Torch! Torch!' I yelled.

'Mr Wallace! Mr Wallace!' Charlie, shouting and banging on the door.

It was winning. I no longer had the option of letting go. *It* had the option of letting go of me. Oh Christ! Somebody was sobbing. Me.

'Mr Wallace! Mr Wallace!'

If Abby had left me and run to open the door, I don't know what I would have done. I was convinced it was only a matter of time before my lower arm was ripped off. Something hard hit my face.

'Argh!'

'Sorry!'

You'd think someone with as much common sense as Abby would turn the bleeding torch on before passing it. I slid the On switch forward and aimed the beam between the boards. Inhuman eyes stared back, frightened, angry, but instantly recognisable.

Eyes from a Polaroid.

'Hello, Handlebars,' I said.

Abby soothed the panicking monkey so that it would let go of my battered hand. She dropped little bribes through the boards, giving him what he'd come for, what he'd come for almost every night, what had been missing from Abby's bag — Abby's Macintosh's toffees.

It was all so obvious when I thought about it. There are no such things as ghosts. Of course there aren't. There was no way any human being could have found a way into our house. There was no motive. But a monkey besotted by toffees could breach its training, slip its collar, climb the three or so metres up to the floorboards without a ladder, and have the strength to hang there while he reached between the floorboards, searching for his prize.

Alongside two prize fools.

Tipping the Scales

Ian Kenny sat in the back row overlooking a sea of heads to the lectern. The speaker's amplified voice rang clear in the hall, no longer having to compete with the sound of rain on the metal roof. Its drumming hadn't mattered. The audience were oblivious to it, eyes and ears fixed on the speaker who held them completely spellbound. He was the fifth author to speak at the Norfolk Island Writers' and Readers' Festival but no mere author. Oh, no. He, Johannes de Benke, was a legend, an adventurer and hero, a man who went where mere mortals feared to tread; a man who'd spent much of his life exploring and exposing myths so successfully that the press referred to him as Johannes de-Bunker. It didn't matter to the audience that it had been quite some time since the speaker had ventured anywhere that didn't boast a five-star hotel or, at the very least, the civilised comforts that merited the sort of prices the speaker was happy for other people to pay. The indisputable fact was he'd done what lesser people only dreamed of doing, and now he was reaping the rewards.

Ian waited patiently while de Benke told his enraptured audience how his boat had been upturned by enraged hippopotami on a Congolese lake while he was searching for evidence of the elusive Mokele-mbembe — a *sauropod* which apparently had failed to become extinct along with all the other dinosaurs seventy million years ago. The story seemed to have grown somewhat since Ian had first read *In the Wake of Lake Monsters & Other Myths*, and then become hooked on reading all of de Benke's books. He didn't mind the elaboration or the apparent exaggeration. He dismissed it simply as the licence authors are granted when extolling the virtues of their wares. He glanced over his shoulder. As he'd suspected, the sun had returned, confirming its presence with a brilliant slash of light that lit up the entrance of Rawson Hall. Someone had failed to close the double doors properly. Ian hoped the intrusion would encourage de Benke to wind up his tales so that question time could begin. He had a question to ask. But de Benke appeared as oblivious to the sun as his audience had been to the showers.

The festival had attracted hundreds of visitors from the mainland as well as the local islanders, and it occurred to Ian that many of the visitors had not yet had the opportunity to see Norfolk Island in all its glory, bathed in sunlight, as green as Ireland at its fairest, a tiny drop of paradise in a seemingly endless ocean. And a bountiful ocean at that. Ian let his mind wander. He'd lived on Norfolk for most of his sixty years but sometimes he honestly believed the sea was more his home. He loved its forever-ness and its capacity to endure; loved its ever-changing colours and moods, feared its rages and rejoiced in its serenity. As a charter-boat operator Ian lived off its generosity, but the truth was he would have gone to sea at every opportunity even if there'd been no keen fishermen among the tourists for him to take out. It was the mystery that attracted him, the sea's infinite capacity to surprise. That was what drew him to the sea and also what had drawn him to Rawson Hall to hear de Benke. He had a question to ask.

The sudden explosion of applause snapped him out of his reverie. De Benke had finished and the Master of Ceremonies was striding to the microphone. Ian leaped to his feet and all but ran down the aisle between the two banks of seats towards the audience microphone. De Benke had grossly exceeded the time allowed for his talk and Ian realised question time would be limited or even cancelled altogether. He was also aware that sometimes people used question time simply to express their admiration for the author and he couldn't allow that to happen. De Benke seemed amused by his haste.

'I was about to say that there was no time left for questions,' said the MC. 'However, it appears I have been pre-empted.' He smiled warningly at Ian. 'Our next speaker is ready and Johannes has other engagements. I'll allow your question on condition that you keep it brief.'

'Mr de Benke,' Ian began, suddenly aware of a dryness in his throat and all the eyes fixed on him. 'Mr de Benke,' he repeated, 'I have a fascination with the sea. I have spent my life gathering curiosities and artifacts, rare books and illustrations, evidence of the sometimes weird and wonderful creatures which over time have inhabited the oceans of the earth.' Ian was aware of the MC rolling his eyes impatiently and a freezing of de Benke's smile. He swallowed and continued. 'You must be aware, Mr de Benke, that from the very beginning of civilisation, writers have spoken of and ancient artists depicted a sea creature which they refer to as ...' Ian hesitated. It was so easy to expose himself to ridicule among strangers. Among the islanders his words would be listened to and respected, even if the listeners did not agree. Ian could feel his face beginning to redden.

'Referred to as what?' cut in de Benke.

'Sea serpents.' Ian said the words so softly he doubted the microphone had picked them up. He was about to repeat them when he saw de Benke's impatient reaction.

'Sea serpents, you said?'

'Yes.'

'And what exactly is your question?'

'Can you categorically deny their existence?'

'For God's sake,' said de Benke, 'do I need to? Hasn't it occurred to you that when ships were few and cameras nonexistent sightings of sea serpents occurred all the time? Mind you, these sightings were by people who'd been so long at sea they mistook manatees and dugongs for mermaids!' De Benke paused to allow the audience to laugh with him and at his questioner. 'Does it not also occur to you that now, when the oceans of the world are positively buzzing with shipping, sea serpents aren't seen at all, at least never by people with cameras? Why do you think that is?'

'Perhaps because when there are many witnesses the question of photographic evidence doesn't immediately arise.'

'What? In this age when television networks and magazines pay fortunes for such photographs?'

'They don't on Norfolk Island.'

'Aha! I suppose you're going to tell me you've seen one of these sea serpents.'

'Yes, and it wasn't just —' Ian wanted to say how it happened, how his guests and people on a nearby boat had seen it too, but de Benke didn't give him a chance.

'I suppose you've seen other phenomena as well. Ghost ships, perhaps?'

Ian gasped. How did de Benke know? But then he guessed de Benke would have checked out the local bookshop, the Golden Orb, flicked through books about the island, flicked through *his* books.

'Well? Have you seen a ghost ship?'

'Yes, myself and my —' Ian wanted to tell him how his wife and two of his grandchildren had also seen it, but again de Benke didn't give him a chance.

'I don't suppose you had your camera with you then either.' De Benke looked away from him and swept the audience imperiously with his eyes. 'The world of cryptozoology exists only in the minds of cryptozoologists. There are no yetis, no bigfoots, no yowies, no mermaids, no Loch Ness monsters and no fire-breathing dragons. Nor are there any sea serpents or ghost ships. How do I know? How can I be so sure? Because I've spent my whole life looking for them. And what did I find? Nothing! Why? Because there is nothing *to* find except a bunch of fanciful, deluded people. Thank you for being such a wonderful audience.'

Ian slunk out of the hall into the sunlight with the sound of the audience's adoration of de Benke ringing in his ears, and the shame of his humiliation burning them.

'I think you'll find Ian Kenny is neither fanciful nor deluded.'

Johannes de Benke's eyes narrowed irritably and focused on his coffee. The Golden Orb bookshop provided free coffee to the festival's speakers and de Benke was not one to let any entitlement pass. He believed he'd earned his coffee and had also earned the right to enjoy it in peace.

'And who might Ian Kenny be?' he asked, looking up and instantly regretting his facetiousness. He found himself staring into a familiar face, a young face in an older man's body. More to the point, he saw both the intelligence in the eyes and the mild reproach.

'Mind if I join you?'

'Not at all,' said de Benke, forcing a smile. The newcomer was his host, Peter Clarke, owner of Shearwater Scenic Villas. Peter had provided de Benke with his best villa for the duration of the writers' festival. He was also painfully aware that he'd inadvertently sat at a table alongside shelves carrying a display of Ian Kenny's books. Ian smiled down at him from the cover of his book *Hooked by the Sea*. Of course de Benke had looked at it. It was the natural thing for someone with his specialisation to do. He was grateful that his host had enough tact to overlook his question.

'I'm not sure if you realise it, but it took a lot of courage for Ian to stand up in front of all those people this morning,' said Peter, getting straight to the point. 'He's not the sort to draw attention to himself.'

'And you think I treated him harshly?'

'I think that's a matter of record,' said Peter wryly.

'Have you any idea how many people come up to me claiming to have seen everything from yowies to pixies, from winged dragons to spiders the size of Volkswagens?'

'I can imagine,' said Peter.

'And you're going to tell me your friend is different?'

'Put it this way, I've been known to have a go at Ian for his lack of imagination.' Once again a wry smile flickered across Peter's face. He leaned back so the waitress could place a cup of coffee in front of him. 'How's your coffee? Need refreshing?'

De Benke nodded and handed his empty cup to the waitress. He never said no to a free coffee. In fact, nobody could remember him saying no to anything that was free.

'Ian's been looking forward to your visit for weeks, you know. He was hoping you'd be able to explain what he saw.'

'The sea serpent or the ghost ship?'

'The ghost ship was very likely a mirage, albeit a pretty convincing one. His wife and grandkids saw it, too. I spoke to each of them and their stories were fairly consistent. They saw a boat with a high stern. The kids thought they were looking at a large junk. Ian thought it looked more like an old Spanish galleon. Both have high, heavy sterns. They had a camera with them but didn't think to take a photo. They were coming down the hill to Emily Bay and figured they'd drive over to Kingston pier after their swim to check the boat out. They were sure they'd find it moored there in the lee. When they found nothing at Kingston, they drove up to the top of Headstone, automatically assuming it would have taken refuge there. But it wasn't there, either. They couldn't find a trace of the boat whichever way they looked. Nor could they find anyone else who'd seen it. That's when Ian realised they'd seen a ghost ship. Thing is, we're talking about a man who spends his life scanning the sea. If he says he saw something, I'm inclined to believe him. He rues the fact that he didn't take a photo but I'm not sure that would have helped. Mirages don't photograph, do they?' Peter paused as the waitress placed de Benke's second coffee on the table. 'No, it's the serpent Ian wants to talk to you about. Will you talk to him?'

'Give me one good reason why I should.'

'I've read your books. Ian put me onto them, in fact. We both feel that you set out in good faith to find the creatures you wrote about. I suspect you'd rather have discovered one of these beasts than proved they don't exist.'

'Of course. What do you think is the more valuable: a good, clear photo of the Loch Ness Monster or no photo of the Loch Ness Monster? True fame awaits the man who finds and can prove the existence of any of these creatures.'

'Perhaps Ian is offering you a chance at true fame.'

'They all do, my friend,' said de Benke bitterly. 'Believe me, I know from experience. They're all plausible at the beginning. Tell me, in your heart of hearts, do you think your friend actually saw a sea serpent?'

'I'm pretty sure.'

'Pretty sure?'

'Very sure.'

'Where does he claim to have seen the creature?'

'On the drop-off, on the western edge of the Norfolk Rise.'

'How close was he?'

'Close enough for a good observation. Fifty metres, maybe less.'

'That's close enough to see that it wasn't a parade of porpoises but not close enough to be sure that it wasn't the trailing arm of a giant squid.'

'I'm sure it wasn't a giant squid,' said Peter.

'How can you be so sure?'

'Ian wasn't the only one out at the drop-off that day. Howard Christian had his boat out there as well and he was a lot closer to the sea serpent than Ian. Howard actually managed to touch the serpent and he's positive it had scales.'

De Benke drove back to his villa, poured himself a beer and sat brooding on his balcony overlooking the beach at Bumboras. Norfolk Island's economy depended on tourism and the writers' festival was a promotion designed to attract visitors to the island in the off-season. The organisers had done the right thing by him by putting him up at Shearwater, which many regarded as the finest accommodation on the island. But de Benke was as blind to their consideration as he was to the fact that only one of the remaining four villas was occupied. He was indulging in what had become his favourite pastime — self-pity. He knew that if things had turned out differently he could have been lording it in New York's finest hotel and being paid handsomely to speak to thousands at the Museum of Natural History, instead of performing for accommodation, coffees and a few hundred book sales at Rawson Hall.

Could he bear to allow himself to dream once more? To be deceived once more? The disappointments had been so many. He'd lost count of the times he had held fame and glory within his grasp, only to be denied by cruel circumstance and deceit.

Early on in his career he had taken what he believed was the only genuine photograph of the yeti in existence, a fact he'd deliberately omitted from his debunking book, *In the Footsteps of the Yeti*. His Sherpa guides had been true to their word and had deserved their exorbitant fee. They'd kept their side of the deal and taken him to a sheer-walled secret valley they called the cradle of Qomolangma, where they insisted the 'yeh-teh' lived. They'd told him that getting there would be a difficult climb but he had failed to grasp just how difficult it would prove to be. He'd been on the point of collapse when they'd reached the edge of the valley where his guides had constructed an ice cave with a narrow slit carved into the opening for observation. Sitting over six thousand metres high and set on a ridge where the northerly wind funnelled between two peaks at express-train speed, the ice cave was by far the coldest place on earth that de Benke had ever had the misfortune to experience. The Sherpas had warned him about that too, but again he'd failed to grasp how desperately cold it would be. The chill factor defied measurement and exposed skin was instantly snap-frozen.

They'd warned him that the cradle of Qomolangma was almost always obscured by cloud whipping across the top of it, but he'd also failed to appreciate how utterly impenetrable the shroud of cloud would be. He was dozing, driven to it by the cold and his exhaustion, when his shoulder was shaken roughly and he heard the excited whispers of the Sherpas. Not only had the clouds lifted, they could see something.

Why were they whispering, he wondered. Even if they'd shouted their voices would not be heard on the valley floor almost four hundred metres below, not in the face of the ceaseless gale. He stumbled to the observation slot, pressed his binoculars hard against his goggles and gasped. There, unmistakeable against the unblemished white backdrop, was a dark shape that could only be a yeti. Even though scale was hard to estimate at that distance, particularly as there was nothing to judge size against, de Benke knew he was looking at a hominid, at least two point three metres tall, its body covered in a thick dark coat of fur or hair and its feet bare. It was walking across the narrow valley and slightly away from him but he could still assess its build: the legs too long to fit any known species of ape, the body — though heavyset — too slight, and the head lacking the protruding eyebrows and heavy jaw associated with apes.

'My God!' he said, barely audibly. He understood now why the Sherpas had whispered. The sight of the yeti invoked awe. His mind yielded to its scientific bent as it tried to classify what his eyes beheld. *Gigantopithecus*, yes! The prehistoric upright ape that had supposedly died out three hundred thousand years earlier, and survived only in rumour and legends of bigfoot, sasquatch, wendigo, yowie, wose, chuchunaa, xueren and other apemen wherever wilderness was still to be found. It was only as the clouds began to tumble back down across the valley, propelled by the relentless wind, that his mind snapped into commercial mode and he remembered THE WHOLE REASON WHY HE WAS THERE!

He screamed for his camera box, fumbled as his gloved hands tried and failed to attach his longest lens onto his Nikon, and almost wept with frustration. But the lens finally seated and with a quick twist he was ready for a shot at immortality. His goggles made sighting through the viewfinder and focusing all but impossible. He set the lens on infinity, the exposure on automatic and did his best to point the camera at the retreating yeti. He clicked. Clicked again and again. Clicked even as the swirling clouds closed in and the valley was once more lost from sight. Frustration made him rash. But he was certain of what he'd seen and the fame and glory that beckoned was worth any price.

'I'll double your fee, triple it!' he'd cried to the Sherpas. 'Just get me down there into the valley. Christ! Just name your price!'

The Sherpas shook their heads sadly.

'There is no way into the valley,' said the head guide. 'We have looked. Our fathers have looked. Our fathers' fathers have looked and their fathers before them.'

'Rock climbers,' said de Benke. 'Rock climbers!'

'The wind would sweep them off the walls to their death.'

'Helicopters!' But even as he uttered the word de Benke knew that no helicopter in existence could survive the winds and the narrowness of the cleft. Neither would parachutes. And even if someone managed to parachute in, how would they get out?

'There must be some way,' he said pleadingly.

'Why?' said the head guide. 'Why must there be a way?'

De Benke had pinned all his hopes on his photographs. Maybe he'd pointed the camera in precisely the right direction at precisely the right time. Maybe the yeti had turned just as he'd clicked, showing convincing details of head and jaw and skin covering. Maybe. Such things happened. People got lucky. Fame, glory and the respect of his peers were just one very happy snap away.

But he hadn't got lucky. Only one shot had captured the yeti at all and the image was blurred and inconclusive. Obviously the camera had slipped slightly as he'd struggled to take the shots, and the slip had been magnified by the telephoto lens. De Benke had to concede that if he'd wanted to fake a shot of a yeti, the photo in his hand was precisely the sort of result he'd have come up with.

He returned twice more to the cradle of Qomolangma, braved the cold, wind and exhaustion, but only once, for a period no longer than two minutes, did the clouds clear. The yeti was nowhere to be seen. De Benke wasted thousands of his own and his backers' dollars on wild-goose chases, prey to every Nepalese shyster looking for a quick buck. He lost the respect of the original guides and everyone else who tried to help him. He risked his life pointlessly on needless ventures, but in doing so also carved out his future career. He was smart enough to realise that one fuzzy photo backed by an unsubstantiated sighting would relegate him to the ranks of over-zealous, crackpot cryptozoologists. His only future lay in playing to the sceptics and debunking everything for which he failed to find indisputable proof of existence. That was what he did in his first book. *In the Footsteps of the Yeti* became an international best-seller.

His debunking brought him fame of a kind and sales of his books provided a comfortable living. But it was neither the fame he craved nor the riches. He still clung to the hope that he would one day find *gigantopithecus*. His hopes took him to Siberia, Mongolia, China, Pakistan and Iran, lured by promises that went unfulfilled. One day he received a letter from North Dakota via his publishers. A schoolteacher claimed to have seen a bigfoot and had managed to take a photograph. The photo was enclosed. De Benke's hands began shaking and he was powerless to stop them. Clearly the subject had been shot on telephoto. The picture was grainy from enlargement. It was useless as scientific evidence but that didn't matter. What was obvious — screamingly obvious — was that the bigfoot in the photo was to all intents and purposes the spitting image of the yeti he'd photographed in the cradle of Qomolangma.

People say Mondays are long but that Thursdays last for ever. In the vast underpopulated expanses of North Dakota, every day is like Thursday, and North Dakota Thursdays last longer than any others. It took de Benke five hours to fly to New York from London, then a day and half to make his way to Dickenson, North Dakota, on the fringe of the Theodore Roosevelt National Park. He then had to endure a four-hour drive in a Chevrolet truck along trails that threatened to jar loose the crowns on his teeth. His hosts were friendly, generous and clearly excited. Despite his tiredness and the fact that they were carrying more beer than food, he couldn't help but be caught up by their optimism and enthusiasm. He let himself believe that this time he'd find the evidence he needed.

His new comrades had built a hide where they could sit and watch for the bigfoot, and carried enough supplies to last a week. They'd brought walkie-talkies fitted with earphones so they could talk without betraying their presence in case they needed to split up, and enough arms to start a small war. They assured him the weapons were not to shoot any bigfoot but to scare away bears and mountain lions. They were well prepared, whatever happened.

It was on the fourth day during the early morning watch that they sighted their quarry. De Benke jammed his binoculars hard against his eyes. The bigfoot was at least one and a half kilometres away and in the shadow of woods, but the clear North Dakota air worked in de Benke's favour. What he saw took his breath away.

'Sweet Jesus!' he said, scarcely able to believe his eyes. The bigfoot had breasts! It was female. Female! Yet the photo he'd been sent was definitely of a male. The magnitude of his discovery was almost too much to take in. He hadn't just found *gigantopithecus*, he'd found a thriving colony!

'We have to get closer,' he said, trying hard to suppress his excitement. 'I want pictures that are beyond question. Pictures of at least two of them. And pictures of whatever it is they call home. I also need some hard evidence. Okay?'

De Benke believed he was on the threshold of scientific acclaim and popular glory. He was oblivious to the flinty stones that gouged his hands and knees as they crept cautiously and silently towards the spot where they'd sighted the female. He made certain that they stayed downwind and did nothing that might give the show away. Yet when they reached the spot of the sighting, there wasn't a trace of the bigfoot to be found.

De Benke wasn't overly concerned. It had taken them more than two cautious hours to cover the one and a half kilometres, and it was reasonable to assume that the bigfoot had continued about her business. It seemed unlikely that she'd have gone very far.

They split up into two groups to try to track her down so that she could lead them to her family or colony. They kept in touch by walkie-talkie. De Benke was a practised tracker and he knew how to move silently through bush. He expected to catch sight of the bigfoot at any moment or hear through his earphones that the others had sighted her. But they never saw her again that day.

Or the next.

Or the next.

De Benke couldn't understand it. They found no footprints, no trails, no evidence of occupation, not even any ape or human-like scat. They found nothing. The following day, an excited voice in his earphones announced that one of his comrades had found tufts of hair snagged on a bush.

De Benke groaned inwardly. His spirits plummeted. It was the last thing he wanted to hear. In Guatemala, after weeks of fruitless hunting, the positive proof he'd been given of the *chupacabras* — a spiny-backed, kangaroo-shaped creature that lived on the blood of goats — had been tufts of the creature's hair snagged on a tree. The hair had proved to be horsehair. The cured scalp of the yeti he'd tracked down to a monastery in Tibet turned out to be from a yak. The piece of skin that was supposed to have come from the Mokele-mbembe turned out to have been cut from the decaying corpse of a hippopotamus. Such were the instruments of deception.

When de Benke was handed the tuft of bigfoot hair, he pulled a couple of strands off it and held a match to them. The tufts shrivelled instantly. They weren't even from a bear or mountain lion, or in fact any living animal. They were synthetic. From a rental fancy-dress suit. His so-called comrades weren't even embarrassed. They laughed hysterically, delighted that they'd carried off their hoax for as long as they had.

On the plane back to London de Benke thought of the similarity between the female bigfoot he'd sighted, the bigfoot in the photo he'd been sent and his only genuine shot of the yeti in existence. The first thing he did when he arrived home was burn his photo of the yeti. It was little consolation that his book *Bigfoot, Big Lie* was also a best-seller.

*   *   *

The breeze swung to the south and freshened, awakening de Benke from his reverie. His eyes lifted across the white-topped waves to the ruins of the penal settlement at Kingston. It looked so innocent now, charming even, as though to make a lie of its horrific history. It sat there as a warning not to take things at face value. But that was exactly what de Benke was being asked to do. He was acutely aware that time was no longer on his side. He'd passed the age at which normal people retire. His host, Peter, appeared genuine enough and there was no doubting Ian Kenny's earnestness. Or was there? He'd been deceived so many times before. Was he being set up for another fall, on this island which had once been the epitome of man's inhumanity to man?

De Benke attended a reception at Government House that evening. Peter Clarke approached him just as the first guests were leaving.

'I've spoken to Ian Kenny,' said Peter. 'He's invited us both over to his house for a beer tomorrow at four. You're under no obligation and Ian won't be offended if you have other commitments. If you decide to accept, let me know and I'll pick you up at three-forty. If nothing else, you might be interested in seeing some of Ian's knick-knacks. Up to you.'

Yes, de Benke thought, it was up to him. To go or not to go? In the end, it was the lack of pressure or any suggestion of a come-on that decided things for him.

'It is easy to believe that sea serpents don't exist,' said Ian Kenny, 'but not so easy to believe that they have never existed.'

He reached over with the bottle and topped up de Benke's beer. De Benke didn't object. The afternoon was pleasantly warm so they sat at a table outside, beneath an extension of the veranda roof. 'Sea serpents occur in literature from too many different cultures, in too many different places and over too great a time span to be simply dismissed.'

De Benke was happy to let Ian do the talking while he tried to get a measure of the man.

'A sea serpent is mentioned in the Old Testament,' said Ian. 'It was named Leviathan or Rahab.'

'Some believe the names refer to a giant dragon,' said de Benke softly.

'True,' said Ian. 'I can't mount an argument either way. But a sea serpent also occurs in Babylonian literature.'

'Marduk, perhaps also a dragon,' said de Benke.

'I'm prepared to concede both are probably myths,' said Ian. 'Along with Jormungandr, the Norse serpent that is supposed to have encircled the world. But there are more recent sightings that are not so easily discarded.'

'Olaus Magnus?' said de Benke.

'1555,' said Ian. *History of the Northern People.* He described a sea serpent that routinely terrified fishermen along the coast of Norway. Bishop Hans Egede described a giant sea serpent he encountered on his way to Greenland in 1734. There are endless reports of sightings among the Nordic people and I'm not prepared to dismiss them all as flights of fancy. Are you aware of the report from Captain McQuhoe of HMS *Daedalus* in 1848?'

'Of course.'

'Why would a captain in the Royal Navy risk his career and livelihood if he wasn't convinced of what he saw? And his description of a hairy mane around the serpent's neck matched the description given by Olaus Magnus three centuries earlier.'

'Have you always been interested in sea serpents?' asked de Benke. 'You've obviously done your research.'

'I wasn't interested at all until I saw one. That's what got me interested. I wanted to know what I saw.'

'Are you certain it wasn't *Architeuthis* you saw?'

'Absolutely. The waters off the rise are two and a half thousand metres deep. We've seen giant squid here before. Besides, *Architeuthis* is estimated to reach around nine metres in length. Nine metres doesn't even get close to what we saw. And *Architeuthis* doesn't have scales.'

'I read the account of your sighting in your book *Fishing Our Way*. Peter showed it to me. There were two boats, right?'

'That's right.'

'Eight people in all, four in each boat?'

'Yes.'

'Tourists?'

'Mostly.'

'And you watched this serpent for, what? Half an hour?'

'Probably a little under.'

'Even so, eight people, mostly tourists, watch something as extraordinary as a giant sea serpent and nobody thinks to take a photograph? Tourists carry cameras like dogs carry fleas. And nobody took a photograph?'

'Nobody had a camera with them. That's not so unusual. There's no room on my boat to put them where they won't get either tossed around or wet. I encourage people to leave their cameras in their car where they're safe, and to take pictures of the catch on our return. It's a practice born of experience. Besides, truth be known, there wasn't a lot to photograph. All a photo would show was a hump in the water. Also, my camera doesn't have much of a zoom. Even if I'd had it with me, I couldn't do it justice.'

'I find it hard to believe no one took a camera. One could easily slip into the pocket of a jacket or hold-all and be quite safe.'

'That's not my experience, but, look, you would've needed an underwater camera anyway. That's where the action was. You've read my piece so you should know that. The water was exceptionally clear. It gets like that on a calm day out on the drop-off. We reckoned we could see down to around twenty metres. The thing was around a metre in diameter and poised like an arch. Neither leg of the arch appeared to get thicker or thinner as it disappeared into the depths. So we don't know which end its head was attached to. We don't know whether it was coming or going. But we do know that whatever it was had to be at least forty metres long plus the few metres that were out of the water.'

'And it definitely had scales?'

'About eight centimetres across. I didn't touch them. Howard Christian did. I wasn't game to get that close.'

De Benke finished his beer and played with his coaster until Ian took the hint and refilled his glass.

'Tell me,' de Benke said, 'why do you think sightings of sea serpents are now so rare? When was the last claimed sighting apart from yours? Canada, wasn't it, 1994?'

'Pollution and overfishing. There are your culprits. Most of the sightings over the past five hundred years have been in the North Sea. You have to assume that a giant creature like a sea serpent would need a vast and constant supply of food. The North Sea cod grounds provided that until they were overfished to the point of no return. Take away the food source and you take away the creatures that feed on it. Sea serpents, if they existed in the North Sea, would have simply died out as the cod were depleted.'

'What happened in the North Sea probably happened elsewhere,' cut in Peter. 'Name the ocean that hasn't been overfished. If we haven't starved the things to death, we've probably killed them with pollution.'

'If sea serpents still exist — and I believe they do — I think it is probable that they would turn up here or in subantarctic waters,' said Ian. 'Both places are isolated, unpolluted and have an abundant food source. Subantarctic waters have, amongst other things, vast shoals of the Patagonian toothfish, seals, penguins, whales and, for all I know, giant squid. Here we have the Norfolk Rise. I don't know what's two and a half thousand metres down off the drop-off, but I do know there's plenty of fish up on the rise. Trumpeter, cod, kingfish, bonito, tuna and sharks, plus all the bait fish. Why do I think sea serpents are still alive here? We have the necessary ingredients to support them: environment, isolation, clean water and a reliable source of food.'

'How many times have you been out to the drop-off?' asked de Benke.

'How many hot dinners have you had?' replied Ian.

'And you've only seen a sea serpent once?'

'Yes, but Howard and I aren't the only ones to have seen it. Other fishermen have seen one too, but like Howard they're pretty guarded when it comes to talking about it. It's too easy to be made out a fool.' If Ian had intended a rebuke for his treatment in Rawson Hall, it slipped by de Benke.

'Tell him about Soupy,' said Peter.

'Who's Soupy?' asked de Benke.

'Was,' said Peter. 'The old bloke died about three years ago. He passed on his collection of curios to Ian.'

'What's his relevance?'

'Soupy was the first local fisherman to see one of the serpents. At least, he was the first to openly talk about seeing them,' said Ian, picking up the story.

'Them,' said de Benke. 'Plural?'

'That's right. Soupy became fascinated by them. He raced out to the drop-off at every excuse. He claimed a dozen or more sightings. Raved about them. Said there was a family out there and that he could tell one from the other.'

'Did you go out with him and look?'

'Yeah. At least a dozen times. Saw nothing except whales, sharks and the occasional marlin. The thing is, Soupy was a wicked raconteur. He had more tales than a tankful of bait fish. You never knew what to believe, and he didn't care one way or the other, so long as he had a good time and a few laughs and we kept the amber fluid up to him. Missed him when he died, though. Think of him every time I look through my display cabinet.'

'May I have a look?'

From past experience de Benke knew that now was about the time he'd be thrown the baited hook and decided to make things easy for them. It was a test. If they offered him the piscatorial equivalent of a tuft of hair he was out of there. Ian and Peter led him to a 1940s' glass display cabinet crammed full of artifacts. Ian had an extensive collection of shells, among them nautilus and paper nautilus shells, descending in size from adult to juvenile.

'Impressive,' said de Benke, but that wasn't what caught his eye. It was the sharks' teeth, ranging from the gigantic to the merely large.

'Great white,' said Ian, pointing to each of the teeth in turn. 'Tiger shark, bronze whaler, hammerhead, grey nurse, thresher.'

'And this?' De Benke pointed to a huge fossilised tooth.

'I thought you'd know,' said Ian.

De Benke picked up the tooth, showed surprise at its weight, and examined it. '*Carcharodon megalodon*, I'd guess. Never expected to see one here. Where did you get it?'

'Part of Soupy's collection.'

'Very impressive,' said de Benke. He thought it was time to cut to the chase. He and some of the other authors had been invited out to the island's best restaurant, as guests of a publishing company. He appreciated good food, especially when he wasn't picking up the tab, and was determined not to let the opportunity slip by. 'Your collection is interesting but I see nothing to convince me to begin a search for your sea serpent. I'm not doubting your word, but it costs a significant amount of money to mount an expedition and my backers would require something more substantial than a reported sighting. I'm sorry if I disappoint you.'

Peter and Ian exchanged glances.

'Let's have a beer for the road,' said Peter.

De Benke returned to the table feeling a weight had been lifted off his shoulders. Ian had failed to convince him. The weakness in his story was that nobody had taken a photograph. People had had cameras, opportunity and incentive and still hadn't taken a picture. That simply did not ring true. He glanced around the walls of the annexe and noticed Maori *meres* and ceremonial sticks fastened there. There were a few Fijian weapons also attached to the wall and a primitive bow with an assortment of arrows. Part of him wished he could stay longer but dinner called.

'Thanks,' he said as Ian once more filled his glass. He took a sip and replaced it on his coaster.

'Hard evidence,' said Ian. 'I can't give you that. All I can give you is my word, which I concede probably isn't enough.'

'As I said, I'm sorry.' De Benke didn't feel the least bit sorry.

'What I can give you is something to think about.'

'What?'

'I'm not sure I should be doing this.'

'For God's sake,' said de Benke, more annoyed than intrigued.

'When you get a second, take a close look at that coaster you've been playing with,' cut in Peter.

'My coaster?' De Benke lifted his beer glass and picked up the mat beneath it. It was hard and unabsorbent, entirely unsuited to its role. He tried to flex it but it resisted his attempt. Now that he looked, there was something very curious about it. He stood and held it up to the light. He recognised what it was immediately and stared at it in disbelief. 'It's a fish scale!'

'Which some fool, probably Soupy, has seen fit to laminate in plastic,' said Peter with an uncharacteristic flash of anger. 'All to make a set of eight beer coasters. Well, that's about where Soupy's mind was at.'

De Benke studied the fish scale with an expression filled with wonder. The scale was almost twelve centimetres across and he couldn't imagine the size of the fish it had come from.

'Was it fossilised?' he asked.

'Can't have been,' said Ian. 'I wondered that myself, but all eight of them are consistent with modern fish scales.'

'You're right,' said de Benke. 'Unquestionably cycloid. God knows what they came from but that probably rules out your sea serpent.'

'Why?' said Ian. 'Who is to say sea serpents haven't evolved along with modern fish? Why shouldn't their scales be cycloid?'

De Benke had no answer. He turned the scale over and over in front of the light, put it back down on the table and picked up another.

'Are you saying this is from a sea serpent?' said de Benke.

'No way,' said Ian. 'I'm just not prepared to exclude the possibility. Soupy claimed he acquired them when one of the sea serpents rubbed up and down along the side of his boat as if scraping off parasites. It scraped off a few scales at the same time. That's what he claimed but I'm not saying I believe him.'

'How did he laminate them?'

'He had relatives in Sydney he visited from time to time. One of them could have had it done for him.'

'Can I take one away with me?' De Benke was loath to part with the scale in his hand. Suddenly he could feel hope, like a flame rekindled, burning through his veins.

'No,' said Ian emphatically. 'I'm not prepared to have my sighting of the sea serpent undermined or discredited on the basis of these scales. I don't know what they're from. They have a hint of green in them and the serpent I saw had a predominantly blue tinge. Besides, who knows what the process of laminating has done to them? Probably all we have left is an impression of the scales, like the fossil outlines of shells found in rocks. No, I'm not prepared to take the chance. I'm no con man and I won't expose myself to the charge of being one.'

De Benke checked each of the eight scales in turn. He noted the slight variations in shape and size. They looked authentic. But what modern fish could possibly have produced them? He looked hard into Ian's face, well aware of the possibility that once again he was being set up.

'Please, let me have one to analyse. It could be the hard evidence we're looking for.'

Ian didn't waver.

'No,' he said firmly. 'I've given you my reasons.'

'Yes, you have,' said de Benke thoughtfully. Ian had also given him the right answer.

De Benke was scheduled to give a lunchtime reading in the Golden Orb bookshop but used the time instead to announce his intention to mount an expedition to prove the existence of the Norfolk Island sea serpent. He was returning directly to London and to a meeting with his backers, who he claimed were 'extremely interested'. A change had come over him. He was a man transformed. The hard-bitten sceptic had become an eager enthusiast. Years had fallen off him.

It didn't matter that he failed to apologise for his earlier treatment of Ian Kenny, or even acknowledge him at all. Both Ian and Peter were relegated to the anonymous role of 'sources'. Neither minded. They'd accomplished what they'd set out to achieve. They sat at the back of the bookstore while de Benke made his speech, dutifully clapped at the end of it and drove back to Peter's house for a beer.

'Now are you going to tell me where you got the coasters?' asked Ian.

'You're not going to believe it,' said Peter. 'About thirty years ago, my company in Melbourne made a television commercial for fish fingers. The idea revolved around a man who was obsessed by fish. Everything in his house had something to do with fish. His clothes had fish patterns. Among other things, the props department had the coasters made up. The actual scales were carved out of resin, I believe. Bit of overkill, really. They were never used.'

'Do you think we've done the right thing?'

'Depends,' said Peter. 'Depends on whether you really saw a sea serpent.'

'I did.'

'Really?'

'Really. Don't you believe me?'

'I don't believe in yetis, yowies, bigfoot, Nessie or black panthers roaming the Blue Mountains, but I'll keep an open mind on your serpent.'

'Gee, thanks.'

'It's not my role to believe,' said Peter.

He thought of all the accommodation lying empty around the island, the duty-free shops that should be busy with customers, the museums, cyclorama and historical re-enactments all in want of a crowd, the glass-bottom boat and fishing charter operators, the restaurants with empty tables. Then he thought of a fired-up de Benke playing to the world's media and all the publicity he would generate for

Norfolk Island, and how quickly the publicity would translate into visitors. He could see the island thriving, see 'No Vacancy' signs becoming permanent fixtures, see restaurants filled to capacity, see Norfolk once again enjoying the year-round popularity its beauty deserved. He turned in his chair so that he could watch the afternoon sun play on Phillip Island, see the brilliant green of the regrowth among the red of bare rock. Somewhere over there, the salvation petrel — thought to be extinct for over a hundred years — had returned to nest and breed. He saw the birds as a symbol of Norfolk Island's renewal. His face lit up with a wry smile.

'No, it wasn't my role to believe,' he repeated. 'My role was simply to tip the scales.'

Walking the Line

Lambert liked to tell people that his wife, Millie, walked out on him the day he retired. Literally walked out on him. Actually Millie walked out a full fortnight after Lambert retired, but the extra few days have no bearing on anything and only a diehard pedant would be picky enough to mention the fact. She'd obviously been making plans for some time but Lambert had been oblivious to them, being entirely caught up in his fishing, the routine of the little township in which he'd spent his entire life, and his last days as a bank manager. The bank's head office closed the branch on Lambert's retirement and replaced it with an ATM that would never require wages, sick leave, holiday loading or a superannuation payout. The banks said that closing branches was progress. When Lambert's bank closed, the little township of Marsden, on the northeast coast of New Zealand's North Island, was suddenly left without any bank. Marsden had progressed as far as it could go.

Lambert and Millie didn't get divorced or formally separate or do any of the usual things people do when they go their own way. Millie simply said that after forty years of marriage, all of which they'd spent in the same three-bedroom weatherboard house, she deserved some time to herself. She must have felt the need pretty keenly because it transpired that her idea of time to herself went far beyond most people's; what Millie had decided to do was take off to the other side of the world and walk the ancient Celtic trails of Great Britain and Ireland. Not only walk them, but walk them alone.

When Millie told Lambert her plans, he was initially stunned, though stunned is an inadequate description. He wasn't just lost for words, his whole thinking process stalled in a monumental seizure of his synapses. It wasn't the plans so much as the fact that they were Millie's. Millie's! Millie, his quiet, uncomplaining wife and mother to his two grown-up and married children. Millie, his constant companion — except when he was working or fishing, which was far more often than was good for any relationship. Nothing in her entire life had even hinted at her intentions. When Lambert realised how serious she was and the degree to which she'd thought things through, his chest swelled with pride and he offered her all the support he could.

'I didn't know you had it in you,' he said admiringly. 'I didn't know she had it in her,' he told his kids and anyone else who was prepared to listen, which was every single soul in Marsden. Nobody had thought Millie had it in her or had ever entertained the possibility. They were, to a man, woman and child, as stunned as Lambert had been and then, just as quickly, as proud and supportive. Nobody from Marsden had ever done anything like that before. Millie was grateful for the support and the good wishes but had no need for either.

Her plans had been forty years in the brewing. She already had everything worked out.

With the help of the internet she'd found enthusiasts with similar interests and, with their eager assistance, identified hundreds of ancient walkways and rights of way crisscrossing Britain, Ireland and northern France. She'd found enough information to keep her walking for the rest of her life if she so chose, without ever retracing her steps.

So Lambert and Millie remained happily married despite being separated by oceans and continents. Millie was happy because she was at last free to follow her own path. Lambert was happy because he was free to continue doing what he'd always done. There was no need to get lawyers involved, or to sell the house, which was located above a tiny kink in the coastline north of Marsden Beach. Millie had often sat out on the veranda looking over the tiny bay that fronted their yard to the fine line where ocean became sky and hinted at the endless possibilities beyond. Lambert also loved the location, but for his own reasons. He loved it because he could launch his boat safely from the tiny beach in almost any wind. They didn't have to sell the Land Rover either, which, while it wasn't the most comfortable of vehicles, was perfect for launching the boat. And they didn't have to sell the boat. That was the main thing. Having to sell the boat would've broken Lambert's heart.

Money wasn't an impediment to their contentment. Lambert retired with adequate superannuation, which was the primary reason his father had encouraged him to join the bank in the first place. It might seem strange today that superannuation had been a priority to a boy just leaving school, but that was the way people thought in those days.

And as things turned out, who's to say Lambert's dad was wrong? Lambert's and Millie's needs were simple, their wants few, and the funds flowing into their separate bank accounts each month were more than enough to cover their outgoings.

Did Lambert miss Millie? Of course he did. He missed the comfort of her presence, their conversation and companionable silences, the sandwiches she cut for his lunches and the dinners she cooked for him. His tea had always hit the table promptly at five thirty and was always followed by pudding. Nobody could make rice pudding, bread-and-butter pudding, trifle or banana custard like Millie could. There were times when he felt Millie's absence acutely, but he never stayed down for long. If friendships are wealth, then Lambert was one of the richest men on earth. He regarded everyone in town as his friend and the sentiment was reciprocated. It may sound a strange thing to say of a bank manager, but Lambert was universally liked.

As a bank manager, Lambert was in a position to know who was doing things tough and it wasn't at all unusual for him to turn up on their doorstep with a few 'surplus' snapper to ease their burden. Sometimes they were young families having a bit of a struggle; other times they were people who, through no fault of their own, suddenly found themselves unemployed or struck down with sickness; sometimes they were just old, often lonely people who welcomed his company as much as the fish that he brought with him. When Lambert retired and Millie disappeared over the horizon, nothing changed in this regard. Lambert kept his ear to the ground and little escaped him. People in need still found fresh snapper and kingfish on their doorsteps.

It's fair to say that Lambert's friends — which is to say, the whole population of Marsden — came to rely upon his largesse. No celebration passed, be it wedding, engagement, anniversary, twenty-first or wake, where Lambert didn't contribute at least two big fish he'd caught and smoked. People took his contribution for granted. Ladies brought a plate bearing their speciality — rolled asparagus sandwiches, creamy sponge cakes, meringues, savoury sausage rolls — and Lambert brought smoked fish. That was the way things happened, as immutable as night follows day.

In the first six months following Millie's departure, Lambert sent her letters regularly, telling her all about the fish he'd caught and who he'd given them to. He wrote to her while she was following an ancient trail through the hills of South Wales, past medieval abbeys, Celtic hill forts and old market towns, across turnstile and footbridge, through wood and pasture, set on a course that would lead her unerringly to Stonehenge. She wrote back asking him to stop writing to her. She didn't do it unkindly. She just pointed out that she knew what the letters would say before she opened them. She knew he'd catch fish and give his 'surplus' away to the needy. That was also as immutable as night following day. She suggested he'd be better off saving the postage and only to contact her in case of sickness or emergency. Lambert might have been miffed except for the fact that he understood her point completely and, anyway, she'd signed off, 'With all my love, Millie'.

For twelve months Lambert had no need to contact her. Then the unthinkable happened. Nobody, least of all Lambert, could believe it. If someone had dropped a section of the old Berlin Wall across the main street in the dead of night it would not have caused a greater disruption to the life of the township. It was as though the earth had suddenly shifted on its axis, as though some Supreme Being had suddenly rewritten the rules, as though nothing could be relied upon any more. And what was the nature of the catastrophe? Unbelievably, incredibly, Lambert stopped catching fish. The most reliable fisherman in Marsden simply stopped catching fish.

The problem came to light when Lambert's old Maori mate, Hika, died. Nobody, but nobody, could believe their eyes when Lambert turned up at the wake empty-handed. Hika had had a passion for Lambert's smoked snapper. Everybody knew that. Whenever Lambert's smoked snapper hit the table, Hika had always been the first to attack it. He liked to rip the fins off and suck out the sweet pieces of flesh between the bones, and then go for the back of the head. If anybody deserved to have Lambert's smoked snapper at his funeral, it had to be Hika. The omission was as glaring as a bride failing to turn up at her wedding.

Lambert told anybody who'd care to listen, which was everybody present and some people twice, how it had come about that he had no fish to bring. None fresh. None in the freezer. None in the smokehouse. None at all. It just didn't seem possible and everybody listened with justifiable concern.

'Every time I get the tides and the phases of the moon right, the wind suddenly springs up from the south,' he said, and everyone nodded sympathetically. They all knew about southerly winds.

'If it doesn't blow from the south, I get hit by squalls just as I'm trying to set the anchor. Anchor doesn't hold.'

Everybody nodded sympathetically. They all knew about squalls.

'When I pick a calm day to go in close after the kelpies, the swell picks up without warning. Tell you what, there've been times when I've been lucky to get away in one piece.'

Everybody nodded sympathetically. They all knew what could happen when the swells came up and you were fishing over kelp close into cliff faces.

'So no fish,' said Lambert unhappily. 'Here I am at Hika's wake with no smoked snapper to commemorate his passing.'

The workers at the local cemetery froze with their shovels in the air. They swore they heard old Hika turn in his grave.

The following Sunday, God's representatives at the local Catholic, Anglican and Presbyterian churches all mentioned Lambert's misfortune and suggested their congregations remember him in their prayers with a plea for normal service to be resumed. Everybody told him he was just going through a bad patch and his luck was bound to change.

It didn't, and all the prayers went unanswered.

Lambert thought he'd give things a rest for a while, so they could settle down and he could start off again afresh. He thought it would be a good opportunity to give his boat a bit of a spring-clean from stem to stern, a lick of paint or varnish where necessary, and also give his twin forty-horsepower Yamaha outboards a service. Although there was virtue in maintenance, in his heart Lambert knew he was just engaging in displacement activity. The world didn't stand still just because his boat was fast on its trailer. Couples still got married or had anniversaries, people celebrated turning twenty-one, turning forty, turning fifty and so on. The townsfolk started dropping by Lambert's house just to warn him that an occasion was coming up which would, of course, require his presence. The subtext was that a contribution of two or three nice smoked snapper had been written into the catering arrangements. Then there were the hard-luck stories. People were still doing it tough and it broke his heart that there was nothing he could do to help.

Lambert readied his boat and filled his bait box with fillets of kahawai, mullet and bonito. He threw in a slab of pilchards for good measure and also made a special pudding with tuatuas, pipis, mussels, flour, a particular brand of cheddar, a sprinkling of blood and bone and several other ingredients which he steadfastly refused to divulge. The result was a pudding the colour of oysters, with a consistency that made it cling to hooks like a spinster to the last eligible man in town, and a flavour which snapper, terakihi and porae found, without wishing to overstate the case, worth dying for. He made a burley by crunching up the shells of the shellfish he'd used in his pudding, added chicken pellets, scraps from the butcher, scrapings from the pub kitchen and brought the mix to a special pungency by stirring in a third of a bottle of tuna oil. He cleaned his reels, serviced the drags until they were silky smooth, sharpened his hooks, renewed his traces and honed his filleting knife. Lambert had never been better prepared for his favourite pursuit. But a howling nor-easter set in that lasted two weeks and blew away any hopes of wetting a line. He couldn't believe his luck. Nobody else could either.

When he was finally able to make it out to his favourite possies, setting out at night to catch the rising tide beneath a clear sky with a first gibbous moon looking as fishy as all hell, the snapper were strangely absent. Either they'd gone deep to escape the turbulence created by the nor-easters or they'd simply gone off the bite. He saw fish on his fish finder but in patterns that were unusual. He caught little red scorpion fish — all mouth and poisonous fins — which the locals ironically referred to as grandfather hapuku. He also caught disgusting yellow eels, which was never a good sign. Lambert hadn't a clue what was going on. When he returned home empty-handed night after night he began to wonder if he'd run over a Chinaman, walked under a ladder or allowed a black cat to cross his path. There was simply no rational explanation for what was happening to him. What was even more galling, tourists up from Auckland launched their boats in broad daylight and fished the bottom of the ebb tide in places that Lambert knew were unproductive, but returned with fish boxes heavy with fish. Not just with snapper but kingfish, kahawai, trevally and the odd John Dory. Nobody could understand it. For the first time in his life, worry lines began to appear on Lambert's normally contented face.

Lambert, for so long a pillar of the little community, lost standing. It was as though he'd changed and was the lesser for it. Lambert the ex-bank manager and provider of fish became Lambert the lost soul. Even worse, he became someone who failed to meet his obligations and who let people down. The townsfolk didn't know how to take him any more and weren't quite so certain where he fitted in. When he went to the pub for a beer, drinkers detoured by his chair on the way to the Gents so they could give him a sympathetic pat on the back, the kind you might give a dog you knew was soon to be put down. It was humiliating. Lambert wore the town's disappointment like a cloak of shame. It wouldn't have surprised him if he'd got home one day to find someone had left a couple of 'surplus' snapper at his front door.

Joni Mitchell said in her song that you don't know what you've got till it's gone. Lambert finally understood what had left his life when Millie had walked off. He missed her dreadfully. She would have known exactly what to say to him to make things better or, if not better, at least bearable. Even their companionable silences would have been a comfort. She'd kept in touch by way of postcards and, in his despair, Lambert turned to the last one she'd sent him. It gave an address in Cornwall through which she could be contacted in an emergency. *In an emergency.* Lambert couldn't imagine circumstances that would constitute a greater emergency. He picked up his pen and wrote to her.

Lambert calculated five days for his letter to reach Britain, another day to reach Cornwall, a day for Millie to post her reply, and a journey of similar duration for it to reach him. In the end he had to wait twenty-one days not thirteen, three fishless weeks of unrelenting rain and blustery winds. When he opened her letter he expected a wave of sympathy and understanding but copped a wake-up call instead.

'Well, what did you expect?' the letter began.

If Lambert had been capable of retort he would've said, 'Anything but this.' He poured himself a calming beer and sat down in his overstuffed armchair, all the better to absorb the shock of her opening words.

'Well, what did you expect?' he read again. The letter continued in much the same tone.

'Ever since I have known you, Lambert, you have taken from the sea and given nothing back. You have consistently taken more fish than meets your needs and have been happy to take the credit for those you have so generously given away. The generosity was not yours, Lambert, the fish were not yours to give. You were simply the instrument of Nature's generosity. It was Her generosity, not yours, something you have consistently abused and failed to acknowledge.

'I know you have no comprehension of what I hope to achieve by following the Celtic path, beyond touching base with my Celtic origins in some mystical way. I also know you have scant respect for ancient wisdoms, and probably regard Stonehenge as simply some primitive people's idea of a garden feature. But I have been to the mountain in Wales where the stones of Stonehenge were quarried, and followed the path all the way to their resting place. Most people with even a casual interest in Stonehenge understand the astronomical significance of the placing of the stones but have absolutely no comprehension of how they got there. Lambert, I have walked the path the stones took and let me tell you, it's no stroll in the woods. How did they do it? How did they carry those monoliths over mountains, across rivers and streams, how did they move them at all?

'In trying to learn more about the Druids I have reached an appreciation of Druidry. I may physically walk the Celtic pathways but I have begun to follow the Druidic Path. The Druidic Path is a way of life, a way of living in harmony with nature.

'Do you know, Lambert, physicists today believe that for the universe to make sense mathematically we have to accept the existence of eleven dimensions. I can think of five: length, width, breadth, time, space. If they are five dimensions, what are the other six? Do you also know that in accepting the existence of eleven dimensions, physicists also believe we should accept the probability of there being parallel universes. What do you think of that? Mind-boggling, isn't it? These are facts I discovered on a late-night BBC program I watched in Polperro and they got me thinking.

'You know, it is easy to discard the wisdoms of old simply because they are old. How can an ancient people possibly be as smart as we are with all our schools, universities, books and technology? The Druids probably never even considered the possibility of there being eleven dimensions or parallel universes, but they were aware that there were forces far beyond their understanding at play, and did their very best to live in harmony with them. They had more gods and goddesses than you can poke a stick at. I'm aware of three hundred and seventy different names of deities and there are almost certainly more. They ascribed responsibilities to each of these gods as a way of bringing order and understanding to their world.

'Why am I telling you this? I am telling you this because the Druids probably experienced what you're going through in the formative years of their beliefs. They learned from their mistakes and the learning became the foundation of their beliefs. Stonehenge played a significant part in their ceremonies but not nearly as much as their groves of trees. I have found remnants of oak groves, the trees clearly planted in Druidic order. Even today, followers of the Druidic Path continue to plant these groves. They are sacred, peaceful places and I delight in just sitting in them. The point is, the Druids took but also gave. The Druids took from Nature but also put back, sometimes in symbolic or sacrificial form, but also by way of new plantings. They did this to appease the forces they could not understand, but also because the system clearly worked. Yes, Lambert, it worked. They didn't plunder and destroy, uproot and leave barren. They worked with Nature. They were farmers and conservationists, hunters and conservationists, hewers and conservationists. They took but they gave back. They kept their lives in balance.

'Now tell me, Lambert, what have you done to compensate for what you have taken? Can you even put a number to the fish you have taken from the sea, the shellfish you have plucked from the sand? What have you put back? What have you done to balance the scales?

'Think about this and let me know your response. All my love, Millie XXX'

'Bloody hell,' said Lambert. He got up, poured himself another beer and went out onto the veranda, sat in Millie's chair and gazed at the fine line where the ocean becomes the sky. He didn't know about the eleven dimensions or the parallel universes but there was something naggingly sensible about what Millie called the Druidic Path and in maintaining a balance with nature. As an ex-bank manager he knew all about balances and he had to concede his fishing ledger was, to say the least, one-sided. He had treated the ocean with disdain, taking all the fish he wanted from it as though he had some kind of divine right. He had assumed that the ocean would always replace what he took and that it would be that way for ever. He'd given the ocean no more consideration than he had the fridge, and treated it in much the same way.

'Bloody hell,' he said again as it occurred to him that nature, or the ocean, had finally rebelled and decided he'd had his lot, that his quota of fish had been filled. He couldn't bear the thought of never catching fish again, of never again having the thrill of a big snapper stripping line off his reel, of never having a big kingfish set off for South America with his hook in its mouth. He immediately went back indoors and wrote to Millie. His letter went on a bit but in essence it said, 'You're right. What do I do?'

It took nineteen days for Millie's reply to reach him, nineteen fretful days during which the seas dropped, the wind dropped and nobody in town could believe Lambert hadn't taken his boat out and caught fish the way he always used to do. When they'd come up to him in the pub to ask why he hadn't gone fishing, he'd been grimly circumspect.

'I have my reasons,' he'd said in a manner calculated to discourage any further discussion. The townsfolk were beginning to think he'd lost it.

Millie's letter was short and to the point. She told him that, beginning the night of the new moon, he had to go out to his favourite and most secret fishing spot and stay there for an hour either side of high tide. Once there, he had to throw into the water exactly the same amount of bait he'd use if he were fishing and at roughly the same rate. On no account was he to take a fishing line or even so much as a fishing hook with him. While there, he was to think about all the fish he'd caught over the span of his life, the cycle of the seasons and the wonderful, precious, regenerative power of an ocean accorded appropriate respect and care. He was to repeat the procedure every night for the entire cycle of the moon, weather permitting. Then, and only then, was he allowed to bait a hook.

Lambert followed Millie's instructions to the letter. As he sat out on his rodless boat alone in the dark, he began to hear and see things he'd never noticed before. One night he heard an almost human gasp, which initially scared him witless, but turned out to be a green turtle taking a breath. It hung around the boat for some ten minutes, probably helping itself to the delicious pieces of bait Lambert tossed overboard. When it finally glided away into the blackness, Lambert felt as if he'd lost a friend.

Over the four weeks that he patiently did his penance, porpoises and sharks came up to make his acquaintance and partake of his generosity. Large schools of pelagic fish swept by and, one night, a river of squid streamed by on either side of his boat. They were iridescent in the light of his torch, an ever-changing ribbon of blue, green, white and silver, their eyes bright and shining like precious stones. It took nearly fifteen minutes for the last of the squid to pass by and Lambert was overcome by the sheer magic of it. He felt privileged and humbled. He felt that in some small way, Nature — that is Nature, Millie's Nature, with a capital N — was letting him know She — with a capital S — was aware and appreciative of what he was doing. Sometimes the timing of the tides kept him out in the boat till dawn and he bore silent witness to the birth of a new day. Of course he'd been out on the water for many dawns but he'd always been going somewhere, deciding which reefs he was going to fish, which rigs he was going to use, and sunrise was merely a cue to turn off his running lights. For the first time in his life, Lambert had nothing to do but simply watch the night fade and the horizon colour up, and was deeply touched by the splendour of the awakening day.

At the end of his penance, with the tide peaking a few minutes after 9 pm and with the slim crescent of a new moon for company, Lambert set off for his most secret reef, this time with rod and reel. His hands shook as he baited his hooks, but why wouldn't they? They'd been shaking since midafternoon when the wind had died and the possibility of going fishing had become a certainty. Lambert had never felt so apprehensive, not even when he'd stood in church awaiting the arrival of his bride, not even when his first child was born, or his second, not even when, heavy with grief, he'd given the eulogy first for his father, then for his mother. Lambert's breath came in shallow gasps as he cast and allowed his line to sink. What if his penance had not been enough? What if his penance had been in vain? What if the fish continued to shun his baits? He actually squealed with fright when his rod suddenly doubled over. Then it was business as usual, yes, business as usual. But not entirely as usual.

Oh, no.

Millie laughed out loud when she read how Lambert had placed a smoked snapper on Hika's grave. Most people take flowers but her husband had taken a fish. Her smile softened to one of affection when she read how he'd watched the seagulls devour the fish and how he'd naively imbued the event with Druidic significance, regarding it as a symbolic act of giving back to Nature. He even used a capital N. Her smile warmed further when she read how he stopped fishing the moment he'd caught all the fish he needed, how he no longer continued fishing purely for the sport, and how he put his rods away and, bit by bit, threw the remaining bait over the side. He also regarded this in a Druidic light as 'giving back for what he'd taken'.

She laughed again when Lambert gave her credit for his change in fortune, and solemnly thanked her with a sincerity bordering on the painful. It amazed and amused her that he couldn't see what he'd done. For forty years she'd listened to her husband's fish stories and knew with blinding certainty that if you burleyed the same fishing spot for four weeks at the same time of the tide, fish would wake up to the fact. She also knew that if you went to that spot to fish on the new moon after all the burleying, a period which the Maori fishing calendar claimed was the hottest time of the month to fish, you really couldn't miss. There was nothing Druidic, Celtic, mystical or magical about it. She laughed again but once more her smile softened to one of affection. She liked the sound of the change that had come over her husband. For the first time in all her wandering she began to think about going home.

Acknowledgements

Writing and fishing are compatible occupations. At no time are they more compatible than when the fishing is slow and night's mantle shields me from the rest of the world. The glowing lights on my fish finder take on a whole new meaning as my mind races trying to imagine exactly what it is that is lurking beneath the hull. One night when the screen went crazy a one-point-three-metre turtle surfaced alongside my boat. A one-point-three-metre turtle in Pittwater? The product of that encounter is included in this collection. But stranger things happen.

On Norfolk Island I met and went fishing with a man who has seen a sea serpent. We were discussing the encounter while a two-metre tiger snake played around our boat like a puppy.

In Mexico I fished with a local skipper and deckie who passed the time between strikes reciting dialogue from the movie *Snatch* in ripe Cockney accents. One of them didn't even speak English. It was the last thing I expected to happen eighty kilometres out to sea off Acapulco.

In Fiji I came across a small fish with a really weird claim to fame. It scares me more than a tank full of starving piranha. It's also in the book.

Inspiration can come from the oddest places, often when it's least expected. The only thing I'm sure of is that the more places I go and the more times I go fishing the more likely I am to find it.

For much appreciated help, advice and hospitality, thanks to:

Peter and Peggy Trethewey, Lionel and Judy Hunt, Peter Clarke, Ian Kenny, Graham Bland and Norman and Valerie Thompson.

Thanks also to my publishers, HarperCollins, agent, Margaret Connolly, and editor, Nicola O'Shea, for their unswerving support and encouragement.

Oh, one more thing.

All the characters in this book are my own creations except for Captain Pete and Miss Peggy, Low Gear Joe, *amigos* XR, Chuy and Pinky, Peter Clarke and Ian Kenny, Howard Christian and Ian Walters.